Released from the Darkness

Gabrielle Arrowsmith

Clean Teen Publishing

This is a work of fiction. The characters, incidents, and dialogues are products of the author's imagination and are not to be construed as real. Any resemblance to actual events or persons, living or dead, is entirely coincidental.

Released from the Darkness

Clean Teen Publishing
PO Box 561326
The Colony, TX 75056

www.cleanteenpublishing.com

ISBN: 978-1-940534-55-8

Content Disclosure

For more information about our content disclosure, please utilize the QR code above with your smart phone or visit us at www.cleanteenpublishing.com.

"Being deeply loved by someone gives you strength, while loving someone deeply gives you courage." -Lao Tzu

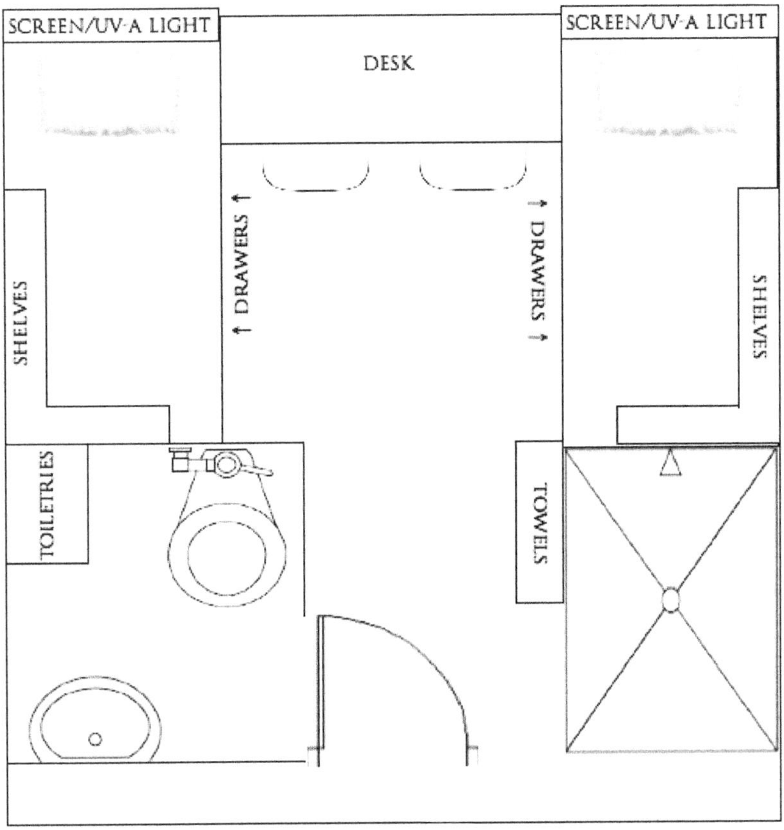
SCREEN/UV-A LIGHT
DESK
SCREEN/UV-A LIGHT
DRAWERS
DRAWERS
SHELVES
SHELVES
TOILETRIES
TOWELS

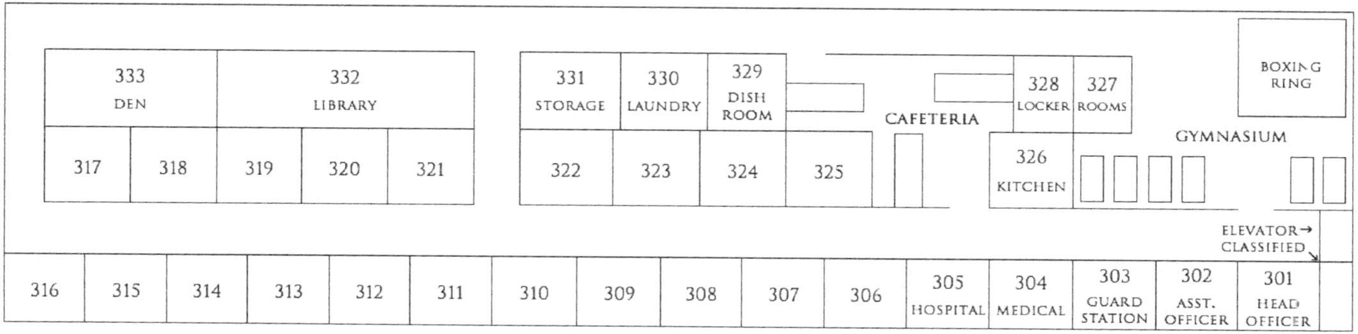
333
DEN
332
LIBRARY
317
318
319
320
321
331
STORAGE
330
LAUNDRY
329
DISH
ROOM
322
323
324
325
CAFETERIA
328
LOCKER
327
ROOMS
326
KITCHEN
BOXING
RING
GYMNASIUM
ELEVATOR →
CLASSIFIED
316
315
314
313
312
311
310
309
308
307
306
305
HOSPITAL
304
MEDICAL
303
GUARD
STATION
302
ASST.
OFFICER
301
HEAD
OFFICER

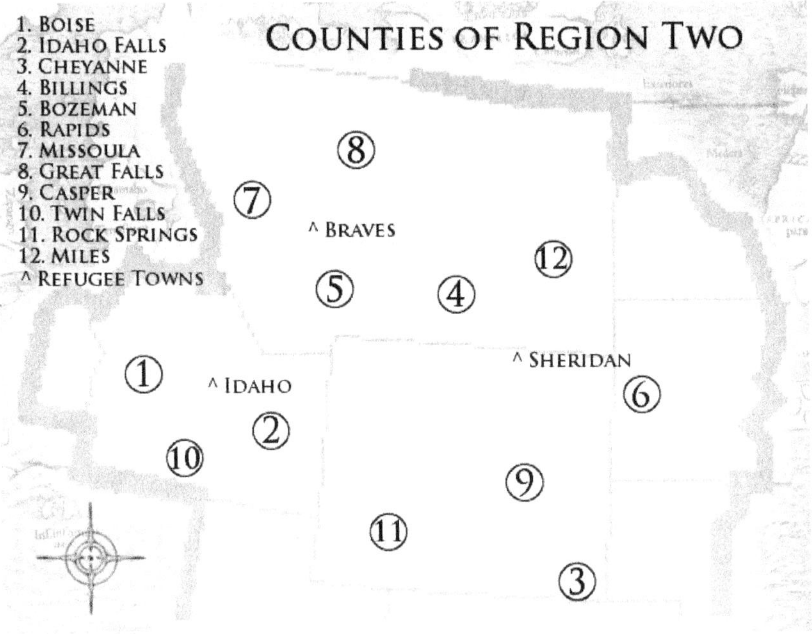
COUNTIES OF REGION TWO
1. BOISE
2. IDAHO FALLS
3. CHEYANNE
4. BILLINGS
5. BOZEMAN
6. RAPIDS
7. MISSOULA
8. GREAT FALLS
9. CASPER
10. TWIN FALLS
11. ROCK SPRINGS
12. MILES
^ REFUGEE TOWNS
^ BRAVES
^ SHERIDAN
^ IDAHO
8
7
5
4
12
1
6
2
10
9
11
3

REGIONS OF THE NATION

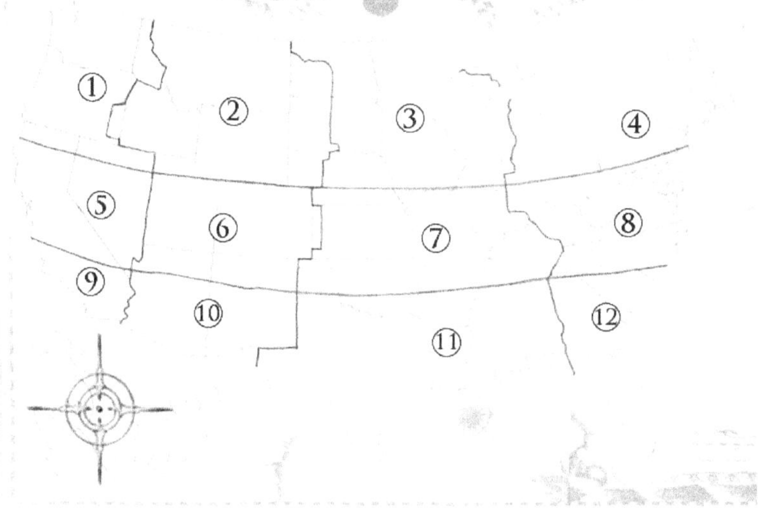

ONE

Darkness surrounds me. I know better than to run from it, as anything could lurk in its shadows. Instead, I wait in the stillness, as if I'm under the surface of the holding pond beyond Miles' barrier, counting the seconds for the camera to pass.

I become aware of a steady, dripping noise. Though its echoes try to fool me, I sense that the source of the drip is close. Strangely, it is my nose—not my ears—that is responsible for determining the rhythm's nearness.

I've come to recognize this odor. I smelled it first at the age of twelve when I discovered my mother's suicide at the institution. The distinguishing scent invaded my nostrils again at the makeshift hospital in Lame Deer where faithful Decklin lied dying, doubly wounded by bullet and flame. I endured the smell as we drove back to Sheridan in a van that carried the caskets of two noble-hearted young men. I buried my face in my lap and covered my head with my arms, not only to guard myself from the sickening stench, but also to keep secret the stream of sorrow that ran from my eyes.

This is the smell of blood. Death.

I try to hold my breath, but I'm quickly choked for air. I

don't have the strength to fight my hunger for oxygen.

A rush of cold air fights its way through my obstructed, sticky throat. I relax my lungs, but I'm unable to do the same for my mind, which is increasingly leery of my dark, mysterious surroundings.

Dim light begins to seep into the obscurity. A shape takes form beside me. I can tell that it's human, but its edges are blurred and its face deeply shadowed. Where did this person come from? Were my eyes not open before? Are they now? I can't find the light source.

"Welcome to Neo-Necropolis." Female. From the voice's smooth texture and deep tone, I'd guess that the woman is older than I am. I warily raise my eyes toward the head of the form, sending a shooting sensation deep into my head. It's dark, but something is also wrong with my eyes. I can't make out any features of the person's face.

"Necropolis is Greek. It means *city of the dead*. Neo is Greek for *new*."

New city of the dead?

I remember. I was halfway to Miles. I should have been driving a truck, but my panic and fate from above had changed that.

The first hour passed too rapidly. I was begging for more time as I still struggled to convince myself that I had made the right decision when I contacted Miles' inner circle to trade places with my sister. I had seriously considered turning the car around not five minutes before a crash that turned the compact car into my steely grave.

I spotted the buck before his hooves hit the pavement, but my perceptiveness didn't matter. There was nothing I could do to change the course of the deer, or the car, at the speed that each was traveling.

I heard that a person's life is supposed to flash before their eyes during a moment like that. Time is supposed to slow so the departing soul can calmly express their final words to their maker. As if the intolerable government ruled it too, time did not alter itself for me. I gasped in terror, pounded the brake, and shut my eyes. That was it. No thought squeezed its way into my mind, not of Evvie, my dad, or Sheridan.

There is time for worries now, though, especially those regarding Evvie's safety. They flood my heart and mind with full force, and my body acts accordingly.

"Relax." The woman gently places a wet cloth on my forehead and guides me to lie back down. "The name of this place is just another way they taunt us. You're not dead; you're going to be just fine."

Fully alert, I find the reflection of low light in the woman's eyes. They're dark, darker than her ebony skin, but kind. I can only focus on them for a second before the splitting headache returns. Of course, I'm not dead—I feel too much pain. I can't imagine the head can sustain this many blows in quick succession without the tissues swelling dangerously to protect the beaten brain.

"You need to rest," urges the unfamiliar woman. I can feel that she's right, but something important is gnawing at my mind like a misplaced itch. What *is* it?

Oh no, the collateral that was forced upon me to make sure that I upheld my end of the agreement with the county. "You don't understand," I stress to the woman. "Miles County BOTs are going to bomb everyone if I don't get there before dawn!"

"Everyone?" she questions. "Who are they going to

bomb? No! Don't tell me," she blurts, just as the answer forms on my lips. She's right. This moment is filled with desperation, but I still need to think before releasing my secrets to a complete stranger. I could jeopardize the safety of Evvie, my father, Crewe, and all other Sheridans with such carelessness.

"I received notice of my new roommate the day before yesterday. Just what day do you think it is?"

She received notice *two days* ago? That's not possible. It was only yesterday that I made contact with Miles. She couldn't have known about my arrival before then. Wait...*roommate*?

The keen woman beside me can tell that my head swells with questions and worries. She bends closer to me, making it easier for me to focus on her eyes as she speaks. "You're *in* Miles County. You've been here at least two days. Today is Wednesday, but I'd rather you not start this day yet. Get a few more hours of sleep while you can."

I've been here *three* days then. That's a long time, considering that I can't remember anything since the accident. I don't even know how I got here. I have many questions that need answering. "I need to know some things," I tell the woman beside me. "I don't sleep much, anyway."

"Well, look at that," she says casually. "I'd already nicknamed you Thrasher. Your nightmarish stirrings have been enough to keep me awake tonight, and I'm usually a rock through all sorts of horrors." The nickname Rock would seem appropriate for her. She certainly has the build for it.

"I wish I could ease your mind, but nothing we say goes unheard." Her eyes flash from wall to wall of the small room. "Do you understand?"

I nod. I understand this well.

The woman removes the wet cloth from my forehead

and slaps it into my hand. "Wipe your face."

I sit up slowly, bringing on a rush of dizziness, nausea, and a sharp pain in my left thumb. I set the cloth on my knee for a minute, to feel a sleek contraption housing my presumably broken thumb. Something warm and wet then touches my upper lip. Blood. I wipe as instructed, first below my nose. The bridge of my nose is unnaturally wide, and I can feel that one side of my face is equally as swollen. There's some tenderness to the touch, but not as much as it seems there should be.

"That's why I stopped you from telling me about the *everyone* whose lives you feared were in danger," the woman continues. "I don't want to know a thing about that."

"They know the name and location of the people they threatened," I say, discarding the wet cloth on the floor with a plop. "I doubt it would be news to anyone listening."

"Yet you still don't name it? It must be me that you don't trust then." She stands, picks up the wet cloth, and disappears around a partial wall at the foot of the bed across from the one on which I sit. I hear a squeak and then interrupted splashes of water as she rinses the cloth. "I don't blame you one bit for that," she calls over the flow of water. "Caution is smart *and* necessary." Water continues to leak from the faucet after it squeaks off, but the woman has presumably left the cloth in the sink to absorb the irritating pings.

Before I opened my eyes, I imagined that blood was the dripping medium. I understand how that morphed into my nightmare, having now learned that I had a nosebleed during my sleep. I heard the leaky faucet, but smelled blood. The bleed also explains the immediate choking I experienced when I attempted to hold my breath. A thin layer of my anxiety has been relieved now that the dripping has lessened.

"What's your name?" I ask as the woman sits on a bed much too small for her frame.

"Edyn with a Y. And you're Sydney. With a Y too," she adds. "Your name is the only thing they told me about you, but I don't see any need to get to know each other this morning. We have our whole lives for that," she says as she slides under the covers and turns toward the wall.

"Our whole lives?" I can't help asking.

"That's right. Once you're a resident here, your days of sunshine are over. I get the feeling you didn't have much sunshine to live for anyway."

"Where *are* we?" If we're truly locked up somewhere, then Edyn will have the rest of her life to sleep. I need answers tonight, and she's the only person who can give them to me. "I lived in Miles my whole life; I've never heard of Neo-Necropolis."

I've gained Edyn's attention. She spins around and props her head up. "That's because no one knows about this place unless they're in it. Most of us call it Neocropolis for short. Actually, a lot of residents call it Neo*crap*olis, even the guards."

"Residents?"

"Prisoners. We're buried below EPA 12-1 on Miles' northernmost border. Citizens have no idea that there is a fully loaded penitentiary right under the county seat."

Another lie fed to Miles' inhabitants. I bet the EduWeb instruction monitors don't even know. As told, they direct their pupils to courses that rave about how well chips deter criminals, so well that Miles County doesn't even need a jail.

"Don't answer this without caution," Edyn warns. "You said that you needed to *arrive* in Miles to prevent a bombing, so I can only assume that you were outside the county. I won't ask where, but I'd like to know how long you've lived beyond

Miles' border."

Suddenly, I realize there is something I need to look into before I can answer Edyn's question. Do the monitors that I need to be aware of exist in the room or directly within us? Before I could be taken from Miles to Sheridan, Galvesten cut into each of my wrists to find and remove my chip, which also served as a tracking device. The wounds had healed enough before I left Sheridan that I would notice had they been reopened. I feel the smoothness of each scar. However, I accidentally notice a fresh incision on my left forearm. There's also the high-tech splint around my thumb that I cannot undo. Both of those injuries could easily occur by impact or debris from the crash, but they could also conveniently cover up a fresh implant.

"I was only outside a week," I answer Edyn. "I lived in Miles until my eighteenth birthday."

"Well, happy belated," Edyn wishes. "I imagine the start to adulthood hasn't been too good for you, seeing as you've incurred enough damage in a week to land yourself in level three."

"Level three of what?" I have to ask.

"Of Neocropolis," she says. "There are five levels here. The depth they hide you in the ground is based on the severity of the crime you committed or the *threat* that you pose. The fifth level is solitary confinement. Very few have been down there, though residents spread rumors like they know the place. Level Fours have a bunkmate, but they don't receive any of the freedoms that we do. Twos above us have committed minor offenses, or they were innocents that put up a fuss. We call Level Ones *Innocents*. They never committed a crime. They were simply at the wrong place at the wrong time. They caught wind of some top-secret information or what have you, and the county couldn't risk that they be among citizens, where they could repeat what they saw or heard. There are even a couple of kids that are Innocents," Edyn sighs.

"Their parents think they're dead, except for one little girl whose momma is in three with us. She was pregnant when they put her down here. Wouldn't make sense for the child of a dead, pregnant lady to be alive. You can change the kid's identity and put her into an orphanage in another county, but they feared her DNA could one day reveal who she really was, and they couldn't have that."

"Couldn't they change her parents' DNA information in the system?" I ask. "Don't they change things like that all the time?" Edyn has been around for a while, and has probably heard many conspiracies through the other residents. I want to affirm that other situations, like when my sister saw a listing of our dead mother's foster children at the courthouse, occur sometimes.

"Without a doubt," Edyn answers. "But there were too many eyes watching this case. The child had to die. Negotiators promised her mother that she'd live in this death as long as she kept providing them the information and services they sought. The little girl gets to come down and visit her mother, and they've promised to take her out to see the sun on her tenth birthday. It's not too far away now. All of us are living for that event—living through that sweet child."

"How long has it been since you've seen the sun, Edyn?"

"Altogether, it's been seven years."

Altogether? There must have been a break between Edyn's time in Neocropolis. Maybe she was generalizing or exaggerating when she explained that imprisonment here is permanent. "Were you out for some time after you'd been in?"

"No." Edyn removes the covers from her side and sits up on the edge of her bed. "That doesn't happen," she says with heavy weight. "It's going to take you some time to accept it, but you will die here, Sydney. You should also understand that you'll never again speak to anyone out there that you care about. It's truth for every one of us, no matter what level we are sentenced to. We are the abandoned dead."

Maybe Edyn is trying to prepare me for the worst-case scenario. I can't accept that this is the beginning of the end for me. Evvie was here, and permanent captivity wasn't true for her. She woke to the sun almost three days ago, and for that, I am glad.

When I contacted Miles, I decided that I was willing to die for my sister, but this isn't the death that I imagined. I didn't expect it to come true, but I held a sliver of hope that I could reason or fight my way out of whatever evil I would encounter. What I did expect is that I would die fighting for the freedom and a better future for the ones I love. I could accept a noble death like the ones fate handed to Cy and Decklin. A slow, passive, unrewarding death buried deep below the enemy's feet is impossible for me to come to terms with.

"It's not right, but it's not all bad here if you keep your head down and try to enjoy the amenities of level three. Don't make the mistake that I made. I started as an Innocent, but you can see I'm not there anymore."

"Why did they move you?" I ask.

"I didn't last four days on One. I couldn't control my anger. I had a loving husband and two beautiful children who needed me. I couldn't give up on getting back to them. Reason got me nowhere, but the riot I brought did. It got me transferred to Two."

So this is what Edyn meant when she said she's been here seven years altogether. She's been moved between different levels.

"I never was an aggressive woman, but anger about the injustices in here built and built in me until one day, I snapped. It was no small thing I did, Sydney." Edyn pauses for a moment to reflect on the incident or to prepare her next words. "It takes a lot longer to be moved up than to be moved down. I can tell you that much. So as mad as you may be, don't do anything that will have you locked up below."

I can't promise that I won't react and get myself into trouble, so I don't respond to Edyn's advice.

I wonder what crime she committed that had her moved down the second time? They've started me on Three, so whatever she did must be considered worse than breaching and living on the outside.

Sometime, I want to hear how Edyn ended up in Neocropolis as an Innocent, but I figure it is both too soon and too odd of an hour to ask. There is just one more thing I have to know before I can allow Edyn to sleep. I have to know if those deemed dead are ever really killed down here. I'm not sure I can ask this outright since our conversation is being recorded, so I'll begin to flush out my answer in a roundabout manner.

"What happened to your last roommate?" I ask.

"She got moved up to Two. She promised to come down and visit sometime, but I imagine it will take her a while to earn enough to do that."

"She wasn't a young girl, was she?"

"Young is a relative term, but no. She was between your age and mine." That makes it clear that her previous roommate wasn't who I was hoping her to be. It's dark, so I can't really approximate Edyn's age, but her old roommate might have been as much as fifteen years older than Evvie. "What are you getting at?" she asks me, apparently reading the additional questions stemming from her answer.

"The girl I'm wondering about is fourteen. She has long, ashen hair with a feathered, neon-green streak." Edyn looks up as she sifts through the young faces she knows. "She would have arrived only a week ago," I add.

"No," she answers quickly. "You were the only recent admittance."

"She may have been on another level, like One or Two," I offer.

"No," Edyn confirms. "Word travels fast around here, even between levels. Unless this girl was in solitary."

Edyn meant nothing by this comment. She may have even been trying to make a joke. She probably couldn't imagine that someone who I thought could have been placed in an upper level could also as easily been locked up in solitary for their association with me. Imagining Evvie being admitted here, and learning her fate from a fellow Neocropolis resident as I have tonight, hurts me enough. It tears me apart to think that she may have spent five days locked up among the worst of sorts, a place about which the prisoners only know rumors. And who knows what the people who run this place can get away with down there?

"Does this girl mean something to you?" Edyn asks.

"Everything," I answer, looking at my lap. "She's my sister." I look up and find the reflection of light in Edyn's eyes. She takes a moment to focus on me, and then shakes her head in sorrow.

"I'm sorry that she's lost to you," she says, "but believe

me, it's better for her than being in here."

"I believe that," I answer. Lying down, I turn myself away from Edyn. I pull the covers around me and close my eyes. My eyelids feel swollen, but not enough to lock in the tears that slide to the corners of my eyes at the thought of never speaking to Evvie again.

"Get some sleep, Thrasher," Edyn says. I can't reply without revealing my emotional state. After a pause, I hear her tuck back in.

I will away my pain with each of Edyn's increasingly steady breaths. After a few minutes of this, she is sound asleep, and I'm alone in my hollowness.

TWO

When I awake later the next morning, I find that I am alone. There are two media screens where windows ought to be, built into the pale wall above the head of each bed. The screens cast an artificial dawn on the features of the congested room.

A narrow desk rests between the two beds. The steel from which it is made connects seamlessly with our bed frames of the same material. Two hard, backless seats are bolted to the floor next to the desk. I wonder if the desk serves as a table as well, or if the prison contains a cafeteria where the inmates eat.

Opposite the media screens are shelves that cover the partial wall at the foot of the bed and extend an equal distance toward the head. Edyn's shelves are full of books and papers, while mine are bare.

In spotting three deep drawers built into Edyn's bedframe, I reach over the bed to open mine. The first and second are barren. I toss the thin blanket covering me toward the wall and crawl to the end of the bed to open the final drawer. A pair of barely-there white shoes rests in the drawer. They're a perfect fit for the navy, standard-issue prison jumpsuit I'm wearing.

Earlier this morning, I hadn't realized that our cell extended beyond the feet of our beds until Edyn disappeared behind a partial wall to rinse the cloth. I swing my feet onto the cold floor to examine the additional features of the room.

Motion-activated lights turn on to reveal a tight shower space behind the wall at the foot of my bed. If there are men in Neocropolis with muscular builds like Crewe, I imagine they are constantly fighting to maneuver their bodies within the tiled shower while they wash up.

Time	Activity	Location
7:00-7:30	Breakfast	313
7:30-8:30	Paperwork	302
8:30-9:30	Officer Meeting	301
9:30-10:30	Tour	Level 3
10:30-11:00	Work System	302
11:00-11:30	Work Offerings	302
11:30-12:00	Medical Exam	305
12:00-1:30	Open Lunch	NC3
TBD-TBD PM	Employment	TBD
5:30-7:30	Open Dinner	NC3
7:30-TBD	Classified	Classified
9:00	Lights Out	313

Although the bathroom opposite the shower did not light earlier when Edyn rinsed the bloodied cloth, it flicks on now as I cross into the congested space. A stingy toilet protrudes from the partial wall directly across from the door to our cell. Thankfully, the hinges of the door are on the bathroom side. It's nice to know that if I'm using the door-less bathroom, I'll be given a few seconds of warning before being embarrassed to death. Engineering a way to close off this opening is near the top of my list of things to do to make this compact cell bearable, right after doing the same for the shower room, which is disadvantaged by the way the door opens.

A steel sink rests to the right of the toilet, and a few drawers extend from the corner of the packed room. Curiosity gets the better of me, and I take a peek inside the top drawer. Metal divides it into multiple sections. An electric toothbrush, toothpaste, hair bands, and others of Edyn's belongings fill the right side. The left half of the drawer has been emptied for my use, as has the entire middle drawer.

The bottom drawer is stocked with various feminine products, among other things. I'm pleased to know that the BOTs, Head of County, or whoever runs this joint, does not mandate that females receive implants that impede the body's natural process. According to Crewe, women's fertility can still be weak long after the implant has been removed. I don't particularly care whether I remain fertile, but I don't trust anything that the government places in my body, especially after learning how grotesquely my rights were violated by a chip that allowed the government to listen in on my conversations.

On my way out of the room, I catch a glimpse of myself in the mirror above the sink. I wonder how awful I looked right after the accident, considering that I've never look as battered as I do today. The bridge of my nose is almost as wide as the tip. It's clear it's been broken. Remnants of this morning's nosebleed still crust the insides of each nostril.

The inner corner of my right eye is blood red from the iris to the tear duct. Both my upper and lower lids are purplish on that eye, and deep bruising spreads to my cheekbone underneath it. The left side of my face is only colorful below the eye, and the colors are more subdued.

My hair is dirty and tangled, but that's nothing new. What is new is its length; it's a few inches shorter than it used to be. Really? Even the length of my hair is at their discretion? Frustrated, I start to pull it back, but stop to examine the laceration on my forehead that creeps into my hairline.

Oddly, it looks better than it did before. Someone from the county improved Galvesten's stitch job. Now that it's neat, I could someday forget getting this wound by head-butting Crewe to free myself from his grasp and go after my kidnapped sister. That was the least of the pain I caused him. The worst of it, I will never forget. Neither will he.

I wish I had decided this fate for myself earlier. I would have complied to live in level five of this place—in solitary confinement—for a hundred years, if it would have saved Cy and Decklin. Unfortunately, I can't go back. All I can do is hope that by coming here to prevent further loss of life, I've taken a step toward righting my wrongs. If my father and Crewe can let me go, as I demanded in the letters I left to each of them, no one else will die in vain.

After the deaths of two of his men, my father found himself in a difficult spot. It was the foundation for why, in my perception, he had given up on rescuing Evvie. Hopefully, he'll act consistently now that his eldest daughter has taken her place.

The last time I spoke to Crewe, he was so distant from me. Then, eyes ablaze with anger, he finally lifted his head to speak a single, cold word to me. *Leave*.

Neither of them will come. I believe and accept what Edyn stated last night. I will breathe my last breath within the steel walls of this tomb.

An alarm blares from the digital clock between the media screens that now painfully illuminate the room. Rushing to it, I tap the clock face, but evidently, the alarm is not configured to turn off this way. I squint to find a button to turn the clock off, but there are none. A back and forth wave of my hands in front of the digital pane also fails. The ringing continues.

Two brisk thuds against the wall adjoining my bed startles me so much that I nearly trip over the chair beside Edyn's half of the desk. Three more thuds, louder than the first pair, follow.

"Turn it off!" a grizzly male in the neighboring cell groans.

"How?" I yell through the wall.

"Stand on the bed and face your screen," he replies unsympathetically. This man has quickly made it known that he is not one to be crossed, even though an impenetrable wall stands between us. I don't hesitate to do as he instructs.

When I stand atop my bed, the media screen changes from a blinding, artificial light source to an enlarged image of my eyeball, through which a red line passes. After the scanner has identified me, a greeting on the screen reads, *Good morning, Sydney Layton*.

This is direly perplexing. Why would the screen say Layton instead of Harter? Obviously, the Neocropolis powers at be know my true identity. For some reason, they intend to keep my family name from the other residents.

Maybe some inhabitants have heard of or have even lived in Sheridan. Many of these people were imprisoned for knowing too much. It's quite possible that someone could have been snatched from Sheridan the way that Evvie was. Someone here could know the captain by his name, Demetri Harter. They may have even known him well enough to hear him speak of his little princess, Sydney, who was left behind in Miles.

If the residents knew they had a bona fide connection to refugee life through me…My heartbeat quickens with the thought. No. No hopes yet. There is much more to learn. I assume I'm expected to keep my true identity secret. I'll abide for the time being.

'Tap anywhere to continue' flashes over and over at the bottom of the media screen. In doing so, I am presented with my schedule for September 24, 2033:

Most of my *activities* for the day seem like first-day prison protocol. The one that both eludes and worries me is the classified activity that I'll have to attend this evening. Even the location is classified. Whoever is hosting this event doesn't want anyone to know where to find us.

"Open up," a voice calls simultaneously as knocks are placed on the door. I jump down from the bed and pull open the narrow door that encloses the tiny space. On the other side are metal bars.

"Breakfast is served," says a gangly boy with bright red hair and a wide grin. He looks a couple of years younger than I am. "Thank you," he says as I take from him a tiny saucer containing a red, rubbery slab.

"Shouldn't I be thanking you?" I ask the second person known to me at Neocropolis.

"For that?" he asks, pointing to the mysterious breakfast. "Take a bite and you'll have your answer," he jokes. "I was thanking you for providing me with two pillows this week." I look at my pillow and back to him with confusion. Does he want me to pay him with my pillow for the meal he just brought to me?

"Not *your* pillow!" he laughs. "That wouldn't be very

neighborly. My roommate and I madc a bet about the new girl. I can see that I won, so I get his extra pillow for a week. Ah, to live like a king!" he says with more sincerity than I can believe in a place like this.

Kings live in the stately upper floors of impressive castles, not in glum cells stomped into the earth. I want to fire that line at him, but my hostility should be chewed on rather than spit at this cheery young man. Instead, I ask, "What was the bet?"

He bounces excitedly at the chance to share. "He bet you'd be a beauty, and I banked on beast."

That's neighborly, I think, and then I remember how I looked in the mirror this morning. I can't argue with his finding.

"You'll have to meet him today, okay? I can't lose a bet to him three weeks in a row," he pleads with me. "I'm tired of picking up his things in our room, and I know he's doing it on purpose," he puffs.

"Well, I don't think I'll look any less hideous tomorrow," I tell him.

"Oh, come on now," he says, perhaps a little hurt that his playfulness hasn't charmed me. He tries a different angle. "Well, promise me that if you do go out of your way to meet anyone other than my roommate you choose…" he comes as close to me as the bars will allow and whispers, "the big dude next door." He thumbs in the direction of the unpleasant neighbor, whose aggressive thuds startled me more than the blaring alarm did. "Maybe your face can do all of us a favor and bring his terrorizing down a notch or two." The boy snickers.

"I doubt I'd have that affect," I confess.

"I wouldn't try to find out," he advises. "Welcome to Neocropolis," he says, raising his eyebrows and grinning. With that, he tiptoes in the direction of my intimidating neighbor, looking over his shoulder to make sure I notice his timid gait.

To his delight, I shake my head in amusement. After he's out of my sight, I take a moment to take him in. His high spirits are awe-worthy after being locked in a place like this for whatever sentence he's served thus far. He reminds me of another person who had a similarly resilient and jovial heart—someone I used to admire for it. Unfortunately, that man's spirit no longer graces this earth.

To remember and honor this fallen friend, my father urged all the Sheridans to find a reason to smile each day. I am still a Sheridan at heart, and forever a friend to the one we lost, so I intend to honor him as the captain suggested. Maybe the gangly, red-haired teen can help me reap some joy from what the rest of my life has to offer.

Any hint of contentment is eradicated as soon as I bite into the gummy slab that the boy served me for breakfast. *What do they put in this?* I make the next bite bigger and swallow the substance without chewing. It isn't much more tolerable this way, but I manage to get it down.

I slurp some water from the sink to round off my underwhelming breakfast. I don't have time to shower before I'm supposed to begin my next activity, so I splash some water on my face instead. I at least have to scrub the dried blood from inside my nose.

Edyn is still a stranger to me, but I've gotten a good enough grasp of her to know that she won't mind if I steal a hair band to pull back my knotted locks and some toothpaste to rid my tongue of the aftertaste left by my breakfast.

I slip on the new white shoes beside my bed. The clock reads 7:27—only a few minutes until I'm supposed to report to room 302 to do paperwork. Since I don't know where it is, I decide to leave now. It's going to take some practice for me to abide by rules so that I don't land myself in solitary, like Edyn warned against. I might as well begin turning over a new leaf today by following what they've forced on me to a tee.

At my room's gate, I discover that finding room 302 isn't the biggest obstacle to arriving there on time. I'm locked in.

"Hello?" I call to anyone who can hear me. No one ceases their light chatter to answer. "Can someone tell me how we open the gates?" I ask aimlessly.

"We don't," a female voice to my right answers. Her response is followed by cruel chuckles from multiple residents. I turn my back to the hallway, rest against the bars, and bitterly watch the clock approach 7:30.

As a new addition to an isolated group, I hoped to be welcomed. During my childhood, a new classmate was added to our section on EduWeb every now and then. Most of the time, the transfer was made because the child's parent made a fuss about their instruction monitor or a classmate who was cyber-bullying them.

Once, a girl who had attended the traditional school was added to my section. Like the others in my class, I was buzzing with excitement to meet her, virtually or otherwise. I had hoped she would be more like myself, having had an upbringing where technology was less of an influence. I reached out in a way that was not normal for me. We were almost friends, but then she stopped talking to me. She messaged me to tell me point-blank that the other girls in my section told her not to be friends with me because I was weird.

"Your gate will unlock when it's time."

I turn to search the rooms across the hall from where

the voice came. A couple of the green, inner cell doors are closed, but most of them are open, exposing parts of the rooms behind the bars.

A young man emerges from the bathroom space of the room directly across from me. "Where do you need to go?" he asks with a toothbrush stuffed in his mouth.

"Room 302," I answer. Just then, my gate buzzes and I'm able to swing it open.

Without additional pleasantries, he points me in the direction that I need to go. My room is fairly close to one end of the building, but it seems my destination is on the opposite end. I'll have to walk down the bright corridor and pass most of the level three occupants to get there.

Many of the residents say nothing to me. A couple of people welcome me amiably. Others give a similar greeting, but with a sarcastic sneer.

There is only one other prisoner in the hallway. As I near the well-built man, I begin to rethink whether he is a prisoner. He wears a navy jumpsuit similar to mine, but his is collared and something is embroidered on the left breast pocket. A thick belt with hooks and compartments wraps around his waist. Edyn mentioned that this place has guards. Could he be one?

He holds a tablet in his hand, but his attention is on me, and not in the informative way that I have been looking at him. To avoid looking at him as I pass, I peer into the open area near which he stands guard. I may have been excited at the sight of a decent-sized gym, if not for the catcall from the guard that makes my skin crawl.

A fit, dark-haired man in his mid-thirties stands outside room 302. With his at-attention stance, he reminds me of a soldier, but his attire in entirely wrong. He wears a red tie that stands out against his black dress shirt, pants, and vest. "Welcome, Sydney," he says, extending his hand to greet me. The gesture is uncommon to Miles, but was used frequently in Sheridan. I offer him my hand, but don't make eye contact with him. Instead, I focus on a subtle reflective quality of his vest. It has buttons and elegant trim in place of straps and practicality, but I can't mistake the material. A multi-layered vest made from strong, synthetic fibers—the kind meant to lessen the damage of a weapon—protects him.

"Come in. Take a seat." He smiles, slides my seat away from a sleek desk, and then settles in his high-backed, leather chair opposite me. "My name is Officer J. I am second in command to Officer Q., who heads level three. I have been instructed to first give you this." He slides a sealed envelope toward me, but does not release his hands from it. He dark eyes lock onto mine, and he studies me briefly. "After I step out of the room, you are to open the envelope, read the classified message, and then burn it." He places a ceramic bowl and a lighter before me. "Knock when you're finished." With that, Officer J. pushes himself out of the large chair and exits the room.

I tear open the envelope and read:

You are Sydney Layton to anyone who inquires, including residents, guards, officers, and all other personnel with whom you will come in contact. You have never had record of your biological parents. You lived in the orphanage until Merideth Layton adopted you in 2030.

Your paperwork indicates that you have been admitted due to an attempt to remove your chip prior to a suspected breaching attempt. This fact should be regarded when conversing with all parties listed above.

Under no circumstances should you mention Sheridan, its captain, your sister, the seeksmen or any other deserters, or your history of breaching. We have our way of enforcing these requirements, as you will find out tonight.

The message is unsigned, but the last sentence leads me to believe it comes from the unspecified person who will host my classified activity tonight. I have good reason to fear that their method of enforcing these demands is going to involve force.

I tear the page to pieces and place all but one in the ceramic bowl. The final piece, I light on fire before dropping it into the bowl with the others. As the fire reduces the scraps to ash, I try to erase the truth from my mind, and bury the unspeakable people deep within my heart.

When the paper is dust, I knock on the door. Officer J. returns to outline the expectations for remaining on level three and the opportunities for upward mobility if I behave well. On his tablet, I place my thumb into a box to verify via electronic signature that I am Sydney Layton. It's remarkable how easily my life has been erased, and how little I decide to care. What difference does it make if I'll never see the ones I love again?

THREE

"Am I interrupting?" a hard-lined woman near fifty asks as she steps through the doorway of Officer J.'s open office.

"Not at all. We've just finished," he says. "Sydney, this is Officer Q., head officer of level three."

That's obvious. Her position is identifiable by her business uniform, which contrasts with the jumpsuits of the prisoners and the navy uniforms of the guards. She also wears a deep purple vest that has a slight iridescence. It's made of the same fibers as Officer J.'s.

"Follow me," Officer Q. says, without extending her hand or waiting for me to rise before she exits. "Close the door," she says with cold superiority after I enter the room. Her office is identical to Officer J.'s, but somehow it feels tighter and the air, staler. "Sit." Officer Q. points to the chair next to hers rather than one on the other side of her desk. She readies her tablet for our meeting while I sit silently, waiting. An uncomfortable minute passes before she swivels her chair around to address me, knee to knee.

She crosses her legs and leans back into her chair. "Tell me about yourself, Sydney."

I've always hated this directive, commonly asked of me

by people like my classmates and instruction monitor when I was young, orphanage staff and potential fosters in my early teens, and later the employees of the restaurant where I worked. Throughout all stages of my life, there has been little to say. I couldn't talk about my parents, I didn't really like the core subjects in school, I wasn't in any sports or clubs, and I didn't have any friends. Turn-of-the-century history and politics were always of interest to me, but speaking of that would be almost as bad as admitting that a favorite pastime of mine was breaching the county barrier. Evvie was the only subject I could talk about when asked about myself. Now that she's been erased from my life, I have no safe answer.

"There isn't much to tell," I finally say. I'm not all that sour in saying it, but Officer Q. is displeased by my response.

"Don't walk in my office with a face like that and tell me you don't have a story to go with it," she says sternly. "You've been admitted to one of the three criminal levels of Neocropolis, so I know what you're not—a drone. But I need more than that." Officer Q. uncrosses her legs and leans toward me. "I need to know who you *are*. It's my job to know my floor."

If she wanted me to confess the action that had me admitted to this prison, then she should have asked that and not used the irritatingly vague *tell me about yourself*.

When I don't answer immediately, she stands and begins to walk about the room. "Stubbornness won't get you anywhere in here, Sydney. Well, that's not true," she decides. "It won't get you anywhere that you want to be." Officer Q. peers at me haughtily.

Hatred for the head officer quickly brings me out of my forced passiveness and into the self I know—Sydney Harter, who is stubborn to a fault, sour by nature, and easily agitated.

"You've seen my paperwork. You already know the answers to what you're asking," I ridicule, "so what's the point?"

She doesn't snap back at me as I expect. She is very collected when she responds, "There is something that the paperwork does not tell me that you will. Actions don't define who we are. Motivation, Sydney. The contemplation behind carefully made decisions tells much more about a person than what it is they did." Officer Q. returns to her seat. Narrowing her gaze, she says, "Let's try again, shall we? Tell me why you're here, Ms. Layton."

Now I intend to create a story that matches my true character, perhaps painting myself to have even greater courage than I do. It'll be a lie, of course, but through the lie, I'll let Officer Q. know *exactly* who I am.

"I was angry," I answer, simply at first. She doesn't beckon more from me, but I'm driven by the truth in this piece. "I was angry all the time. Adults who didn't stand up to the county's crude systems and corrupt leaders disgusted me. My foster irritated me because she thought that loving me could erase the evil that Miles handed me. I couldn't make friends with classmates or neighbors. People disliked me because I *wouldn't* accept imprisonment. The electric barrier was no different than the metal bars of this place."

Officer Q. smiles and relaxes into her chair again. Her cool delight eggs me on.

"That was my motivation for taking a knife and cutting into my arm to dig out my chip. Unfortunately, I damaged my chip while trying to extract it, and so they came. The blow that took me down broke my nose. I knew it was a lost cause as they pinned me, but that was no reason to quit. A quitter is *not* who I am." Officer Q. seems to be getting a peculiar satisfaction as I feed her the lie. She says nothing, so I continue to let the fabrication roll off my tongue. "I struggled with everything I am as they tried to cuff me. I broke my thumb against their force and gashed my forehead on the knife that still lay on the floor. That's the story that goes with my face. Does that tell you who I am?" My pulse rises as I sneer at the head officer.

"I think you've told a tale of who you want to be," she retorts. "Either way, it's enough for today." Officer Q. stands and taps her tablet a few times as she heads to the door. Opening it, she says, "I'll watch you go back to your room." Her face is unreadable as she rigidly gestures for me to leave. "Your tour guide will pick you up in ten minutes."

Surprised, angry, and embarrassed that she's called my bluff, I rise quickly and exit. The heat of her smile burns into the flesh on my back as I walk through the long hallway toward my cell. Most of the rooms I pass appear empty, so I'm glad I don't have to endure additional hostile stares.

From her tablet, Officer Q. unlocks my cell and relocks it as the weighted gate slams behind me.

Officer Q. was right. The girl in the tale is the person that I wish I could be. Even still, the phonily courageous Sydney *Layton* failed in her escape and wound up in more complete captivity than the one she started in.

The only edge that Sydney *Harter* has is that she did succeed in freeing herself time and again. My largest victory may have come by the hands of Crewe and Cy Davids, but it wouldn't have been possible if I hadn't escaped into my haven first. With the seeksmen's help, I experienced true freedom in Sheridan. When they were dead, dispersed, or downtrodden, I created a way to return someone I love more than myself to that free civilization.

It's too soon to imagine her happy, but someday I'll be able to picture Evvie gabbing away with her friends in the school cafeteria, or making up for lost time with our dad over breakfast in the restaurant below the meeting space where the seeksmen devised their plans.

Hopefully, Evvie has been able to meet the captain by now. I want her to have more people than just Crewe to trust. I'm sure the first thing Merick did when he woke and found me missing was call the captain in Braves, which would certainly have sent him hightailing back to Sheridan. Meanwhile, Evvie would have woken and urgently asked around until she found Crewe. Once with him, she would also meet Merick, who would have called my father with an update. Through the letters, Merick would know and would have to tell my father that my disappearance was planned.

My hope is that, in that moment, my father stayed his course toward Miles rather than turning around to continue making invasion plans with the leaders of Braves. I hope that meeting his other daughter, and the words in my letter to him, were together enough to keep him from acting rashly.

I hadn't yet thought about how strange it must have been for Evvie to hold in her hand a letter addressed to herself, Crewe, and *Dad*. After opening her envelope and reading the text by my hand, she would suddenly learn that our father was truly alive and usually right there in Sheridan, her new home. Soon, she would also understand why I hadn't addressed a letter to Cy. I pray to God she doesn't feel any guilt, though his death came from an effort to save her.

The buzz of my cell gate alerts me back to my present reality. Someone knocks lightly on the inner door, and then opens it.

"Hi, Sydney. I'm Emanda, your tour guide," says an amiable woman in a jumpsuit designed to imitate business wear. Her hair is dark and almost as curly as Gwen's, the woman I worked with at the laundromat in Miles. It's hard to tell her age. She could fall anywhere between twenty-five and thirty-five.

"We're actually going to begin right here in your apartment, so you can stay there if you like." Emanda seems very nice, but calling this *cell* an apartment pricks me some. "Do you mind if I turn on the overhead lights?" she asks.

"Oh, sure," I answer. Emanda slides her finger along a vertical metal strip below the shelving unit at the end of my bed, illuminating part of the ceiling.

"There's another signal to the side of your screen," she says, pointing. "A sliding stroke will cause the lights to function as a dimmer, while tapping the lower, middle, or upper portion in a staccato fashion will turn on the corresponding section to its fullest capacity."

Emanda approaches the strip to demonstrate. "Let's say you're in bed reading and you want only the light near your head on, but dimly so because your roommate is asleep. You'll want to tap the top of the strip once to choose the light's location, then once more to slide to your desired softness."

Apathetically, I try the light as instructed. I'm surprised that Merideth didn't have this latest, functional lighting in her home. Visiting Evvie at her foster's the few times that I had kept me current on technological home furnishings. The transitions building was always far behind.

"I trust you figured out this morning how your screen works?" she asks. I nod. "They actually have heat—not motion—sensors, so they turn off automatically if both residents are out of the apartment. You can turn the screen off by holding your thumb here." She demonstrates. "It's recommended that you be exposed to this light source at least one hour each day, but no more than three."

"Why?" I ask the guide.

"Behind the glass are UV-A light bulbs. The UV-A rays provide us some benefits that are traditional of the sun, like the production of vitamin D3 to help our bodies absorb calcium and other minerals from food. The lights also stimulate the production of endorphins to guard against depression and melatonin to regulate sleep. They improve blood circulation, metabolism, and pulse, liver, and kidney function. Avoid looking directly into the light, and be sure to use protective lotion each day."

"Where do I get the lotion?" I ask.

"Here," she says, signaling me to follow her toward the shower room. "You have a dispenser for shampoo, conditioner, body wash, and lotion. Once a week, your shower and bathroom will be scrubbed and the dispensers refilled. It's one of the many jobs available to earn points."

"Points?"

"Yes. On level three, residents earn points by working. The points buy you privileges like warm shower water, minted toothpaste, or an extra pillow. They can also purchase passes to watch selected media programs in the den, use the gymnasium, or check out a paper book from the library. We'll cover much of that during the rest of the tour."

"What do workers earn on other levels?" I ask Emanda.

"Well, I might as well give you the grounds rundown now. There are a total of six levels in Neo-Necropolis," she begins. My ears perk up with that fact. I thought there were five. "Each level is approximately 7,750 square feet. The bottom level houses residents labeled *Level Five*. Those residents live in solitary confinement. There are forty five-by-nine foot cells, of which seventeen are in permanent use and twelve are in semi-permanent use. Five is the least populated level."

Many questions come to mind. "What is the difference between permanent and semi-permanent use?" I ask first.

"Permanent Fives have no chance for upward mobility. Semi-permanent Fives have a chance to move to Level Four, but they are often converted to a permanent."

"I have another question," I admit.

"Residents always ask the most questions about level five," Emanda responds. "Go ahead," she smiles.

Forty closet-sized cells can only take up a fraction of the square footage down there. Edyn mentioned that Level Fours don't have the amenities we have on three, so I doubt Fives have any. "What else is there on Level Five besides the cells?" I ask Emanda.

"I'm not privy to the layout of the bottom level," she says, shooting me a warning. "I know there are no luxuries like there are on this level. I also know that Level Four receives Level Five's AM dishes and laundry for cleaning, and that Level Three receives its PM workload, so it seems there are no workplaces either. Perhaps additional offices or storage," she says, but I can tell she doesn't believe that possibility herself.

"Aren't there people who have lived in solitary but have been moved up?" I begin.

"I know what you are getting at," Emanda interjects, "but it's not something that can be answered. I imagine those residents are under orders not to speak about the unknown parts of Level Five, so it would be best if you don't ask about it again," she advises.

"Let's get back to the grounds sketch, shall we?" Emanda continues without waiting for me to respond. "Levels Three and Four are nearly identical in layout, except that Level Four has storage in place of a library and den. There are thirty-six inhabitants of Four. They work for rights while Level Threes work for privileges. Fours' points go toward meals, clothing, towels, bedding, running water in the shower, toiletries, et cetera. The only privileges they can earn are the abilities to exercise in the gymnasium and to check out paper books from the library on your level."

Edyn has several books on her shelf, and she's built in a way that tells me she makes a trip to the gym daily, but I can't assume points will be so easy for me to earn. Edyn has had seven years to accumulate points.

"You'll learn about your own level during your work systems and offerings meeting today, so I'll tell you about Levels One and Two. On those levels, we work to earn paper bills that allow us to pay our apartment rent, purchase specialty meals from a restaurant, a gym membership, paper books, or films or programs on our home media screens. We can also rent one of the dens for a birthday party, visit the salon…the list goes on," she says, not meaning to brag.

How can they have the space for multiple dens, restaurants in addition to the cafeteria, a gymnasium, and a *salon*? Are there that few residents on levels one and two? "Are One and Two designed differently than three?" I ask Emanda.

"Well, I should first explain that the level directly below EPA 1-12's basement is Level One, sometimes referred to as Innocence," Emanda says with a slight eye roll. "Below that is Neo-Necropolis' little metropolis. We call it *The Main*. It contains the gym, cafeteria, library, dens, offices, and businesses to which Levels One and Two have access. Level One above and Two below The Main are solely apartments, many of which are large. There are thirty-six Ones and thirty-five on my level. Two," she adds. "The main differences between Ones and Twos are that Ones make a greater wage and there are no gates, meaning no nighttime curfew."

No bars on Level One. Noted. "Do you earn your income through these tours?" I ask Emanda, covering my secret, devious thought.

"Part of it. I give tours to new residents, those who have been moved up or down a level, and occasionally to Ones or Twos whose curiosity has gotten the better of them." How tragic that Innocents and Twos have nothing better to do with their time and money than to tour the locked up of a lower level. "I also act as an accountant for my husband's business and another friend's."

"Your husband lives in Neocropolis too?" I inquire, surprised.

"Well, he's my second husband. After my first husband remarried out there, I began dating the man who is now my husband."

"How did you know your first husband had remarried?" I ask with my deepest intrigue yet.

"The internet. On One and Two, you're allowed to conduct a supervised search of your family or anything else that suits your fancy on the tablets in the library." I wish this luxury were allowed on Level Three. I wonder what the county has falsified for the disappearances of my sister and me. Truthfully, staying up to date on my family is impossible. They're *really* on the outside, so even if I were able to move up to Two, I'll never know what has become of them.

"You can't post, of course." Emanda lets out a chuckle at the obvious, but some depressing thought stifles it. Maybe she's thinking of her first husband—possibly their children. Being able to use a tablet like that must be so tempting. In all of its years, and with all of its condemned-to-death prisoners, not one post has been transmitted from Neocropolis. I can imagine what any resident would give to post just one more time.

"You live on the most populated level," Emanda continues, returning to her spirits. "There is bound to be some movement soon." She winks. "Let's get out there and have a look, shall we?"

In the course of touring the level, I learn that the male cells on the opposite side of my level are a pinch bigger, but that there are more males on my level than females, so a few of the male residents live in the female row. Unfortunately, that includes the crotchety man whose bed is a wall away from mine.

In addition to a slew of information, I obtain a bundle of provisions during the tour. From the storage room, I receive five bland jumpsuits, a supply of socks and undergarments, and a plastic bag labeled *female*. It contains a small, electric toothbrush, toothpaste, a hairbrush and a few hair ties, deodorant, cotton swabs, a nail file, lip balm, a tiny tube of antibiotic ointment, bandages, and feminine products.

When I ask about a razor, I'm told that when I've saved enough points, the Level Two barber can come down to give me an electric shave or wax. Before learning that fact, I was pleased to see that two of my jumpsuits are sleeveless and cropped above the knee. Now, I've decided I'll be wearing the standard jumpsuit to the gym.

"Thank you, Emanda," I say at the conclusion of the tour. "You've been very helpful."

"You're welcome, Sydney," she says sincerely. "Stay grounded, and maybe I'll see you on Two." Emanda smiles and heads to the elevator, leaving me at Officer J.'s door. The door closes to lift her to the only sort of society she'll know again.

FOUR

Officer J. spends the first part of our second meeting today elaborating on the work system and what I can get with the points I earn. Even though the items we work for on Level Three are viewed as privileges, working is not really optional unless I want to stay locked in a box all day without a thing to do but think about all my problems. I would be allowed a half-hour lunch and dinner in the cafeteria each day, but would taste nothing but white rice, baked beans, and sliced bread for the rest of my life. Oh, I can't forget the disgusting, vitamin-infused breakfast chew.

There are only four labor choices, as most of the positions already have more than enough residents assigned to them. I can scrub showers and bathrooms, as well as restock the necessary supplies, like a prison housekeeper, prepare food for the inmates, collect and wash dishes, or work in the Level Three laundry facility. Although it would keep me busy, I have no interest in scrubbing away at mildew and scum or food scraps all day. I'll continue working in the industries I know.

From 10:00 to 2:30 each day, I'll work in food service, preparing lunches and cleaning the tiny cafeteria kitchen before the dinner shift arrives. It won't be at all like serving at Tiana's, but at least it's something familiar.

I'll then work in laundry from 3:00 to 7:30. My job duties there will include collecting, washing, folding, and returning clothing, bedding, and towels used in the cells, kitchen, and gym. I'll also be responsible for organizing a more efficient wash cycle, and for determining when individuals merit the issuing of new clothing items from storage. I agree to begin this assignment this afternoon. Right afterward, I'll be summoned to my classified activity, something of which Officer J. hastily reminds me as he ushers me out of the door.

Room 305 of Level Three is what must be the tiniest hospital on earth. A woman in a white coat enters. She says hello, but is then silent as she stirs about the room, readying instruments and medications. Because of the way she carries herself, I decide that she must be a resident of Neocropolis rather than a medic from the outside. An outside physician would not be so nervous during a routine underground appointment. I only hope she's not nervous because she's new to the medical field.

I soon realize that the woman is purposely avoiding eye contact and delaying necessary conversation with me. Maybe she's an Innocent, and doctoring wayward patients on Level Three terrifies her. Maybe it's my face. The woman pauses to gather herself before forcing herself to speak to me.

"How do you feel today?" she asks with her back to me, her face only partially turned in my direction.

"I'm okay," I answer, my voice cracking with tension. She crosses to one of the beds and holds down a button, changing it to an upright position.

"Take a seat." The medic distances herself as much as she can from me as soon as I'm seated. "Are you experiencing any muscle weakness, balance problems, or nausea?"

"No," I answer.

"Dizziness, confusion, or headache?" she asks from behind a tablet.

"Maybe a little." I've had a perpetual headache since I was captured by the seeksmen a week and a half ago.

"I'm told you were up for a bit this morning. Were you able to fall back asleep?" She looks up at me for a fleeting moment, and then dives deeper into the chart on her tablet. It's uncomfortable to watch her try to steady her breathing. I wonder if *she* shouldn't be the one being doctored.

"Yeah." I was quite surprised that I had fallen back asleep after learning from Edyn my fate in this place.

"That's good." The woman approaches me, pulls the connected tray out from the side of the bed, and places two plastic cups before me. The smaller of the two contains a few pills, and the larger is filled with water. "Take those," she says before walking back to her tablet. "They're a low dose of painkillers. When you're through, roll up your sleeve above your elbow, please. You're here to do an intravenous steroid that will manage any residual swelling around your brain from the severe concussion you suffered. It should also help reduce the swelling around your nose and eye."

Without wasting any time, she inserts an IV into my arm. Once the drip is going, she looks me in the eye for the first time, but only because it's required of her job today. "Have you been experiencing any flashing lights?" she asks as she moves a bright light between my eyes. Suddenly, I feel like there is something vaguely familiar about the woman.

"No," I answer. "Are you a nurse or a doctor?" I ask.

"A doctor. Doctor McClain," she responds simply.

"I'm Sydney," I tell her.

At this, she rests her instrument and examines me with strange bewilderment. Her expression morphs into a deep sadness as her eyes begin to well and she says, "I know."

The way she says those words gives me the impression that she doesn't know my name from my chart or chatter between residents. Have I met this woman before? I imagine most, if not all, of Neocropolis' residents are from Miles.

"Excuse me," the doctor says as she stands abruptly to leave the room. I can hear her in the hallway talking to Officer J. Their conversation is brief but emotional. It results in Officer J. entering the hospital room instead of Doctor McClain returning.

"Doctor McClain wasn't feeling well and needed to step out," Officer J. tells me. "I'll send for our other doctor to come down and remove the IV in about twenty minutes."

Officer J. isn't out of the room thirty seconds before his superior steps in.

"Hello again, Sydney. Eventful morning?"

What is she *really* asking this time? Though Officer Q. is the last person I want to make conversation with, I decide to answer her thoroughly to cover all bases. I also drop my attitude considerably from the end of our last exchange—even border on demonstrating respect. "There was a lot of information to take in during the tour and my meeting with Officer J., but I think I'm understanding and adjusting well."

"And Doctor McClain was assessing your recovery just now?"

"Yes, and I feel fine," I tell her.

"Well, I guess that makes only one of you. Ironic, isn't it? The doctor being more ill than the patient?"

"I guess," I answer.

"You guess?" Officer Q. questions. "Did she not seem ill to you?"

It's not my place to make a conjecture as to what was really wrong with Doctor McClain. I don't know her, and I don't why Officer Q. needs me to verify whether I believed she was feeling ill. I don't want to get anyone in trouble, so I answer as safely as I can. "It's hard to tell when you don't know someone, but something must have been wrong."

"Hmm. So it seems," the head officer remarks. "Enjoy the rest of your day," she says without a hint of sincerity.

When the door closes behind Officer Q., I rest my heavy eyelids. The morning began stressfully and continued busily, leaving me little time to digest and process. I wish I had the means of escaping my worries with a long run in the wild like I used to. Sleep has never provided me this grace, but perhaps it can today since this steroid is making me tired. My thoughts become fragmented, lost. They give way to a dream.

The woman looking down at me is sad, yet she forces a sweet smile. She is holding my shaking shoulders and telling me that my mother loved my sister and me very much. The woman fights to restrain tears in the same way that she did minutes ago.

My heart races, and I force my eyes open. Regretfully, I had forgotten the face of the woman in the dream too soon after she had kindly tried to comfort me the day I discovered my mother's body at the institution. Not even my subconscious could reproduce the memory of her. That is, until today, when the same expression formed on the face that I saw once ten years ago.

Doctor McClain was only a nurse then. In the orphanage, I used to pray that she would come and take Evvie and me home with her. She was the first person in a long time to really look at me and *care*. The kind nurse was the piece of the memory I tried to hold onto after that tragic day. Instead, the pieces I desperately tried to will away were those that became burned into my mind.

Though my face and name has changed since that day, Doctor McClain recognized me. She knows at least part of the truth about who I am. She will never buy the story that I concocted for Officer Q. this morning.

Could Officer Q. have known that Doctor McClain was a small part of my past? She must have stepped in to try to assess whether I had recognized the doctor in the way that she recognized me. I'm glad that the realization had not yet come to me. Officer Q. has already proven that she can see through me.

The Level Two doctor comes in, removes the IV, and gives me a little bag of medical provisions. Specific to me are a nighttime dose of the pain medication and an anti-inflammatory, as well as cream for the lacerations on my head and forearm. The other pills, aspirin, sleep aids, and menstrual symptom reducers come standard-packed, but in small quantities. The new doctor explains and mandates use of the final, pre-stocked item; two drops of the liquid in each eye every morning will protect my eyes from harmful UV-A exposure.

He tells me to go back to my room and rest for a half hour, but to make sure that I get to the cafeteria for lunch. The doctor goes freely to the elevator, but I am assigned an escort to walk me back to my cell.

"How's Neocropolis treating you so far, doll face?" asks the guard who made a vile comment toward me this morning.

Officer J. explained in my work systems meeting this morning that only the head officer of each level is a non-resident. All the assistant officers and guards are workers from one of the two non-criminal levels. He let me know that if I have any problems with guards or himself, that I should report it to Officer Q. The guard walking me to my cell seems more like the type to belong on Three than Edyn or the cheery, redheaded boy who served me breakfast. I can't imagine this guard could be an Innocent.

"What?" he says when I don't answer his question. "Don't you like my nickname for you, doll face?"

"My name is Sydney," I say sourly.

"Now that's not how a doll ought to be." We've arrived at my room but he doesn't unlock the gate. "I think somebody needs to sweeten you up," he says, leaning an arm against the bars over my head so that his face and body become uncomfortably close.

"You can let me in now," I say bitterly. Even if he's harmless, I have a lot of hatred stored up for this type of man; the type of man I feared could become a foster of my sister or me.

"You can be that way to me," he says without budging, "but I'm still going to be sweet to you." I glare at him as he flashes a suggestive smile at me. Finally, I hear the gate buzz, though it couldn't have been his doing. He backs away to allow me to pull the gate out, but then places his hand on the small of my back to usher me into my cell. "Get some beauty rest, doll face. I'll be back at one to let you out for lunch. As a matter of fact, I might switch my lunch break to join you."

I pull the gate closed and quickly follow with the inner door of my cell. I'm especially grateful for this door. My stomach writhes imagining the guard being able to look in on me any time he pleased.

I drop the plastic medical bag from the doctor in the

middle drawer of the bathroom cabinet alongside the items I received from the tour this morning. Opening two of the drawers under my bed, I haphazardly slide all the clothing items I received off the bed and into the drawers.

I've only completed half a day in this place. I have infinitely more to go. I don't know how I'm going to hold on to my sanity.

I know I'll be able to keep myself from doing something that would require me moving me to Five—I couldn't stand being confined to a cell only half the size of this. I wouldn't mind the solitude at first, but how long can someone be alone before they fill the void with imaginary company? I fear being sent to solitary because I'm certain that doing time down there would change me. I'm afraid I would go insane like my mother.

What I need to find is motivation to stay on Three. I need something that I can remind myself of when I have the urge to lip off to Officer Q. or kick a certain guard where he'd regret his words.

Edyn. Edyn seems like a good roommate. Who knows what type of person might be waiting for a cellmate on Four? The redheaded guy too. If anyone has a chance to pull a smile out of me, it's him. Even Officer J. is okay. I'm sure they send less compassionate guards and officers to the lowest levels.

There. I have three people to remind myself about if that guard pushes my buttons when he comes back to wake me for lunch. I won't respond to him. I doubt he'll persist in preying on me for long if I don't give him the gratification of a reaction.

With an action plan in mind, I can close my eyes and rest to refuel for the afternoon. I wish I knew a way to prepare myself for the unknown of this evening.

FIVE

At 12:58 PM, the alarm in my room sounds, causing me to jump to my feet on the bed. I don't want to disturb my grizzly neighbor again, especially if he also takes his lunch at one. I'm glad my alarm was set rather than being awoken by an ominous knock on the door. Hopefully, that means I'll be fortunate enough to avoid the guard for the rest of the day.

Just as I finish brushing my teeth in the bathroom, I hear the gate outside of my cell buzz. I hurry to pull the inner door open so that I don't miss my opportunity to walk to lunch alone.

A few other gates on either side of the hallway open at the same time as mine. The residents who file out quickly form little clusters as they walk through the hall towards the cafeteria. Though many study me with their eyes, none attempts to engage me in conversation. They pass harsh judgment on me as soon as they look upon my broken, bruised, and cut face.

A few of the residents in line before me hand the worker in the kitchen window a plastic card with which they are allowed to upgrade one item of their lunch meal. It's not so much of an upgrade as it is a variation, which must have a certain luster to people who eat the same mush every day. Some select dry mashed potatoes instead of rice, some swap green beans for baked beans, and others trade the slice of plain, white bread for a cut of heartier wheat.

The worker at the window doesn't waste her time to welcome me either. Residents of Neocropolis are very different from those in Sheridan, who crowded the car to welcome Evvie and me. Crewe was forced to stop and let them reach their hands in to shake ours. I shouldn't have expected a friendly welcome from those that were born and bred in the same cold county where I grew up. Citizens of Miles are never looking to make new friends, at least not with the likes of me.

"Sydney!" calls a jolly voice in the back of the tiny cafeteria kitchen. I'm glad one of my food service coworkers will be the friendly boy who served me breakfast this morning. "Hey, come over to the door on the side quickly." His invitation is largely welcomed. He spared me the difficulty of determining the direction of my next step. If one of the three cafeteria tables were empty, I would have gone toward it. Since they are all occupied, I'm hoping that he can point me toward the least uncomfortable place to sit.

"Gauge!" he yells across the cafeteria as I'm wrapping around to the side of the kitchen. His eyes are fixed on someone whom he has to wave over persistently before a lean young man in a black jumpsuit reluctantly stands. I saw him briefly this morning, and through two sets of bars, as he explained to me that my gate would open when it was time.

"That's my roommate, Gauge," my acquaintance says, pointing to the resident who is dismissing himself from the older residents around him.

"You live across from me," I say to the redheaded cafeteria worker.

"Well, yeah! I called you neighbor," he teases.

"I don't know your name," I realize.

"What?" he exclaims. "It's written all over me!" I examine his jumpsuit for an embroidered name, but I don't see one.

"We call him Red," says the resident in black as he approaches us. His blue eyes make a piecing contrast with his dark garment and dark hair. "He's a pain, but we all tolerate him," Red's roommate dryly banters. "I know your name, and you've heard mine," he says simply.

"Is Gauge you're real name?" I ask him.

"Yep," he nods.

"Alright, enough chatter," Red interrupts. "Let's get down to business—beauty or beast?"

"You're a piece of work," Gauge tells his roommate. "Are we getting the eye?" Gauge asks Red more seriously. I follow Red's gaze to a portly guard standing at the opening on the opposite side of the cafeteria.

"Back to work!" Red answers as he flies back into the kitchen.

"Come on," Gauge says as he walks away. "You can sit by us."

Though I don't see her among the faces, I decide to ask Gauge about my roommate. "Does Edyn eat this lunch?"

"Nope. She's training." Gauge sits at the end of the table and motions to his friends to slide his tray over. I'm glad to be sitting *with* rather than *by* someone. Emanda's tour this morning gave me the dry facts, but an insider is needed to answer most of my questions.

"What is Edyn training for?" I ask Gauge.

"No, she's providing the training," he corrects me. "It's her job. Have you learned yet that the rooms are miked?" he asks, surprising me with the sudden change in our exchange. I answer with a nod. "Good." Gauge scoops as much mashed potatoes as he can fit onto his recycled spork and jams it into his mouth. "You should know that they can distinguish all the individual conversations going on in here; mikes are planted everywhere."

"Wouldn't it be easier to mike us through chips?"

Gauge looks a little startled by my comment. He swallows before continuing. "We don't have chips in here. Chips are archives, you know, and we're supposed to be dead. Mikes are coming soon for people out there, though. They've tried some prototypes, but the sound is muffled. It'll clear up when they start implanting into the neck."

Planting the chip closer to the vocal chords would definitely improve the sound. It will also make it more difficult for Galvesten to remove chips so that the BOTs can't track new refugees. Convenient.

"So how did you die?" I ask Gauge. He stops chewing. The muscles in his jaw tighten, and he clenches the handle of his spork.

"Suicide," he answers shortly.

I understand quickly that it was rude for me to ask. Even though it's a lie, the way a resident's family and friends above perceive their death could become a very personal matter. Maybe I should apologize. Instead, I start eating.

"That's how Red ended up here," Gauge says.

I don't understand what he means. "Did he try to commit suicide?" I ask.

"No, no. Red was brought in as an Innocent when he was eleven. A school project landed him here. Can you believe that?"

"How?" I ask.

"He and some other kids in his section were grouped together to research Billings County for geography credit hours. He was responsible for statistics: original and current population, racial breakdown, number orphaned—standard stuff." I nod. I've completed similar projects for credit hours. Gauge leans over his tray and lowers his voice. "Well, he comes across this bizarre article on statistics for causes of death before and after the population bill and establishment of counties. Suicide, fast-acting illnesses, and accidental deaths had more than quadrupled."

I immediately understand. It's people like us—people buried below the earth—that account for the change. The County's figures must also include anyone who did escape and was brought to Sheridan by the seeksmen that survey the outskirts of Billings. The government would have lied to their loved ones in order to account for their sudden disappearances too. Some from the statistics must truly be dead, but that's not saying that their given causes of death are true.

I'm sure Miles County has had a similar trend. There are one hundred seventy-five of us locked up down here. There are many former citizens that are now in Sheridan, like my father, Crewe, and even Cy, whose death record probably reads accidental. Nothing could be farther from the truth.

Suddenly, an eerie thought creeps into my mind. I saw clearly that my mother really was dead. The gashes in her wrists and the blood on the floor certainly indicated suicide, but was that the *truth*, or was it only made to look that way? For the first time in the ten years that she's been dead, I find myself questioning whether my mother really took her own life.

"It's a lot to take in," Gauge says.

"Yeah," I say as I pull myself back to our conversation. "Yeah, it is." I want to tell Gauge about my personal experience with such statistics, but I'm not supposed to know anything about my mother or father. Anyone I meet is supposed to believe that I was raised in the orphanage and adopted by Merideth Layton sometime in 2030.

"Anyway," Gauge continues, "Red was visited by a few strange men with questions. Red is a pretty odd character, but his IQ is off the charts. So the kid won't stop asking *them* questions. He's brilliant, yet too stupid to know when to shut up," Gauge explains. "I think he scared them. I think they mistook his idiocy for boldness. They were afraid to let a kid like that grow more aware and courageous, so they dragged him from his house to this tomb."

I want to ask what lie was told to Red's family to cover his disappearance, but maybe it's better to ask Red himself at an appropriate time. The question I replace my initial curiosity with may not be appropriate either, but I ask it anyway. "You said Red was brought in as an Innocent. Why did he get moved to Level Three?"

"No, *Five*," Gauge reveals, his blue eyes wide and intense.

"Red's been in *solitary*?" I ask, stunned that I'm asking such a question. He sticks out like a sore thumb on Level Three... for being *nice*. How could Red be capable of doing something to get moved down to Five?

Edyn told me that it takes a long time to be moved up a level, comparative to how quickly you can cause yourself to be moved down. Whatever Red did must have happened a long time ago for him to live on Three now. What terrible thing could such a young child do?

"It started out that Red was just an upset little kid who

missed his family," Gauge tells me. "He carried on a bit, and so he was moved to Two. But then he stuck a tablet utensil into his new officer during their first meeting!" Now I understand the need for the officers' protective vests. "He meant to just threaten him," Gauge adds to ease my worry. "The authorities watched and re-watched the event and finally determined that there was no way the kid anticipated that the officer was going to lunge at him in the same moment that he stabbed at the air. Protocol required that he be moved to solitary since he was acting in a threatening manner. They meant to move him to Four after a week or so, but the kid went ballistic. He stayed down there a long time."

With this information, I feel both sorry for Red and a bit unnerved about him, even though it happened long ago. I never imagined Red would be the next person that I would feel uneasy around.

"I suspect he already had issues," Gauge continues, "but Red developed a dissociative identity disorder while in solitary. The Red we see is very different from the other side of him—a side that he doesn't even know exists," Gauge says, nodding subtly.

"How can he not know?" I ask. The mental illness that I am familiar with after trying to take care of my mom is very different from this. She was diagnosed with severe schizophrenia due to her delusions and the manic state that overcame her because of them.

"He thinks that he has a seizure disorder. He comes back to us very tired and confused, but it's actually because he's been raging while under the influence of his second identity. Red believes that the meds he takes are a preventative for seizures, but they're actually treatment for his split personality."

"No one has told him?" I ask. There are some mean-spirits around here; it surprises me that none of them taunts Red with the truth about himself.

"No. Nobody wants that. Everyone feels lucky to have Red around. I mean, some call him crazy now and again, but he thinks they're just teasing him for being off beat."

"How often does he shift personalities?" I ask.

"I can't remember the last time," Gauge observes. "But, no matter how long he goes without an episode, he can never move up. Wouldn't want to upset the non-delinquents above," he cracks. "Red sets up a meeting with Officer Q. just about every week to ask what he can do to improve his chances of being moved up to Two. He's frustrated like mad while I, and the rest of Three, are glad he's here to stay."

"Is there anyone else on our level that's been to Five?" Gauge's shoulders drop, and he squints his eyes as he studies me for some time. Finally, he decides how to best answer my question.

"Both of the people who have been down there are the last ones that you would expect."

Both. Two. Red and only one other resident on Level Three have spent time in solitary. I haven't met enough of the residents to have an expectation about who would or wouldn't belong on Five. Either Gauge is coding his answer because he doesn't believe it's his business to tell, or because he's mindful of the microphones, and this is something that is not supposed to be shared.

Most of the conversation between Gauge and me has been unhindered. At the same time, I know there were items that I could have added to my end of the conversation, but couldn't due to the demands in the message I burned this morning. I'm sure what Gauge has been able to share with me this afternoon is only part of his truth as well.

While Gauge was telling me about Red's downfall, I immediately wondered if Rico Aves, *a man for true freedom*, wrote the article that the astute eleven-year-old stumbled upon. If Rico knew that his propaganda became a death sentence for those who came by them, he would stop infiltrating county systems.

Rico. I hope he hasn't enraged the captain by helping me switch places with Evvie. Even so, my father can't isolate him for long—they need him more than ever. With Cy gone, Rico is the only one who can keep Sheridan communicating with the other tribes of refugees and with the counties, if need be.

After Gauge and I have spent some time eating, I decide there is one more thing I have to ask him before our lunchtime expires. "Gauge?" I wait for him to break from his food. "How did you end up here?"

He wipes his mouth and rests the spork on his tray. "I'm no Innocent. I earned my place here."

If Gauge were a real criminal, Miles would have flown him to a county with an *official* penitentiary to do time. Citizens need the gratification of knowing justice is being served, so no real felon would be in Neocropolis. Still, I wish I hadn't asked the question. Maybe I will not want to know the answer. "You don't have to tell me," I decide.

"Jeez, Sydney," he laughs. "I didn't hurt anybody. Those are Fours or Fives. I've always been a Three. Sucking up to the officers to get moved up isn't something I agree with. It condones this system, and I don't."

The additional freedoms of One and Two are appealing. No one can blame me for feeling that way. But, like Gauge, it is simply not in me to appease Officer Q. or to live among the weak-hearted conformists above.

"I'm a decent engineer," Gauge says as he scratches his neck. "Good enough that they've finally allowed it to be my specialized occupation. They wouldn't let me near anything mechanical at first."

My eyes are brought to Gauge's neck as he scratches it forcefully. Then, I realize that he's tapping his neck with his index finger as he pretends to relieve an itch. He's giving me a covert signal, but I don't understand it. He raises his eyebrows, and I shake my head ever so slightly from side to side.

No, I don't understand. I know how it feels to be frustrated when your hints are lost on someone. I often felt this way by Evvie's lack of understanding. It's going to take me a while to decipher the code they use here. I'm glad I'm getting started on day one.

"My voice is kind of scratchy today. I hope I'm not getting sick," Gauge clarifies.

The neck tapping didn't clue me in, but the reference to his voice does. I nod to show him that I understand his gesture now. Earlier, he spoke of the counties placing chips into citizens' necks in order to gain clearer audio of their conversations. Gauge is letting me know that because of the mikes, he can't tell me more about why he is in Neocropolis. At least, he can't tell me the *truth*.

The same hand that reddened Gauge's neck is now irritatingly tapping the table as Gauge nonchalantly finishes his beans. His first signal didn't mean the end of our exchange on this topic. As soon as my eyes are drawn to his hand, he makes a tight fist and then violently expands his fingers. He repeats the gesture a second time to make sure I comprehend.

Understanding now what he did to get himself in Neocropolis, I want to draw Gauge's eyes to mine, but he continues to scrape away at the food on his tray. I lift the slice of bread to eat so that I, too, can appear casual. It's important that whoever listens to and watches us doesn't find out that I know why Gauge wasn't allowed near anything mechanical when he was first admitted to Neocropolis. Those that keep us here feared that Gauge would find a way to use what was available to engineer, and then release, the energy of an explosive.

SIX

My leave for dinner is given separately from my coworker in the laundry room. I don't spot Edyn, Red, or Gauge in the cafeteria, but this time I am content sitting alone. With my classified activity weighing heavily on my mind, I'm glad there is no one to interrupt my thought process with questions or chatter. I can't rouse an appetite to eat anything more than a few bites. I pass the half hour nervously twirling my spork in the spaghetti.

After dinner, I decide to stop by Officer J.'s office to ask where I need to go at 7:30 for my classified meeting. When I arrive, I see that neither he nor Officer Q. is in their office. Officer J. is a resident of Neocropolis so, like the rest of us, he probably only works eight hours each day. Perhaps that's also true for Officer Q., only she is permitted to return to life above ground at the end of her workday.

It's also possible that Officer Q. has gone to help prepare whatever misery I will be brought into at 7:30 tonight. Though I dislike her, I don't feel physically threatened by the head officer. I doubt I'll be lucky enough to find her the sole host of whatever punishment awaits in some dark corner of this place.

Back in the laundry room, my palms sweat profusely as

I try to focus on performing my work duties. I can't help tainting the heaps of clean clothes as I fold and deliver them.

"Laundry," I announce as I knock on room 307 of the women's side.

"Hey!" says a tall, slender woman as she opens the narrow, green door on the inside for me. She immediately halts her greeting when she sees that I am not my coworker, Andriette. "Oh," she says abruptly. The woman takes the items from me through the gate without another word.

Andriette said that residents are normally a little unwelcoming on Three, but that the hostility I have been facing is unique. She explained that my face and the fact that I had been admitted directly to Three are warnings signs. Other Threes see me as a fresh criminal, many of which naturally cause level-dropping trouble when delivered into their new captivity. The residents don't want to be associated with someone who could bring them down.

My coworker predicts that residents will warm up to me in time as long as I stay composed. I guess showboating my admittance tale the way I did to Officer Q. would be a mistake. I never cared about fitting in while living in Miles, but social isolation feels different here. It's more painful when everyone knows and is constantly bumping shoulders with you, only to turn their back. It hurts the way it did when I was very young, alone, and afraid, riding the high-speed rail all over the city to provide for and protect my family. Passengers were so close, yet far from caring.

When I return to the laundry facility on the other side of the men's cells, I expect to see some burly, menacing man dressed in black. Instead, Andriette waits outside the door.

"A message on the screen told me to step out," she says

with disdain. "Shut the door," she adds, shaking her head like I've caused this uncanny circumstance. Apparently, now Andriette feels the same contempt for me as the other standoffish Threes.

After the door closes, the small laundry room screen displays the words: *The elevator next to Q.'s office will be opened for you as soon as the hall and gym entrance are clear. Enter it unheard and unseen. We know you're capable of this.*

My heart sinks. The elevator. My classified activity will not take place on Level Three. I bet I know which direction the shaft will take me.

The screen reverts to showing the time and a slideshow of peaceful, outdoor images taken around Miles County. I take a deep breath and exit the laundry facility.

"I'm finished for the day," I tell Andriette. She doesn't question my leaving a half hour early, as she understands I've been summoned away. She reenters the laundry room without a response.

I force my feet to move through the halls toward the elevator. My sweaty palms tremble at my sides. I stop to gather my breath and my tremors. I can't let them see that I'm frightened. *This is for Evvie*, I remind myself. I round the corner to walk toward the elevator with sure footing and head held high. I am thick-skinned and courageous. I wouldn't be here if I were too afraid to face these people.

They forced my dad out of Miles, caused my mother's insanity, kidnapped my sister, and killed two of my friends. Let them inflict outer harm; they can't put so much as a scratch on my heart. It is strong for the ones I love.

The elevator opens soundlessly as I approach it. There is no one in sight, so I enter it swiftly. As the door slides closed, the lights in the elevator turn off, leaving me in absolute darkness.

I hear a sound and feel an impossible breeze. I wish it were a dream, but I am awake and my senses are sharp. I'm not alone.

All at once, a cloth swallows my head and a forceful hand smothers my instinctive cry. My body is pressed into a corner, and my arms are pulled and cuffed behind me. I don't struggle against the two or more captors. What good would it do?

I'm turned and squeezed into the body of the one whose hand covers my mouth, leaving no room for error.

Surprisingly, the elevator begins to rise. I was convinced that I'd sink further into the ground for this classified activity. What business could they have with me on One, Two, or The Main? It doesn't make sense, unless I'm traveling beyond Neocropolis' ceiling.

So odd to this circumstance is the trace of excitement I feel at being brought above ground. I haven't been underground long, but I've been sentenced to living an eternity there, so the prospect of breathing fresher, freer air enlivens me.

My hint of joy is quickly and completely eradicated as I continue to speculate on the elevator moving upward. The possibilities of where I am being taken, and whom I will meet there, have now expanded. My heart believes that Evvie is still safe, but my greatest fear is that my father is not. I'm petrified that we'll meet in some dark room, both of us chained, and I'll be harmed in order to extract information from my father. That type of punishment would cut deeply into his heart.

The elevator stops, but only briefly, before it begins to sink again. Perhaps we only rose to pick up another assaulter. The oppressor that holds me begins to spin the two of us around and around as the elevator rises and falls erratically. Finally, the elevator rests when their intent is achieved. I have no idea which level I'm on when I'm pushed from the elevator.

"You are in a soundproof location," the man restraining me says in my ear before lifting his hold on my mouth. I hadn't planned on screaming anyway. Who would come?

My cuffed hands are chained to a cool, metal bar behind me. There is a dim light in the room, but I can't make anything out from behind the mesh bag that covers my face. The design of this *activity* is the handiwork of professionals—a black-operations team or their leader.

"Sydney," says a gravelly voiced male at my side. "First of all, we would like to say thank you. You've made our operation profoundly easy by returning to Miles."

The words have an icy superiority, but the man beside me who speaks them does not. He's reading someone else's poisonous words. If that leader were here, I would declare with matched condescension that I knew what they wanted when I deliberately came here. I, the captain's eldest daughter—the one he once knew and recently reunited with—am the bait to lure in the leader of the three refugee towns.

They think they've made an advantageous trade, but they don't know that I was the driving force behind the mission to rescue Evvie. The captain was reluctant then, and now I've begged him to let me go for the sake of my sister, the other seeksmen, and the whole town. I've demanded that my father endure whatever is done to me. If he obeys, they won't get what they want.

"You know, Sydney, there was a way that you could have stagnated the operation, but we gambled that you hadn't thought of it or couldn't go through with it," continues the reader. "Of course, we never thought a deer would throw a wrench in the plan." He and the other assailant chuckle. "We sure are glad you've made a full recovery."

Their gamble was sound. It had never crossed my mind to crash the little car into a tree because I believed Sheridan would pay the price. My guess is that had I died accidentally by that deer, a bombing still would have been Sheridan's undeserved consequence.

"My father won't come," I say. I hope someone, besides the two in the room, is listening. I hope my poise flusters their malevolent leader.

Silence fills the room. It's not a speculative, but an empty one. The courier's script is in development. "Your new haircut is very becoming," he says at last. "Did you notice it?"

"Yes," I answer.

"Those few inches may seem trivial, but they are of great significance. You see, Sydney, hair growth indicates the passing of time. We admit that such a task as we completed with you would have been very difficult with your sister. Evvie was very still, very compliant."

I admire my sister's composure and understand that such a disposition would only interfere with one type of task—inflicting harm. What did the messenger say? The task *would have* been difficult with Evvie. My sister may have been afraid and alone, but she was not physically hurt.

"You were infinitely more tranquil than we expected you to be, but that's because you were barely conscious."

The messages being relayed to me have no point. Why is the person behind the inscriptions delaying the purpose of our meeting? Surely, the only purpose can't be to irritate me. Toxic words swim in my mouth, but I swallow them. With my hands bound, words are the only defense I have, but I won't speak a single one if they could have me moved down permanently. If that's the goal of this meeting tonight, I'll make it harder to reach by sitting still, being mindful, and forcing myself to have Evvie's impeccable patience.

"You're similarly silent tonight, but I can feel the life within you. Just the other night you were so far away and quite gruesome looking," the orator says. "You were unaware, but the chopper that dropped your sister off trailed you during your journey. There was no medic on board, so you did not have an examination until you were on site. We only attended to you with the quick and necessary, because the accident provided us an opportunity that we ran with. You were the subject of a little photo shoot."

My photograph wasn't taken in that condition for Neocropolis records. "What did you do with the picture?" I ask, less calmly than I would've liked.

"Don't speak unless you're asked a question," I'm directly warned by the man doing the talking. He clears his throat and resumes his role as a vessel for his superior. "There were many pictures, Sydney, not just one. We've selected one from each batch of photos where your hair was cut a different length. We changed your wounds with makeup and the assistance of technology and, as you know, we made a significant improvement to the scar near your hairline. All of this together sends the impression that you continue to sustain greater and deadlier punishment as time passes, and your father refuses to come for you."

Now I know the purpose the photos will serve. I'm enraged and afraid that my letter will not hold up against the vivid blood that must cover my face in the pictures that, over time, they'll give to my father. I remind myself of the people in Neocropolis whom I am lucky to have near—Edyn, Red, Officer

J., and now Gauge. Still, I struggle not to lift my arsenic tongue.

"Two photos have already been given to your pal Rico," the moderator says. "As instructed, he delivered the first when your father returned."

"You threatened him," I accuse.

"No, not at all," he answers fairly quickly. "Our message to Rico was explained that we would further threaten *you* if the first one was not delivered. Apparently, you made a friend in our middleman, as it seems he did not want more harm done to you. But it's only a matter of time, Sydney. Demetri Harter will come."

"And then what, you'll kill him?" I yell wildly. The second man in the room quickly and forcefully covers my mouth. I fight to free myself, but I'm made to listen. Finally, I cease my struggle, but only because I see a loophole.

"We're not the bad guys, Sydney. We just want to talk."

My plan worked. The agent covering my mouth lets up ever so slightly once I become still. It is enough that I am able to lower my jaw and bite his hand. There is a layer of fabric between my teeth and his flesh, so I really dig in to make it count. The captor roars in pain and anger.

"The same way you talked to the seeksmen who came to rescue my sister?" I scream at the one absent from the room. If they only wanted to talk, they could have captured the captain or any one of the seeksmen. Instead, they open fired, killing two of them.

To my astonishment, the bitten agent is the one who returns an answer to my accusation.

"That wasn't supposed to happen," the man says, the power of his words biting back.

"Shut up," urges the messenger straight from himself.

I address the leader again. "Don't tell me you're not the

bad guys; you killed two innocent men! They were practically kids," I charge.

"I know!" the man agent in the room yells with all his might. I hear a scuffle between the two agents in the room. Something small, maybe a tablet, hits the floor just before a body does. Something is very wrong here, but it's still unclear whether it's to my advantage.

"I know everything those boys were." His words are coated in pain. "But, innocent wasn't one of them. They knew seeking was a crime," he snaps.

"It wasn't a crime they had to die for!" I shout back, now at this man rather than his leader.

"I know it!" he yells back. "I tried to protect all of them, even you, but you're impossible to reason with. Look where it got everyone, Sydney."

Hearing my name spoken by this agent sucks the air from my lungs. My heart drops to try and fill the void. I know who I'm speaking with.

"You killed them, you traitor!" I scream, flailing within my chains. "You killed Cy and—" Rage within takes over when my mouth is re-covered. Jerus could be the one smothering me, so I jerk and kick at him as much as I can. I might be hurting myself against the restraints, but I can't feel it. All I can feel is the burning need to make Jerus pay for betraying his fellow seeksmen and his captain, my father.

"I know," Jerus says quietly from the other side of the room. He takes two more steps away, and then I distinctly hear the elevator sink to take him away.

I stop thrashing against the other agent, who has already taken a beating from Jerus. "Don't say a single word," he says angrily as he lets me go. Heavy-footed, he crosses the small room and picks up whatever fell. "It says that I'll accompany you on the elevator," the agent tells me, exasperated. "I'll open the elevator when it's clear. You're supposed to go directly to your cell, which I will open, and observe your roommate." The agent puts down the tablet with a careless thump. "I'm guessing you've been told that we have ways of enforcing what you do and don't say around here. Think about that and act accordingly."

With that, the agent removes the connection between my handcuff chain and metal bar, pulls me onto my feet, and pushes me into the elevator. Again, it rises and falls as I'm roughly spun this way and that after an already dizzying experience. The shackles and bag over my head are removed in the final moment, and I'm shoved toward my cell. My feet follow a quiet path, and I do not look behind me.

SEVEN

Edyn barely looks up from behind the pad on which she busily sketches when I enter. I observe her like I was told, but I don't see traces of the BOTs on her being or in her demeanor. I try to be discrete with my evaluating eyes, but Edyn senses my gaze. Her brows furrow in irritation.

"I'm Edyn, your roommate," she says, breaking my fixation. "You must be Sydney," she says flatly. *Must be*? Of course I'm Sydney. We covered introductions and much more before the artificial sunrise this morning. Edyn was helpful and plenty friendly then, why is she so aloof now? Quite unaffected by my return, my roommate continues with tedious strokes of her pencil. They must have done something or told Edyn something to change the way she interacts with me.

"This is for you," my roommate says, without looking up from her artwork. Like Doctor McClain, she now avoids my eyes like they are black holes that will suck her to the bedrock of Neocropolis. With unmasked displeasure, Edyn holds out to me a brightly decorated card that is clearly not from her.

In precise handwriting filling the cover of the card are the words *Welcome to Neocropolis*. The inside houses the most brilliant sky and sun that crayons and a hopeful spirit could form. Beneath the horizon is the inscription: *This picture is to help you remember your sunshine in dark places. Your friend, Gracen Ray.*

How thoughtful to make a card to welcome me. Though simple, the words are very wise. I find it interesting that the sunshine is referred to as mine. Is that because the sun's nutrients still live within my cells or was sunshine meant to be a metaphor for something else? However the child intended it, the card will remind me of Evvie. I examine the card a second time and then rest it, my reminder of truth, on the shelf above my bed. "Did the little girl who was born here make that?" I ask Edyn.

"You've heard about her already, huh?" Edyn remarks. "You've probably heard some things about me today too," she says with suspicion. I've actually heard nothing about my roommate today, other than she works as a trainer. For what, I don't know.

"I try to lead a good life in here to honor my family," she says. "It's a shame I can't remember them well enough to draw their faces just right." Each of our eyes scan the many sketches that cover the wall between her bed and the shelf overhead. "There isn't much else I need to tell you about me."

Edyn already told me about her family, and I'm certain she was the one who told me about the girl who was born in Neocropolis. Doesn't she remember?

"Do you have family out there?" Edyn asks me. She is somewhat disinterested, but she asks the question genuinely. If my roommate were to remember anything of our conversation during the wee hours of this morning, it would be that I had a little sister who I thought might have lived in Neocropolis for a short time. Either Edyn has a short-term memory problem or, more likely, I've just discovered how BOTs or Neocropolis agents enforce their expectations. Before I received the note this morning demanding that I change my name and background, I had told Edyn pieces of the truth. As a result, her memory of our initial meeting has been erased.

"No," I answer calmly, though my heart drowns in anger. "No real family. Just a foster."

"Did they do that to you?" Edyn asks, referring to my face.

"Who?" I ask her.

"Your foster."

"No," I say quickly, but I see Edyn's mind turning. Since the foster is not real, and my recent classified activity was, I assumed Edyn was asking if the unknown *they* that run this place were responsible for the swelling and discoloration of my face. I need to conceal my blunder so that they don't have to. "I did something illegal. A black ops team came, and I struggled against them," I lie.

"You're young. You tried to escape," Edyn guesses.

"No. I planned to, but I knew I'd need to remove my chip first if I planned to get anywhere. Their system detected my tampering, though. They came and brought me here."

She nods her head. To me, it communicates that she's decided I'm all right, that I'm safe to be around. Like last night, Edyn decides she knows all she needs to know about my past. "Did you get employment today?"

"Yes. Food service from 10:00 to 2:30 and laundry from 3:00 to 7:30. What do you do?" I ask, since Gauge started talking about planted mikes when I asked about Edyn at lunch.

"I clean grounds from 6:00 to 8:00 each morning. I mop, vacuum, dust, and disinfect the entire level," Edyn says with an eye roll and a smirk. "My specialty employment varies each day of the week depending on who I'm training."

"What type of training do you provide?" I ask.

"Boxing." My eyes widen. "Are you surprised they let me?" she asks a bit sharply after my reaction.

The way that Edyn asks the question makes me think I should be alarmed that *she* is a trainer, not just that the sport is allowed. "Should I be?" I ask her tentatively.

"So they *didn't* tell you?" Edyn asks, breaking from her drawing.

"Tell me what?" I ask, again wondering what *they* she is referring to.

"All the residents like to blab, so I assumed you already knew." Edyn studies me intently. After a moment, she places her sketchpad and pencil on the desk joining our beds. "There is one more thing you need to know about me then. Being my roommate, I think you ought to know so I'm just going to tell it to you straight. I am a former resident of Level Five."

Gauge informed me that neither of the two people from Level Three who had been in solitary were individuals who I would suspect. Still, I can't believe what Edyn has disclosed. During our first acquaintance, my roommate compassionately held a cold cloth to my forehead and urged me to rest after we had finished talking. Besides Red, who cannot be contended with, she was the most inviting occupant of Neocropolis.

"I was *some* boxer before I was locked up in this place," Edyn says with a proud grin. "I claimed the title of my division for three straight years. Might have continued the streak if I had the chance," she reflects. It isn't difficult for me to imagine Edyn as a champion boxer. Her power and discipline are very evident.

"One day, I lost my control and let my skill loose on an

untrained guard," Edyn tells me, her words heavy with regret. "Sydney, understand that I am not proud of what I did, but also that he had it coming. He bothered girls in here in the worst of ways. I was defending someone I cared about, but I took it too far. Because of the attack, I was considered unstable and dangerous. Regret was my only company for the year that I spent in that cell."

"Does the guard still work on this level?" I ask Edyn, wondering if the one she beat might be the man who calls me doll face.

"He doesn't work anymore," Edyn says gravely. "I put that man in a coma that he'll probably never wake up from. Like I said, I'm ashamed that I unleashed my anger and power to that extent."

Edyn kneels on her bed and reaches up to select a thick book from the collection on the shelf. She flips the light pages to find the predetermined text that she wishes to study. With her earnest reflection on what must be Bible verses, I can see that Edyn still pleads to be forgiven for her transgression so many years ago.

Since my roommate needs her peace and I need something to do, I open the drawers under my bed to straighten the jumpsuits, socks, and undergarments that I received during the tour with Emanda this morning. When I finish, I spend some time in the bathroom, arranging my items in those drawers and preparing for bed.

"Do you ever read the Bible?" Edyn calls from the other side of the partial wall. She doesn't wait for my answer to continue. "I'd like to read something aloud if you don't mind. I do every night."

"That's fine," I tell her.

"Get settled in and then I'll begin," she says. Edyn and I each lie down and rest our heads on our pillows. She holds her Bible above her face and reads:

Here is my servant, whom I uphold,
My chosen one with whom I am pleased.
I have sent my spirit upon him;
He shall bring forth justice to the nations.

Edyn suddenly interrupts the verse. "Listen to me carefully, Sydney, but keep an even-tempered expression while I speak. For a few minutes each night, the microphones in this room are muted, courtesy of one of the guards. He inserts prerecorded audio of me reading scripture, so I must continue to look like I'm reading to you, and you must continue to look like you are listening to Bible verses."

"I'm going to look at you quickly, and I want you to blink twice if we've met prior to your return from your employment this evening, once if we haven't." Edyn looks at me, and I blink twice as instructed. "I was afraid so," she says, looking at the passage again. "If the answer is yes to the question I'm about to ask you, pretend to yawn. Are you are here because you breached? If the answer is yes," Edyn interjects, "and it was a single, short breech, make it a short yawn. If you were out for days or more, make it a long one. I usually read people well, but if you're in for something else, do nothing."

I answer Edyn with a drawn-out yawn, as if to indicate for breaching and much, much more.

"Alright, now I'm going to give you some instructions. You need to save the points you earn in order to check out a book from the library. I'll work on getting you an opportunity to record some cover audio so that it looks like we are taking turns reading to each other. Twice a week, the second shift guards hold a boxing match in the gym. The microphones and cameras are not active because no one is supposed to be in there after close."

"The next female fight is this Friday night. The match is set, but I'm sure I can talk them into letting you fight if they know that I trained you. After I close my Bible, we can segue the conversation into boxing again so that I can begin training you tonight. I need you to win the fight so that you advance to next week's match too. It won't be easy."

Edyn reads the final verse of the chapter.

In his ways, they refused to walk,
His law they disobeyed.
So he poured out wrath upon them,
His anger, and the fury of battle;
Fire blazed all around, yet they did not realize.
It burned them, but they took it not to heart.

My roommate closes her Bible. At the same moment, the lights in the room are shut off.

"What part of the Bible was that, Edyn?"

"Isaiah," she answers. "A very powerful book. That was chapter forty-two." Isaiah was the book Decklin had marked in the Bible that he passed on to me. The chapter I read from his was different, but the writer's message seemed similar.

"Can I read it again sometime?" I ask my roommate.

"Help yourself anytime, even if I'm here and not off training." Edyn provides the opportunity to transition into boxing talk, so I use it.

"Who do you train for your job?" I ask her.

"Men and women from levels One and Two. They have tournaments up there, which enables me to hold the perfect specialty job."

"What types of things do you teach them?" I ask.

"First, I teach my fighters the stances and basic footwork for attacking and guarding. Technique for the fundamental punches—jabs, straights, hooks, and uppercuts—is also important in the beginning. Later, I get into reading your opponents' style and weaknesses and executing combinations accordingly."

"Could you teach me some things?"

"I suppose," Edyn says as she sits up. "But you better promise me that you'll never use what I teach you to attack anyone. Defending yourself is fine, but hopefully, you'll never need to in here like you did out there. Someone with a face like yours ought to be taught to duck at the least."

Edyn and I stand between the shower room and bathroom, where there is a faint light that comes in under the door from the hallway. Her training isn't hindered at all by the lack of light. She begins by fine-tuning my natural stance, teaching me the importance of raising my lead shoulder and tucking my chin for protection. She also tightens the distance between my feet and increases the bend in my knees and the bounce on the balls of my feet to improve my agility. The sound of her feet against the floor dictates my footwork as we shuffle around the tiny space like dueling phantoms.

Late into the night, my trainer teaches me how to simultaneously throw my body into my punches and guard myself with the opposite arm. Though I hit nothing but air tonight, my opponent materializes between my trainer and me.

It's any one of the faceless BOTs who gunned down my friends less than a week ago. Sometimes, my imaginary opponent does have a face and a name, and instead of wearing heavy, black gear, he wears hunting camouflage. I imagine myself dodging the punch he threw at his partner tonight and hitting Jerus with an uppercut forceful enough to put him in a coma for the pain he has caused me and the other Sheridans, especially Crewe.

EIGHT

The alarm jolts me awake, and I hurriedly stand atop my bed. Thankfully, my muscles feel strong. They easily sustained Edyn's late-night boxing fundamentals session. I'm not to expect such ease when she coaches me today.

Now that I've completed my enrollment meetings and chosen employment positions, my schedule is fixed. Edyn's is more variable but luckily, some of our free time overlaps. She'll work with me from the time she returns from her morning employment until ten o'clock, when I have to report to the cafeteria kitchen to begin my food service job.

Edyn decided that I should use my combined points from yesterday's laundry employment and today's food service work to purchase a pass for thirty minutes in the gym. I won't earn enough from my evening employment to check out a book from the library, but she decided that getting in the ring today is detrimental to my success there tomorrow night. If I can beat my opponent, the opportunity for unmonitored speech will follow. I want her to know who I really am as soon as possible, but I have to trust her on the matter of the delay.

Synthetic sunlight is supposed to shoot from the screen after my schedule is shown to me, but instead of the makeshift dawn, an image follows. I hardly recognize myself in it.

Fresh blood flows from the top of my skull, but on the opposite side of where my real laceration is. Technology has cleaned up that scar to where I can hardly see it. Likewise, the blood from my broken nose streams across my mouth, chin, and even my neck. The wet, crimson fluid pools on the shirt, much like sweat after a long, hard run. My hair must have been in a ponytail when I was taken from the scene of the accident, but it deliberately hangs below my shoulders—its former length—in the horrific snapshot. There is also a streak of blood on my arm and a noticeably crooked thumb. This must be the final photo in the series. It's only a matter of time now. My father can't possibly stay away after seeing this.

How will I really feel about it if the days tick by, and he doesn't come? I was bewildered for a fleeting moment when I first met my supposedly deceased father. Then feelings of disappointment and resentment poured in after considering all the years Evvie and I lived under unstable and harmful caretakers. Our lives were dependent on our psychotic mother, negligent, orphanage personages, and then Trista, our wicked foster. Although it is truly for the best, and is what I want, part of me will feel heartbreakingly forgotten if my father leaves me at the county's mercy again. I am bound to pass enough time down here to hate him.

Even if the situation above changes for the better, I can't imagine the government will release its prisoners. We make evident the fact that the nation has been engaged in warfare just like other parts of the world, only the battle is civil, and their opposition never stood a chance. The leaders wouldn't allow such controversy to taint their spotless, conscientious reputation.

I begin to accept that I may never see Gracen Ray's cherished sun again, and suddenly I feel very claustrophobic. I open the inner door of my cell to get some air, but it doesn't help. Picking up the card from my shelf, I look at the bright sun Gracen Ray drew for me, but it will never do after being in the presence of the real thing. The tortuous image on the screen above my bed is replaced by the Neocropolis version of sunlight, which only fuels my panic.

I was too charged to notice the sun the last time I walked under its setting warmth and light. I rushed to my provisional residence from the laundromat, focusing only on what I would say in each of the three letters I was going to write. Had I known I would also be saying goodbye to the sun, I would have looked at it directly and savored its non-judgmental affection.

I crunch against the wall next to my bed to try to calm myself where no one can see me. Then I remember that there are watchers behind camera lenses, camouflaged into the features of this room. Truly, they're more responsible for my growing discomfort than the lack of sun. The constriction in my chest lessens just enough to breathe when I remember that I'll escape the relentless peer of the unknown onlookers during the fight tomorrow night. With cameras and microphone being powered down, the ring will become my new haven.

"Good morning, neighbor," Red greets me as he wobbles a plate containing another red, gummy slab through the small opening in the gate. "How are you on this fine morning?"

If it were anyone but Red asking the question, I'd return nothing but a glare. How can I be anything but melancholy in this place? "Not as happy as you, Red, but tolerating," I answer.

"I'm sorry, Sydney," he says with soft sincerity. "I've been acting over-the-top to try and cheer you up, but it seems

I've had the opposite effect."

"No, Red, you do cheer me up," I tell him truthfully. "Thank you," I add. I'm surprised how easy it is to be comfortable and amiable with Red after learning yesterday about the incident that relegated him to solitary confinement.

"Oh now, don't charm me, Sydney," he smirks. "Save that smile for my roommate," he calls toward the cell across the hall. "He wants to know if you'll have lunch with him today."

"Oh shut up, Red," Gauge calls coolly from across the hall. "I apologize for my pest's fat mouth and imagination," he says as he approaches the bars of his call. "I told him to tell you that I take lunch at one in case you needed someone to sit with since you're new. That's all."

"See, he was listening carefully to us. He's a little bashful, I guess," Red whispers. "Didn't know it. Not too many girls to peak his interest around here, you know?" Red elbows at my hand, which is wrapped around a bar of the gate.

"You're so dead, man," Gauge warns, a bit more flustered by the mysterious whispering. "Don't listen to him," he urges me. I might smile at Red's playfulness, if I only knew whether or not he is joking.

"Yeah, don't listen to the crazy redhead." I don't have to see Red's change in demeanor to know who approaches. His voice alone sends a prickling sensation down my spine. I'm aware of every step as the guard's heavy shoes connect with the floor. "Next time I catch you making conversation on the job, I'll report it," he reprimands Red. Red is quick to back away from my gate, but he fidgets with the prepared plates on the wheeled cart a few feet away. The guard scowls at him until he picks up a plate and turns away.

"Looking better this morning, doll face." To avoid

reaction, I train my eyes on Red. Gauge slaps at him through his own gate for embarrassing him, but the expectant Red dodges every attempt. "Oh now, don't be shy. Let me have a look at you." The boys stop fooling around when the guard reaches in to hold my chin.

I'm not flustered this time. I look him directly in the eyes. "Take a good look," I scorn.

"Why is that?" he asks. I step away and slam the inside door. How's that for an answer? Angrily, I bite off half of my breakfast and struggle to swallow it. I rest the plate with the other half on the desk.

My cell door buzzes. I look up at the clock. I'm not authorized to leave my cell until ten, and it's too early for Edyn to be returning. The guard is coming in. I loathe my shortsightedness.

"Still all spice, I see." He closes the inside door. I doubt I ever will again, but right now, I appreciate the cameras and microphones in my cell. "You're little fantasies may point otherwise, but I came to visit you because I was told to examine the swelling in that doll face and decide if you need to see the doctor today. I will do my job, and you will show respect for your superiors. Now come here," he orders. I compose the turmoil within me and lock my tongue in place. Begrudgingly, I move toward the guard.

"Closer," he grins. "I won't bite." I take another maddening step toward him. "That's a good girl," he says. The guard runs each of his hands up my arms to hold me in place by the shoulders. He leans in to examine my face, though I believe he pays no attention to the swelling or bruising. He releases one of my shoulders only to brush his thumb over my cheek as he pretends to fulfill his duty. The guard halves what little space is left between us.

"I need you to relax this frown, doll face." His thumb inches over to trace the curve of my upper lip. Just as I slap his hand away, my cell door buzzes and the inner door is thrust open.

"What's going on in here?" Officer J. asks neither of us in particular. No one answers. "Sydney, is he bothering you?"

"Bothering her?" the guard contests. "She slammed the door in my face when I was trying to get a look at her swelling like I was asked. I had no choice but to come in here and do it."

"Get out of here," Officer J. says without looking at the guard.

"Gladly," he responds.

Officer J. studies me a moment before he speaks. "You can't do stuff like that, Sydney. My limited understanding is that you're lucky to be on this level. Don't push that luck."

Maybe it's because I spent so much time thinking about my dad this morning that I find myself wondering if Officer J. is a father, either in or outside of Neocropolis. He seems like he would make a good one. He's firm, but only because he cares.

"If he bothers you, you come to me," Officer J. stresses. I nod, and that's good enough for him to exit.

I choke down the rest of my breakfast and with it, the anti-inflammatory medication that Doctor McClain prescribed.

The two drops of chemicals that I pinch into each eye cause them to sting and tear up. Though I'm a bit shielded by the partial wall in the bathroom, I blink rapidly when I hear the door buzz. I don't want Edyn to misconstrue the effect of the drops for vulnerability. I need to show her that I am strong, ready, and deserving of this fight.

"Good morning, Thrasher," Edyn says. "I won't ask

how you slept because I already know."

Sorry," I offer, understanding that my restlessness must have kept her awake again.

"You *will* be sorry when sleep deprivation slows you down, and you can't dodge your opponent's blows. You take one of your sleep aides tonight," she says. I nod. "Ready?"

"Yes," I tell her.

"Good. Let's get to it."

Now that we have light, Edyn again examines my form, making small but important adjustments, like heightening my lead shoulder to protect my chin. Since my ribcage isn't bruised the way my face is, Edyn balls up a towel and administers the hits in order to teach me how to block and absorb the inevitable blows. She withholds a lot of her power, leaving me unsure of the caliber of the raps I should expect in a real fight.

We review the punches I learned last night, but, today, Edyn demonstrates the common counter punches that correspond with the weak spots that emerge when I attack. Her reactions to each of my throws are automatic and precise. She capitalizes on the gaps so thoroughly that I am forced to learn quickly.

"Here." Edyn hands me her water bottle, and I squirt some into my mouth. "You're doing well, but you'll be defeated if you're even an instant behind your opponent. We need to increase the agility of your hands and feet." I hand the bottle to Edyn, but she discards it.

Edyn has me bounce on the balls of my feet for the next half hour. At first, my hands hang loosely at my sides, waiting for her to command a type of punch to deliver. I have to react quickly enough to deliver a hit and block hers. Next, we do a series of bobbing and weaving or lunges, while she throws straight punches and hooks. The agility session concludes when I tire too much to make the required quick lunge, and Edyn's left hook makes solid contact with my inflamed and sensitive face.

Thankfully, we are taking a second water break when our gate buzzes. Edyn opens the door, and Gauge enters. My surprise that he was the person at the door is surpassed by his surprise at the sight of Edyn teaching me to box. Everyone on Three knows about the fights. He's aware that there's a female match tomorrow night, and must guess that Edyn is training me for it. His surprise is definitely warranted. Not only do I lack experience with the sport, but I also have a battered face and a broken thumb. At least my power arm is free of injury.

"I'm here to fix a leak," he says. "Sink right?" Gauge asks Edyn.

"Yeah, and it's about time," she says.

"You okay?" he asks me with concerned eyes.

"Yeah," I answer, a bit taken aback. "Edyn was just training me," I explain.

"I'm not asking about that," he states.

"Oh the guard," I realize. "I can handle him."

"Well, I can't. I hate that perverted lowlife." Gauge catches eye contact with Edyn.

She puts her hands up in surrender and says, "I don't want to know. Leave me out of it." Right. Edyn was housed on Level Five after attacking a guard who bothered her female friends. She is probably trying to control a justifiable hatred that she already has for this other guard. Now more than ever, I know it's imperative that I keep my current roommate. Edyn and I can't be moved away from one another, so each of us needs to do our best to tolerate the guard.

"I'll let you two get back at it." Gauge winks, his concern somewhat alleviated either because I'm not worried, or because he's mentioned the incident in front of Edyn who, despite her plea to remain uninformed, will probably be watchful of the guard's interactions with me.

Gauge has the sink fixed and is out of our cell in time for me to bathe away the sweat from the final half hour of training. Because Edyn and I don't know exactly where the cameras are embedded in our cell, I shower in my underwear and afterward, change them out discretely. Edyn laughs at this. I'm not sure nakedness is something I'll ever become used to, as she and the other residents evidently have.

"Hey! There she is," Red exclaims when I enter the cafeteria kitchen at ten. "Have you two met?" he asks his other coworker.

"I'm Sydney," I tell the sour-faced woman who handed me lunch yesterday. She doesn't care, nor does she respond. She goes on measuring the appropriate amount of rice and pouring it into the pots that she or Red have brought to a boil.

"What can I do?" I ask Red, looking at all the lunch ingredients scattered about.

"You can open these up," he tells me, patting the collection of canned baked and green beans. "We don't really need an extra hand, but I suppose they had to find somewhere to put you. I'm glad it's here," he says, patting me on the back and smiling. I'm glad too, but I don't say so.

"So what's it like out there these days?" Red asks. "We got this last week." Red hands me a laser-operated can opener that fits in the palm of my hand. "Did you have one?"

Ever since my father's feigned death, I was among the poorest class of society. Though I was far too young for such a thing, I had to learn from my grandmother about rationing my father's inheritance so that I could do the same with hers when her date came up. When a railcar scanner missed the chip in my arm and my mother's condition was brought to light, my grandmother's remaining inheritance was turned over to the state and used to admit her to the institution, and Evvie and me to the orphanage. The only technology given to us there was an outdated tablet needed to complete our county-mandated EduWeb quotas.

Living with Trista, the foster Evvie and I shared for a year, was the worst of all. She boozed away her tax break—the only reason she fostered us—instead of providing for us.

The living I earned by working in Tiana's restaurant in the most recent stage of my county life was barely enough to keep my head above water. There was too little cushion to purchase the high-tech conveniences that others owned.

"There was probably one in the restaurant I worked in," I answer Red.

"You worked in a restaurant?" Red asks enthusiastically.

"As a server," I answer. "I didn't do much. Tables were assigned by online reservations and built-in screens were responsible for taking orders. All I had to do was place the entrees at the appropriate places and bring refills and the occasional forgotten item, both of which were usually ordered via screen."

"Wow. So you barely had to speak to the customers," Red observes.

"Perfect for me, right?" I jest.

"I wasn't going to say anything," Red teases back.

"Was it even any better out there?" the woman asks seriously.

I'm not sure whether she means to ask if things have gotten better comparative to whatever year she was incarcerated, or if she wants to know if life in Miles County is preferable to living in Neocropolis. Either way, the answer is the same. "Life in Miles has never been good for me."

"Doesn't look like it," she comments.

The kitchen work is tight but agreeable, especially with Red's constant banter. The chatter between us is also much more dimensional than it was with Tiana during our down time.

This is also true with Gauge. He and I pass another lunch break whispering about the history of different residents around us. Most have come down from Levels One or Two but, like me, some were admitted directly to Three. Gauge tells me what he can about the secret information the residents heard or occurrences they witnessed that landed them here. Judging by my own story, I assume these are only partially true.

I'm sure to catch the same portly cafeteria guard from yesterday at the end of my lunch break to purchase a thirty-minute pass for the gym.

Time passes very slowly during the last hour of clean-up work in the kitchen. This is partly because a quiet man has replaced Red, and partly because of my anticipation to get in the ring with Edyn. Finally, 2:30 rolls around, and I'm seen to the gym by a second-shift guard.

Edyn is already warming up in the ring. She looks fiercer than ever, bobbing and throwing combinations in the air. Seeing the power behind her warm-up, I wonder if any of her opponents ever threw in the towel *before* they stepped in the ring. I might have.

"I won't be able to get in here with you tomorrow," Edyn says when she spots me. She lifts the ropes, and I crawl into the ring. "Leave it all on the platform." I put on the heavy gloves and begin to look around for the protective headgear that Edyn wears before she says, "Just body shots from me. I want you to see clearly. I'm going to outline an opponent for you," Edyn briefs me. "For today, let's say your contender exceeds your weight but is a couple of inches shorter. Got it?" she asks with a telling manner.

"Got it," I answer, understanding that these are the attributes of the person who will meet me in the ring tomorrow night. Edyn and her guard friend, who has authorized my participation in the fight, might not have allowed it if our heights were reversed and strikes to my face were more likely.

"Good. I'm going to show you how to operate according to their style. Seventy-five percent of boxing is mental," she says as she begins bounding around. "You need to master your advantages to be successful."

Edyn teaches me everything she can during the short lesson and I give everything I have, leaving with a jumpsuit saturated in sweat as I head to my evening employment. Six more hours, I tell myself as I walk to the laundry room. Just before nine o'clock, when lights go out, false audio will play in my cell and I'll feel less stifled.

I can get through each day by reminding myself of the freedom the night brings, and I can get through the weeks by looking forward to my fights in the ring, assuming I'm good enough to keep fighting. But how long will those incentives succeed in calming me? What will I use to get me through the months, years, and *decades* in Neocropolis? The only thing I can look forward to for that length of time is the opportunity to escape so I can see my sister again.

NINE

At three o'clock, I part from Edyn and, drenched in sweat, head to my second employment of the day. After the way Andriette was removed from the laundry room so I could be summoned to my classified encounter last night, I don't blame her for not speaking to me this afternoon. Word does travel quickly around here. If it's possible, the other residents show more cold disapproval as I sit alone through another meal.

Since I'm new, I've assumed the detested task of descending to Level Five after dinner to collect the men's garments and shower towels. Fours handle the AM wash load, which consists of the female garments and towels.

As Andriette instructed, I ask the stout cafeteria guard to open the elevator for me. He uses his tablet to do so, watches me inside, and then remotely closes the door and sends me deeper into the earth.

I feel incredibly uneasy in the elevator, partly due to where it's taking me, and partly because I'm afraid the lights will turn off and a ghostly BOT will seize, hood, and chain me again.

A guard is waiting for me when I arrive on Five. "Looks like we have a new worker," he says with surprise. "You must be Neo*crap*olis' latest resident."

Passing on the opportunity to exchange pleasantries with the guard, I begin to fiercely analyze my surroundings. There are two rooms on each side of the hallway next to the elevator. They are about the same size and in the same location as the spaces for officers or physicians on Three, but I can't be sure if that's their purpose since they're unlabeled and shut up for the night.

The end of the row is much closer to me than on Level Three. Assuming this deepest level is indeed as large as the others are, nearly three-fourths of its area is closed off by an ominous, windowless door opposite me.

A bit irritated by my indifference to him, the guard stuffs a mesh bag and a pair of gloves into my hands. Laundry collection must work differently on this level since the rooms ahead have no bars through which the inmates can slide their dirty clothes. The steel doors would otherwise melt into the surrounding wall if not for the hinges on the side and a small, glass window.

The guard makes a few strokes on his tablet to initiate a message that reaches the inmates through a speaker in their rooms. Faintly, I hear the computerized woman's aristocratic voice calling for laundry.

"I give them a minute to gather it, and then I open their windows," the guard says, lifting his tablet. "After the windows are closed, you can go collect what they've dropped." The guard startles me by forcefully extending a baton. "The windows have sensors so they can't go back up until everybody's hands are out. They've been up to something lately. Whether it's an intelligent scheme or an idiotic game, I don't know."

"Please state your task," the guard's tablet requires.

"Men's windows down," he responds.

"Approximate duration?" the voice asks.

"Thirty seconds."

"Would you like to begin this task now?"

"Yes." With his baton firmly gripped, the guard takes a few powerful strides toward the cells as the steel door swallows the thick panes of glass. The inmates drop their laundry, but many do not retract their arms. This hallway being narrower than the one on my level, hands on either side of the guard could easily grab him as he strikes away at the rascally arms.

The guard curses at the inmates and threatens to install Tasers into the doors themselves. I wouldn't be surprised if the technology exists. It would certainly save him a hassle.

Finally, the arms have all been beaten enough to retreat into their steel shell. Now substantially irritated, the guard rushes me to put on the gloves and sweep the laundry from the floor.

"Get the towels at the end of the hall too," he says breathlessly. I wonder how anyone can possibly succeed in feeding these prisoners their food.

I'm afraid to make eye contact with anyone so hardened as to endure a severe beating purely for entertainment, so I avoid looking at the windows as I gather items from the floor and deposit them into the bag. They probably think of Threes the same way that I think of Innocents—feeble-minded and spineless.

Near the end of the row, I hear running water over the still-riled shouts of the men. The towels are heaped together there rather than being dropped from individual rooms because there are no showers in the solitary cells.

The water shuts off in the tiny, barred shower cell just as I reach the end of the hallway.

"Do me a favor and slide her a towel," the guard calls from his post near the elevator. "On the ground and don't get too close." This is normally his job? I shoot him a disapprovingly glare, to which he responds, "It's not my design. No cameras in there. Got to have a way to watch them."

I drop the mesh bag next to the pile of damp towels and pull a fresh one from the stack on the shelf across from the single-stall shower. Trying to avert my eyes, I push the towel along the floor until it's less than a foot from the bars that lock in the naked woman. While she dries, I wipe splashes of water from the floor with one of the towels from the heap, and then shove it and the others into the overflowing laundry bag.

"Her clothes now," the guard requests after the woman has dropped her towel through the bars. I take her jumpsuit, undergarments, socks, and shoes off the shelf and slide them toward the barred gate. The woman nods in thanks to me and begins to dress.

She doesn't seem the least bit like the men with the flailing arms. She must be a semi-permanent looking to move up, but how can she stand it down here? I can't imagine Edyn or Red living on this level like caged animals. How did they endure these conditions well enough to be moved up? I wouldn't have had the control or the patience to wait months, or maybe even a year, to make it to Level Four. I'd surely become a permanent. I can't allow myself to be sent down here.

"Come on, let's get you back up," the guard calls to me. "I'll deal with her next," he says, referring to the dressing woman.

I lug the heavy bag toward the elevator. As we stand waiting, an unexpected noise catches my attention. All the inmates are locked up, what other door could I hear opening than the one between the row and the rest of Five?

By his attire, I can tell that the man who opens the door is a Neocropolis officer—probably for this level. I look passed the officer and deeper into the space beyond the door. A wave of disbelief wrenches through my body and then freezes it solid. The mesh bag drops from my arms.

The elevator behind me opens. The guard beside me tugs at the sleeve of my jumpsuit and says something to try to break my gaze, but he can't. The officer turns toward the ruckus and, just as quickly, back toward the door behind which I was never meant to see.

The ice inside me bursts, causing an explosive madness that moves me through the short hallway toward the closing door. In response to my piercing scream, the man behind the door on whom my eyes are fixed looks up, his guileful smile fading. Shock crosses his face, and right afterward, the edge of the shutting door.

With one swift move, the officer who I was paying no attention to slams my back against the bedrock of Neocropolis. He pins my torso, but can't quiet my feet as they slam into the door or my voice as I scream with more power than I knew I possessed.

Even before I found out for sure last night, I had already suspected that Jerus was a double-crosser. One person told me that it might be the case, and I believed him. One thousand people could have told me that the man before me a moment ago was a traitor to Sheridan, but still I wouldn't have believed it. My love for him would have blinded me. Until a moment ago, I believed my father had it in him to become a hero.

The door is violently opened into my kicking feet. "Help me hold her," the officer begs the unfamiliar man who emerges.

"Get the restraints and open the resistor cell," the man

tells the guard as he rips my arm out from under the officer.

"I hate you! I hate you!" I'm screaming when the two flip me over and pin me into a hammerlock hold. From there, one of them covers my mouth until the guard returns and assists them in latching some kind of muzzle around my head. I scream, but the sound is only heard in my head. The mask swallows the rest.

I thrash about in the arms of the three men as they carry me into the tiny cell, but they overpower me. Within a minute, I'm strapped so tightly to a bed that I can hardly breathe. Just as I have that thought, the guard and the officer hold my head, while the other man fastens something with tubular protrusions near the mouth of the muzzle. The tubes wiggle before my eyes, and then the man forces them deep into my swollen nostrils. The tubes irritate my nasal cavity, but I guess it's better than suffocating from this muzzle. With their conquering complete, the three men finally leave me.

Now I know why it was so hard to convince the captain to go after my sister, and why he was reluctant to try again after the first mission failed. It had nothing to do with sadness over the men he lost or fear that he would lose more seeksmen. My father is a member of this organization, one that steals people from their homes and buries them in Neocropolis, never to see the sun again. One that killed young men who fought to rescue my stolen sister—his daughter! Crewe and Cy *trusted* the captain as if he were their own father, and he led them and the others into a deadly conflict from which he knew he and Jerus would emerge unscathed.

The people of Sheridan are in grave danger because they wholeheartedly trust their captain, who has repulsively betrayed them, along with the people in the free towns of Braves and Idaho. Seeing my father smiling comfortably in the heart of enemy territory crushes my hope for the free people. Whether through actual death or a feigned one, Evvie, Crewe, and the rest of the refugees will not survive unless they learn the truth.

I am the only one who can alert them, and it is absolutely imperative that I find a way to do so. In her letter, I told Evvie to trust our father. I thought she was safe with him.

Possibilities flood my mind. Could have Evvie seen our father before I did when she was locked away here? That traitor could have been aboard the helicopter that returned Evvie's limp body to Sheridan, and then apparently tailed me as I rode into Miles County. Would she have recognized his face from the few photographs online, or the printed photo that we peeked at every now and again? I was certainly never meant to see him, but my little sister is so much more compliant and impressionable than I am.

Merick and the other seeksmen trusted that their captain travelled to Braves or Idaho when he was away from Sheridan. How frequently was he actually involved in similar thieving trips similar to Evvie's, or in the hidden corridors of this place, scheming with his murderous cronies?

I have to get out of here, get to Sheridan, and convince them to trust *me* instead of the captain. If the refugee towns were to fall because of my father's treachery, what resistance would there be to the conniving, oppressive regime in Region Two? Suddenly, the future of the entire region falls singularly in my hands.

What is someone of my age and experience to do with that kind of responsibility? Seeing as I'm now bound by restraints in a steel-walled, solitary cell buried six stories below the earth's surface, with my only previous hope for rescue in bed with the organization that holds me captive, I don't imagine

I'll ever have that chance.

If there were only myself to consider, I'd have reason to give up. But since Evvie's safety and well-being are again at stake, I have to keep fighting. I will find a way out of this Godforsaken place, and I *will* return to Sheridan.

But would I even find Evvie there? I understand now that she and I were never collateral to bring my father in—he had been here all along. Either he removed us from Sheridan to satisfy a filthy desire to watch his own children suffer his heinous oppression, or he got us out because the plans for destroying the refugee towns are soon to be enacted. God forbid his flesh and blood be subjugated to that.

The door to my cell opens. Because my head is strapped down, I can't see who has entered, nor can I guess why they've come. They chain my feet. A blanket is thrown over my face. They reach under it, loosen the straps restraining my head, and then jostle a bag over my still-silenced face.

The restraints are removed, and then I'm abrasively flipped over. Someone tightly fastens the bag around my neck, while another drives my hands into barred handcuffs. After chaining my feet, they pull me onto them and drag me from the cell.

We pause while a door is opened. The only one in this direction leads to the rest of Five. I'm being taken to my father. Masked, cuffed, and dragged, that's how my merciless father sends for me.

After they've towed me a bit further, we pause again and pass through a second, narrower door. A few steps into the room, I'm made to sit while the chain around my ankles is linked to something on the bottom of the secure seat.

One of my hands is un-cuffed. I react instantly, grabbing

a fistful of someone's clothing. The person chops at my arm, frees their self of my grasp, and succeeds in returning my hand to the cuff after the bar between my wrists has been fed through a high slot in the column behind me. Additionally, a contraption resting behind my neck is bolted around my risen biceps and latched to the column, so that I cannot move my arms or stand. The most I can do is flail my legs until those, too, are pinned in.

The bag is undone and taken off. I turn quickly, but my raised arms and the column behind me prevent me from seeing anything behind me. The only things in the room are the column, the attached chair, and an uncovered bulb that hangs from the ceiling.

Since they didn't remove the muzzle, I can assume that whoever will come to meet me doesn't want to hear me speak. Because of the pains that they've taken and the area in which I find myself, I believe I'll soon look upon one of two people, my father or the leader of the BOTs.

The door opens and slow, solemn footsteps approach. This time, I don't try to look over my shoulders. In fact, I close my eyes. I'm not ready to see him.

"Look at me, Sydney," the man says. I know his voice. I open my eyes to glare at my disgusting father.

TEN

"I'm not the man you think I am," my father says.

Obviously not, I think.

"There are many things about our nation and the world that you do not yet understand, Sydney." My father clasps his hands behind his back and begins to walk methodically about the small room. "I know it must be difficult for you to accept me as I stand before you in Neo-Necropolis, among the black-operations teams that you so deeply fear."

He carries himself with arrogance and speaks to me with condescension. Here, my father's true nature is revealed. This personality is entirely different from the one he played in Sheridan, yet somehow, his mannerisms are strikingly familiar.

"It's a daunting task, but I'm going to attempt to widen your perception of things and hopefully sway your impression of me for the better." He stops abruptly and faces me. "I will not have you hating me."

Impossible. He can never take back what he did to Cy and Decklin. He didn't fire the bullet himself, but in my eyes, his actions make him more responsible for their execution than whoever did fire those rounds.

The captain said so many meaningful words at Cy's

funeral. He told the heartbroken crowd that he *loved* Cy as his own son, and that he was forever indebted to him for bringing hope and happiness to all—namely me. How could he have been *involved* in the callous murder of someone so valiant and caring, and then acted as if he cared when he spoke at his grave?

"First, I want you to know is that your sister is safe. You and Evvie have always been my primary concern. I have looked out for you, especially after your grandmother's passing. I had various preparations if you and Evvie ran into any trouble, but you did so well that I found it unnecessary to uproot you."

Don't compliment me. I don't want to listen to this. If only I could close my ears to show him. I can't stand his words or his voice.

"I had no choice when your mother's mind deteriorated," he says, beginning to tread back and forth again. "She needed care, so I intervened when the opportunity presented itself. I grieved that this meant sending you and your sister to the orphanage, but I trusted that I could find a suitable foster for you. Against my efforts, which did include denying requests by deviant men, I failed you both—you especially."

Shut up! I need it to stop. I don't want to hear another word uttered by the lying tongue of *this deviant*.

"I was quite troubled when your foster harmed you. After that, I had a microphone chip inserted to better monitor your well-being. There were obstacles with the courts, but I worked to return you and Evvie to a safer situation at the orphanage. I only approved Merideth's fostering request because of your microphone, but then you convinced her to use her parenting years for Evvie alone. That dismantled my plan, but I admired your trust and selflessness."

His compliments are poison. There isn't a hint of

sincerity in his weaseling ways. I don't care what he says or does; I won't change my mind about him in a lifetime, let alone a sitting.

"You kept us awfully busy with your breaches," he laughs. "I had to answer to the Head of County." He reads my contempt and explains, "We all found your pride at discovering a gap in the system humorous." His pleasure fades, and his eyes become cold. "There are no gaps, Sydney. *I* protected you from harm and allowed you certain freedoms so that you could keep your sanity about you."

I was harmed, stifled, and unhappy, so he failed there too. But could my life really have been worse without his vigilance? Could I have been hurt more by my mother, neglected longer in the orphanage, adopted or fostered by someone more damaging than Trista, or captured and jailed years ago when I first breached?

I can tell he isn't lying about having known about my breaches from the beginning. I was never alone in my haven. In fact, there may have been even more eyes on me on the outside than there were when I was inside. My past and future have been turned upside down by this man, and I'm afraid he's only begun to scratch the surface of what I thought I knew and what really was, or *is*.

"I know you do not agree with this establishment," my father says, gesturing around us, "but in this shifting world, there have to be harsh consequences for breaking the law. Without them, our civilization would crumble. We do our best to be humane and accommodating."

If it's possible, my brows crunch closer to my burning eyes. I sit before him not only restrained completely, but also muted. How is this or anything about Level Five *humane*?

"Let me tell you the truth about Sheridan," my father says, becoming agitated by my continued loyalty to them. "They are selfish rebels who refuse to think about the common good. Their resistance is going to give other nations the opportunity to intervene on behalf of the supposed oppressed, as our nation has done historically."

He steps closer and bends to my eye level. "Those are the corrupt and power-hungry governments. They are watching and waiting for their opportunity to attack and, let me tell you," he chuckles eerily, "if they do, it will *not* be by armed forces." He shakes his head violently. "They won't waste money and men when chemical warfare can diminish our population effectively, without contaminating our resources. And believe me, they will not save the refugees, Sydney, oh no. They mean to slaughter us all." My father stands and smooths his shirt and hair.

"You see, we cannot allow refugees to interfere with our delicate design. A black-operations team must be assigned to track, collect, and incarcerate every criminal escapee. You might view it as a sad fate, especially for the little or innocent ones, but our nation would be infinitely sadder if *all* the families were exterminated by a noxious phantom."

My father believes he's doing our nation a favor, but his explanation of it has a major flaw. There would be no resistance if our nation went back to the way it was before I was born. What oppression could the foreign governments use as a catalyst for war, if the people were freed from county control?

"No one wanted this for our nation, Sydney. The system was to be temporary, but we did make more permanent preparations in case the battles beyond our coasts grew direr. We knew that as time went on, the likelihood of a civil uprising would grow. We disguised the construction of Neo-Necropolis and the underground line—both of which were used almost immediately—as mining sites. No one questioned this. People were especially dependent on the earth's raw materials then, and they understood the counties would need to be self-sufficient. I hope I've widened your perception of our nation's current circumstance."

My father pauses and rubs his hands together as he studies me. "You maintain a very skewed perception of Sheridan, which I mean to correct. Let me bring it closer to home for you. I'm going to tell you the truth about your capture by the seeksmen and your stay in their town."

He speaks of my time in Sheridan as if he were absent from it altogether. It's like the man before me now and the one that pretended to be Sheridan's stronghold are split entities—each unaware of the other side. The evil side proved stronger, and so it overcame the one I thought I loved.

"Against the strictest orders, the agent assigned to your detail decided to let fate—rather than particular control—take charge of your life. Those young men never should have been able to lay a hand on you."

It makes me sick to think my father was given the honor of delivering Cy's eulogy, since it was all lies. In the opening lines, he referred to Cy as a son and later called him a hero for being a seeksman. But, although he had known the Davids brothers for years, he would have executed them without hesitation had he been the agent monitoring their movement toward me in the woods.

"I am sorry they were allowed to stalk you over the years, but my greater regret is that they hurt you and forced you to join their faction. I suppose maybe they didn't need to force you," he entertains, "because you were treated quite differently than most captives, since one or both of them had developed twisted affection for you."

At this, I vehemently clang my shackles. How dare he speak of the seeksmen that way? Even he can't deny their upstanding gentility. It rattles my bones to hear him speak ill of Cy, the deceased seeksmen, for whom this was especially true.

"Were you not there?" he questions, as flustered as I. "They abduct our citizens and inject them with the same substance we had to use on your roommate yesterday. The doctor told you that you had amnesia, right?" Of course, I can't answer, so he continues with the assumption that he is correct. Distressingly, he is. "They do it to put distance between the victim and their family. They concoct a story for the abductee's missing memory, one that tells of the county government murdering their family and the seeksmen coming to their rescue. Conveniently, new Sheridans have no access to tablets to check in on their *living* family members. Evvie would be lamenting your loss and you hers right now, neither of you the wiser, had they not broken their rule for you."

I vividly remember shoving Crewe against the gravelly roadside and demand he let me go back for Evvie. He conceded, and then Cy convinced his brother that they go with me. It had never been done before. Could my father be telling the truth about the normal procedure?

Crewe told me that the injections had to be used because talking to the wanderer and allowing them free will regarding Sheridan would have terrible ramifications both for that individual and for their town if the refugee decided to return to Miles. I don't want to think that seeksmen abduct, lie to, and hold people against their will the same way that Miles' agents do, but it would be unwise to ignore valid points. What would the Davids brothers have done with me if they refused to go after Evvie?

To my dismay, it seems both the counties and the refugee towns are evildoers. My father wants me to believe that his unit is the lesser of the evils because by being involved in sanctioned politics, they better understand the dangerous world and the repercussions for ignorant actions.

"I can see you are at least questioning your previous perceptions. That's good, Sydney. An inquisitive mind and an untrusting heart are qualities to keep. I would not expect you to trust me wholly or to have immediate faith in this operation, but I do hope you believe I care about you, and that I would never hurt you. Or Evvie," he adds.

I shake my head from side to side to show him that I don't grant the least of his wishes either.

"Do you believe that I watched over you and attempted to keep you safe while you were growing up?" he asks me. I don't want to disclose this, but I nod because I want him to keep asking me questions until he discovers why I don't trust him. I need to hear his attempt to explain himself on that matter.

"Do you believe that I have watched over Evvie as well, and that she is safe now?" No matter how much I despise my father, I do feel as though her safekeeping is true. I nod.

"Have I physically hurt you? I know the way you are being treated now is not ideal, but I have done all of this," he gestures to the column and my shackles, "because I know you, Sydney. I know your resolve to be free." Tight-jawed, I shake my head no.

He raises his brows and head, mouthing a silent *aha*. He plants his feet and hooks his hands behind his back again. "It's the seeksmen who passed."

A gesture of my head is not necessary this time. He seems to notice the sorrow that seeps into my angry eyes. I continue to hate and distrust him because of what he did to Cy and Decklin. They trusted him. They believed that he would never intentionally harm them, but he did. He was their leader, and he purposefully led them to their death.

After he rescued and virtually raised Crewe and Cy, they came to love my father like their own. The captain made the Davids brothers and the entire town of Sheridan believe that he had loved them like his own sons. Yet he had so easily killed Cy and did nothing while we believed Crewe had gone to risk his life to avenge his brother's death.

"I wish that did not happen, but the black-operations teams were under an obligation to protect Evvie, as well as the general county population. They were to inflict non-fatal wounds if possible. An agent aimed for a lower leg, and unintentionally hit the bike's gas tank. He saw the flames and made a judgment call to end their suffering rather than see such young men burned alive. Hopefully this time, when those pictures of you are used to convince all the seeksmen to venture here again, my agents will not need to fire."

I don't believe his excuse for the rounds that passed through Cy and Decklin's weakened, expired vests. Decklin, for one, wasn't even burned severely. If they hadn't been shot, they could have abandoned the bike and rolled to smother the flames. The BOTs intended to make an example of Cy and Decklin by adding to their suffering, in the end killing them.

The door behind me swings open. My father lifts his hand to catch something thrown to him by the one who entered.

"I am going to leave now, Sydney, and this agent is going to aid you in enacting your decision about where we go from here. You have two choices. You can receive this," he says, showing me a bagged kit labeled *recall inhibitor*, "and return to the comforts of Level Three, or you can retain your new knowledge, in which case you'll have to remain on Level Five."

No! I've been given an impossible choice. If I remain on Five, I won't be able to use Edyn's connections and Gauge's expertise to plan an escape. But what good will an escape do if I lead these people to trust the captain, who is an inside agent?

My decisions always come down to Evvie. This has all proven that I can't trust anyone but myself to take care of her. I need to be with her. Since she's not in Neocropolis, I'll need to get out. I have to return to Three, and to the way I thought of the world before the impossible changed everything. I signal toward the kit. My father raises it to cheek, and I nod.

"Very well," he says, with no disappointment. "The two-hour dosage." He leaves the room as easily as he had come in, as if this entire episode were completely routine.

"Yes sir," the agent replies.

Sir? Just where does my father rank in this force? Without contemplation, the answer washes over me like a paralyzing vapor. Although he was a completely different person in Sheridan, there was something familiar about the words my father chose, and the cool haughtiness with which he said them, when he first began speaking tonight. Now, I've placed the distinguishing characteristic.

The same diction and air were used in the message Rico and I received that set the parameters for Evvie's release. The same mind formulated the discourse given by the agent who led my classified meeting last night. Tonight, I heard it from his very tongue. Demetri Harter is not simply an agent of the county; he is the leader of the entire black-operations program.

Stunned. Sickened. Heart beating out of control. My head feels light, and the room begins to tip. Anguish and anxiety fight for control of my insides. I cannot believe I am the daughter of the leader of the BOTs, who has the authority to bring everything down with a whisper.

Learning of my father's immeasurable power changes things. It's something I can't afford to forget. I calm my breathing and steady myself just in time to see the syringe coming toward my leg. I move as much as I can in the restraints until the agent rests the recall inhibitor and looks up at me.

No. With all my might, I shake my head from side to side, increasing my wooziness. *I changed my mind*.

The room seems to brighten, and the agent's face blurs. I try to hang on, but there's little left to hold. I've lost the feeling in my arms, and my ability to breathe through these tubes. My eyes are open, but all I see are auras whirling like a dream.

ELEVEN

Much of the last twenty-four hours has been clouded and peculiar. I woke up this morning to the blaring alarm as usual. My schedule appeared on the screen, followed by another horrific picture of myself. After that, I realized that I couldn't remember anything about the previous evening.

At first, I thought that Edyn and I had exchanged information while she pretended to read her Bible verses before lights out. I feared that our charade was somehow discovered until Edyn asked me in passing today if I'd be around tonight to hear the scripture. Discretely, she helped me understand a piece of the puzzle. Something had to have occurred earlier, maybe during my dinner break or the latter half of my evening employment.

Red was all business when he came to pass me breakfast. Likewise, his usual playfulness was replaced with deep pensiveness later in the morning when I joined him to work in the cafeteria kitchen.

I had hoped to ask Gauge at lunch what was wrong with Red today, but he didn't eat at his usual time. I sat alone, and apprehension ate at me.

Andriette avoided me like the plague during my PM employment, so it's possible that she was involved in yesterday's untold incident.

I was hyperaware of each resident's gaze at dinner tonight, but none seemed to focus on me any more than usual. If I had sat with anyone at dinner yesterday and learned something that was meant to be kept secret, the teller is following his or her order to appear inconspicuous well.

Now, I anxiously await Edyn's return to our cell so that we can talk. My focus should be on preparing for the match, but it's impossible to do so when I know that something important was revealed yesterday—information so significant that I'll never be able to recall it.

I wash up and brush my teeth as if I'm heading to bed for the night. Since I'm a contender in the boxing match tonight, I'll leave my cell sometime after lights out. Faking the small details is crucial. Edyn stressed that, but it's something I've always known to be true.

While I wait, I pull Edyn's Bible from her shelf and open to the book of Isaiah. I page to chapter forty-two, from where she read last night. She has the sixth and seventh verses circled, so I skip ahead to those. They read:

I, the Lord, have called you for a righteous purpose,
And I will hold your hand and keep you;
I will give you as a covenant to the people,
And as a light to the nations.
You will open blind eyes,
And release those bound to dungeon cells,
And those sitting in darkness from the prison house.

This book has again proven hauntingly applicable to the current world and our particular situation. I'm surprised those who listen to the false audio feed allow Edyn to read such words night after night.

For the sake of the cameras, my roommate attempts to conceal her anxiety when she returns at quarter to nine but, to my eyes, she's failing. She looks as if she'll burst if she doesn't soon release the dire information swarming inside her. My composure now slipping, I counteract our uneasy display by casually slumping into bed.

Edyn begins the verses as she did two nights ago, then cuts in with words I could have never expected. "It's not as well-planned as we wished, but we've decided to make our escape attempt tonight."

I actively try to keep my eyes from bulging and my jaw from dropping, but the racing of my heart and the sweat that quickly lines my palms is out of my control. We're going to escape *tonight*. Well, we're going to try.

"Andriette also had her memory wiped last night. She suspected that she sent you down to Level Five to collect the PM laundry load. That suspicion was confirmed when the guard couldn't remember which of you two came down yesterday. His memory had been deleted too."

Questions race through my mind, but I'm unable to ask them. I'm astonished that I descended to Five last night. Afterward, three minds were muddled with, so something severe occurred. I hope Edyn has an inkling as to what.

"The only witnesses whose minds were not tampered with were the solitary residents. They give the guard a hard time, so he was reluctant to ask something of them, but eventually he agreed to do some digging."

"There was a woman trapped in the shower cell who told him that you saw someone behind the door that closes off most of the level. Apparently, you went nuts, shouting that this person was a traitor and that you hated him."

Jerus. The rage rises in me now just thinking about him. Yes, I would have been wild with anger if I saw him continuing to make plans with the enemy, threatening the people I care about in Sheridan.

"You were put in the resistor cell for a bit and then taken into the unknown section of Five." Edyn's tone changes from quick and factual, to particular and intense. "I'm now sure that you've been outside of Miles and that you told me something of the sort that first night, but were forced to change your story. I also believe you got to know the leaders out there well, if you were charged enough to cuss this person out for being a double agent."

I want to tell Edyn everything. I want her to know that I indeed know the leaders of Sheridan well. How could I not when their leader is my father? I also want to assure her that the timing of our escape couldn't be better. It's urgent that I get out of here before the leader of the BOTs uses those awful photographs to lure my father here where he, and any others that come, could meet brutal death.

"Sydney, think what you will about this, but I am telling you the reason I was brought to Neocropolis. I have a strange gift—one I hadn't believed in before. I'm aware of souls that have passed on, and the guidance they bring me gets me in trouble sometimes."

It's strange in itself, but stranger to picture Edyn with psychic abilities. Most of the people in Miles who claim to be mediums have an eerie, mystical quality about them. Edyn is so grounded and levelheaded. I trust her enough to be interested in how her gift fits into our current predicament.

"A young man visited me last night while you were below. They can befuddle a mind, but they can't erase the impression one soul has on another. I recognized that I'd been in his presence before, likely the night you entered this cell."

Though Cy and Decklin died in body, one of them is still not finished looking after the ones he cares about. I think I know which one. Happy tears warm my eyes, but I blink them away. I'm supposed to be listening to scripture.

I wish I could feel his presence as Edyn can. If I could speak right now, I'd tell him everything that I whispered to his corpse that horrible day—that he had become my best friend, that I couldn't thank him enough for bringing me to Sheridan—to my father, and for risking his life to save my sister. Above the rest, I would apologize for getting him killed through my stubbornness and selfishness. I would tell him that I'm sorry for the pain I've since caused his brother.

"This young man is also why I believe you know people out there well—people that they hurt. Your friend is panicked, Sydney. I'm not always right, but this one feels clear. He's worried about someone who is coming here after you."

My father, Sheridan's captain, *is* coming for me. Although I asked it of him, he couldn't forget his little princess. I'm happy to be cared for enough to be rescued, but likewise panicked that something terrible could happen to my dad and any men who travel with him.

"Now for the plan," Edyn continues. "Vic, one of the nightshift guards, will type a code to freeze the audio and video feed in our cell for ten seconds at exactly 10:40. Make sure your blanket and pillow cover you completely before that. Like usual, the other two guards will replace you and your opponent in your beds. They're not aware of our plan, nor are they necessarily with us, so don't give them anything to suspect."

Edyn is running out of time, so she abbreviates and rushes the rest of the information. "Red will have a breakdown during the match. Posing as a guard, you'll meet Vic in the guards' station to open Doctor McClain's gate, room 310, by tablet. You'll escort her to the hospital room. Vic will enlist Gauge to help control Red. The guard who'll be in this room takes his job very seriously, so you'll have to be careful about getting me out. Do it as late as possible."

I'm glad both of my neighbors across the hall and Doctor McClain will be among those escaping. Even though most of the residents have been unwelcoming toward me, it will be hard to leave so many behind. I wish we could bring them all out of the dungeon, like the Bible verse said, but we can't. That is, not tonight.

"Once you're in the hospital, Gauge will get the final element he needs to make his explosive function. The attempt to settle Red should look plausible to anyone watching, but they'll come to control the situation if it's carried on too long. If the BOTs haven't seized us by then, Vic will open the elevator for us and override nighttime lock-in to get us to One. We'll duck into an apartment while Gauge sets and activates the bomb on top of the hydraulic elevator. After the blow, it'll be mass chaos as the Innocents and the group of us fights BOTs and flames to climb out of the hole in Neocropolis."

After rescuing Evvie from Miles with the Davids brothers, Galvesten, and Della, Crewe redirected us to plan B, the safe house. If we have a backup plan for this escape attempt, Edyn doesn't go over it. Perhaps none can exist within the restrictive walls of Neocropolis. If the BOTs come down to Three or meet us on One, we'll be lucky to be condemned to a deeper level of this inferno. More likely, we'll be dead.

"I'll see you on the other side," Edyn says. "Don't let your opponent knock you out beforehand." Our cell goes black. She couldn't have cut it any closer. "I'll see you at dawn," Edyn says. "Goodnight and God bless."

The blessing is something new. I'm glad to have it since the most hazardous moments of my life are a mere hour away. "Goodnight, Edyn," I return.

I replay Edyn's directions over and over. Quickly switch places with the guard at exactly 10:40. Listen for Red's wails and don't get knocked out in the meantime. Posing as a guard, release Doctor McClain from room 310 and escort her to the hospital. After Gauge is set with what he needs, retrieve Edyn. Rise to level One. Get into an apartment before the bomb blows. Fight the BOTs to get above ground.

Each time I repeat the scenario, I find myself focusing on the missing pieces. What do we do if the elevator door opens to a slew of BOTs on level One? If we do manage the escape without resistance from them, it won't be for long. What is the plan once we're on foot in Miles?

Dispersing into Miles to expose the government's best-kept secret makes the most sense to me. This will not only be the desire of any in our group with family inside the county, but getting Miles' citizens on our side is necessary to build resistance against confinement and coercion. It wouldn't make sense to flee Miles and come back after they've had the opportunity to regroup and invest more personnel in watching for us.

We should get lost within the population fairly quickly, who start to flock to the county's center right around the eleven o'clock hour. But where do we go from there? They'll sniff us out if we stay under their noses for any length of time. We'll need to move out of the county eventually. Unfortunately, we can't free any of the citizens with us. A tiny piece of metal in their wrists prevents us from being able to grant them independence. The only bodies that can cross the barrier are those without chips. God willing, there will still be six of us.

Six warm-blooded bodies blazing red in the cool September night. I know some of my companions have been jailed for many years, but they know that infrared technology exists. Thermal imaging is something that we can't deny, but we also can't let it deny us our opportunity for freedom.

I hate to think it, but the dreadful reality is that not all the bunch from Level Three is likely to make it out. Edyn and the guard, Vic, seem to be behind most of the plans. How are we supposed to get on if something were to happen to them? I sure hope Gauge, Red, and Doctor McClain know more than I do.

TWELVE

Against my greatest efforts, I've glanced at the clock much more than would be considered normal tonight. I have no choice but to stare at the clock as it changes from 10:38 to 10:39. Then, I toss and turn, finally placing my pillow over my head. Although my counting is near accurate to real time after years of practice with the camera mounted on EPA 7-8, I count sixty two seconds to allow for some error.

With the last second counted, I spring from my bed and make for the door. The gate buzzes. The guard swings the outer gate open at the exact moment that I pull open the inner door. I don't even see his face as he slaps a cap on my head, hands me his belt, and closes the inner door. The cap and belt are my keys to temporarily change lives with the guard, without allowing those behind the cameras to recognize the swap. I tuck my ponytail into the hat, buckle the belt, close the gate, and continue his loop around the level.

I'm surprised the nightshift guards are allowed to congregate in the gymnasium since the cameras and microphones are turned off after it closes. They're Innocents or maybe Twos, so I suppose the higher ups trust them with particular freedoms that residents of Three do not enjoy.

Edyn's guard friend enters the gym from the opposite doorway. "I'm Vic," he says. "Big fight, bigger night." After I drop the guard belt, he removes my cap and hands me a face guard and a pair of gloves. "Can't have inmates waking up with mysterious cuts and bruises," he says, apparently reading my surprise at using a mask. "Wouldn't have let you fight otherwise," he says, noting my colorful face.

Wearing the mask even for a shortened match will better my chances of withstanding my opponent. Not only that, but increased swelling would blur my vision. We can't afford any impairment to my reactions to the bomb and the BOTs.

Vic lifts the ropes for me to enter the ring, but stops me abruptly when he spots the little splint on my thumb. He lifts my hand to examine it. "It's fine," I tell him.

"It's not the boxing I'm worried about," he says. "It's the possibility of a chip being in the splint or in you. We'll have to add getting that thing off discreetly to Doctor McClain's challenges. Jump in," he says, patting the mat. "Remember, Rhoma doesn't know what's happening tonight. Fight like a contender would, but save some for the agents if you can."

Vic has given me something to think about, something that I haven't fretted over since I first awoke in Neocropolis. I wouldn't put it past whoever runs this place to make sure that, unlike the rest of the residents, Demetri Harter's daughter received a chip implant.

What will happen if they remove the splint and find an incision on my thumb? It would not necessarily be indicative of a chip; breaks sometimes do require surgery, even to remove bone splinters. They wouldn't be able to take that risk, and I wouldn't expect them to.

But I can't stay behind and entrust the task of finding

my father and preventing him from coming to Miles to them. I haven't even been able to tell Edyn about the captain. What I did tell her about my family when we first met, she doesn't remember. Even if in the end I'd be recaptured and imprisoned on a lower level, I would escape with the others, but then take my signal far away from them. I'd travel toward Sheridan with desperate hope that I would meet the captain, and Galvesten, along the way.

My feet notice that my competition has entered the ring before my fixed eyes do. I quickly tuck my injured thumb into a fist in order to hide it from her sight. I don't want to reveal any weaknesses.

Rhoma doesn't spend time looking me over. She heads straight to her corner to gear up. She reminds me of Alix, only shorter and perhaps a little older. She is visibly strong and confident. The bottom half of her hair is blond like Alix's, but her natural color has grown in past her chin. The contrasting hair colors show how long she's lived below ground. Maybe she doesn't have it cut because it's something by which she can remember her prior life.

"We'll box ten-minute-and-a-half rounds if you last that long," she informs me as she makes her way toward the center of the ring. The comment is more matter-of-fact than insulting. I take no offense, especially knowing that I won't need to last half that many.

"We count for each other on knockouts, but keep track of our own clean hits to score each round. I'll keep time. Come on, let's tap gloves," she says, waving me toward the center of the ring. Rhoma's bump is much more forceful than mine is. It doesn't seem to be a show of superiority; I think her toughness is just ingrained physically. For my sister's sake, I've always internalized my strength.

Rhoma bounces back to her corner, where a timer hangs from the rope. She leans over, clicks it with her nose, and shuffles at me, her lead glove making tight circles as if she's winding it up for power.

I had no idea how fast the hits would come. Three jabs in, I drop my lead hand to better protect my ribcage. Wrong decision. Rhoma instinctively capitalizes on my mistake, landing two blows to my face before I can get my gloves back up and tuck my chin.

She continues to throw all the punches, but thankfully, many land on my gloves. I try to shuffle away to regain a proper stance where I can see my foe, but Rhoma's feet follow faster than my own shadow. Every time I throw a glove toward her, it's smashed back into my face.

Finally, the timer buzzes to end my embarrassment. I don't care that Rhoma is the only one witnessing my overwhelming defeat or that, if all goes according to plan, I won't be here tomorrow when the result is coded between residents. I can do better than the pathetic fight I just put up. Rhoma certainly has the advantage of experience, but my height should allow me to dodge more of the blows than I am.

What am I doing wrong that I can fix? This is mostly a mental sport, so there must be a strategy I can use to step up my game. *Absorb the blows*. I need to lean into the attacks, causing a reverberation that will give me more time and space to predict her next move. I'll never get away, let alone keep up with her, if all I see are green gloves coming at me.

"Round two," Rhoma announces as she drops the ticking timer. I quickly get off the ropes in my corner and shuffle my feet toward her. Our feet dance around each other only a second longer than the first round before she lands a combination of jabs and a hook. She shoots for the next succession of blows, but this time, I lean into the first body punch, scooting her an extra inch away. It's just enough for me to lean away from the straight she throws toward my face.

Finally, I land a single jab on Rhoma's exposed side under her extended arm. Instantaneously, two are returned to me. I try to toss a hook with my power hand. Though it lands on her, opening myself up for the straight that follows proves that I've again made a mistake, this time in my guarding. Propelled by the force of Rhoma's quick strikes, I slide along the ropes. The blows come too fast. There's no room for me to focus and use the techniques that Edyn taught me.

Acting as both adversary and referee, Rhoma says, "Come on, off the ropes," as she bounds back toward the center of the ring. "Come on," she repeats, when I don't move quickly enough for her liking.

In the middle, I meet a well-executed series that sends me straight back to the edge of the ring. My own gloves pummel and blind me as Rhoma unleashes her power on them. Backed into a corner, all I can do is wait for the timer to sound.

Rhoma stops hitting me and walks toward her corner. At first, I think that the protective mask and the ringing in my ears must have masked the timer's sound. After Rhoma reaches her corner, it buzzes. I'm not even worth her fight.

I wish she were trustworthy enough to be let in on the plan. Then I wouldn't have to put up with any of this. I'm sure Edyn, Vic, and the others weren't worried about her sharing the news with the authorities or even spreading it among the residents of Level Three. I assume they chose not to disclose their intention to my opponent because Rhoma wouldn't have accepted being left behind. Like any fed-up inmate, she would demand to go with us.

I guess no matter how shameful my defeat in the ring is—I have still beaten her in some way. Tonight, I will be freed from this place, while she will remain cemented within it. This victory, however, is nothing I can be proud of. There is no glory in leaving others behind to suffer.

Rhoma comes at me to begin round three. I shuffle away from her first jab, which throws a wrench in her premeditated combination. I land a hook with my power hand, which seems to ignite her prowess. Again, I retreat rather than attack. Even though this match is not my primary concern right now, I am stubborn enough not to allow such a pitiable score as the first two rounds. Five clean hits this round, that's my goal.

You know how to fight, I tell myself. One way or another, I've been fighting all my life. Since my grandmother was euthanized. Jab. That's two. I absorb a combination and shuffle away. This time, I lead the attack toward Rhoma. Since my mother committed suicide. Right straight. Rhoma easily ducks away and returns a body hit. Since Evvie and I were put into the orphanage. Two jabs with my lead hand can be counted, but my attempt to finish the combination with a power hook is blocked.

Rhoma goes on the offensive again, backing me into a corner. How can she so easily overcome the ground that I have to work so hard to hold? Is it boxing or, like me, something else that propels my opponent? Is it her former life, or the torture of a mundane life since being locked up that drives her?

The bell sounds. Close. Four hits. I don't expect to be a threat in the next round, but at least I can be a competitor. I have loads of anger that I can misappropriate on my foe in the opposite corner. My movements definitely aren't ingrained like Rhoma's are, but every now and again, I get a feel for what I need to do next. Now if I could only execute more often.

Seconds into the fourth round, I think about Trista, the foster parent that beat me. Without realizing the progression, I pound my glove straight into Rhoma's face. For the first time, her feet are closer to the ropes than mine are—and she knows it.

Before I retract the arm that delivered the blow, Rhoma replies with two hard jabs to my exposed ribcage. I fight the natural reactions to either step back—giving up the ground I've earned—or tuck my power arm against my side for protection. Instead, I remain on the attack, pounding the left side of Rhoma's headgear with a right hook. Unbelievably, my more experienced opponent is the first to stumble.

I attempt to capitalize on her instability, but it is very short-lived. By the time my feet shuffle over to hers, Rhoma looks composed and strong. Instead of attacking, she waits patiently for me to decide on a punch.

My effort is sloppy. Rhoma easily blocks the first two hits in my combination. She doesn't allow me the opportunity to deliver the third. The hit isn't a clean uppercut, but it's too angled to qualify as a straight punch.

Blurred strokes of light cross between Rhoma and me, but I manage to stay on my feet. My opponent shifts her position so that I am once again closer to the ropes than she is. The muscles in Rhoma's power arm tense, and she starts to twist into what could be the final blow of the match, but a piercing scream delays her execution the split second that I need to drop to my knees and avoid the strike. Red has given us the signal. It's time to escape.

By design, my opponent doesn't know what is about to

occur. Wails from the cells must be somewhat regular, because she rips me up, steps back, and pounds a left hook into the side of my head. Rather than putting my arms up in protection, I try to tell Rhoma to stop. Wrong decision. She throws another hook with the same precision as the first, but with greater power from her dominant arm.

She's done it. Her successive hooks to the opposite sides of my head, both undefended, send me to the ring floor. Agonizing pain erupts through my skull. This wasn't supposed to happen. We weren't supposed to fight long enough for my more experienced opponent to deliver a knock out.

Dizzily, I get on my hands and knees, and crawl toward the ropes. Rhoma appears before me, blocking my way. "You aren't through yet. Come on!" she yells, dragging me up again.

I open my mouth to tell her that I'm throwing in the towel, but I'm silenced by yet another ruthless hit. Finally, the timer sounds, leaving an indisputable winner. Rhoma has reduced me to a stumbling idiot, able to think only of the pain in my head.

Red's screams grow louder, wilder, closer, each one a splinter in my brain, but also a reminder that in this situation where every *second* is imperative, I've wasted a minute or more. *Get up*. I need to protect my family. I need to see the sun again. No amount of pain and disorientation will prevent me from following the plan. I will not let this opportunity for freedom slip away.

THIRTEEN

Stumbling out of the ring, I shed the boxing gloves and headgear. I stand up a bit too quickly after bending to grab the discarded guard belt. After securing my bearings, I strap it around my waist and tuck my ponytail into the cap. I don't have the embroidery on my jumpsuit, but at least it's the same color as the guards'. Before heading into the hallway, I cross my arms to hide my splinted thumb.

Vic's expression as I arrive to the guard's station is a mix of impatience and concern. "Here," he says anxiously over Red's convincing wails. He hands me a tablet, and I struggle to handle it without exposing the splint. "We need Doctor McClain right away. I'm going to get Red and try bringing him to 305."

"Let Gauge help you," I suggest.

"Good idea. I will." Vic speeds down the hallway toward the cell across the hall from mine.

"Come give us a hand," I call to Rhoma, who is frozen in the gymnasium opening. The confidence I saw in her eyes during the fight has receded.

I hustle towards room 310 without waiting to see what Rhoma does. Every piece of this mission needs to be executed intelligently and quickly. Because of Rhoma's willpower to take me down, it has begun more slowly than planned, giving the agents more time to reach us if they've noticed that something is off.

Doctor McClain's inner door is opened, and her hands clench the bars of her gate. "I need to settle him down right away," she says earnestly. I don't notice how frenzied I am until my unsteady hands fail to touch the correct commands on the tablet's surface.

Rhoma snatches the tablet from my hands, opens Doctor McClain's gate, and rushes back down the hall. I am still for a moment as both sympathy and panic seep in at the sight of Red thrashing uncontrollably as Vic and Gauge try to pull him from his cell.

"Get Edyn," Vic commands. Rhoma is quicker than I would have been with the responsibility. She sprints to my cell and produces Edyn within a breath. I see alarm in every pair of eyes, except for Rhoma's—whose should show the most shock. Something is wrong. Thankfully, Rhoma is composed and driving those of us who are not—namely me.

Rhoma and Doctor McClain push past me into the tiny hospital. Rhoma undoes the straps of a bed restraint while Doctor McClain digs through a small refrigerator. Some liquids she hurriedly pushes aside, while others she strategically places on the adjacent countertop. These are the substances that Gauge needs to complete his explosive.

Gauge's eyes meet mine for a moment as Vic, Edyn, and Rhoma struggle to restrain the thrashing teenager. I know now why their eyes have a greater sense of nervousness than I had anticipated—Red isn't acting. The stress of the situation, or perhaps the hysterical wails themselves, must have caused the Red I know to fade. If there's a silver lining, it's that his darker side has continued to scream according to the plan.

They toss him onto the narrow, wheeled bed and begin strapping down his violent limbs. Although his body is secured, we can't contain his screams—screams that are no doubt stirring the residents of Level Three.

What does this look like from the agents' point of view? To them, three guards, two residents, and a resident doctor are fighting to subdue an unstable adolescent. Of course, they know well that the raging resident is the one who once impaled an officer. They can see that the guards have let out his roommate, who was brought to Neocropolis for creating an explosive and Edyn, who they remember spent time in solitary for nearly beating a guard to death. I have no doubt that they are watching us very closely.

How long will it take for one of the agents to notice mine and Rhoma's unlikely stature and shape, the fact that our chins seem glued to our chests as not to give away a glimpse of our faces, or that the light in the room has been dimmed suspiciously for a doctor to do her work. Doctor McClain guides a needle into the vein of Red's latched arm.

"Edyn?" Vic says to my roommate.

Edyn looks up from the other side of the bed, where she's been holding Red's abdomen down against his lurches. "Gauge?" she says, redirecting Vic's question. Gauge nods to Edyn, who in turn passes the gesture to Vic. "I'll take Red," she says.

"McClain, take care of her." Vic points to me before exiting the hospital. I hold up my thumb to explain Vic's command to the Doctor. She grabs my arm and pulls me toward the counter, where Gauge works tediously. I still can't believe this was the same woman who sat me on her lap and told me that my mother loved me after I had discovered her bled-out body. There is no time for the gentleness that she possessed that day.

"What is this?" Rhoma demands. No one needs to answer. Rhoma knows that we wouldn't do anything that would have us locked in a deeper level of Neocropolis. She has to know Red's outburst was planned and that those released to help control him was strategic. This is an escape attempt—perhaps the first that has a chance of success.

"Open the elevator," Edyn tells Rhoma, who still holds the tablet.

Rhoma nearly collides with Vic at the doorway. He pushes past her to hand Edyn a semi-automatic pistol. Over my shoulder, I watch him set an identical .22-caliber handgun on the counter between Gauge and me. I wonder which of us the weapon is meant for until he clips a belt with an empty holster and additional magazines around Gauge's waist.

My attention is ripped back to my thumb, where the doctor has made an incision. At first, the skin around the incision is white, but then it flushes as the wound begins to bleed.

"Gauge! I need you to hold her," the doctor orders. Gauge slides the pistol into his holster and whips around to the other side of Doctor McClain and me. "Look at me," he says as he turns my face away from my thumb. He squeezes my wrist and arm so tightly in his hands that I worry about the pain that is to come.

I nervously glance over my left shoulder at the drops of blood on the counter and the tool in Doctor McClain's hand. "Look at my eyes," Gauge beckons. The words are hard, but his light, blue eyes are soft and welcoming.

I simultaneously feel two things that I could not

have expected. The first is a hint of affection for Gauge—the intelligent, passionate young man who has been looking out for me. The second is a breath-stopping pain as Doctor McClain removes a tiny piece of metal from my thumb. I held the same suspicion as Vic, and we were right. They placed a tracking chip in my thumb. Thankfully, there was no microphone, or this escape would have been ended before it could start. Meaning the people behind the attempt would have been ended.

Doctor McClain hastily fastens a strip of medical tape across the wound. Without an oral order, we rush out of the hospital room and cram into the tiny elevator, where Vic enters his code on the touch screen. I had a chip in my thumb, which means they've been watching intently since I stepped out of my cell. They're prepared.

It wasn't supposed to be like this. Our escape began late because of my inability to hold my ground in the ring. Again, I slowed our progress due to the splint on my thumb. And now, we have a comatose Red to tow around. How can we possibly make it out without BOT resistance? I'm amazed they haven't stopped us already. Unless, of course, they are waiting patiently for us above.

The elevator opens to a calm row. Vic gives Gauge a boost into the hatch on the ceiling before following the rest of us out of the elevator. The first door handle I try is locked firm, but the next one gives. I help Edyn drag Red into the home of two wide-eyed Innocents.

"What's going on?" the man asks fearfully.

"We're escaping," Vic answers with a grin. "Join at your own risk." The owners of the unit begin an onslaught of questions. It reminds me of the panic that I stirred in the citizens of Sheridan at the hospital when I yelled at Della. *People are dying*. I wish those words hadn't come true.

"Where is Doctor McClain?" I ask over the couple's chatter, suddenly aware that she is not among us.

"She's getting her daughter," Edyn answers. "God be with us." Edyn deliberately places her loaded handgun in my hand. I don't know why she trusts me with this type of firearm, which I've never held, let alone fired, before. "I can't handle it and carry him," she explains. "Don't be afraid to use it. There's no waiting out the punches in this," Edyn says with remarkable calm and focus. "You've got to throw them." She adjusts my grip on the weapon, looks me in the eye, and firmly says, "Remember what they've done to you."

Edyn's steadfast confidence boosts my own. I can't hesitate because they won't. We're already dead down here. Why would they show us any mercy? They won't. Shoot or get shot. Kill or be killed.

It would be easy to act on these thoughts if my sister was the target of a BOT's aim. This situation is indirect, but it's not that different. Evvie could still be in danger. I certainly know that my father is and perhaps Crewe too. Cy's soul revisited this world to aid us in what is just. For strength, I picture that he's beside me. I wish I could feel his presence the way Edyn can. It would give me comfort to know that he's with me, like a guardian angel. I think about asking my roommate, but Gauge's rapid entrance and the slam of the apartment door causes the breath I'd inhaled for the question to solidify and sink in my lungs.

"I found a—" Gauge's frenzied piece of information is cut off by the thunderous blast whose energy rattles the ceiling and cracks the light fixture. He tries to continue the statement, but his voice is lost in the sea of screams. He frantically thrusts his pointer finger upward. I make out only part of the phrase on his lips…*saw them coming down*. Even before he detonated the bomb, our resistance was coming.

Vic is the first to make for the door. Gauge and I follow his lead, but he brushes us back against the wall. Sounds of pandemonium—screams from the residents and the heavy boots of the BOTs—form a dreadful image in my mind. Despite the explosion above, they've made it down. One shouts an order right outside the door. "On the floor!"

Although the vests worn by the seeksmen proved too old and thin to save their lives when fired upon, I wish I had one around me now. I feel so unprotected in only the Neocropolis-issued jumpsuit.

With Edyn, Red, and the man and woman of the apartment lining the wall alongside Gauge and me, Vic pulls open the door and heads gun-first into the hallway. He's only taken a step beyond the doorway when a round explodes. A shrill scream erupts from the woman who lives in this apartment and resonates with others throughout the level. Gauge reacts by drawing his pistol and turning off the safety.

A cloud of debris from the explosion masks all but a triangle of white elastic on the side of Vic's prison shoes. I wait for his body to crumble, but it doesn't fall. Instead, his feet move forward in the direction of the elevator. Like magnets, Gauge's follow. Mine, however, are bound by fear to this spot.

Somehow, I think I'd have the courage to leave if it were someone else in front of me. I trust Gauge, but trust and the opportunity for freedom are not enough for me run past BOTs who could fire at me point blank. Love, however, is enough to inspire the courage I need. If it were my father in front of me, I would follow to provide him with whatever protection

I could. If it were Crewe, and not Gauge who slipped out the door before me…

Another gunshot. This one comes from the opposite end of Level One, though I can't tell which direction the round was fired. Doctor McClain was the only member of our company that traveled deeper down the row, and she was not armed. An agent has traveled to the opposite end and is firing, but on who? Residents of *Innocence*? Men, woman, and *children* who never committed a crime, yet have paid an incredible price without a complaint. What cause would a BOT have to fire, unless the formerly tame residents have risen up against an armed agent?

The thought shames me. I am acting more cowardly than an Innocent and the citizens of Miles, who failed to act at the injustices inside the county.

"Cover us, Sydney." Edyn gives me the last, little push that I need to step out of the apartment. The weapon in my hand is needed to protect more than just myself. While my love for these people is no match for certain people of Sheridan, they have become my friends, and I do care for them.

"Come on!" Gauge screams.

I step into the hallway, falling right behind Doctor McClain and her little girl. I sweep my weapon toward the far end of the row. When I see that it's clear, I turn to join the others in a mad rush toward the debris-filled elevator.

A sizeable hole has been blown in the top of the shaft. Good thing this wasn't a cable-system elevator. The blast would've obliterated cables, dropped the car, and left us no way to get up and out.

"Hurry!" Gauge yells with arms stretching below. Edyn drops Red, and helps Doctor McClain lift her daughter to Vic's and Gauge's waiting hands. They scoop up the nine-year-old effortlessly.

"Red next," Vic orders. "Sydney, watch that hallway." Doctor McClain and Edyn grunt as they struggle to lift Red's limp body high enough for the men's arms to grab him.

"Mom!" Gracen Ray cries from above, and it's enough that Edyn decides Doctor McClain should be next. When she struggles to lift her on her own, I set the gun down and help.

I know who should be lifted next. This operation is largely Edyn's. She knows what to do once we have exited Neocropolis and are free, either within the borders of Miles County or outside of them. I certainly bring knowledge to the table, but the others aren't aware of where I've been and why I'm important to the county, so they have no reason to need me the way they need her.

Edyn's mass is another reason that I should be last. She'll need a boost from the floor to make it to the men's hands more than I will. With Edyn's arms added to the lifters, they'll have no problem lifting me if only I can jump high enough.

"Go!" Edyn screams at me suddenly. She looks over her shoulder and says it again, but not before picking up my discarded handgun. I jump up and grab hold of the men's arms. Once they've dragged me up, I spin around, determined to help Edyn, but she's not there.

"Edyn!" I yell below. My call is answered with a gunshot.

FOURTEEN

"Get out of here!" Vic commands, before suddenly jumping atop the rubble below to follow the sound of the exploded round. Just like that, our other leader has left us.

"Do you have a plan?" a man urgently asks Gauge. Apparently, Rhoma and two other men were lifted from captivity while my cowardice delayed our escape. If I had moved sooner, the imminent danger that Edyn snatched my weapon to confront may not have presented itself. Vic would not have been compelled to jump down after Edyn, his long-time friend. Both of our leaders would be beside us, telling us where we go from here.

"Yes," Gauge answers, swiftly stepping into command.

"Then go. We'll stay and help others out," the man says.

"More of them will come," Gauge argues. "You know—"

"If she shot him, more of *us* will come. We'll stay," the man affirms. "Go now!" he demands.

Gauge and I stand and start toward Rhoma, Doctor McClain, her daughter, and an unconscious Red.

"Help." The faint plea reaches my ears and causes me to stop. Where did the voice come from? The room is dark, except for some small, multicolored lights scattered about the switchboards and media screens that dominate the space. "Please," the hoarse voice calls again.

"Sydney," Gauge warns after hearing the man and noticing that I'm navigating the darkness to follow his voice.

I smell him before I see him, and painful memories take hold of my heart. The man is a county agent. One of his duties is to contain the captives of Neocropolis. He must have been close to the elevator when Gauge's bomb ignited, but has since scooted away. The flesh of his lower body is badly burned. I did notice two other bodies beside the opening in the ground when I was lifted to this level, but I tried to ignore them and focus on helping Edyn up. This suffering man I cannot ignore.

A most fearful *click*, the hammer of a gun being cocked, sounds right behind me. I can sense that the loaded weapon is pointed in my direction. Of course, there would be other BOTs remaining on this level. They were either also injured from the explosion or, like me, were too afraid to act after it. Or perhaps an agent was ordered to stay and to make sure that no residents escaped Neo-Necropolis.

No shot is fired. I slowly turn to face my assailant, and am shocked to see that it is Gauge behind the gun. At first, I'm terrified, but I quickly realize the barrel of his weapon is not focused on me, but rather on the injured agent beside me.

"Gauge, don't," I plead.

"Move," Gauge says uncertainly. The gun shakes in his unsteady hand.

"Wait. Don't kill me," the burned agent begs.

"You would have killed me for trying to regain my God-given freedom," Gauge says through gritted teeth. "Why shouldn't I kill you?"

"You don't understand," the threatened man says. "We don't have a choice. Sydney, please," he says, reaching to take hold of my arm.

Shivers ripple down my spine. How does this man know who I am?

"Wait," I tell Gauge. "Who are you?" I ask the agent.

"I was the one with Jerus that night," he mutters through his pain. Yes, his was the voice reading the poisonous words of whatever ruthless man leads the BOTs. "Most of us don't want to hurt anyone, but we have no choice," he continues.

"You always have a choice," Gauge accuses.

"So do you," the man returns calmly. "Right now." He turns to me again. "Jerus made a poor choice, a deadly one—for the seeksmen and for himself. He wasn't the *real* traitor to Sheridan, but he felt that way. He couldn't live with the guilt this job brings."

"What are you saying?" I ask the agent.

He neglects to answer. Instead, he says, "If you want to know who the real traitor is, and want to know how to get yourselves and the others to safety, you can't kill me."

"Tell us," Gauge demands, stepping around me to bring the barrel of the gun closer to the agent.

"In good faith," the agent says after a tense, silent moment. "I'll tell you one. I'll reveal the other if you help me."

Gauge looks between the man and me, deliberating. Although my strongest desire is to hear who the real traitor to Sheridan is, I know that's not the right choice. Gauge knows it too.

Rhoma interrupts. "The exit's through a long corridor over there."

"Careful. That's the way we come in," the agent says,

proving his value.

Gauge finally lowers his handgun and hands it to Rhoma. "Get Red through it, and watch the door," he tells her. "How do we get them to safety?" Gauge asks the agent.

"We've had our eyes on a tribe of seeksmen from Sheridan who travelled up the Tongue River." The agent pauses to take a deep breath, but tenses in pain. How did Cy manage to get on his brother's bike after being burned more severely than this man?

"We lost their heat signatures about six miles south of the county border," he continues. "We assume they're hiding underground." The agent turns to me. "Breach at EPA 7-8 so you can avoid the cameras. Travel the river's bank, cutting across its meanderings where you can. Even if the seeksmen have hidden themselves in the water, you shouldn't miss them."

His theory is not a bad one. For a moment, I picture it. I picture my father, Crewe, Merick, Alix, Cheng and his seeking partner, and perhaps even Rico and Galvesten, dressed in the neoprene suits and floating along with the current. It's an excellent way to both stay off the open road and to beat the county's heat-seeking technology.

"We need him," Rhoma says, unexpectedly returning. "Or his thumb. There's a scanner to get out."

"I got it," says a young man more lumbering than Crewe from near the hole. Another man takes his spot to help out the trickle of prisoners, while the young man hoists the body of a dead agent and carries him toward the exit. The agent closes his eyes in grief.

"What if we don't meet these *seeksmen* in or by the Tongue?" Gauge asks, paying little attention to the rest. The word seeksmen, which holds so much hope for me, is clearly foreign to my friend. He has heard of the people outside, but he must not know much about them. "Where else would we be likely to find them?"

"After a large oxbow lake, the river will meander due west and then hairpin back around. Travel due east after this curve and cross the highway. You'll find a collection of buildings. If God's on *your* side, you'll at least find their suspected hideaway and be somewhat safe from the teams sent after you."

As if he were reading my mind, the agent says, "I realize you already have one to slow you down. Instead, take my wife and kids with you. Do that for me, and I'll disable the infrared energy sensors around EPA 7-8 to give you better chances."

"Why should we trust you?" Gauge asks.

"You have no reason to, but Sydney does." The agent focuses on me. "In Jerus' honor, I'll do for you what he wished he had the courage to do, which was be a traitor to the county side. He wasn't a man to show it, but I know now that he cared deeply for the people of Sheridan."

"Where can we find your family?" I ask, letting him know I trust him.

"The Neu Vu Condominiums in Sector Seven. Room 407. You all need to go now. If there are any others, I'll tell them to meet you at EPA 7-8 in hopes that they'll not kill me either. When I have proof that my family is safe in Sheridan, I'll send word about the real traitor."

"I heard," says the man who first took Gauge's place helping others out. "It's quiet down there. I don't think any more are coming out."

"Let's go," Gauge and I say in unison.

There is enough space, monitors, and other gadgets in this open room to be the workspace for a couple of dozen agents, yet only a quarter of that amount seemed to be on duty tonight. I imagine the rest are hidden in the forests along the Tongue River or circling above in stealthy choppers.

If they are in choppers, it won't take them long to arrive back here so the BOTs can put the Neocropolis uprising to an abrupt rest. We've wasted too much time. Again, it's my fault for stopping, but at least this time we've gained something useful.

The others and I follow Gauge up several steep stairs, and then through a long, upward sloping corridor. Finally, I see the reflection of the others' faces in the glow of a pale blue light ahead.

"This everyone?" asks the large man holding the corpse of an agent.

"Do it," Gauge answers. The man lifts the agent's arm and presses his thumb to the screen. The light turns red and the recording *access denied* is shot from the device, crushing all of our hopes at once. Gauge curses and pounds the metal door beside the scanner.

"What are we going to do?" asks the woman from the apartment where we took cover as the bomb went off. I wonder what became of the male who shared that space with her? He isn't one of the men among us.

Without answering, Gauge pushes his own thumb against the device, this time causing a beeping that sounds like the warning before an alarm begins to sound.

"Why did you do that?" a man in his early fifties asks.

"What else was I supposed to do?" Gauge fires back with irritation.

"Anything but that! What did you think your fingerprint was going to do, idiot kid?"

"Hey, it was this idiot kid whose explosive got you out of

that hell hole, so back off him," Rhoma warns.

"Out? Does it look like we're out?" The pace of the beeping quickens. "See what you've done?" the man charges. "We have nowhere to go but right back down, and that's if we're lucky!" he charges bitterly.

We didn't know nearly enough when we attempted this mission. Although I don't like the blame and anger he's placing upon Gauge, the older man is right. And while I might live, considering I'm still collateral for the captain, it's not likely that the others will be allowed that mercy. I don't want to think about Gauge or Red being killed. I couldn't accept another friend dying by the hand of the government's secret force.

A loud alarm begins to sound throughout the corridor and the level below us. Either I am hearing echoes of the blaring alarm on the level below, or there are alarms sounding on every level of Neocropolis. If the residents down in solitary didn't awaken from the blast or the screams that probably passed from level to level, they've been awoken now. The whole place must be nuts.

"Perfect," the older man grumbles, loudly enough for all to hear over the alarm.

"Shut up!" the hefty young man booms, silencing him and even little Gracen Ray's sobs. He takes hold of the dead man's thumb, rubs it rapidly against the bright fabric of his own jumpsuit, and presses it against the scanner for a second time.

The alarm quiets. When the scanner light turns green, the man drops the body and turns the door handle. Before he opens it, he turns and faces the group, now ten strong. "Let's do this the right way, huh?" he says with every ounce of accusation that is owed us.

Every one of us, except for the child, deserves to be

shamed by the idiocy that just occurred. Some bickered while the others of us watched, but none besides this man held enough hope and pride to think of an obvious solution to the dilemma. This time, my feet are the first to move, regardless of what's on the other side of that door. I step over the body in the corridor and follow the sharp man outside.

Air. Fresh air. I used to hate any air breathed inside the county's barrier, but not anymore. I'll never take this air for granted again.

After each of the ten has exited, Gauge closes the metal door. The moonlight reflects off a bright, yellow circle on the door, the rectangular container jutting from the building. Below the symbol is a sign that reads *Hazardous Waste*. So this is how they keep the agents and the existence of Neocropolis hidden? How infrequently and stealthily must the agents come and go, so that not even the employees of the actual Environmental Protection Agency standing above ground know they exist? How soundproof are the floors beneath their feet? I wonder if the alarm has ever sounded during daylight hours before.

"We're splitting up," Gauge announces. "Rhoma and Sydney, you'll take Monya with you," he says, pointing to the woman from the apartment. "Find the family in the condominiums and try to convince them to leave with you. Gather some dark clothes for all of us while you're there, but do it quickly," he says, eyeing us. I nod to let him know that I won't stall our progress again.

"Rhett and Jarod, take care of my best friend." Gauge pats the two eldest men in the group on their backs, even the one who ridiculed him minutes ago. They messily heave Red into their arms and, unlike my party, immediately take off.

"Jaxon," Gauge addresses the man in his late twenties

who stopped the alarm, "you go with Doctor McClain and Gracen Ray. You'll arrive first, so be cautious while you wait."

I don't think this young man will have difficulty thinking on the fly if anyone takes notice of their lingering around the EPA late at night. He squats down and allows Doctor McClain to lift her daughter onto his back. Then they hustle toward the noisy city center.

"What are you doing, Gauge?" I ask suspiciously, noting that he has not included himself in any of the groups.

"There's something I have to do, Sydney. Don't wait for me," he orders. Our eyes meet for a minute, and I recognize in them the same mixture of anxiety and longing that I saw in Crewe's eyes just before he kissed me. Crewe propelled himself through his fear toward me, but Gauge turns forthwith and runs away.

"Gauge!" I call after him, protesting whatever it is that he's setting off alone to do. At my call, he quickens his pace and doesn't turn back.

FIFTEEN

Darting between the shadowy buildings as if there were a helicopter overhead, I lead Rhoma and Monya across the county. A spotlight would alert the citizens that something is wrong, so just because one doesn't shine on the ground doesn't mean that a BOT isn't seeking us out from above. Instead, they would use the ever-present infrared technology to watch for a group travelling with suspicious movements. We'll have to blend better.

The first part of our journey is relatively quiet, but as we approach the center of Miles, the crowd of hooting and hollering people enjoying the county's nightlife swells. I don't have to worry about anyone in the crowd recognizing me, because I was never out among them, or anyone for that matter. Miles County declared me dead, but it made no difference to anyone.

I wonder if any type of service was held in my honor. Who would have come? Merideth, for sure. She would have been the only one in tears, though maybe not for me. She would be distraught that Evvie was missing and had possibly succumbed to the same fate that I supposedly had.

My boss, Tiana, from the restaurant where I was a server would have attended. She chatted incessantly with me, but she never took a breath to ask about me and find out who I was. A couple of the kitchen employees might have accompanied her, though I don't even think they knew my name.

My instruction monitor probably felt obligated to go. Perhaps a couple of my EduWeb classmates were present. Though I never developed friendships with anyone, a few didn't seem to be the gossips to message one another about how strange I was. At best, a handful of the classmates I had worked with for years might have come. Most of them would have been content posting a superficial *rest in peace* message to my TabFile.

I doubt that Trista, my only foster parent, would have showed up. Evvie and I never heard a word from her after we were removed from her care. Neither of us minded.

There was an employee at the orphanage who was really nice, but she was that way with all the boys and girls who came and went, so I doubt if she would have remembered my name—that is, if the orphanage was even notified about my death. It seemed that whenever I made a friend at the orphanage, they were adopted or taken into the care of a foster right afterward. I never used my tablet as a means of staying in touch with people, so any friendship I made faded quickly. I focused instead on caring for Evvie.

Rhoma and Monya don't seem to be hiding their faces either as we weave through the crowd. They've probably been gone too long to be remembered by many. On the off chance that someone who did care for one of them was out here and spotted them moving through the crowd, they'd think their mind was playing tricks on them. They'd be used to the mirages of their loved one fading the next time the face turned their direction. I experienced this for a while after my mother died.

Before the crowd thins, I slow to pass a message to

Rhoma, who is closest behind me. "Don't follow too close," I tell her, and then continue at pace on my path. I'm using a tactic that the Davids brothers taught me in Sheridan. They brought Evvie and me into the school during passing time so that our heat signatures were lost among the hundred students and adults who moved around between the school, hospital, and nearby residences. If our heat signatures have been tracked during this journey, it's imperative that we sever that tail before heading to the Neu Vu Condominiums in Sector Seven.

In zigzagging somewhat aimlessly through the center of Miles, we happen upon a building with turquoise-tinted glass walls. It's the coffee shop where I met Merideth before Evvie's guardianship hearing at the courthouse. Sitting there that morning, I could never have imagined that in only two weeks, my life and my knowledge of the world could have changed so much.

During these first two weeks of my eighteenth year, I have been a citizen of a refugee town that is fighting the county system. I have seen firsthand that I had no idea the extent to which county leaders hold their people captive. After living underground as a resident of Neocropolis, I know better the evil of which they are capable. One day, I'll be among a party that will bring justice to the leader the black-operations teams. Even if I have to do it myself, I will find a way to bring him down.

A welcomed quiet begins to grow as we approach the outskirts of Miles County. The Neu Vu Condominiums are only a few blocks from the transitions building where I lived for two years, so I know well the alleyways and dark corners through which to lead my company.

"What can I do for you, ladies?" The question comes from a man on a small screen outside the main entrance of the condominiums. On the screen, he seems to be giving us his attention, but in looking through the glass of the doors, I can see he's busy typing something on his personal tablet.

"We're visitors," I answer.

"You think I don't know that?" he replies. "Which room?"

"407," I answer.

"Scan your chips while I transfer you," he says.

Scan our chips? There's a chip reader beside the little media screen. We're in trouble; none of us have a chip. We can't let this man know that, or we'll be caught.

"Why do we have to scan?" I ask the man.

"The fee times are in place for a reason. It's after midnight. Got to pay if you want to come in."

"But our friend asked us to come over. Make her pay the fees," Rhoma laughs, pretending to be somewhat intoxicated. I wish I could think on my feet the way she can.

"Alright, I'll ask her. You ladies sure you have the right room?" he asks. He knows the residents of the building well. His question makes it apparent that it's out of character for the burned agent's wife to have visitors late at night, even on the weekends.

"I don't know, maybe," Rhoma laughs.

"Who are you looking for," he asks.

"Just call our friend!" Rhoma shout obnoxiously, and immediately follows with giggles. She plays the part well—well enough for me to wonder if Rhoma led an outwardly blissful and inwardly numb life before falling into Neocropolis.

"Hello?" the burned agent's wife calls from the screen.

"Hi," I answer. "We need to come in and speak with you."

"About what?" she demands. "I don't even know you," she adds with irritation.

"We need to talk to you about your husband," I tell her.

"Well, what about him?"

"Let us up and we'll tell you," I say.

"I don't think so," she snaps. "Goodnight."

"Wait!" I plead. The woman huffs and waits for me to say something. How can I get her to agree to see us without revealing our secret to the listening guard?

Rhoma chimes in when I don't follow with anything. "Do you know where your husband is right now?" she asks with a mischievous grin.

"He's at work," the woman says. "What is this?" she asks, concern growing in her features.

"Well, he is now, yes, but con-sha-rary to your belief," she slurs, "his shift only just started. Isn't that right, Marleigh?" she says, nudging Monya with the alias. It's clear that Monya doesn't understand what's going on, but the agent's wife and I do. Rhoma is suggesting that her husband was with this Marleigh earlier in the night.

"What do you want?" the woman asks.

"Just to talk about some things that a good, loving wife has the right to know. We're not asking for much," she says playfully. "I think paying our way in should do."

"My kids are asleep," the woman says, indicating that she agrees to us coming up so long as we bring no trouble.

"We'll be very quiet," Rhoma teases, holding her pointer finger up to cross her lips.

The media screen goes dark for a moment and then plays advertisements, while the agent's wife speaks with the guard. I think about complimenting Rhoma on her impressive improvisation, but praising the woman who beat me to a pulp in the ring doesn't come easily.

The doors of the condominiums make a buzzing sound that I will forever associate with the barred gates of our cells in Neocropolis. Rhoma and I each push a door open.

"Hold up a minute," the guard says as we enter. He is now standing and his personal tablet has none of his attention. "That was some sweet talking you did there," he says, addressing Rhoma. "This better not be some kind of con act," he says seriously. "I have all of your faces and voices recorded."

"Oh, don't worry yourself," Rhoma replies flatly. "Elevator?" The building guard points and watches Monya and me head in that direction. "Thanks, sweetie," Rhoma says, blowing a kiss his way before following. Was she acting, or is this her true nature?

The agent's wife is waiting in her doorway when we exit the elevator on the fourth floor. Rhoma leads us confidently into her condo, but her demeanor changes as soon as the wife closes the door behind us.

"We're not here for the reason that we told you," Rhoma begins.

"Oh thank God," the woman follows, rubbing her blotchy neck.

"Well, I wouldn't do that just yet," Rhoma says, warning the woman that she still has reason to fret the message with which we've come.

"Monya, gather dark clothing for all of us," I order. Monya nods and breaks away into the woman's bedroom.

"I'm not sure what you think your husband does for a living," Rhoma says before the woman can protest our takeover of her apartment, "but he's actually a secret agent of the county government." I try to read the woman's face, but it's rather stoic. Perhaps she already knew.

"Among other things, one of his duties is to manage people that have been unjustly imprisoned underground. We are three of those people. We escaped the prison tonight. Unfortunately, your husband was injured in the process."

"What did you do to him?" the woman accuses.

"It was an accident," I interject. "We didn't know there was a level of agents above us. We used an explosive to get out, and he must have caught fire from it. Much of the lower half of his body is badly burned."

"You burned him!" Anger and pain are clear in the woman's raised voice.

Rhoma returns the bite. "Don't forget that your husband was responsible for keeping one hundred and seventy-five people below ground, the majority of who were innocent of any real crime."

I speak up before more heat rises from either of them. "We're here because your husband knows that what the county government is doing is wrong. We promised him that we would take his family with us into freedom in exchange for vital information and his assistance in our escape."

"You threatened him," the woman says, incriminating me.

"Sydney *stopped* another escapee from shooting your husband point blank," Rhoma returns. "He offered us help afterward. Look, we don't have the time to gain your trust. We're leaving in two minutes. Whether or not you and your children come with us is up to you."

"What about my husband?" the woman asks, her stance beginning to shift.

"I don't know," I answer honestly. "But this is what he wants for you and your children."

"I can't leave him," she says, her words tight.

"His injuries aren't fatal, just too severe for him to be able to come with us," Rhoma explains. "He'll either recover and attempt to join your family one day, or he'll be locked up—maybe killed—by one of his own for assisting us. I'm sorry, but that's the truth. There's no use in you staying behind. You'll never get to him."

Monya returns with a heap of dark clothing. She has already changed out of her jumpsuit and into garments to help her blend.

The woman's stare is the same as the deer that I hit when traveling to Miles. Terror has frozen her so that she can't decide which way to go. Should she believe complete strangers about outrageous things and follow them in a dangerous breach, or should she stay in the county and wait for her husband to come home? I know the fate for the creature that hesitates.

"Time's up," Rhoma tells her. "Choose."

"You and your children aren't safe here," I insist. "Come with us."

The woman stares into my eyes for another moment. It's remarkable that I've made the effort to convince her and that I'm now trying to convey trustworthiness as she scans my eyes. As a kid, I was always angry that strangers didn't notice my struggle and come to my aid. But both then, and as I grew older, I was just as guilty of carelessness toward those around me. Cy Davids changed that about me. In doing so for me, he taught me to open my heart to strangers.

"We'll come with you," the woman decides. She hurtles off for her children, Monya a step behind to help.

Rhoma and I quickly sift through the heap of clothing to find items to wear. I wonder how long it's been since she wore real clothing like this, rather than a Neocropolis-issued jumpsuit.

The agent's wife pulls a sleepy little boy across the hallway into another bedroom. Monya follows with miniature garments in hand.

I hate to see such a little thing's life in danger as we cross the barrier. I sure hope his father is able to disable the section of the barrier through which we will escape. A body so small couldn't endure the shocks the way that mine could when I'd soar above the electric line.

A chime stills us. Someone is requesting to be let up to this condo. The agent's wife peeks out of the second child's bedroom. "More of yours?" she asks.

Everyone should be meeting at EPA 7-8, not here. "I don't think so." But if it were anyone other than ours, there would be no chime. If it were BOTs, the door would be kicked in without warning, they'd be upon us instantly, and we'd be seized with nowhere to go but back to Neocropolis, likely to solitary for Rhoma and me.

Tentatively, I tap the media screen to stop the chime and light it up. Before my hand leaves the screen, I see the bright lights of the condominium entrance reflecting in his blue eyes.

"It's Gauge," I tell Rhoma, relief washing over me.

"One of ours—we're fine," she tells the woman.

Excitement flows from my heart at seeing Gauge alive and well so much sooner than I'd expected. Dressed in black behind him are an older man, woman, and a young girl. Even through the small media screen, I can infer who these people are. Gauge went alone to seek out his family, a luxury he didn't grant to any of the other escapees. Yet, I can't blame him for taking the risk that he didn't allow any of the rest. I would have done the same.

I push the option on the screen to allow the visitors in. Gauge's father steps in front of his son and holds his wrist up to the chip reader, covering much of my view with his fingertips. The door buzzes once the fare is paid, and the mother opens the door to usher her daughter in. Gauge takes hold of the door for his mother then, and she kisses his cheek before stepping inside.

I can't imagine what it must feel like for Gauge's mother to be reunited with her son, who she believed committed suicide. Her years without him have been shadowed by sorrow, and probably weighted with guilt. And now, miraculously, all of that pain has been alleviated. Her son never took his own life. He never died at all. He has been alive, and growing in character through the suffering he endured underground. Her boy is now a brave young man. How could a mother be more proud?

When I hear their approach, I open the door to let Gauge and his family in. Immediately, my eyes are drawn to his mother. "Mrs. Gallagher?" I ask, dumbfounded. Standing in front of me is my EduWeb instruction monitor. What a small world that Gauge's mother is a woman that I have known, sort of, for about five years.

"Sydney Harter?" she responds. She immediately envelops me in a hug. "They told me you were dead. I had to tell your classmates," she stammers. "Is it really this bad? How many are there?" she asks her son. But when she releases me from the hug to hear his response, we both see that something is terribly wrong.

Gauge's eyes are fixed on me in disbelief. "Sydney," he says slowly and carefully, "what is your last name?"

"Harter," his mother answers for me. "Gauge, Sydney is one of my students." Gauge doesn't listen to a word that his mother is saying.

"What's your last name?" he asks again, the space between us tightening.

"Your mother just told you. I am Sydney Harter." In telling him this, I feel the same way I felt when I told Cy that I had been lying about my last name. Gauge's reaction, however, does not match the worry that Cy held, but the intense anger and distrust that Crewe had for me when he found out that my microphone contained a chip.

Why does my last name fill Gauge's eyes with distrust? My father, the man from whom my last name comes, is the captain of three refugee towns in Region Two. I don't see how Gauge would have any way of knowing that, but if he did, how could he think that being that man's daughter is a bad thing? Once again, I'm in the dark around my last name's importance. By the looks of it, I'm not going to want to hear what Gauge has to say.

SIXTEEN

"Let's meet the others," Gauge says to the group. Instead of the astuteness and willpower I'm used to seeing in his light eyes, an icy coolness comes over them when he speaks to me. "We'll talk en route."

"Wait," I say, slowing his progress toward the door. "We need to talk about the plan now—we won't have time out there." With the addition of the agent's and Gauge's families, there will be sixteen of us gathered near EPA 7-8. By now, the county agents know that Demetri Harter's daughter is among the escapees. They'll be watching my old escape route. If we hang around there while we decide what to do, we'll never make it across the border.

"Let's hear it," Gauge replies flatly.

He wants *me* to produce the plan? The getaway leg was never discussed, at least not with me. I wish Edyn or Vic were here. Then again, maybe I was always the best candidate to lead the barrier breach. Edyn knew that I'd been out before; maybe I'm the only one who can show the others how.

"First we'll need someone with a chip to test the barrier," I say. "We have to make sure it's been turned off so that we can pass through it."

"Turned off?" Gauge's father questions me.

"Her husband is a county agent," I say, nodding to the mother who holds the hands of two small children. "But he's on our side now."

"We'll see about that," Rhoma says skeptically.

"He stayed behind to monitor his family's chips. He'll turn a section of the barrier off as they cross through it. If your family sticks with them, you shouldn't have any problem getting through."

"I'll test the barrier then," Gauge's father declares. "What are we going to do if it's on?"

"We're going to jump from the top of EPA 7-8 into a holding pond across the barrier. I've done it a hundred times," I assure them. "It hurts, but you'll be safe if you commit to the jump." Fear and doubt are evident in many of their eyes, especially the mother of the two small children.

"My little sister has also made the jump," I say, trying to comfort Gauge's little sister, and the two women who may doubt their own athleticism. "I'll jump too to ease your minds. It has to be done like our lives depend on it."

"Sounds like they do," Gauge's father comments.

"What about my sons?" the agent's wife asks. Monya kneels to comfort the older one who nibbles on his shirtsleeve.

"I'll take the youngest," I tell her. "Mr. Gallagher, do you think you could carry the older boy?"

"Yes, I'll take him," Gauge's father answers.

"Whether we can cross on foot or if we have to jump, we'll use the water and the tree coverage to avoid being spotted by the camera. Follow my lead," I tell them.

"Your plan has a big problem," Rhoma criticizes. Everyone's attention, including mine, shifts to her. "They're going to track the chips like mad tonight. An inch within the barrier, and they'll know. We'll be lucky to be out a minute."

Rhoma's right. I've been thinking the same thing, but what else can I do? Citizens with chips weren't part of the group we'd planned on. Neither were children. Their addition makes a failed escape ten times more likely.

"We understand that," Gauge's father responds. "It's a risk my family and I are willing to take. I think those of us with chips should separate from those without, even if it's only by a small amount of time and space."

"I second that," Rhoma says. Her selfishness is understandable. For some of us, being captured by a BOT would mean a lifetime of solitary confinement or worse.

"Rhoma, Jarod heard the whole plan, and I think you caught enough. You two will lead the others. I'm going to stay with my family. Since their chips will likely bring out the BOTs, you should go before us. Now, even."

"Gauge, explain the route to me and I'll lead our group," Mr. Gallagher says. "I don't want you—"

"I'm staying with you, Dad. I belong with my family," he says boldly.

"I suppose you can always run when trouble comes." I don't think Gauge would run from his family, but he doesn't say so. Maybe he's allowing his dad to think that breaking away safely would be an option, so that his father will allow him to lead the group with dangerous chip implants.

"Sydney would be able to run too," Gauge says. His eyes are still cold when they look upon mine. "You'll need to be with our group in case we have to jump." That's true, but I suspect discussing my last name will also be in order.

"Well, I guess this is goodbye," Rhoma says irreverently.

"Let's go, Monya." Monya takes a minute to hug the child and whisper something to their mother.

"Hey, Rhoma," Gauge says as she reaches the door. She turns the knob, opens the door, and impatiently turns in the doorway to face him. "If something happens...if we don't make it there..."

"What? What?" Rhoma spews in annoyance.

"Just tell Red that I love him."

Rhoma's demeanor softens. She nods and pats Gauge on the back. "Good luck, Gauge." With that, she and Monya are out the door and on their way to EPA 7-8 where, hopefully, the other two parties discreetly wait.

If not for her attitude and for time being so precious, I might have asked Rhoma to relay some messages myself. She has a better chance of reaching my father and the seeksmen than I do. But, anything that I would want to say to him or to Crewe I have already written in their letters.

Rhoma knows all the new information about Neocropolis that I would bring to the seeksmen. Hopefully, it can be of use in rescuing the other residents, especially if Gauge and I fail our group and get recaptured.

"Sydney, let's talk for two minutes," Gauge says before walking toward the master bedroom. He opens the door for me, but the gesture is more intimidating than gentlemanly. I step inside, and he closes it behind us. He pays close attention to the light as he slides it on so that he doesn't have to make eye contact with me. "What do you know about your father?" he asks flatly.

"My father worked for the government; I was never sure in what respect. I was almost four when my mother was told that he had died."

Gauge leans against the wall and looks at me at last. "Sydney, what you've been told is a lie. Your father is alive," he says heavily.

"I know." Gauge's face twists with surprise and confusion. "I met my father a week and a half ago in Sheridan, the refugee town," I add, in case he didn't know. "My father is the captain of it and the two others in Region Two that we know exist. He travels between the three to collaborate with their leaders. They discuss ways to protect their people from the county governments, but mostly they strategize. My father is working to bring down the system, freeing everyone."

Gauge is unmoved by this, which I take such pride in. "Sounds like a good man, but I'm not sure he's your father."

"Well, I'm one hundred percent certain," I declare. I didn't recognize his aged face at first, but when I met my father in Sheridan, I heard the same voice that once fell sweetly on my ears.

"Let me tell you what I'm one hundred percent certain of," Gauge says, pushing himself off the wall. "Then we'll try to make sense of our contrasting beliefs."

I feared this. I could tell by the way he looked at me when Gauge learned my last name. If his beliefs about my father are different from mine, then he is about to tell me something I won't be able to accept.

"Your father *is* the leader of a large number of people, but not free people. He is the leader of a highly trained body of people on the inside. Sydney, Commander Harter, as we know him, is the head of the Miles County black-operations teams and all the government's special agents."

Relief lightens my heart so much that I find myself smiling, something that must perplex Gauge something terrible after his proclamation. My friend is mistaken. I know my father. I've seen him in action, defending his fellow seeksmen. There is no validity in Gauge's words. "No, you're wrong. I've communicated with the leader of the BOTs. That evil man is not my father."

"You've seen him—spoken with him—in person?" Gauge asks.

"Well, no, but I still know he's not my father."

Gauge becomes angered that I have sloughed off his revelation. "I know too, Sydney! Unlike you, I lived in that hell for *years*. Harter used to be an agent before he became the commander." Gauge pauses and then lowers his voice. "I know your father too. He *is* capable of evil. Sydney, I'm sorry."

"I'll prove you wrong," I tell him calmly. "We'll meet him out there, and you'll see that he's a good man." I wish the conviction in my voice were stronger.

When I first met my father, I was disappointed. After he escaped the county, he turned a blind eye to my mother and me. He had the chance to make up for that when Evvie was taken, but his hope was diminished and his willpower easily lost after the first attempt. It would be too much to call him great, but evil is just absurd. Good is a suitable description for the type of man my father is.

"I have an idea," Gauge says. "It would be too risky to use a tablet right now to search for your father. That activity could be trailed. Do you have a printed photograph of him?"

"I have a picture of him and my mother in my apartment in the transitions building."

"That's close. Let's split from the others and find it so we can resolve this. We're going to have to know the truth if and when we run into this captain."

"Won't they have eyes on my apartment?" I ask. The possibility of being caught isn't really what makes me hesitant to go. I don't want Gauge to think that he's right—or be right—about my father.

"I don't know another way. Do you?" Nothing better comes to mind, so I shake my head. "We have to know whether he's a friend of foe."

I nod. Gauge is right. I set my stubbornness aside and open myself up for an investigation I never thought we'd need to conduct. The safety of the newly escaped residents, as well as the seeksmen and townspeople of Sheridan, depends on the truth. No more mistakes from me. We're going to do this the right way.

"Lead the way. I'll follow at a distance. If we meet trouble and have to separate, you know where to meet me." Gauge turns and opens the bedroom door for me, this time with care.

The Gallagher family is now seated with the agent's wife and her children in the center of the media room. Their conversation has hushed, and they look to the two of us for the order of *it's time*. However, that's no longer appropriate.

"Something has come up that Sydney and I need to sort out before we can go," Gauge tells them. "If we're not back in ten minutes, you'll need to test the barrier on your own. If it's on, it's up to you to decide whether or not to make the jump without Sydney's example." Gauge walks over to them, kneels down, and grabs the hands from the laps of his mother and little sister. "I love you."

"We love you, Gauge," his mother replies. "We never stopped loving you and never will." Tears well in her eyes. Suddenly, I feel guilty for not offering my condolences when my instruction monitor lost her young son. I never especially liked

Mrs. Gallagher, but that's because I was no model student like Evvie. She constantly had to get on my case for not completing my course work. Whether I liked her or not, I'm ashamed that I didn't reach out to her. The world's apathy toward me didn't condone my apathy to the world.

"This isn't goodbye," Gauge says as he squeezes their hands.

"We're proud of you," his father says with a strong hand gripping his son's shoulder. "Now go." Gauge squeezes their hands and lets them go reluctantly. He stands, and drops behind me at the door.

"Be careful," his mother says, she and her husband now standing with the difficulty of letting their son go again.

My eyes meet Gauge's for a moment. They look certain, assured. "We'll be back," he says. I take that as my directive to lead us out.

The county agents have had a lot of time to regroup and organize a manhunt. They'll be focusing on the border, where there is no crowd in which to become lost. One sighting, and it's back to the dungeon.

As we dart between buildings, never really coming to a stop, I try to focus on the sounds around us and the spotlights that *are* now present overhead. However, I mostly find myself worrying about the words of the injured agent back in Neocropolis. He clearly stated that Jerus was not the biggest traitor to Sheridan.

Could my father really be playing dual roles? The seeksmen told me that he is away on captain duties an awful lot. Was he really visiting the other refugee towns when he was away, or was he in Miles County, dishing all the thoughts and plans of the refugee leaders to his agents?

I've already assumed that my father was not a political representative or something of the sort as I once believed him to be. Demetri Harter's role was deeper inside the government than that. Either he never abandoned the principles of the county and works for them still, or something caused him to flip sides, as I believed minutes ago and still hope is true.

I should have asked my father more about his past while I was in Sheridan. I wish I had more time with him before he left for Braves. Maybe then, I would have more to go on, and Gauge and I wouldn't need to be risking so much out here.

Though I'm dressed to match my dark surroundings, I don't feel well concealed. At any second, a bright light could flood the ground on which I run, and I would be caught. The agents could easily shoot me or swallow me back into their underground belly.

I see the transitions building ahead. Perhaps my things haven't been cleared out of my old unit. Maybe it's been preserved as evidence. The better the agents understood me, the more likely they were to know how best to lure my father in to rescue me.

Why would the leader of the BOTs tell me about the purpose of my haircut and the photographs taken—to lure the captain in—if it were him I was talking to? That doesn't make sense, but neither does the night in Neocropolis when my memory was erased. I remember working in the laundromat before dinner, and then waking up the next morning. What did I learn in between that had to be wiped?

Regardless of whether or not my father is Commander Harter, leader of the BOTs, I am a wanted person in Miles County. If my apartment does look just as I left it, it's probably booby-trapped.

Stop, I tell myself. Yes, there is a huge risk, but this has to be done. If Gauge verifies the picture is of a man that he saw working as an agent in Neocropolis only a couple of years ago, then my father lied to me. I have to know the truth.

Unlike the Neu Vu Condominiums, the front door of the transitions building is always open. No high security needed for the likes of its residents. As I make my way to the window at the end of the hall, I hear the main door swing open behind me. I tuck toward the wall until I'm sure it's Gauge. Once he sees me, I quietly boost myself onto the window ledge and lift the ceiling tile, like I've done a hundred times. The key is right where I left it two weeks ago. I grab it, hop down, and unlock the apartment door.

"Wait," he whispers, scooting in and gently placing his hand on my abdomen to stop me from entering. Gauge takes off a shoe and tosses it through the doorway. Apparently, I wasn't the only one thinking that the agents could have set traps in here. Just because the shoe didn't ignite some kind of energy or set off an alarm doesn't mean that it didn't signal something silently. We move quickly into my congested bedroom.

The decrepit dresser drawer is as stubborn as always. After Gauge helps me yank it open, I pull out the small, wooden box that contains my most valued items. I stuff the contents of the box into my pants pockets, until there is only the picture that rests at the bottom. I peek at my smiling father first, and then hand it to Gauge.

Although my father is much younger in the photograph, Gauge doesn't need much time to study it. He also doesn't need to say anything for me to read his eyes when they look up at mine. He recognizes the man in the photo as one who worked as an agent sometimes seen in Neocropolis—the agent who is now the leader of the force we oppose.

Gauge hands me the photo. What do I want with it now? Instead of shoving it into a pocket, I neatly place it in the bottom of the box and close the lid. I return the box to the drawer and attempt again and again to slam it closed.

"Sydney, hey..." he whispers sympathetically as I fight to close the drawer. "Stop."

I turn on him. "What do I do now, Gauge? What am I supposed to do when we cross his path? Just let someone kill my father, who I've only known to be a good man?"

"I can't speak for the others who've joined us, but those of us who planned the escape don't mean to kill anyone. Sydney, you have no idea how sick I feel after seeing what my bomb did to those agents." Gauge takes a breath to calm the ache that comes with his recollection. He reaches into the stubborn drawer and removes the small memento box. After removing the picture from the box, he gently places it back in the drawer. "But if any of them, including Commander Harter," he says, waving the photograph in his hand, "raise a weapon toward any one of us, I will bear the sickness to do what is right—to protect my own. If that situation presents itself to you, you'll have to decide what to do. I can't help you with that."

After pocketing the picture, Gauge taps the doorframe twice as if to say *let's go*. He leads me out of the apartment, the door of which I don't even bother to close. Who cares if they know where we've been? *They* sure has taken on another meaning, I note. *They* now includes my double-crossing father, who leads the evil force.

SEVENTEEN

I lag a good distance behind Gauge during the dash back to the Neu Vu Condominiums. Trying to recollect what I've learned about my father is a serious strain on my mind. Some things just don't add up, like the fact that my father deliberately brought the Davids brothers into Sheridan when they were young. Why would he do that if his loyalty belonged to the Miles County government?

Many of the points I try to raise in the captain's defense, however, lack depth. He rode into Miles County with a band of seeksmen to attempt to rescue Evvie from their grips. However, only one side of the line of soldiers was fired upon. While some had injuries that claimed their lives, my father came out unscathed. Did Jerus raise his hands to signal his own presence, or was the signal meant to indicate which bike had Commander Harter aboard? My stomach twists with how easily I can raise contradictions to his good character.

I push thoughts of my father out of my mind. After all, there are immediate dangers that I should be focusing on.

Gauge doesn't bother to wait for me at the entrance to the condominiums ahead. I accelerate my pace, but the glass door closes just before I nearly collide with the building.

"Another charge to 407?" the front desk guard grumbles through the speaker outside.

"No. I'll wait," I answer. He should be back down with the two families soon.

The guard slouches in his chair and pulls one ankle across to the opposite knee. He slides his tablet onto his lap, and returns to whatever brainless activity he had been conducting on it before our return interrupted him.

It's cool outside, but the air is refreshing. I walk a few feet from the glass doors and lean against the building to rest. With deep breaths, I relax my body, but my mind and my senses are as alert as ever. One helicopter's spotlight search comes too close for comfort. I ought to go inside after all.

Strangely, the guard is already standing when I tap the bell icon on the screen beside the doors. When he turns in my direction, wide-eyed, I see what has sprung the lazy man to his feet. Gauge's face fills the media screen behind him. The county has issued an escaped felon warning, though Gauge Gallagher is not the name listed below his picture.

"Don't move," the guard yells from inside. Clearly, he's matched the picture to the young man who he just readmitted into room 407, the same room that Rhoma, Monya, and I requested entrance into when we first arrived. He knows we're from the same party.

My first instinct is to scream Gauge's name to warn him that something is wrong, but I change my mind as the guard fumbles to pull his gun on me. The guard doesn't realize how easily the agents will be able to catch us if he calls them to give up our whereabouts. All he needs to do is tap a few buttons on his tablet to alert the police, who will inform their secret superiors. In his panic, I hope the guard will forget that it's not his job to detain us.

Before he can grasp his gun, I take off and run alongside the building, hoping to draw him outside and away from his tablet. My plan works. I hear the doors open, followed by the sounds of his heavy feet along the walkway. "Hey!" he yells as I round the corner. "Freeze!"

I bend around another corner of the building and slow to a stop a few yards from the center of its backside. I raise my arms in surrender and wait for the guard. He rounds the back corner at full speed, as he must have done around the first corner in order to be so close behind me. I could have stopped at the corner and blindsided him as he came around it, but seeing how untrained he is, and knowing that he carries a loaded weapon, I'm glad that I didn't surprise him.

"Down on your knees!" he screams when he spots me. "Do it, or I'll shoot!" he adds when I don't budge.

"I didn't do anything," I return as loudly as I can. I hope the commotion alerts Gauge and the others. It wasn't by happenstance that I stopped to surrender right below the condo where they are.

"Get down," he commands again. This time he approaches me with the barrel of his handgun pointed. I do as he says. "Don't move. Keep your hands where I can see them." Worried residents have awoken and have flicked on their lights, allowing me to see the beads of sweat on the guard's forehead as he approaches me slowly. "On your stomach. Hands behind your back."

"I thought I wasn't supposed to move," I sass, trying to delay the inevitable handcuffs.

Then, I see something that I hope none of the residents who might be peeking around their shades can see. A figure dressed in black slides around the corner and along the building, until he's only a few yards behind the nervous guard.

"I said, get down!" the guard repeats.

Gauge takes two quick steps toward the guard, places a firm hand on the back of his shoulder, and cocks his own gun right behind the guard's head. "Drop it," he orders. "Now!" he yells when the guard fails to lower the weapon that's fixed on me. With the severity and impatience in Gauge's voice, the guard follows the command and places the weapon on the ground.

"Go cuff yourself," Gauge says, indicating the railed deck of one of the first-floor condos. "Do I look like I'm kidding?" he warns, raising his gun.

"Alright, I'm going. I'm going," the guard repeats, begging Gauge to lower the firearm. He takes the cuffs from his belt and snaps one side around the railing.

"Tight," Gauge orders as the guard snaps the other end around his wrist. "Keys," he demands.

"We don't have keys," the guard pleads. "We only use the cuff when we're taking someone into custody. Officers at the processing room have the cuff keys."

"Did they teach you to say that in the academy?" Gauge remarks. "You can hand them over, or I can make being held at gunpoint feel very real while you strip naked so that she can search for them."

Luckily, the guard doesn't waste our time deliberating which way he wants to act. We'll get what we want either way, so he decides to spare himself—and us—the embarrassment. The key he tosses at Gauge's feet comes from a concealed key keeper on the inside of his belt.

I pick up the .40-caliber pistol that was drawn on me and pull the slide to check for a round. Empty. I load it and point it at the guard. "Toss your belt too." The guard rolls his eyes. Whether the gesture is made in disgust at having to lose his Taser, mace, and radio backup, or if it's because he's under the command of a teenage girl, I don't know. Either way, the belt gets tossed toward us.

"Good call," Gauge tells me as he picks up the belt. "They're out front; let's go." He turns the safety on the .22-caliber, and trades it with me. He returns the more damaging gun to the holster and tightens the belt around his far narrower waist as we continue the lap around the building.

Behind us, the guard begins to scream for help and to make a racket with the handcuffs around the railing. If by some miracle no resident had yet called the police regarding the emergency, some certainly will now. We shouldn't have taken the liberties with time that we did.

Instead of heading toward EPA 7-8, Gauge leads us on a direct route to the barrier. He's right. Maybe we can make up for lost time if we don't have to make the jump and conduct the timing game. I hope the agent back in EPA 12-1 has been tracking the chips of his family members. I hope he will be able to turn off the barrier wherever we approach it.

We stop at the high-speed rail station that lies between EPA 7-8 and 8-9, less than a quarter mile from my usual exiting point. There doesn't seem to be a lot of overhead toward the wilderness. Either that means the others made it out before the helicopters caught up with them, or that they've already been seized.

Gauge was the only escapee labeled as wanted, making me fear that the others may have already been captured. Either that, or the county agents are focusing their manpower on whoever remains inside. Have they somehow been able to trace me this entire time? Even though Gauge's face was the one labeled wanted, I have a feeling that I'm the one they're really after. If they find the bomber, they find his more valuable accomplice.

"Gauge, listen to me," Mr. Gallagher addresses his son. "They're going to track our chips when we cross. We've already decided that we're going to split into three groups, each adult taking a child. You and Sydney will make a fourth group."

"Dad," Gauge protests.

"You've told us the way to the meeting place and about the free town farther south. If we're captured, the adults will probably be placed in the same level of that place where you were kept. The kids should be allowed to live in a freer level, don't you think?" Gauge's father nods himself, and then continues without his son's affirmation. "If either of you two are captured. . ." he trails off. "I won't allow that fate for my son. I'm still your father, so you'll do as I tell you. If something happens, then you and the others can come back for us some day, deal?"

Gauge nods in submission. Mr. Gallagher embraces his son tightly, and then his daughter, with whom he will evidently split. A heart-rending kiss is shared between husband and wife, while the agent's wife douses her oldest boy with affection of the same type.

While Mr. Gallagher runs toward the barrier, Mrs. Gallagher wraps Gauge into her arms. His little sister quickly divides them and holds her long-lost big brother. Unexpectedly, I am brought into the hugging affair as Mrs. Gallagher, my instruction monitor, pulls me into her arms. "Be safe," she whispers in my ear.

We mutually break the embrace in time to see her husband's arm penetrate the barrier. He yields no reaction.

They'll be able to cross safely, but what then?

Gauge scoops up the older of the agent's children, and runs with him toward the barrier where his father waits. The agent's wife lifts her youngest toddler into her arms and follows. Mrs. Gallagher clasps her daughter's hand into her own, and pulls her in a slightly different direction than the others.

After handing the older boy off to his father, Gauge changes his course. He glances over his shoulder to see that I'm following him.

All four groups cross the barrier safely and continue to the grassy marsh north of Spotted-Eagle Lake, where I used to reenter Miles County after visiting my haven. Afterward, the forest cover thins considerably. That makes it easier for me to follow Gauge's movements, but if I can see him better so can the whispering choppers above. And there's no mistake; the spotlights have crept closer.

They were alerted to chips crossing the border, and they know that the fleeing citizens must be related to the Neocropolis prison break. Find those citizens, and find me. That is, if I'm still important to the county now that I know I was never bait to lure in the captain.

The choppers remain close, but they don't speed up to reach us. Why aren't they seizing at least the people with GPS signaling from within their flesh?

Regrettably, I believe it could be because they can capture those citizens any time they want. Why not wait until their heat signatures meet up with others that are undocumented—that is, those of us who no longer have chip implants.

A spotlight sweeps across Gauge just in front of me. He doesn't attempt to hide, doesn't falter or slow. He just keeps running, so I do the same. All at once, the dancing beams of light disappear, leaving the rocky plane dark and distrustful. The county government wouldn't want their citizens to become alarmed by a show of lights crossing through the trees this far outside the border. Worse than that, they wouldn't want them to become *daring* after assuming the county is searching for escapees.

The BOTs have our heat signatures to follow now, and there's no way to dodge those. I keep waiting for an agent to tackle me from behind any of the scattered trees or shrubs that we pass, but they don't. I'm certain now that we're bait for the others. I suspect that any other Necropolis escapees who make it out are just another model. All of us being used to trap the trophy catch—the seeksmen.

It's the only logical conclusion to letting us go on. The BOTs are keeping their distance, so we continue on our path. But how would they know that the agent told us about the seeksmen's location? Have they already pulled this information from the scarred agent?

"They're following us," I call to Gauge, loudly enough that he can hear me, but quietly enough that the other pairs who must be near cannot.

Gauge slows a bit, and I easily catch him. "I know," he says. "It doesn't make sense."

"No, it does," I correct him. "After what just happened in Neocropolis, they can't risk sending many BOTs out to keep looking for the seeksmen. They're letting all of us do that job for them."

"That's got to be it," Gauge says after a few strides. "And if they had to be spread out in order to find the group, it would give the seeksmen better chances against BOTs arriving separately. Now, they can wait within the county," he says between breaths, "and put forth a united attack when we meet up. We've handed the best of both worlds right to them."

I hadn't thought of it that way. Gauge is right; we've truly given them the upper hand. "What do we do?" I ask him.

"Let me think," Gauge answers. He remains silent until we've pushed around the south side of the lake, and have come to a point where we have to make a decision. "We won't make it alone, Sydney. My family definitely won't make it. We need to find the people from outside if we want to have a chance. I say we stick to the plan and all fight them together."

There are three possibilities at play. In scenario one, we lead the agents off course. After they've realized this, they'll capture each pair. Like Gauge's father noted, that would likely land Gauge and me in a lifetime of solitary confinement.

Scenario two is the worst of the possibilities. In sticking to the plan and meeting up with the seeksmen, we could all be captured, or worse. The town of Sheridan would also be stripped of its leaders. Just like that, the liberation effort would be lost.

The third scenario is why Gauge is willing to proceed with our plan. What if the county agents have made a mistake in using us as bait? What if we strengthen Sheridan's fighting force enough to evade county capture? We would bring not only numbers, but also important knowledge back to the people of Sheridan, and the other refugee towns in Region Two.

If we could convince the leaders of Braves and Idaho to fight with us, we could go back for all those left behind in Neocropolis. We could raise the tribes of proclaimed dead from beneath every county in the region, further populating the free civilizations and fortifying their ranks. Just like that, the liberation effort could tip in *our* favor.

"To the Tongue," I say, fervor rising in my heart. Armed with pistols and passion, the two of us continue boldly toward the river.

It's incredible to think that we, two teenagers, could have such a huge impact on the struggle within Region Two. It's astounding and yet, the responsibility doesn't overwhelm me as much as it should. My rebellious spirit has always been alive, but it's like it's finally being put to use, being set free itself.

But, my fortitude to bring justice could die in an instant. How can I advance the fight if I learn that my father is indeed the leader of the force that I oppose?

If he is not a member of the group that we meet, then it will be clear to me that he is not loyal to Sheridan. Their captain should be in the front lines, leading the others in a noble fight.

If he leads or at least accompanies the group that is either hiding or traveling somewhere along the river, then I will be faced with a dilemma. I alone have been in both Sheridan and Neocropolis. Only I have heard both sides of my father's history. It will be up to me to determine where his allegiance lies and to convince the others of this so that we can unite against our foe, whether or not it includes Demetri Harter.

EIGHTEEN

After crossing below an old bridge not far from the county border, Gauge slows our run. Even though we no longer have evidence of the choppers above, they are probably still nearby. I don't want to lessen the gap that they're allowing us.

"Shouldn't we keep pace?" I ask Gauge. "I've seen a county chopper appear out of thin air, and hover without a sound."

They either turned back to trace our heat signatures remotely, or they continue their stealthy stalking of us. There's no way of knowing, so I've stopped trying to listen for a faint whisper of the blades cutting through the still morning air. My attention is instead given to thoughts of the next step, about the potential of crossing paths with my father.

"I think that's what they've done—gone invisible," Gauge says. "They can close in anytime they want, so we might as well catch our breath a little here. Then we can push hard for the next five miles to see if we can catch up to the Neocropolis group before they come in contact with people from Sheridan."

Catching the first group could be possible, even though our start came much later than theirs did. I have no doubt about

Rhoma's athleticism; she proved it in the ring. Jarod, one of the men who were helping others out of the hole blown at the top of the elevator shaft, and Jaxon, the younger man who lugged a dead agent's body through the corridor so we could escape, both proved their strength.

I'm not sure how fit Doctor McClain or the older man Rhett are, but I know Monya's endurance is inadequate for such a long run. That's also true of the group that carries the burdens of nine-year-old Gracen Ray and the comatose Red. Gauge and I will have to push to our limits, but it's possible for us to catch the earlier groups before they reach the seeksmen's hideaway.

"I don't need a breather," I tell Gauge. The sooner we begin this sprint, the more likely we are to prevent something catastrophic from happening between the escapees and the seeksmen. If Gauge recognized my father from the picture, some of the other former Neocropolis residents could recognize him as a county agent. However, they won't know that he's my father, so they may not give him the same chance to explain himself that we would allow. My father's life could depend on my speed.

"I haven't been able to run on real land in years," Gauge says, admitting his deficiency in stamina. "But, I'll try to keep up."

For the next half hour, I run the way I used to run in my haven—so hard that I can think of nothing but fighting the urge to slow. Every now and again, I lose track of the sound of Gauge's footsteps behind me, so I look over my shoulder to search for him in the dark. He takes the glance as my insistence for him to catch up, which he does every time. His training and motivation are no match for mine, but what he's lacking there he's able to make up for with his strength and the embarrassment that might come from being outrun by a girl.

Finally, I see what I've been watching for ahead—movement. I sprint toward the slinking cluster. I need to be sure I'm approaching the correct group before I say anything.

"Hey!" Gauge calls, evidently noticing the group too. He catches up to me, and we run together toward the others, who have now stopped.

As we get closer, I notice that two in the group are significantly shorter and smaller in stature than the others are. They are children, but not toddlers like the agent's boys. One must be Gracen Ray. It seems we've caught up to the others from Neocropolis, but the group is larger than I expected.

"It's Gauge," someone says, and some in the group celebrate by running to meet us.

"How's he doing?" Gauge calls, before we meet.

"He's been in and out," Jaxon says, "mostly out. And heavier than you'd think." Jaxon and Jarod hoist Red into an upright position, each wrapping and arm around their neck. I see now that two new men, a new woman, a tall, preteen boy, and short girl in her early teens have been added to the group.

"Hey man," Gauge says, squeezing Red's shoulder. Slowly, Red lifts his head and opens his heavy eyes.

"Hey butthead," he says. His head drops again.

Gauge bites a smile, and pokes Red again. "Hey Red. Hey buddy," he says, lifting his head.

"Yeah?" Red replies with groggy irritation.

Gauge digs into his pocket and pulls out the picture of my mother and father. "I need you to open your eyes for just a second."

"Why?" Red complains, his eyes still closed.

Gauge hands the picture to me and searches the guard's belt on his waist. Finally, he frees a flashlight.

"I need you to look at a picture and tell me if you know the person in it." Gauge hands the flashlight to me. "Come on buddy," he pleads.

Red opens his eyes with exaggeration, and tries hard to focus on the picture. "Pretty blonde lady," he says. "I don't know any of those." He snickers.

Gauge grabs Red's chin aggressively and looks him in the eyes. "The man, Red, I need you to tell me who the man is."

"Okay," Red says seriously. If it's possible, his eyes open even wider to concentrate on the picture as I light it again. "That's, uh, that's...that's Agent Harter, Gauge."

Gauge rubs Red's ginger hair. "Thanks, buddy. Good job," he says, as if praising a small child or dog.

"He, I...I saw him on five," Red adds before he falls back out of it.

"Where did the picture come from?" Rhoma asks with concern.

"Sydney's apartment," Gauge answers. "Harter's her father."

"Her father is an *agent*?" Rhoma groans.

"Not just any agent," Gauge corrects. "*The* agent. He was promoted to Commander. Her father leads them all."

Before I have a chance to defend my father, I find myself pounded to the ground.

"I would've had you knocked out in the first round!" Rhoma growls while pinning me. With Gauge's help, I squirm out from under her.

"She didn't know," Gauge says as he pushes Rhoma back so I'm able to stand.

"Don't," I correct him. "I don't know."

"There's no mistake, Sydney. You've heard it from him

too," he says, gesturing to where Red has been laid on the ground.

"You've also heard it from me that the man in the photograph is also the captain of three refugee towns in Region Two." I eye random members of the group. "I do believe that he's been seen acting as an agent in Neocropolis," I tell them, "but I still believe that one could be the act, and that he's loyal to Sheridan."

Gauge takes the flashlight from my hand and passes it, along with the picture, to Rhoma. "Memorize his face, and then pass the picture on." He puts out his palm and gestures for me to hand over the .22-caliber pistol I carry. He passes that to Rhoma as well. "We're going to split up and search for the group of free people that the agents believe to be hiding below ground about a half-mile east of here. Do *not* trust Harter. If you meet a group that doesn't include him, try to convince them to take you to the free town without letting this *captain* of theirs know."

"How do we know that they're not all county agents?" Jaxon asks.

"Because I've lived with them out there," I answer. "I know them."

"You thought you knew your father too," Rhoma sourly reminds me. I ignore her.

"Let's say these people you know are really for freedom," Jaxon says, "is there something that we can ask them that only free people would know the answer to?" he asks me. "That way, if agents have descended from the choppers to pose as refugees and recapture us, we can know to fight them if they don't have the answer."

A possibility comes to me easily. "Ask them what Decklin read."

"What's the answer?" Doctor McClain asks.

"The Bible," I tell the group.

"Read?" The oldest member of the group, Rhett, notes my use of past tense, and maybe the sorrow in the way I said it. "Doesn't sound like it did him much good."

"I'm sure it did him a world of good," Monya speaks up. "If your friend passed, I'm sure he's with the Lord now."

"Agents?" Jaxon says, inquiring about Decklin's cause of death.

I nod. "He and another seeksmen were shot as they crossed the county border to rescue my little sister, who the BOTs had stolen from our new home in Sheridan. The other soldier that died was a young man who my father had brought into Sheridan seven years prior. My father began the seeking program, eventually training pairs to search for and assist in getting out people who had breached the county barrier. It doesn't make sense that the leader of the BOTs would do that."

"BOTs. Is that short for robots or something?" Jarod asks.

"Black-Operations Teams," I answer.

"So yes," he quips. "They sure seem to do whatever they're told."

"We'll know soon enough about her dad and the rest," Gauge says, giving me a gentle pat on the back. "Alright, let's get into groups of three or four. Make sure we pair Red and the youngest children with the strongest men." This order, Gauge must give in case any group needs to flee agents. The group as a whole might be faster with those mentioned being carried.

Doctor McClain breaks from her daughter, and approaches me as the others start to form groups. "Sydney, there is something I need to tell you," she says hurriedly. "I know you recognized me some time after your appointment with me. I could see the change in your eyes when I took that splint off. Your mother was under my care at the institution. She used to rant about her husband being a county agent, and how he had *doubts* about the *work* he was doing. She never believed his death was accidental. She believed he was killed because of his doubts. She also feared they would come for her one day for knowing too much. As the weeks went on, my take on her sanity shifted. I started to believe her."

Looking back, my take on my mother's sanity has shifted too. There's no mistaking that her constant chatter and inability to properly care for herself and her children was abnormal, but more and more, I am seeing that any normal person would have been led to the same state of justified paranoia.

"Your mother was particularly convinced that they were coming for her one day. She frantically begged me to override the health monitors of her chip, which we can do for some patients whose frequent panic attacks cause the chips read like heart attacks. I didn't know how disabling this aspect of her chip would keep them from finding her, but I did it anyway because I wanted to help her in case she was right. That's how she was able to kill herself without our timely action to save her. I made a huge mistake, and I can't express to you how sorry I am for that."

I'm too stunned to say anything, and I don't have to because Gauge ushers each of us into our respective groups before I have the chance. I'm pleased to see that I'll continue to travel with him. Our group, the smallest of the four, only includes the new, preteen boy and the two of us. Gauge leads us away, and the others follow behind in clusters.

"What's your name?" Gauge asks the boy.

Though he tries to speak confidently, his voice cracks as

he answers, "Wezden."

"Do you know how to swim?" Gauge asks Wezden as we arrive at the riverbank. When the boy shakes his head shamefully, it occurs to me that I might not know the proper way to swim either. Evvie and I never got to go to the amusement park in Sector Three like other kids, so my only experiences with a body of water were when I would sink, not really swim, under the surface of the holding pond outside the county barrier.

"The current travels eastbound along this meander. If we get in here, we'll have plenty of time to swim to the south bank without much extra effort," Gauge tells me. "I'll go first so I can help you out before the bend," Gauge tells Wezden. "Will you be okay?" he asks me. I'm uncertain, but I nod anyway. Gauge and the boy couldn't have swum for years. If they can do it, so can I.

The three of us make it across the river without any trouble. With our clothes dripping wet and sticking to us uncomfortably, we hurry into a field.

The tall grasses once thrived, but have since become dry. They struggle to hang on to precious life before the winter's first freeze arrives and, in a single night, depletes their dwindled strength and exhausts their will to persevere.

As we run through the field, I recall something that Edyn told me about the mother of the child who was born in Neocropolis, before I knew she was Doctor McClain. She told me there were many eyes watching the pregnant nurse's alleged death. She also told me that agents promised her that she would live, for the sake of her daughter, as long as she provided them with the information and services that they sought from her. Were my mother's ramblings what they were trying to pull from her back then? A mother's love for her child knows no bounds.

I'm sure Doctor McClain would do anything to protect her, as I would for Evvie. Which leads me to the question, could she be helping them still?

We cross a road less than half as wide as the bridge that we went under just outside of Miles. Instead of continuing east, we change our course and begin heading south along the road's ditch. The hideaway must be close.

"I think that's it," Gauge says after we've jogged in the overgrown ditch for only about five hundred feet. I follow Gauge's finger to a silver roof that shines in the moonlight. He stops, unsnaps the holster on the belt, and pulls out the pistol. Gauge pulls the slide back to load a round. With the safety still on, he returns the weapon to the belt but doesn't secure the snap.

Anxiety wells in my chest. I hope that the agent was right and the seeksmen are here somewhere, because all of these people's freedom depends on them. I'd also like to know once and for all who my father is, but I'm equally hesitant. I'll never be ready to learn that Gauge and Red are right.

I've only barely finished the thought when two dark figures burst from a cluster of trees at the start of the long driveway leading to the buildings. It's too dark, and they're too far away and too covered up for me to make out their faces, but I can distinguish the long guns they point at us as one of them shouts, "Freeze!"

Gauge protectively pushes Wezden and me behind him, and then puts his arms up in surrender. "What did Decklin read?" Gauge shouts.

"What?" one of them calls back.

"Sydney," Gauge whispers over his shoulder, "if they don't answer, draw the gun and shoot." The steps of the two men are quick and trained as they approach us. "What did Decklin read?" Gauge annunciates.

"Don't you talk about him, you murdering—"

"Crewe!" I shout when I recognize his voice. Thankfully, his fearless, threatening progression toward us is halted when I step out from behind Gauge.

Crewe relaxes his grip on the weapon that is pressed into his shoulder, but he doesn't lower it. I expected him to run to me and wrap me in his arms, like a person should after seeing that someone for whom they had dire concern is alive and well. I guess I was wrong about many things.

The man beside Crewe is the one to slide his rifle around to his back. He pulls off the facemask portion of the neoprene suit. It's him. He's here, with the seeksmen. He eagerly runs toward me and probably expects me to do the same. He is shocked and shaken when, at close range, I pull Gauge's handgun on him and return the command, "Freeze!"

NINETEEN

"Sydney, what are you doing?" Crewe steps forward just a little. He tightens his grip around the rifle again and shifts the barrel from Gauge to me.

"Do you work for the county?" I ask my father, more accusatory than inquisitive.

"What?" he says, either mystified or acting to be. My father takes a gingerly step toward me.

"Don't!" I order as I disengage the grip safety on the pistol. "What did you do before you escaped Miles?" I ask from behind gritted teeth. "What was your job?"

"Sydney, put the gun down," Crewe pleads as he advances carefully.

"He was an agent, Crewe," I say. "Weren't you?" I ask my father.

"Crewe already knows that," my father reveals. "They all do."

"Yeah? Do they know that you, not Jerus, are the real traitor to Sheridan? Do they know that you're *still* working for the inside?"

"I haven't worked for the county for a long time, Sydney," my father protests. "Could you really think that?"

"Then why have people from inside Neocropolis identified you as the leader of the BOTs? Why have they seen you in that prison in recent years?"

My question has struck chord with someone who has greater right to be enraged at my father than Gauge and me. Crewe continues to advance and to hold his weapon drawn, but it's no longer as a means to stabilize and cool the conflict. He's now more heated than we are.

"Crewe, I've never been down there," my father says, apparently sensing that Crewe, too, has turned on him.

"No? Then how is that you know so much about it, Captain?" Crewe circles to the front side of my father. "Tell me again how one flank of the riders, my brother's side," he says vehemently, "was attacked while your side met no fire at all." Crewe's gun shakes in his unsteady hands. His eyes must burn into the captain's.

"You know why I think that happened. I believe Jerus was dirty, and signaled to them his whereabouts."

"That's convenient, since he was your passenger," Crewe spits.

"Crewe, I wish every damn day that your bother had been on that bike with Jerus instead of me. I loved Cy like he was my own son, Crewe, same as I love you. Have I ever given you any reason to doubt that, to doubt me?"

When Crewe doesn't answer, Gauge speaks up. "It's going to take more than that to convince me," he says, unimpressed by what he believes to be a show of false emotion. "I've seen you enough times with my own eyes to be certain, but I had my roommate—who spent some time in solitary—confirm for Sydney that you are indeed an agent. He used to see you all the time. Since those days, word has made its way to us that you're now the one that gives the black-operations teams, or BOTs, their orders. Isn't that right, Commander Harter?"

"It's *Captain* Harter, and no, that's not right," my father retorts.

"Sydney had her memory erased about thirty hours ago, but a Level Five guard said she went nuts down there, yelling something about a traitor. This was after she'd already interacted with Jerus in Neocropolis," Gauge explains.

"You're always leaving Sheridan, Captain," Crewe accuses. "You were away thirty hours ago. Tell me it isn't true," Crewe demands.

"I'm going to take a cell phone out of my pocket to toss to Crewe," my father tells Gauge before slowly doing so. Crewe holds the rifle out with just one hand while he picks up the phone. "I told you that I was meeting Braves at a safe house outside Billings County," my father reminds Crewe, who appears to be already trying to get Braves on the line.

My father shifts his attention back to Gauge. "It could be entirely true that you've seen my *face* down there, boy," he says condescendingly, "but not *me*. Your generation wouldn't know much about it, but identical twins were permitted when my brother and I were born."

"Braves, it's Crewe. Is there any way the captain could have been in Miles about thirty hours ago?" You're absolutely positive about the time? Did he ever tell you his brother was a twin? No, everything's fine. He'll let you know soon."

"It sounds like 'ol Ted has been promoted," my father says.

Crewe finally lowers his weapon, and so do I. "You never told me you were a twin. I'm sorry," he says with embarrassment.

"Well, he never felt like one," my father says simply.

Looking my father square in the eyes, Crewe says, "The answer is no, Captain. You've never given me a reason to doubt you. You've given me a million reasons to trust you. I'm sorry, sir." He averts his eyes and hangs his head.

"I know it," my father says, patting him on the back. "And I'm still sorry about your brother. I always will be." Crewe nods a few times and pushes his lower jaw forward, as if tensing will mask or push away the signs of heartbreak. My father holds his hand out to Crewe, who lifts his head and firmly shakes it.

That's my father. There's no denying he *is* a good man.

After all is forgiven between the two seeksmen, my father turns toward me. "Are you going to shoot me if I try to give you a hug?" My weapon has sagged and my stance loosened, but his joke is still coated in discomfort. Though I'm also embarrassed for doubting my father, I don't become sheepish like Crewe did. I disengage the gun, hand it back to Gauge, and walk toward my father. With no trace of disappointment, he pulls me into a warm hug.

"I'm sorry," I tell him awkwardly.

"No," he starts, squeezing me more tightly. "Look at you, Sydney," he sighs. "I'm sorry I let you lose hope in me. I know I made you feel like you had no choice but to exchange places with Evvie."

"Is she okay?" I ask him.

"She's perfectly safe." My father breaks away to look into my eyes. "You were never the one the fire wanted. My brother wants me, and like the coward that he is, he hurt you to get to me. My mistake allowed him that chance, but I can promise you I'll never let him hurt you again."

My father gazes upon me for a moment, and then brushes away the bangs that stick to my sweaty face. "Don't be sorry about what happened here. I haven't proved myself to you yet, so I don't blame you for believing what looked to be true. I think I'd like to know the young man's name," he says more to Gauge than to me. "That is, if he's done trying to turn my people on me."

"My name is Gauge, but I'm afraid I'm not done doing that. We're just three of a group of fifteen that escaped from Neocropolis. The others groups shouldn't be far now. They'll be searching this place for your seeksmen, with my order to try to convince your men to take them to Sheridan without telling you. We thought we had the facts."

"Yeah, everybody does," my father groans. "Fifteen, huh?"

"We also think that choppers followed us out here," I add. "I think the agents were hoping we'd flush you out instead of them having to come down and do it."

"What do you mean, flush us out?" Crewe asks me. Though his eyes meet mine, he still hasn't really *looked* at me. I want him to so badly. I apologized for everything from the depths of my heart in the letter I wrote him, but my words don't appear to have put a chip in the wall he's put up between us.

"They know you're here," Gauge tells Crewe and my father. "They lost sight of your heat signatures at some point, but they suspected that you hadn't traveled far."

"Then I guess it's time to move," my father says. "Maybe in the opposite direction than we planned if the prison is on a higher-security lockdown and there are kids among the escapees," he says as he looks at the boy with us. "Well, younger kids. What's your name, son?" my dad asks the nervous boy.

"Wezden," he replies quietly.

"There's a girl just a little older than him, several women, and my roommate who was sedated earlier," Gauge tells my father. "He might still be in bad shape. My family and another escaped with us. They were citizens, not Neocropolis residents, so they have chips. They'll be quite a bit farther behind the other groups."

"That complicates things," my father says, "but we have doctors who will prepare for their arrival. Crewe, let's get these suits off," my father says as he begins to peel off his outer gear. "Sydney, after you and Wezden suit up, run down the drive and keep on it until you get to two connected buildings. In front of them, you'll want to veer right so you're running parallel to them. When you come to a small pond on your left, run toward it. You should find an underground storm shelter running along that line."

I take off Monya's dark jacket and strip Wezden of the sweatshirt he put over his jump so we can slide into the now-discarded heat signature masks. Our garments are a little bunched, but these larger suits allow us to remain mostly dressed. "When you get inside, tell Galv and Della to get suited right away. Send them out with their med kits and all the suits but one. Tell Cheng to put on the last one, and to find and bring me as much rope as he can get his hands on."

Once Wezden has finished zipping the suit, I lead the two of us on the route my father has described. The network of crossing dirt roads is expansive and confusing, especially in the dark. When I see the two connected buildings, I veer to the right as directed, and hope that I've chosen the correct path.

"Hey, is that the pond?" Wezden calls from behind me. I look ahead and to my left, but I don't see it. I turn to Wezden, but he's already traveled off the road. "Here it is," he says, bending over to try to lift a rusty cellar door. I'm glad to have the boy's eyes—an extra set never hurts. From the looks of it, he'll be glad he has my arms to help lift the heavy door.

"Who is it?" a man's voice asks from the pitch-black void beneath our feet.

"Sydney Harte. I'm back, and I brought a lot of friends," I say, a shameless smile spreading across my face. Now I know how Cy Davids felt when he proclaimed the new town population as Evvie and I were paraded down Main Street in Sheridan. I'll always remember his smile as he climbed halfway out the passenger window to shout, *two-fifty one*!

"Sydney!" Della's voice is unmistakable. "How in the devil's name?" A few familiar faces emerge beneath my feet, and visibly share Della's sentiments. My smile sticks, as I've never felt so welcomed. It feels good, even if I know that some soldiers celebrate just because now they won't have to risk their lives to try to rescue the captain's daughter from BOT control.

"Later, Della. My father will tell you what you need to know out there. He needs you and Galvesten to suit up right away."

Galvesten and Della disappear into the darkness. Cheng, his seeking partner whose name I never did learn, and an unfamiliar male, create a tight circle and reach their arms up towards us.

"Sit on the edge first," I tell Wezden, seeing that there are no stairs to descend into this bizarre shelter. "Give me your arm." Although the men don't need my help from this side, giving Wezden a hand to hold onto as he drops below seems to comfort him. I follow, using the edge of the opening to support myself as the others pull me down into the hole.

"Are you taking your suit off, Wezden?" His name comes out a little funny as Della unexpectedly squeezes me into a tight hug.

"Hey Del." I smile and hug her back. I practically have to shake her off me so I can remove my suit and pass along the rest of my father's orders. "You two need to bring the med kits and all the suits except for one. Cheng, the last suit is for you. You need to find as much rope as you can and bring it to the captain at the end of the drive."

"Were you in Neo-Necropolis?" Cheng asks as removes his jacket.

"Yes. That's where we escaped from," I tell him.

"How many?" he asks.

"Fifteen, plus six Miles' citizens who are also on their way here."

"With chips, I presume," Galvesten states.

"That'll draw the agents if the rest hasn't," Cheng says bitterly. I want to return that the agents already knew their hideout, but I don't want to worry the other with the snarky comment. It might scare Della too much to follow my father's orders. "Put the inner lock on this door, then," Cheng orders the others. "It won't be much help if you're discovered, but it might buy those of us out there a little time to get here and keep them from springing in on you."

"Assuming there's any of you left out there," Cheng's partner mumbles.

"What do you mean?" Della asks. "Do you think there are agents out there?" Great. Exactly what I was sure to avoid. I can't see why my father chose him as one of the higher-ranking seeksmen.

The truthful answer to Della's question is yes, but instead I say, "There were no signs of any agents out there, Della," which is also true. If they continued to follow us out of Miles, they were both invisible and silent.

"Lift me out first so I can help the others," Cheng says. The men quickly boost Cheng out of the storm cellar. Galv hands him the two medical kits and a number of suits before he is lifted out. Lastly, Cheng's partner and the new seeksman hoist Della to the sets of waiting arms above.

Cheng's partner speaks up just before the others close the cellar door. "We should pick a word for her friends or any of us to say so that we know to unchain the door for allies only."

"Bible," I say. "I had told the others from Neocropolis to ask anyone they met what Decklin read. That's how they were going to be sure they were with people from Sheridan."

"Alright, Bible it is," Cheng says before letting the door slam us into complete darkness.

"Wezden," one of the two remaining men says, "I have a job for you."

"Yeah?" Wezden replies tentatively.

"There you are. Here, hop on my shoulders. Tate, help me out, will ya? Ready?" The man releases a small grunt as he stands with the weight of a growing boy on his shoulders. "Reach up and see if you can find a length of chain."

"Got it," Wezden says right away.

"Okay. Now there's a metal handle on the ceiling next to the door hinge. Can you reach the ceiling?"

"Yeah, I found it," Wezden says.

"Good. Thread the chain through the handle. Then you're going to use this lock to connect the chain back on itself."

There is some clanking and finally Wezden says, "It's locked."

"Alright, that's our job every time, okay? How old are ya, kid?"

"Twelve," Wezden answers.

"How long did they have ya down there?"

"Almost nine months."

"What'd you do?"

"I was walking my dog along the barrier, and I saw a man moving in the woods. I called 911. The dispatcher lady transferred me to a man who told me not to tell anyone what I saw, to go back to my house, and to wait for him to get there. He interviewed me, and afterward he took me into Neocropolis."

"I bet you wish you didn't give him details. He probably could have convinced you that you saw a deer," one of the two men says.

"When I was in Neocropolis, both my roommate and I had a short time span of our memory erased," I tell the men. "Why wouldn't they have just erased his memory, so they didn't have to commit him to lifetime in prison?"

"Hmm. I didn't know they could do that," one of the men observes. His comment seems genuine, yet—inexplicably—a prickle of skepticism presents itself to me.

The seeksman with a deeper voice adds, "Must be a pretty new practice. I suppose they didn't use it on Wezden here because he would have noticed the memory gap and told his parents. If they used it a lot on the inside, doctors could start forming conspiracies about governmental practices. That's the last group of people they'd want to become suspicious—doctors. If more of them started removing chips, well, that wouldn't be good for the County's side."

"Neocropolis is starting to fill up," Wezden says. "Maybe they'll be forced to start erasing more people's memories once they're out of space, at least for the Innocents who didn't really do anything."

"Everybody down there is innocent as far as I'm

concerned," the man replies. "People who commit real crimes, like murder, go to the penitentiary in Boise. Citizens want to follow the news and see that justice is served. How many people are there in Neo-Necropolis anyway?"

Since it's dark, I'm not sure who the seeksman is asking, but I answer when Wezden doesn't. "I was the one hundred and seventy-fifth person."

"So one hundred and sixty after you take away the escapees," the other man says.

"My dad said we're going to return to Sheridan instead of going into Miles. Do you think he'll regroup and go back for the other prisoners?" I ask anyone.

"The prisoners will want to go back for their friends below and their families on the inside. Captain's a good man—he'll respect that—but all in due time, Sydney. We're on one of history's slipperiest slopes, so everything has to be done with care."

A few knocks on the cellar door bring the four of us to our feet. "Decklin read the Bible." I recognize the voice and the authority behind it. Crewe.

After Wezden removes the lock and chain, Crewe easily pulls open the heavy cellar door. He rests it on the ground and starts helping a group to our waiting hands.

Gracen Ray is the first. She is followed by two new additions to the group: the teenaged girl and the woman. The last of the group is Rhoma. Although she isn't sold on me, I see the impressive young woman as much more than a champion of the ring. Like Alix, the female seeksmen who suffered bad burns, I have a deep respect, even admiration, for Rhoma.

Unexpectedly, Crewe lowers himself into the hole without the help of anyone above or below him, unintentionally making a show of his strength. He alights into the little room and uses the moonlight to find me. "Come here," he says as he assertively pulls my body against his. I wrap my arms around his waist and shiver with the movement of each of his hands, one on my lower back and the other laced into the hair at the nape of my neck. "You're safe now," he says. Enveloped by his arms, the smell of his sweat-dampened gear filling our space, I do feel safe. I want him to hold me a just a few seconds more, but he lets me go to be elevated by the others.

"Four more in two minutes," he says as he catches the neoprene suits that are thrown to him. "But lock up anyway," he says, finding my eyes in the dim moonlight. For a fleeting moment, his expression softens, but then his eyes revert to the hardened and vengeful ones that I couldn't get to look at me before I exchanged places with my sister. I would do anything to make the first of his expressions last.

TWENTY

"You have always worn your hair long, Evvie," says Ted, the leader of the BOTs and my father's twin brother. "I think it is time we see if a shorter style becomes you."

I try to stop the snips of his sharpened scissor, but can't move. I look at metal column behind me, and am horrified to find my hands melted into it. I look down at my feet that also don't budge, but find that my legs stop at my ankles, the rest presumably cemented into the floor. I arch my back away from the column behind me, but then a serpent begins to wind itself around my abdomen. I flail my midsection violently, but to no gain.

"Hush, Sydney," he says after cutting a few inches from my sister's locks. "A haircut never hurt anyone." He lifts a mirror from a crimson tray of tools and walks toward me with it in hand. "You and your sister may match soon, and you know I am not talking about your hair length." He holds the mirror up to my face, revealing swelling, cuts, and deep bruises from the nose up. Beneath my nose, I wear a muzzle that hides the rest of my face.

"I am not asking you to tell me much, Sydney," he says as he returns the mirror to the tray across from Evvie. "I am

certain you will tell me what I need to know in the end, so why not save your sister the pain and tell me now?" Commander Harter holds a pair of brass knuckles up from the tray, making his point to me. He holds them out to Evvie in the same way, but she doesn't react.

"So sweet and naive," he says, stroking her hair. "She does not know what it is," he sneers in my direction. "It will be a pity if you choose to educate her." He slides the metal around his fingers as he walks toward me again. He removes the muzzle from my face with sickening care. "Where are your father and the others, Sydney?"

"Don't tell him, Syd," Evvie sobs. Her words are brave, but her eyes beg the opposite of me.

Would he really hurt her, his own innocent niece? He told me once that it would've been a lot harder if I hadn't switched places with Evvie. I have to hope that it will be too hard. I can't tell him where my father, Crewe, and the others are. The BOTs are ready. My father's force is not.

Tight lipped, I stare back at him. He is physically identical to my father in every way but one—his eyes. Where my father's are rational, truthful, and caring, his are wild, deceitful, and merciless. His lips curl into a wry smile as he turns his back to me and walks toward my sister.

"Sydney?" Evvie cries quietly in fear. I'm equally afraid, as his stony eyes gave him away. Evvie and I are nothing to him. Her precious virtue won't deter him at all. She might as well have my sharp tongue and cross character. He wants to do this.

Evvie looks at me again, cringing away from the fist that he opens and closes, readjusting his grip around the brass knuckles.

Commander Harter turns to me again. "Last chance,

big sis," he says with a sardonic grin. "Nothing to say?" He turns back toward Evvie and shrugs his shoulders.

I try to tell him to wait. Though the muzzle is off, no sound escapes my lips. In fact, the lips I had a minute ago have been removed and replaced with thick stiches that lock my mouth shut. I scream in my throat, but he lifts his fist and draws it back. I shriek with all my might, but it doesn't affect him. The snake around me begins to coil itself more tightly, crushing my ribcage and lungs. I try to twist and flail in the restraints, but my body doesn't move a millimeter. I'm completely paralyzed.

He throws a powerful right hook toward my little sister's face. Helplessly, I close my eyes right before he makes contact. When I hear no sound, I open my eyes to see whether he actually hit her, but I see nothing but darkness. I try to speak, but still can't make a sound. I try to inhale, but my breath fails me.

Finally, I'm able to gasp for air and even make sound with my exacerbated effort. The only sense that doesn't follow is my sight. My eyes are opened, but all I see is black. Then I realize it's not because my sight is lacking that I cannot see, but because there is even less light here than in level three of Neocropolis.

I'm in a storm cellar below ground with the seeksmen and the Neocropolis escapees, and Evvie is safe in Sheridan. It was only a nightmare, but one that awakened something important. I've remembered just a glimpse of being in a purposefully designed room of Level Five in front of the leader of the BOTs. My uncle and I are not strangers after all.

A few knocks startle the others who were awake, and cause them to stir. "Decklin read the Bible." Crewe again.

"Wezden, wake up. I need you again."

Several other occupants of the cellar rise to their feet as Wezden frees the chain. I stand too, bumping into someone on each of my sides. Even without any light, I can tell there are more of us packed in here than there were after the last group was added. I must have slept through additional arrivals. We haven't left yet, and Crewe is still out there, meaning that we're still waiting for someone. I wonder which group, or groups, haven't made it here yet.

Light from the gray dawn shines in on us as Crewe opens the door above.

"I'm sorry," Crewe says regretfully. I quickly follow his eyes to the woman they are locked on—the agent's wife, who holds only her youngest son.

I keep my ear trained on her pleas and Crewe's sorrowful responses while I shuffle through the others to find Red. Finally, I spot him being assisted to his feet by Jaxon and a newcomer. All the Neocropolis escapees made it here safely.

"You didn't find them?" Red pipes in, more alert and able-bodied than I expect him to be.

Crewe shakes his head. "We have to go."

"Is Gauge going too?" Red asks. He's even more serious than during my AM employment when he was quiet and pensive due the pending escape.

"He's yours to convince," Crewe answers. "All of yours," he adds, his gaze crossing the seas of faces in the den. I wish his eyes would meet mine again, with purpose, but he doesn't linger on my face any longer than anyone else's.

"Someone has to stay," the agent's wife says. "I can stay if you take my baby with you. I'll—"

"You'll both come with us where you'll be safe," Crewe says sternly. "You're too easy of a target to stay here."

"But this is where they're coming!" she cries. Her words are rushed and desperate. "We know that. Someone needs to stay so that Mr. Gallagher will know that we've already met with you all and that he and my son should move south. Shouldn't it be the doctor? You wouldn't want their chip signals heading toward your town, would you?"

"I'm not comfortable leaving anyone who would otherwise be safe behind. We have to consider how many hours have passed. Come on guys, let's get them up," Crewe says before the agent's wife can say any more to delay our exodus.

Jaxon, Jarod, and Cheng's seeking partner work together to lift each of us up to Crewe, who ushers us into the daylight.

"Where's my mom?" Gauge's little sister asks me after we've both been lifted from the cellar.

"I don't know. Didn't you come with her?" I ask.

"Yes, but she wasn't in the cellar anymore when I woke up," she answers calmly and maturely.

"What's your name again?" I ask, even though I don't believe I ever learned it.

"Attalie Gallagher. I'm Gauge's sister."

"I know. I'm sure your mom is with Gauge, the doctor, and my father, the captain. She must have gone out when another group came in." There's a strong possibility that as time passed and her husband and the child did not arrive, she became worried and desperate to add another pair of eyes to the search for them.

"What's going to happen to my dad if they captured him?" she asks me, her lip quivering this time.

"Nothing bad, Attalie," I tell her, wrapping her into an embrace as if she were my own teenaged sister. "He'll be put in the same place they held Gauge and me, but thcy won't hurt him, okay?" She breaks away from me, wipes a stray tear, and nods.

"We are going back for all of them soon; I promise you that," I tell her. This time, she lifts her head and eyes when she nods, showing me that I've assured her.

"Our heat signatures have caught their attention by now," Cheng's partner tells Crewe.

"Alright everybody," Crewe says, calling our attention, "there are four vehicles parked alongside that building ahead. Make your way quickly to one and buckle up—it's going to be a fast ride. Adam, make sure we put one of the spare suits in each one," he tells Cheng's partner.

"I'm on it," he responds as he turns and runs toward the vehicles, setting the rest of our feet in motion behind him.

"Hey," Crewe says as he lightly grabs my arm. I slow and jog at his side. "Captain's in the gray truck. He wants to talk to you during the ride down."

"Okay. You?" I ask.

"I'm driving the van. See you there," he says, and splits ways with me as quickly as he appeared at my side. I watch him tell Red something, which sends Red toward the gray truck as well. For some reason, he seems quite leery as he hops into the cab seat. Gauge and his troubled mother meet up with Attalie, and begin to usher her into the opposite side of the cab.

"This isn't going to be the place for her, is it, Gauge?" my father asks. He's trying to protect Gauge's young sister from what he plans to talk about as we ride back to Sheridan. "I'd go with Crewe or Galv instead."

"Gauge, take your sister to one of the other vehicles and stay with her, please," Mrs. Gallagher says.

"Mom, I have some things to say," Gauge protests.

"Red can tell him all the same things you can. Stay with your sister," she repeats more authoritatively.

"Have the mother with the little boy join us, will you?" my father adds, minimizing Gauge's room to argue with his mother.

"Come on, Attie." Gauge helps his sister back out of the truck and, reluctantly, takes her away.

"I can never explain how good it feels to hear his voice," Gauge's mother says. "Even when he's arguing with me."

"You don't have to explain that to me," my father says. He looks at Gauge's mom in the rearview mirror for a moment, and then pats my knee.

"How long were you two separated?" Mrs. Gallagher asks.

"Almost fifteen years," my father answers.

"That sure dwarfs my time away from my son."

"But your situation was different. I always knew Sydney was *alive*, and I thought she was well. I should have known better than to believe that."

The agent's wife hoists herself into the last spot in the cab, sits her toddler on her lap, and pulls the door closed.

"Alright," my father starts as he leads the caravan of vehicles along the dirt road, "Red, I want to talk to you about Level Five. Gauge told me you spent some time down there?"

"That's right, sir," Red replies.

"You two are here because I think you deserve to know what we believe the fate of your family members will be," he says to the two women in the back seat. "So you recognize me then, Red?" he asks, switching gears.

"You do look identical to him," Red replies.

"Do you have any proof that my brother has become the leader of the BOTs?"

"Our trust in the word that traveled from level to level down there was of the highest sort. I've heard them call him Commander Harter, which was the last name of the agent I saw with your same face when I was a resident of that level. But no, I have no first-hand proof because I haven't been on Five since I was a kid."

"You still are a kid," my father remarks.

"I have proof, Dad," I declare. I can feel that my words are unexpected by everyone in the vehicle. "I was down there on Thursday night. I'm almost sure of it."

"Almost sure?" my father questions.

"I woke up Friday morning with no memory of the night before, but I think some if it came back in a dream I just had."

"What happened in the dream?" my father asks.

"Evvie was cuffed and chained to a beam that reached from the ceiling to the floor. The column and the seat she was restrained to looked like it was designed specifically to hold, maybe torture, someone. In the dream I wore a muzzle, like a dog would wear, that completely silenced my scream."

"I don't know about the rest," Red interrupts, "but the muzzles aren't something your imagination created. They're real."

"I can assure you that your sister's safe," my father adds, building from my dream. "She's in good hands back home. I don't want you to worry about her."

It's a nice notion, but it's ridiculous to think that I could ever stop worrying about Evvie. Her safety, happiness, and awareness have been the basis of my life.

"What happened to you in the dream, Sydney?" Mrs.

Gallagher asks. The agent's wife does not need to worry about her older son, who if captured will become an Innocent, but Mrs. Gallagher has good reason to fear that her husband would be brought into a situation similar to my dream.

"The leader of the BOTs, who looked exactly like you, Dad, threatened to hurt my sister if I didn't give up your location. He wore brass knuckles. I woke up right before his fist hit her face." Red reaches from behind me to squeeze my shoulder a little as if to say *I'm sorry* or *It's okay; it was only a dream.*

"Well, between Neocropolis testimony and your dream, it could be that my brother has been promoted to commander. It's good to know what we're up against."

"What do you plan to do, sir?" Red asks my father.

"You can call me Captain if you like, Red. Sir sounds a little too formal for our kind." His mouth breaks into a smile, but it fades quickly. "Most of our troupe is going to regroup in Sheridan while a few of us travel to the other two refugee towns to recruit more trained men and women. Then the lot of us—gosh, we could be fifty strong," he reflects, "are going to ambush Neocropolis and free the residents into Miles."

"Into the county?" I ask. Had we not needed to get to my father and the seeksmen, I had thought that would be a good plan for our first escaped group.

"That's right. Sneaking them out to Sheridan does little besides grow our population. They're trying like mad to initiate this war, but we can't follow until we have more on our side. If all the residents find their loved ones and tell where and how they've been *living* for however long they were supposed to have been dead, and if we make sure they get active on their tablets with the news, word will spread very quickly. It's my hope that the wrongdoings of Miles County will be read or heard in the other counties in Region Two. In less than an hour, we will have exposed the government's schemes to all the people in the region and we'll have introduced our refugee civilizations as a better option."

"But how will people escape with the barrier and the chips?" Mrs. Gallagher asks, thinking about her husband.

"We'll have to rely on the other Neocropolis doctor and maybe some disgruntled county doctors for that. The end goal is to have all the Neocropolis escapees, their families, and other rebels join us in Sheridan. We can't promise all of that, of course, but at least the people will be freed from that underground prison and the masses will become skeptical of governmental practices. It'll be a huge step in the right direction for our cause."

"Dad, how did you and your brother become involved in all of this?" I ask.

My father lets out a heavy sigh. "Ted and I both wanted to work in county intelligence. It was about patriotism then, protecting our nation from other countries. Because of our patriotism, intelligence, and physical aptitude, we were recruited into a force where once you were in, you were in forever. We were dumb to blindly believe in every aspect of our cause and to follow our orders without question."

My father takes his eyes of the road to look at me. "Sydney, please understand that I was never proud of the things I did. Never. I did them out of necessity only, because I believed I was protecting something, our nation or the people's greater good. My brother, on the other hand, took pride in his actions, and started to get competitive with me and the other agents. I was worried about him, but I never thought they could twist him so much that he'd one day rise to the *they* that we're talking about." My father shakes his head in disbelief.

"How did you get out, Captain?" Red asks, sure to address him the way he was invited to.

"I was sent to retrieve a man who had escaped Miles County and was gathering a small number of other refugees who had been living off the land in solidarity or in pairs. We didn't use the technology as systematically as they do now, so my job was to get him to tell me how he was locating other escapees and where they were gathering. He was so obstinate when I was," my father pauses and frowns, "*questioning* him." He stops speaking and stares at the road ahead.

"You're not that man anymore, Dad," I say, trying to comfort him.

He nods. "I know, but it was Merick, Sydney. I was sent to torture Merick for information and kill him if he didn't give it to me. There was no Neocropolis then. We didn't hold people; we were even more ruthless then."

My father shakes his head in shame. "I was going to do it. I was going to kill him because every time I asked a question, he told me something about the county rather than answering me. Conspiracies, I thought. At first, I didn't even hear his words, but soon his obstinacy and courage convinced me to really listen. I never escaped. They sent me out, and I just didn't come back. Merick didn't kill me, didn't even lock me up when he brought me to his group of people. Against all reason, he trusted me. Over time, I shared my knowledge, skill, and fervor to take charge of the fight against county captivity. And here we are."

"What will you do when you're up against county agents, possibly your own flesh and blood?" the agent's wife asks.

"I don't think of Ted that way. My family is here," he says, patting my knee again. "I'll fight for them no matter who we face. They've proven that they'll show no mercy to us in battle, so we can't be hesitant to do the same. Lives will be lost on both sides. I don't doubt that. I just hope the casualty count is heavier for them than us."

TWENTY-ONE

During the ride back to Sheridan, my father called Merick to let him know what time to expect the caravan of escapees, including Neocropolis residents and county residents. My favorite part of the conversation was the grin that stretched across my father's face when he told Merick, "Yes, I have her back." I wonder whose smile was wider, his or mine.

When we pull into The Lot where vehicles are parked in Sheridan, Merick and Alix come out from the storehouse to greet us. The handshake-turned-hug that Merick and my father exchange means something entirely different to me now.

While my father was away and Merick was looking over me, I didn't care for him because he sided with my father's reluctance to go after Evvie. Like the captain, I thought Merick was being somewhat of a coward. Now I know some of Merick's story. He risked death by my father's hand in order to protect his people and his belief in freedom. My father disobeyed his order and spared Merick. In return, Merick saved my father by shaping him into a wiser and morally admirable man. Neither of them were ever cowards, they were just more levelheaded and patient with their passion for justice than I am.

After exchanging a few words in private, my father

returns to the waiting mass of us and announces, "Drivers, each of us is responsible for situating our carful. Rest for a few hours first this morning if you'd like. Then, enroll any kids in school and assign jobs to the adults. Be conservative when you arrange housing; we're expecting more soon," he says proudly. The seeksmen, Doc, and Della begin to clap and cheer. A few of the escapees join in, but many are too awed by all of this to celebrate with us.

"If anyone has questions or concerns, talk to whoever drove you here. This is Merick," my father says as he places a hand on Merick's shoulder. "He is in charge of defending our growing town."

"I thought you were the captain," Jarod says.

"I am, but that means that I'm in the other refugee towns frequently. I'll be away in a matter of hours, as will my daughter, Sydney, Adam, who most of you met in the cellar," my father points to Cheng's seeking partner, "and Alix, another seeksman who's on injury leave right now." Alix nods to my father to acknowledge his order. "A small force of us attempted to rescue Sydney's younger sister who the county had captured from this very town. We had shown no physical threat when they fired upon us, killing two of our young men. Alix here heroically tried to save one of them who was swathed in flame."

No one claps this time to honor Alix's deed. Like me, those who would clap for her are probably thinking of the one she tried to save. That sadness overshadows Alix's valiant effort.

"That should tell you two things," Merick says after a beat. "One—we're in a state where we're never fully safe, so listen to the man who has been given charge of you and don't wander off on your own. Two—know that if you wish to join our force, it is absolutely certain that we'll go to war against the county who held you captive, that they will show no mercy to any of us, and that you could be harmed or killed. While the captain is away, I'll be preparing anyone who chooses to enlist."

My father nods to acknowledge Merick's statements and then says, "I need four from Neocropolis to join the two groups of us that are leaving today to go to the two other refugee towns. I'd prefer people from Level Three or Ones who know some things about the people who are running the place and their practices. My goal is to convince the leaders of Braves and Idaho to lend us their men for an assault on Neocropolis."

"If that's the plan, you can enlist me now," Jarod tells Merick. "I was on One," he admits, "but I believe I know enough to convince anyone that our cause is worthy."

"I'm good to travel and to enlist," Gauge tells the Sheridan leaders.

Merick frowns. "I'm not so sure about that. How old are you, son?"

Gauge's jaw tenses and his brows crease. "Those are my friends down there, and now probably my father too. I'm old enough," he answers.

"Captain?" Merick says, passing the buck.

My father was looking at Gauge, but he looks away to answer. "Eighteen. That's the rule."

"There's also a rule about family," I remind my father.

My father doesn't hide his disappointment in my raising the argument. "That rule only applies to untrained *adults* who want to join the force to fight for an immediate family member."

"The seeksmen agreed on that rule so I could fight for Evvie. We make the rules out here, Dad, so we can change them any time," I argue.

"They're made for a reason," my father says snappishly.

"Leniency was already pushed on me to allow that one." He looks around the crown and then to me. "Everybody here has a reason to fight. You want the ranks open to kids?"

"Parental consent," I wager. "If they're under eighteen, a parent has to agree that they can enlist."

"We could use the numbers, Captain," Cheng says.

My father crosses his arm and bites his thumb. Finally, he looks up and surrenders. "Parents by blood only." He finds Mrs. Gallagher in the crowd. "Well?" he asks regretfully.

It's clear that Gauge's mother feels not only the heat of the situation, but also that of the multitude of Neocropolis residents that feel for Gauge—people who know him as a man, not a child.

"Gauge," she says slowly, "I wouldn't want to lose you again."

"Mom, I've been dead for years because I couldn't do a damn thing to stop everything they were doing in the prison, the county, and apparently beyond," Gauge fumes. "I'm dead still if you make me stay back here and what, go to school, make new friends, join a club? I can't do it." Gauge composes himself before saying, "I'm as good as dead doing all that, Mom. I'm not alive if I'm not fighting to fix this."

"You wouldn't be dead to us!" Attalie interjects, tears suddenly streaming down her cheeks. "Not to me. We'll help you, Gauge," she says, "I promise. Please, don't go—I don't want you to die again." Attalie wraps her arms around her brother, and pushes her face into his chest. Gauge's eyes well at his little sister's sobs, but he doesn't allow a tear to fall.

Attalie's pleas are hard for me to bear because I know Evvie will feel the same way. Removing myself from the force for my sister's sake never even crossed my mind. Evvie won't be able to understand how much it will hurt me to leave her, how scared I will be, and yet how necessary it is that I remain part of this force. I *have* to fight for her, for the new friends I've made, and even for those I don't know who are suffering because of this system. Like Gauge, I wouldn't feel right staying behind. I'll always *need* to be involved in this war until it is finished.

"Attie," Gauge says once his voice is steady enough for words, "you know I'll do my best to stay alive for you and for Mom." Since his sister doesn't pull her face from his chest while she listens, Gauge centers on his mother while he says, "I have to do this for Dad, and for my friends who helped me escape from that place. I promised."

Mrs. Gallagher nods and wipes her tears before speaking to my father. "My son is not a boy anymore. I give my permission."

Perhaps emotionally strained from watching Mrs. Gallagher's reaction to her son's enlistment, my father moves on. "We'll need two more."

"Red and I will go," Rhoma tells my father. "And just me for enlistment unless you'll believe that I'm Red's biological parent." Rhoma chuckles and pats Red hard on the back, but he remains disappointed by the fact that he won't be allowed to fight for his friends in Neocropolis or return to his family on the inside like my father explained on the ride back here.

"Townsfolk will be out and about shortly," my father says. "I'd like to have us away from Main Street before then. No sense on stirring up emotions and questions from them when we all have a lot ahead of us this morning. Those of you who rode with me will stay with Merick instead since I'll be leaving."

"Captain, I have to ask my wife before I can have company," Merick laughs. "Who do we have?" he asks the group.

"The two of us and one kid each," Mrs. Gallagher says, "assuming my daughter can switch from the driver she and Gauge rode down with since her brother will be leaving."

"Of course," Merick answers. He leads his group away at the same time that Galvesten does.

Neither Cheng nor Crewe have made a move to take their group away. Instead, Cheng stalks up to our little group and asks, "Why Adam, Captain? I should be going to Idaho."

"Because of this right here, Cheng," my father says impatiently. "You're not quite to Jerus' level, but you argue too much and it's off-putting. You're not the best man for this job, and the same goes for you, Crewe," my father says to his son-like seeksmen who stands nearby with his ears perked and arms crossed. "They won't think your motives are sound. Understand?" my father asks Crewe.

As a means of answering that he is following his orders, but that he doesn't agree with them, Crewe turns and tells his group members to follow him. I agree with my father though. Braves himself had to chase Crewe's racing car to Miles County after Braves didn't agree to send men with him to avenge Cy's death. I can see why Crewe, though higher in the ranks than Alix and Adam, shouldn't be selected this time.

"Convince them instead," my father tells Cheng, motioning to his group of escapees. "Go," he says, waving him away.

"Alix, can you drive with one arm?" my father asks, looking at her sling.

"Course," she says, with a mischievous smile.

"Good. Adam, Rhoma, and Jarod, you'll be headed to Idaho so you'll leave straightaway. You three haven't had much rest," he says to Adam, Rhoma, and Jarod, "so try to sleep in the van if you can."

"I'll fill it up and stock some gas," Adam says. "You two go with Alix to get some foodstuff and whatever else you need from the storehouse. Good luck, Captain," Adam says, shaking my father's hand. "Hopefully, we'll each bring back carloads."

"Let's hope," my father says. Then he strides away with Gauge, Red, and me on his heels.

"I need to sleep some before the drive, and Gauge, I know you haven't had any rest either. Red, do you think you need to see the doctor before we leave?"

"No, sir, I mean, Captain," he corrects. "This has been worse than the usual fatigue and confusion I feel after seizures, but it's not too bad. Plus, Doctor McClain pocketed some meds for me when we escaped." He pulls the pill bottle from the back pocket of the baggy black jeans he is wearing and shakes it with delight.

"Red, now that we're out, I feel like I have to tell you something," Gauge says. "I think it might be a point in our favor when we talk to the people of Braves about the horrors of Neocropolis." Red says nothing, but rather waits for Gauge to continue.

"You had it pretty bad down there," Gauge says after a beat. "You were just a kid, and didn't know what to do with that kind of frustration, you know?"

"I know, man. I was there," Red kids.

"You sort of were. Red, you don't have a seizure disorder," Gauge discloses.

Red stops walking. "What are you talking about?" he asks his friend calmly.

"You're tired and have sore limbs sometimes when you come back to us because you've been screaming and thrashing about. You have a multiple personality disorder, Red. That's why you can't remember your seizures and why you sometimes get confused trying to remember other things."

Red starts walking again, and we follow. "Wouldn't I know that?" he asks finally.

"You didn't, and the other Red doesn't know about you either," Gauge answers.

"Did other people know?" Red asks.

"Yeah," Gauge replies simply.

"I always knew there was something off about me. I just thought it was my blazing red hair," Red jokes. "Alright well, now I know," he says, assuring us that he's okay. "I wondered why you guys wanted me to scream and carry on to initiate the escape."

"Yeah, but we didn't know faking it would bring out the other side," I say.

"Hmm," Red reflects. "Maybe knowing about this can help me. Why didn't you tell me before?" Red asks Gauge.

"Stress and worry about your other personality wouldn't have been good for your stability in this personality. I know, because I'd probably asked Doctor McClain ten times since bunking with you why no one told you the truth. It was a risk they didn't want to take since everything had become well managed, you know? No one wanted you to end up in a deeper level again."

"Makes sense," Red says.

"What time does school start?" I ask my father as we enter the other side of town where the hospital, school, and the majority of residences are located.

"I'm guessing you're asking about the high school's start time," my father smirks. That's right. Evvie is in a more rigid, numerical grade out here. Ninth grade, the beginning of high school, was probably a big milestone for her classmates when school started this fall. For Evvie, the milestone lays in attending class in a physical building with classmates whose voices she can hear in real-time.

"Traditional school runs on Saturdays?" Gauge asks. After so much time in Neocropolis, where every day is the same, how is it that Gauge has kept better track of time passing than I have?

"In its own respect," my father answers. "The younger kids can't stay home by themselves while their parents or guardians work, so they have an activity day. The preteen kids lead the activities or help the teachers. The high school students have service Saturday obligations, where they go into one of the requesting workplaces to help catch them up. No traditional weekend when there's work to be done by all."

"Do you know where Evvie will be serving?" I ask my dad.

"They go to the school first and divide up from there. She'll be up at about eight, which means you'll have a couple of hours before you can see her, if you can stand to let her sleep."

"You don't know her well enough yet, Dad. She knew you were outside of Miles and trying to rescue me; I doubt she's slept much. I'll stay away anyway in case she has. Do you have an alarm so that I can try to fall asleep in the meantime?"

"Yes I do," my father answers as he grins. "This one is us," he tells the guys as he veers off the road toward our little house.

"You can get to sleep right away since you'll be driving again," I tell my father when we get inside. "I'll get these guys set up."

"Alright." My father squeezes me tightly in his arms for a

moment. "It's good to have you back," he says when he comes away from the embrace.

"It's good to be back," I tell him. "Water?" I ask the guys.

"Parched," Red answers with a dramatically scratchy voice. I'm glad Red's back too, not to Sheridan, but to Red.

"Alarm!" my father calls from his bedroom. He tosses me the little, battery-operated device. "Wake me at nine if I'm not already up."

I nod, place the alarm in my pocket, and continue playing hostess for Red and Gauge. It's unlike me, but then again, it's unlike me to have friends, and these boys have become my friends.

"I knew things would change when your ugly face opened the cell door of 313 for breakfast that first morning in Neocropolis," Red comments after he's had a satisfying glass of water. "Alright, naptime. Do you have a pillow for the couch here?" he asks.

"Yeah, Evvie has an extra," I tell him. "She's still a little spoiled."

"Isn't she using it?" Red asks.

"No, at least I don't think she brought it with her. She's been staying with a townswoman while my father has been away. Gauge, will you be alright sleeping in a twin bed?"

Gauge rolls his eyes. Right. He's slept in a prison bed for years. "A twin bed isn't too small for a guy my size," he says, a little self-masochistically. "I blame that on cell and bunk size though. I think Neocropolis stunted my growth."

"Oh, I feel so sorry for you," Red says sarcastically. "In fact, I think I'll honor the bet you think you won and let you keep Evvie's extra pillow since you keep insisting this thing," Red nudges me off the arm of the couch, "is such a beauty."

Over my laughter, I hear the front door close. I spin around in momentary fright. Crewe. When had he opened the door and stepped in?

"Sorry, I didn't mean to startle you," he says. "We're all just used to coming and going from places."

"We're used to the exact opposite," Gauge remarks.

"My dad has gone to bed already," I tell Crewe.

"Actually, I'm here to talk to you." His eyes flash uneasily from mine, to the opposite side of the couch where Gauge sits, and then to mine again.

"Sure," I answer, a little unsure of how to proceed.

"Maybe outside?" he suggests. Crewe opens the door for me, and I walk through. He reaches into his pocket and takes out a piece of paper, which, by the handwriting, I recognize to be the letter that I wrote him before exchanging places with Evvie.

"I read this like ten times," he admits, his tanned cheeks reddening a bit. "I don't know why I kept reading it, because I realized from the very first that I screwed up. You came over to talk to me, and I made you feel like you played a part in my brother's death. I made you feel like you had no other choice than to turn yourself over to the BOTs." My father used the same line after I lowered the pistol I pulled on him. I wonder which of the two men was the original expresser and who was the mimicker. "I let them hurt you." A vein in Crewe's temple bulges. "I should have listened to you and talked to you. I should have helped somehow."

"The captain's reluctance to go after Evvie again drove my decision to go," I confess, "But nothing you did made me leave."

"But I didn't make you stay," he argues, his eyes locked

onto mine. "And I think I could have."

"You were grieving Cy's loss," I tell him, trying to let him know that I understood why he wasn't focused on saving my sister anymore.

"I still am. I mean, I brought those people in our house," he stops and swallows hard, "and I expected my smiley kid brother to come out of his room to shake each of their hands. Seconds passed…and it just killed me that he didn't come. I had to leave them. I just couldn't stay there. I ended up here instead. I'm sorry."

"Don't be sorry," I insist. "I should be the one apologizing, Crewe. Things might have been different if I was more patient, but I just didn't know what could be happening to Evvie."

Crewe steps in a little closer to me. "No, you were wrong to write that in here," he says, shaking the letter in his hand. "Things would have been different if they hadn't shot my brother. That's what all the *what ifs* boil down to, Sydney. I've decided that for my own sanity. Anyway, I wanted to apologize if I made you feel," he pauses to think, "alone," he says finally.

I forgive you isn't appropriate because I've already told him that he had nothing to be sorry for. What do I say? Okay? I stand there uncomfortably until he fills in the gap with, "Well, I'll let you get some rest."

"Do you want to stay here? You said that you needed to get out of your house," I explain quickly.

"No, I'll be fine," he says immediately, taking a step away.

"You're welcome to come back if you can't sleep and change your mind," I tell him.

He takes a step toward me again, and this time his eyes are soft and warm. "Thank you, Sydney." As he speaks my name, he lifts the hand that grasps my letter and lightly touches my forearm. He removes it sooner than I want him to, but he doesn't go anywhere.

"You're welcome," I say. I nervously reach up and touch the shirtsleeve of his opposite arm. He looks deeply into my eyes and swallows hard again. I let my hand fall gently down across the skin of his arm. His eyes shift to my hand on him and so do mine, my face growing warm. Crewe reaches for my elbow, while the hand with the letter takes hold of my hip.

He looks back at me for a moment before his eyes close, and his lips focus on me instead. They carefully surround my upper lip. The kiss is a mix of passion and sorrow, but I love it, and hold him so that he doesn't pull away as quickly as last time.

He kisses me softly twice more and then hugs me tightly. "I missed you, Sydney." He stands tall, looks down at me, and smiles. "I've felt connected to you since the first time I saw you on one of your routine runs outside of Miles. I only wish I hadn't screwed up so much the first time you saw me," he chuckles.

It feels even better to see him laugh than it does to kiss him. If I can't sleep now, it'll be because my excitement has doubled. Last time that he kissed me, all I wanted to do was run to tell Evvie what had happened, but I couldn't. In a couple of hours, I'll finally be able to share my first romance with her.

"Get some sleep," Crewe says before parting with me. My heart feels fluttery, and the smile on my face is difficult to subdue as I enter the house. I allow it to linger when I step inside and see that Red is sleeping on the couch and Gauge is presumably shut into mine and Evvie's room. After a moment, I tiptoe in to find Gauge already asleep.

Inspired by the kiss, I begin wishing the impossible as I lie in bed and attempt to get some rest. I wish Miles would release the Neocropolis residents. I wish Region Two would declare Sheridan, Braves, and Idaho their own, separately governed counties. I wish all the counties in Region Two would allow desiring citizens to join their nearest, barrier-free town. Sure, leaving might need to have limitations, but maybe that would be okay. Maybe it would be enough to prevent a civil war that will jeopardize the security of the nation and the lives of its citizens. If those problems could be solved, then maybe all of my wildest dreams could come true.

TWENTY-TWO

Even though my father's alarm doesn't blare like the one in Neocropolis did, I still feel a little panicked and find myself standing erect atop my bed after it sounds. Thank goodness Gauge didn't wake to see. After my slumber, it feels like a new day, and I've already fulfilled Sheridan's way to honor Cy Davids by finding a reason to smile each day. This time, I'm amused by my own self—something that hasn't happened for a long time.

I jump down from the bed, landing as silently as I used to when I would sneak out of the transitions building in the wee hours of the morning.

Red hasn't shifted an inch from how he laid on the couch hours ago. He's been sleeping in an extremely narrow bed since he was about eleven. He's probably been conditioned to sleep motionlessly.

The sun is bright this morning, and it warms my skin deliciously. I soak in its rays and wonder again why war has to be on the horizon. Then I remember all the people still trapped in Neocropolis and how they haven't seen the sun, felt a breeze, or heard the birds chirping and singing overhead in years.

Although Gwen's house is not far from mine, I decide to

run there. My body has to be ready when war dawns.

Once Gwen's house is in sight, I increase my pace to almost a sprint. I see it, and then I'm on its porch before I've blinked or breathed. My quick and demanding knocks on the door also correspond with my excitement to see my sister, awake and breathing, for the first time since we entered Sheridan together ten days ago.

The door bursts open and someone squashes their self into me so quickly that I hardly have time to see that it's my sister.

"They're back, Gwen, they're back," someone shrieks from inside the house. Little Lysia tromps toward Evvie and me, but Gwen grabs her by the arm just before she reaches us.

"One hug and one question," Gwen tells her adopted daughter. "Do you understand me? Then it's off to school, or you'll be late."

"Is my. . .is Crewe okay?" she asks, careful not to call him her dad like she'd done before.

Evvie comes away from me so that I can answer Lysia's question. We look into one another's eyes, both of us crying, then laughing, then hugging once more.

Lysia wiggles her way into the hug, but probably only so she can be as close as possible to me to impatiently say, "Well?"

"Everyone is okay," I tell her.

"Everyone?" Gwen marvels. Her eyes and smile are wide with astonishment and joy.

"What happed to your face?" Lysia asks, her own little face twisted in disgust.

"I said one question," Gwen scolds. "You get going now."

"But Gwen, I want to hear," Lysia whines.

"Get those feet moving," Gwen says as she guides her

daughter to the road.

"Don't worry, they didn't hurt me," I tell Evvie, answering Lysia's question that my sister evidently shares. "I hit a deer on my way to Miles, but I'm fine."

"Faster, young lady, or no painting when you get home tonight." Gwen shouts to Lysia. She continues to watch her perpetually testing daughter slump along to school before she returns to us.

"Sydney, can you take two minutes to tell me what happened and what's coming before I head to the laundromat? I want you two to have some time to yourselves before Evvie has to be off, but I just have to know," she says apologetically.

"The Seeksmen didn't have to come into Miles to rescue me. A band of us who were being held captive underground had planned an escape. We were lucky that an agent told us where my father and the others were hiding, but also unlucky because a few of the other captives and two Miles County citizens were left behind in the process."

"Not harmed though?" she asks.

"There were a few shots fired as we tried to escape. I'm not sure whether it was guards or prisoners who were hit." I wish I felt more uncertain about the last shot that was fired. I had an immediate and terrible feeling that the fired round hit Edyn.

"I'm sorry to hear that," Gwen offers. "I suppose Demetri still plans to rescue the rest held captive?" Gwen nervously shifts her weight from one leg to the other.

"That's our plan. But for now, we're going to try to convince Braves and Idaho to fight alongside us," I tell her, aware that the use of *us* will upset Evvie.

"Are you leaving?" Evvie asks.

"I am going, yes, but I'll be back tonight."

"Good luck, Sydney," Gwen says as she takes her leave. "If you or your father need anything…"

"We will," I say, putting my arm around my sister, "and we'll let you know when." Gwen nods to let me know that she'll look after Evvie again when my father and I invade Miles County. She has incredible love for and patience with Lysia, despite the eight-year-old's toothy spunk, so I think my father made a great choice. In fact, getting to know Evvie by providing for and comforting her the last two days has probably helped Gwen pull her mind away from Decklin's passing. He was like a son to her.

"So, our dad's alive," I joke with my sister once we're alone.

"I noticed," she says, but only a hint of a smile shows. "Sydney, I worry that it won't be for long. I'm afraid for both of you, but mostly for you."

What can I say to comfort my sister? I don't want to tell her that everything is going to be all right, because I don't know that it is. I would never promise her something that I can't guarantee. "We're doing the right thing," I say at last.

"I know," she says. "I knew you would want to fight. It's who you've always been, but I guess you have even more reason now."

"I do. Do you remember anything after you were taken away?" I ask.

"I don't even remember being taken away," my sister answers. I suspected that she wouldn't remember her stay in Neocropolis, if that's even where she was, but they've erased even more of her memory than that.

"You remember coming here though, right?" I ask her.

"Yes. The captain asked me the same thing, and I told

him that the last thing I remember was Cy making me pancakes before I went to bed."

"He made you pancakes?" I ask. The warm vision is accompanied by sorrow.

Evvie nods, and then begins to fight back tears. "I feel like all of this is our fault, Syd. BOTs killing seeksmen and everyone preparing for war...I feel like none of it would have happened if it weren't for us."

I sit down on the steps of Gwen's front porch and take hold of my sister's hands, inviting her to join me. She sits beside me, but doesn't let go of my hand. "I feel the same way sometimes, Evvie. This morning when we got in, I told Crewe that I feel like Cy's death was my fault because I convinced the seeksmen to go after you. And you're my flesh and blood so I know that you feel some responsibility because of that too."

With each little, successive nod, Evvie's chin lowers. "Hey," I say, pulling her chin up so that she looks me in the eyes. "Crewe said that he felt like he was to blame. Dad feels like it was his fault because those are his men. Alix probably feels like she could have done more to save him, and the same with Galvesten and Della. Cy's death is just an example of how we can all find a way to blame ourselves if we look for it, rather than at whom we should really be blaming."

"Which is them," Evvie says.

"That's right."

"And is that also why you feel like you have to fight? Because of them?"

"Because of what they do and will continue doing if no one challenges them," I answer. "I've always thought a resistance should form to create a better future, but I never knew then about the people who had a *present* much worse than ours was.

There are people being held captive in a prison underground. Some of them have been down there a long, long time. There are even kid prisoners younger than you."

"The captain told me a little about what he thought the place was like to see if it jogged my memory at all. Do you think that's where I was?" my sister asks me.

"I think so. They erased my memory too, but I think parts of it came back to me in a dream. Have you had any unusual dreams?"

"Only one that I can remember. We were at a funeral, and then it began to storm. I didn't want to close the lid to the... what do you call those wooden things that they put bodies into again?"

"A coffin," I tell her. Although cremation is the only option inside Miles County, I would think Evvie should know the word from Halloween festivities. Then again, we never celebrated the way that other kids did.

"I didn't want to close the lid to the coffin because you looked so pretty," she says, looking up at me with welling eyes. "I couldn't let it be the last time I saw you."

A lump forms in my throat. "*I* was in the coffin?"

She nods sorrowfully. "Wearing the black dress and Mom's Tahitian pearls, just like you wore in court. I've had that dream over and over ever since I woke up holding a letter that basically said goodbye forever."

I swallow hard and hug my sister, maybe as much for my own comfort as for hers. "What do you need to do to get ready for school?" I ask her, unable to listen to anything more about her dream and unwilling to let her become mad at me for leaving the way I did.

"I'll go change. Then I'll just need to eat, brush, and do

something with my hair," she answers.

With energy conservation in the forefront, I suppose the high school girls don't perfect their hair with products and electronics the way most did on the inside. It's ironic that the students who are actually in one another's physical presence when they attend school do less to get ready for it. I also know Evvie can't spend twenty minutes deciding on an outfit when she only owns three and doesn't particularly care for any. She can't take a shower every day, nor can she wear makeup. All those things considered, getting ready to be seen by her peers takes a fraction of the time it took on the inside.

Normally, I'd like that my sister can put the time and energy into more worthy things, but today her extra time before school is going to be spent worrying that I am war bound—that there is a chance I might die—if I don't find a better subject to talk with her about.

"How do you like the school? Have you made some friends?" I call to my sister, who changes in another room.

"It's okay," she responds. "I still miss my friends back home, I mean, in Miles," she corrects, "but most of the kids are pretty nice."

"Most of them?" My sister has always fit in better than I did, so I'm surprised to hear that anyone, especially here, has treated her poorly.

"Not everyone in the town agrees with the captain's decisions. There are some kids whose caretakers, friends, or relatives are training to join the Sheridan army. They understand but can't help disliking that someone they care about is going to war. So being the captain's daughter is a little tough."

Evvie emerges from the room in an outfit I know she didn't have before I left. "I didn't think you could grow any cuter, especially in Sheridan. How'd you manage that?" I tease her.

The corners of her lips turn up in a guilty smile. "I made another trip to the storehouse," she confesses.

"It's not a mall, Ev," I say, both in seriousness and in fun.

"I put a few things back," she defends.

"Yeah? And how many did you pick up?" Evvie's cheeks redden, and I have my answer. Probably a thing or two more than her fair share. The best thing about my sister is that I've already said enough. It might take her a while to choose between what she has, but she'll get around to correcting this. "Well, I'm glad you like most of the kids. So how many boyfriends do you have?" I clown.

"Just one," she says, trying to busy herself with breakfast as not to leak her contained smile.

"Liar. I didn't believe you for a second. But keep looking that good and you might," I warn. Evvie stirs orange powder into the two glasses of water. "Thanks," I tell her, but I miss the county imports right now. Like Neocropolis, the diet out here is limited.

"I do want to talk about one boy, though," my sister says.

Two pieces of toast pop. It's as if we're back in my apartment in the transitions building during one of Evvie's overnights away from her foster home with Merideth. She's buttering our breakfast and wanting to spill the beans about some boy in school to whom she's already taken a liking. "Oh, here we go." With my poking-fun eye roll comes an easy, genuine smile. With my sister around, I'll never have to work to honor Cy.

"No, no. Here *you* go," she says, tossing a piece of toast at me. "You're the one doing the talking."

"About what?" I ask, guilt flashing in my cheeks.

"How many boyfriends do you have?" Evvie responds, a grin erupting across her face. "I know he likes you, and I think you like him back. Now spill!" she demands.

"Alright," I laugh. "You're right...on both accounts," I admit.

"I knew it and couldn't believe it at the same time. I don't think you've ever liked anyone before, have you? Does he know that you like him?"

"I think he knows," I tell her in a way that indicates he certainly does know I like him.

Evvie's had practice picking up on this type of clue from her friends. She's much quicker to pick it up than the coded escape plans I had to deliver when she first breached with me. "Tell me," my sister begs.

"Eat your breakfast," I tell her.

"Tell me!"

"Can't you chew and listen at the same time?" I joke. Evvie folds her piece of toast in half and shoves a huge bite into her mouth. I can't very well stay quiet now. "Crewe and I had to trust each other when we first decided to go back toward Miles after the seeksmen had taken me. I guess we connected. When we came back to Sheridan with you, my heart felt kind of light, and I think he played a part in that."

"Ooooh, the butterflies," Evvie mocks with a mouthful of toast.

"Shut up," I say, not really meaning it, or thinking that she would stop if I did. "When they took you, I was the most scared I've ever been, Ev." Evvie swallows a large lump of toast and listens carefully. "That fear grew with every day that you were in the hands of the Miles County BOTs, and we were sitting here doing nothing. Crewe assured me that we'd get you back.

He also made sure I wasn't part of the group that went after you. He coerced Alix into volunteering so they wouldn't have room for me. Who knows how the riders may have been rearranged if I were among them," I reflect. "It could have easily been me who the BOTs shot and killed that day."

"Then I'm thankful to him too, but mostly to you for everything that you did to get me back." My sister throws her hair into a ponytail and finishes her crude orange juice. "I have been awake a lot at night, thinking about everything that you've done for me in your life. I've decided that there's never been a sister who has proven her love more than you have."

"Love brings that need, I guess. God knows I love you, even with that neon stripe in your hair." I shake my head and smile. Evvie gives me a hug and kiss on the cheek before she disappears into the bathroom to brush her teeth.

"Walk with me?" she asks when she's finished.

"I have to go back and wake Dad and two of my friends up, but I can walk with you for a minute," I say as we head through the door.

"You have friends and a boyfriend!" Evvie exclaims. "I think they've replaced my sister, but I like you just as well."

"I never said I had a boyfriend," I reply.

"You also never said you didn't. Even just there," Evvie points out. "Are your friends people from the underground prison?"

"Yes, they're from Neocropolis. They're coming with us today to help convince Braves that we need to fight to free all the people Miles County is holding down there."

"How many prisoners are there?" my sister asks.

"One hundred and sixty now."

"One hundred and sixty? That's a lot of people to lock

up," she says in disbelief.

"Not to mention all their fake deaths," I add.

"Is that what they do? The county makes up a death like they did with the captain?"

"Yes, exactly," I answer. I can see I've really opened my sister's eyes with this. "Even though some of the kids give you a hard time about him, you like Dad, right?" I ask my sister.

"I haven't gotten to know him that well yet but, yes, I like him. Will you tell the captain good luck from me?" Evvie asks.

"I will tell *Dad*, yes," I say.

"I'm sorry, I'm still getting used to having a dad, having *Dad*," she says.

"I am too, but it's a miraculous and great thing to have to get used to."

Evvie nods. "Good luck today." My sister turns and gives me a hug. "I love you, Sydney.

"I love you too, Ev. Have a good day at school."

I look over my shoulder three times before my view of Evvie becomes obstructed. It's hard to take my eyes off her, both with what has happened and what is coming. I want to cherish every moment with her, even those where she doesn't know I'm watching.

Twenty-Three

At this time of day, most of the townspeople of Braves are inside their places of business, so there aren't many to greet the captain and inquire as to who Gauge, Red, and I are as we walk the short distance from their lot to the designated meeting place. However, one short, middle-aged man spots us from inside the butcher shop we pass.

"Captain!" he calls after making his way outside. As not to delay us, he catches up to our group. "What brings you here today?" the man asks.

"We're meeting with Braves right now," my father says without slowing. "Hopefully, you'll know why once we're finished."

"Your new recruits look pretty young," he says, thinking he's made a joke.

My father stops and studies the man for a moment. "Well, I might as well tell you exactly who these three are and let small-town gossip do its work while we meet with Braves."

The man raises his eyebrows in honored surprise and then nods. "I can spread the word on whatever you like, Captain."

My father places his strong hand on the top of my head. "This here is Sydney, my daughter."

Astonished, the man asks, "You got her back from BOTs?"

"No, she escaped from beneath them," my father says. "And so did her friends here."

"Well, welcome to Braves," the stunned man says as he shakes all of our hands. "Braves always tells us that the name of our town was never meant to reflect his surname, but to proclaim to the world the type of people who can be found here." The man focuses on me and says, "You are truly a brave soul, Sydney Harter. Someone who willingly hands herself over to the BOTs after being in freedom is certainly welcome in our town. And then you escaped from them! This news won't take an hour to spread. You'll be a hero, young lady."

I smile to acknowledge his praise, but I don't believe I deserve it. Trading places with Evvie was a necessity. I was willing to lay down my life for the person I love the most, but I may not have even risked my life had anyone else been in danger the way that Evvie was. I am not as brave as the Davids brothers, the other seeksmen, Galvesten, or even Della, who have been putting their lives on the line for strangers since they chose their professions.

I learned the shortcomings of my bravery when I hesitated to leave the apartment room on Level One of Neocropolis after Gauge's bomb exploded. Even though Evvie is now safe in Sheridan, I hope I can still find courage enough to fight for others who are being treated unjustly, are imprisoned, or are in danger.

"Actually, it's not the fifteen escapees that I want you to talk about," the captain says.

"Fifteen?" the man seeks to verify. The number is enough to strike hope and excitement.

"I need you to let the townsmen know that there are one

hundred and sixty former citizens being held in a penitentiary beneath EPA 12-1 in Miles County. They're imprisoned because they have knowledge of things that the government wishes to keep secret, not because they've committed real crimes. Their loved ones believe they're dead, but it's all been faked. Most of the causes of death were suicide or freak accident. It's important the people know that too."

"Fifteen escaped, including Sydney Harter. One hundred and sixty remain imprisoned under an EPA in Miles County—their only crime that they knew the truth. The government faked their suicides or accidental death because of this. How's that?" the man asks.

"Good," my father answers.

"I think you'll convince him this time, Captain," the man says. "Braves knows our boys are ready. Today's the day."

"I hope so," my father replies. He turns and we continue to walk, more quickly now, until we reach a restaurant. With how busy my father and the other leaders are, they'd probably forget to eat if meetings weren't held in or near eating establishments.

A young woman greets us and brings us to a private dining area where a man about my father's age waits.

"I finally get to meet the famous daughter," he says in a deep and grainy voice. "Edson Braves. Good to meet you. And you two must also come from Neocropolis," he says, while shaking hands with Gauge and Red.

"Yes, sir. I'm Red, sir."

"Braves will do, young man," he tells Red. "And you?" he asks Gauge.

"Gauge Gallagher."

"You were the one down in solitary?" Braves asks.

"No, that was me, sir," Red says. "Ugh, Braves. Sorry."

Red pounds his fist against his head as if that will help him skip the formality of addressing his superiors as sir. I'm sure Red had to be extremely polite and compliant in order to move up to higher levels of Neocropolis. It took him years to make it to Three, so the habit is well ingrained.

"I wouldn't have guessed," Braves remarks. He sits back down and passes a handwritten menu across the table.

Red excitedly lifts it to examine the options. "Meaty pizza, California burger, chicken Caesar salad, ham and cheese sandwich, or crusty macaroni and bacon," he reads out loud.

"Have you ever heard of California?" Braves asks Red.

"No, sorry," Red apologizes. "My education stopped when I was placed in Neocropolis. I was only eleven when I was put in Level Five. By the time I ascended to Three," he smiles and lifts his hands as if he floated there divinely, "I'd saved some points that I could have used for tutoring sessions, but I used them to check out books from the library instead. That way I could learn about the things that interested me. I know I've heard the word before, but I don't think I ever read what a California is."

My dad, Braves, and I all try to withhold a chuckle, but Gauge looks as if he has the same question in mind as Red, even with his mother being an instruction monitor.

I always had more than double the necessary history credits, so I know all about the former states. Gauge, on the other hand, may have studied the bare minimum if he didn't like history as much. His required credit hours likely included colonialism, the American Revolution, the Civil War, World War I, the Great Depression, World War II, the Cold War, the War on Terror, and the Great Recession, which led into the contemporary age. Special emphasis was always placed on the costliness of war.

The uniformly designed EduWeb courses didn't name states, but rather talked about the old regions of the nation before time zones and lines of latitude were used to divide and rename them. A student would have to know the regions numbers, and which counties in each were most populated. They'd have to know the reasons for, and benefits from, shifting from united states to disjoint counties, as taught by the government. Memorization of the former states was never a course expectation.

Most would learn about the former states and some of their major cities over time, by listening to those who were alive when the shift was made, but Gauge, and certainly Red, weren't given as much of a chance for that due to their imprisonment.

"California was a large and populated state on the west coast," Braves says. "Out here, certain foods are only available after the harvest. That California burger includes fresh lettuce and tomato, which makes it much better than the cheeseburger that's offered when those two crops aren't in season. That's one of the few downsides of living in one of the free towns—we can't trade with other regions to get more variety in our diet like the counties can."

"That's no problem for us," Gauge says. "We've been eating the same mush over and over in Neocropolis."

Braves made the California burger sound so delicious and exquisite that Red, Gauge, and I all end up ordering it.

While my grandma was still alive, Evvie and I got to dine out twice a year, on each of our birthdays. After that, I made my family a lot of bland sandwiches until my sister and I were placed in the orphanage. The food there was similar to the dishes in Neocropolis. I'd order something from Tiana's restaurant every now and again, when the temptation at work got to be too much, but the majority of the time my diet remained plain. All the years of my frugality make my appetite for a California burger just as wet as the boys'.

"So you want men," Braves says to my father after the waitress leaves. "The burden is on you, as always. Convince me."

"When my youngest daughter was taken from *our* free soil, you didn't aid us in going after her. We gathered a small force anyway and went. Now I know he was unsanctioned and unstable, but when Crewe came to you after that force was fired upon and two of them killed, you still refused to fight. However, as one of your townsmen pointed out earlier, my eighteen-year-old daughter had the guts to go straight to them while I was here trying to convince you to fight with us."

"Now that's not my fault," Braves begins gruffly.

"I know," my father retorts. "I'm not saying it was your fault, Braves," he says more calmly. "I'm just saying that if she had the courage to go, I know there are men and women in this town, the town of the brave, who are willing to aid us."

Braves crosses his arms, but the gesture doesn't conceal the shame that's written on his face.

"I didn't even ask for your help to rescue Sydney, because I was tired of hearing the same answer. You always say there aren't enough of us and that the seeksmen lack training. Eddie, we're never going to match their numbers and your troops are never going to have battlefield experience until you let them go to battle. Mine have gained that now. Sydney's probably more qualified after two weeks of confrontations with BOTs than some of your guys who have been seeksmen for years."

Braves rolls his eyes, but I don't get defensive. I have my father to defend me now.

"For the first time we have firsthand accounts of

Neocropolis, which we have speculated about for years. With the recent additions to my town, our force is bigger than we could have imagined it would be today. And Eddie," the captain says, leaning forward on his elbows, "we also know who their commander is. This *is* the time, Braves. I'd rather make war than find it upon us."

"Who's their commander?" Braves asks, deeply interested.

"My brother, Ted." My father sits back in his chair.

"And that's supposed to be a good thing?" Braves asks critically.

"I knew him a long time, so I might be able to predict his moves against us."

"Yeah, you knew him a long time, Demetri—as brothers and best friends," Braves charges.

"Look, I know what you're afraid of." My father's voice becomes louder, and his tone aggravated. "If it comes down to me versus Ted and I can't do it, then you have my permission to kill him, and so does every other soldier we acquire for our force. If you found out it was your brother, father, or best friend who killed your little girls, would you hesitate to kill them?"

"Not for a second," Braves answers through a clenched jaw.

Tuli and Tigonee, the two names that Evvie came across on my mother's parenting account long after she'd been dead, were Braves' daughters. Merick told me the story of how Braves saw a cluster of free people on a satellite image and broadcasted the news by infecting citizens' technological devices with a virus. County agents forced Braves to recant his findings by threatening to harm his wife and twin daughters. He did everything they said, but in the end, his family still tragically died of carbon monoxide poisoning.

"My brother didn't kill my daughters," my father says, "but he could have, and might have if he needed to. He did kill two of my seeksmen and, after what Sydney told me on the ride here, I think his predecessor left my wife no choice other than to kill herself. If it comes down to it, I don't think I'll have a problem putting a bullet in my brother."

"Can I ask you something?" I ask Braves, a little worried about the risk in my question. I've had a realization that could make the difference for us. It could mean that this is the time Braves will say yes to aiding Sheridan with his forces. It could also upset him enough that he sends us on our way.

"Go ahead," Braves says.

"I know the deaths of your family members is a sensitive matter," I start.

"It is, but it's also been a long time, Sydney, and I've told the tale many times."

"Did you see their bodies?" I ask bluntly.

Braves rubs his facial hair as he thinks. "I never did. Because my family had been in the public eye, the media got a hold of the story and broadcasted their death before I'd even been notified. I was angry enough to kill, and sad enough to die, but I didn't know how to find the BOT who had been threatening us for the month prior. I figured I was next unless I got myself out. I said my farewells to them in my heart, and then escaped."

"My family never saw my body," Gauge says fervently. "They told them that I'd committed suicide and my remains were nothing to see and have to remember."

"My family never saw my body either," Red adds. "How could they? I'm *alive*."

"Had you stayed, you might have been next," I tell Braves.

"But what if death wasn't what you were next in line for? What if the agents planned to send you to an underground prison?"

"No, Sydney," Gauge says, stopping this from going any farther. "No one in Neocropolis was from another county."

"Gauge, they force us to tell lies about ourselves in Neocropolis," I argue. "I told Edyn about my sister and about Sheridan when I first woke up in my cell. Later, I had a classified meeting where the commander told me to lie about my name, my family, and what crime I committed that sank me in Neocropolis."

"Even so," Gauge says, "we know everyone in Neocropolis. There are no twins."

"He's right Sydney," Red says. "We knew all one hundred and seventy-five residents. Sorry, Braves." Red apologizes for what he sees as unreasonable hope I've given to a father and husband whose family was taken from him.

Braves sighs and waves Red off. "One hundred and seventy-five," he whispers and shakes his head. "Are there really that many people below ground?"

"Yes sir, I mean, Braves," Red says. "Less now that some have escaped. There were five different levels. The deeper you were, the worse your crime against the county was."

"What could have you done to be on the deepest level?" Braves asks Red.

"I committed an actual crime, and I deserved to be punished."

"That's not true," Gauge interrupts. "It was an accident, man." It's clear Gauge has had to remind Red of this often since they became roommates. Braves raises his eyebrows, encouraging Red to go on.

"When I was gathering research for a school report, I

came across an article about the huge rise in suicide and accidental deaths in every county in Region Two. I looked for more on the same topic, but found it odd that I couldn't find any other sources providing causes of death statistics after the year 2015. That's how I wound up in Neocropolis."

"That might have been Rico," my father tells Braves. I'd thought the same thing when Gauge first told me the story.

"Rico is our technology guru," the captain tells my friends. "He infiltrates the county system with articles like the one you described."

Red nods and continues his story without any hard feelings toward Rico or his work. "I was young, confused, and afraid in there. I became very angry one day at the officer of my level. I never meant to hurt him, but it ended up that I stabbed him with a tablet pen. And so I was put in solitary confinement. I just found out today that I developed a multiple personality disorder while down there."

"The conditions are that bad," Gauge says, defending the mind of his best friend.

Now is a good time for me to chime in on the conditions. "During that classified meeting I told you about, my head was bagged and my hands were cuffed," I say. "I spent less than an evening in solitary confinement, but I believe I met my uncle Ted while chained and silenced by a muzzle."

"You believe?" Braves questions, seeking further explanation.

"My memory was erased afterward, but I dreamed about the encounter."

"And I can vouch that the muzzles do exist," Red adds.

The waitress knocks on the wall before bringing in a tray with our meals. She happily passes each of us our plates, which we eagerly dig into. After a few bites, I look up from my plate to thank Braves for the suggestion, but follow his gaze to my father, who hasn't touched his food.

"What's on your mind, Captain?" Braves asks.

"To tell you the truth, Braves, I haven't gotten Sydney's speculation about your family being alive off my mind."

"They closed that possibility themselves," Braves says, confused by my father's persistent thought on the topic.

"In Miles, yes, but not in Bozeman, Braves." My father notices that all of us have stopped eating to hear him out, but he doesn't appear to be talking to any of us when he says, "If the smallest, least-populated, and least-funded county in Region Two built an underground prison to contain one hundred and seventy-five offenders, then don't you think the larger ones could, and in fact *would*, have needed to hide enemies of the government in a similar way?"

My father's eyes meet Braves' for only a moment, and then he begins to eat his meal.

Braves suddenly slams his silverware down. "You think you can use my family to manipulate me into giving you *my forces*? You're no better than your brother if you can't have more respect for the dead and the ones they've left behind," he charges.

"Braves," my father snaps back, "if I had the slightest idea about the suffering my wife and daughters endured after I escaped, I would've done things differently." He stands up and leans over the table. "I regret that I didn't make sure with my own eyes what the county systems said to be true. My wife has been dead for ten years, and I had *no* idea. What if your wife and daughters have been *alive* all this time? What if they've been hoping you'd come to free them someday?"

My father shakes his head and sits back down. He picks up his fork, but then drops it back on the napkin. "I'm not trying to manipulate *you* as much as I'm trying to help *them*. Those one hundred and sixty people belong to someone. They're someone's husband, wife, child, or friend. I do believe there could be more prisons, and I do believe that your family could be alive in one of them. My soldiers and I are going with or without yours," he says flatly, "but we'll have a better chance of not only freeing Miles' prisoners, but also continuing on to other counties with you."

After a tense minute, my father starts to eat. Even Red withholds his usual, friendly chatter during the awkward meal. The California burger is hard to enjoy when I feel as though the sounds of my chewing need to be silent.

"Promise me that the next county we look into is Bozeman," Braves says when he's finished eating. "Swear that we'll attack them right afterwards, so their forces don't have the opportunity to prepare after seeing what we did in Miles."

"You have my word," my father says.

I feel like this progression calls for celebration, but my father doesn't even smile after finally convincing Braves to join forces with him for the first time. I suppose it would be different if two sports teams were merging to make one super team, but this is not a game, it is war. There is no cause for my father to be happy now that Braves' soldiers will lose their lives along with Sheridan's.

TWENTY-FOUR

"You did, huh? How many?" my father excitedly asks whoever is on the other side of the cell phone conversation. It's probably Adam, Cheng's seeking partner, or Alix, whose place in my father ranks I am determined to take now that she's injured.

"Well, I can understand that. He sent you and the others away with the best supplies though, right?"

The fifteen of us—our foursome from Sheridan, Edson Braves, all nine of his seeksmen, and one of his town's doctors—spent about an hour loading this truck and the three vehicles behind us with gasoline, guns, ammunition, neoprene suits, bulletproof vests, and two motorcycles. My father is probably making sure that they are reaping similar war necessities from the free town of Idaho.

"*Really*? No kidding. We'll have to find somebody who can get it running. True. All right, let me know. See you then."

"What do you need to get running?" Gauge asks my dad when he's finished talking on the phone.

"That's right, you're a pretty good mechanic, aren't you?" he remarks. "One of their seeksmen found a small, personal plane shut up in a big garage yesterday. If we can get that running, we'll certainly put it to use." My father scratches his chin and smiles slightly. "It could make a huge difference for us."

"How many seeksmen are coming from Idaho?"

My father doesn't realize that I've asked him a question. He's seems stuck in the clouds, thinking about the advantages the plane could bring. "What?" he says when my question finally sinks in. "Oh, we have eight coming from Idaho, two of their three seeking teams, a doctor, and their tech person. I'm going to call Merick and see what the force is amounting to back home.

My father's phone conversation with Merick is as fragmented and hard to understand as the last one was, so I pay attention instead to some murmurings from Red in the back seat.

"I feel useless. You get to help by fixing things and since your mom is out here to permit it, you get to fight too. So does Sydney," he says, meeting my eyes in the rearview mirror. "Just about everyone from Neocropolis who would want the option to enlist has it, except for me. I'm no good anywhere else," he explains. "All I know how to do is make food and scrub pots and pans. That won't help us free our friends. I need to be out there with you guys."

"Six soldiers from Idaho, ten from Braves, nine from Sheridan, and seven from Neocropolis," my father announces when he's hung up with Merick. "Then add five doctors and two techies."

"That makes a force of thirty-nine," Red says. "You could make it a flat forty if you'd let me fight, Captain."

"You've got a good heart, son, but you know my age requirement," my father says. "I could round out the number by having Alix help Della," my father considers.

"What about the Miles' citizens who escaped with us?"

Gauge asks. "Did you include them with the Neocropolis count?"

"You mean your mother and the woman with the two little boys? Though the two women have good reason to fight, they each also have good reason to help behind the scenes rather than in the ranks with us."

Though my father doesn't look at me, I feel like he's trying to tell me that Gauge's mom is doing the *right thing* by staying behind for the sake of her daughter, who is Evvie's age, and that Monya is likewise choosing correctly because of her young son who is accounted for. Though they each have a missing family member, they didn't enlist because, if the worst should happen, Attalie and the toddler would have no family left alive.

Likewise, if my father and I were both to perish, Evvie will be left alone. As the captain of the three refugee towns, my father is responsible for leading the men and women into battle. I, on the other hand, am not required to fight. My father thinks I'm making the wrong choice by going into combat, and he's trying to tell me in a roundabout way.

For so long, I've wanted to bring people into true freedom. My desire has deepened since learning some of the government's many secrets. The truth needs to be exposed. Going to battle is what's right *for me*. To make it right by my father and Evvie, I'll just have to stay alive.

Moreover, if I stayed back and we lost, if we were all forced back into a Petri-dish county or worse—an underground jail—then I'd never forgive myself for having remained here while the others fought.

"What do you kids say we brainstorm for a bit?" my father suggests. "If we wait until the morning when we all meet, we'll end up with thirty-nine different attack strategies.

The way I see it, I know the fighting tactics of the BOTs and the seeksmen better than anybody. Sydney knows Miles County and its breaching points. You two boys know the Neocropolis layout and personnel. Of course, we'll hear from the others tomorrow, but I'd like to start the meeting with a rough plan. I think we have the resources right here to draw it up. The only other men whose specialty would warrant input would be Rico or Cy."

"Happy to help, Captain." Red perks up while my father and I slump under the mention of Cy's name.

"What's their specialty, the men you wished were here with us?" Gauge asks.

"Just one man. Rico. Cy was one of the young men they killed." My father shakes his head at the slip up. My thoughts are pulled to Crewe. I wonder how he's doing with the former prisoners staying in his house, maybe even in Cy's room. Hopefully, the process of getting them situated and then training with Merick has kept them out of the house and busied him today.

"Rico is our tech man," my father continues. "Their infrared cameras have always been the biggest obstacle for us. We have no element of surprise. The neoprene suits are only good when worn by a small number and for a short amount of time. With this many, they'll be able to watch us all the way in."

"The agent inside Neocropolis—the one who turned off the barrier for his family and mine to get out—he said that they didn't know your group's exact location. They had an idea, but they had lost you at some point. How was that?" Gauge asks.

"I guess we did a good job getting from the Tongue to that cellar to rest before our assault," he answers.

"So you had come up by river," I reflect. "They suspected as much."

"They did, huh? We'll have to improve our camouflage," the captain sighs. I can't imagine the pressure he's under to lead an attack against such an all-seeing foe.

"Suspicion is fine," Gauge says encouragingly. "They couldn't pinpoint your location. That has to be the best you can expect to do against their imaging systems."

"And the barrier is no problem for any of us since we don't have chips," Red adds. "That's another plus."

Red is right. Not having chip implants gives us an edge. Our force could easily be lost among the bustle of bodies during the rush hours or buzz hour in Miles. The BOTs in the choppers above couldn't find us when they first started searching for us. If they didn't know to be looking for anyone, then small clusters of us moving through the crowds toward EPA 12-1 would go unnoticed.

"Dad, I have an idea. When Crewe and Cy first brought Evvie and me into Sheridan, they had us go into the school during passing time to get lost amongst the heat signatures. What if on the day that we choose to attack, we had all the residents of Sheridan travel far outside of the town in the direction of Miles. There would be so many heat signatures; they wouldn't know which ones belonged to soldiers."

"Not bad, Sydney," my father starts, "but you're operating under the assumption that they wouldn't open fire on anyone and everyone who crosses our city limits in the direction of theirs. I know they've been watching us closely, expecting that we'll come for the rest of the Neocropolis residents."

My father flashes a glance to the boys in the back through the rearview mirror. "As they see it, you all attacked them from within when you broke out. And you killed members of their forces, right?" Without meaning to, I catch Gauge's eyes.

He nods, and then lowers his head.

"There's no shame in doing what you needed to do to be free," my father says. "Freedom is an unalienable right, Gauge. They had no right to take it from you, or from anyone else." My father searches for more assurance for my friend. "Look at it this way—it sounds like your escape may have saved my life and the lives of the seeksmen who were with me. Without your distraction in Neocropolis, they may have found us that very night."

"I didn't mean for anyone to die," Gauge says. "I know I act tough but...I thought the floor above Innocence was just the EPA, and that it'd be empty that time of night."

"We know you didn't try to, Gauge," Red says, avoiding the word kill as if that'll help his roommate forget. "But the problem now is that they might think we did try to. Right, Captain?"

My father made a brief effort to comfort Gauge, but has since moved on to planning our attack. "If we were to make your move, Sydney, we would risk losing an awful lot of innocent people. It would become more and more dangerous for our citizens the closer they got to Miles. And if they were spared, we may not even have the fuel to get them home."

"What if we could be hidden in the river before Sheridan citizens had to travel that much? It wouldn't be too dangerous then," I argue.

"Wouldn't work," my father maintains. "Apparently, they suspected we were in the river. They'll be sure to catch us between infrared or satellite images if they are watching more closely, which you can bet they are."

"Would it make a difference which they catch you by?" Red asks genuinely.

My father scratches the shadow on his chin. "They had to have been monitoring the wilderness between Sheridan and Miles carefully, whether by infrared systems or a man's eye behind the satellite images. Probably both." He shakes his head. He cuts into his own disillusionment. "But we may have an advantage if they stay trained on the Tongue. They don't know that we know that they knew we traveled up it."

"Come again, sir?" Red asks politely. The question is on all of our minds.

"They probably think that we believe we fooled their technology by traveling up the river," the captain explains.

"Right," Red follows. "So they'll expect you to use it again."

"Sheridan has north-flowing rivers to its west and east, both of which flow into the Yellowstone right outside of Miles," my father says eagerly. "Their manpower will be focused on watching the Tongue. Meanwhile, we'll be outside of their sights initially, but with the potential to slip into their backyard quickly via the Yellowstone."

"Then the Sheridan citizens wouldn't have to go north toward Miles at all," I say. "We could disappear without the BOTs noticing that those rivers were our vanishing points."

"Not only that," my father clarifies, "but without knowing that we're up to anything in particular, if we space our teams and our citizens well."

"How's that?" Gauge asks.

"We have people that travel out from our town all the time on supply searches and pick-ups from the farms."

"Farms?" I ask.

"Where'd you think we get our meat from, the county's suppliers?" my father teases.

"Do you think it could work?" Red asks the captain.

"I think Gauge was right. This idea is about all we have to work with, save for causing a total power outage in Miles, which we haven't been able to accomplish. There are so many backups to power nowadays. Well done, you three. We're on our way to initiating a battle."

Half of me feels like saying *Good, let's do this*, while the other half wants to retract my suggestions by pointing out the evident flaws or major risks. I guess I won't know how I really feel until the heat of the moment arrives. Hopefully, that heat isn't the same one that the fallen seeksmen experienced. That was an acceptable fate for me once, when I had no choice but to throw myself at the claws of death to save Evvie. Now that she's relatively safe, my next objective is to ensure her happiness. Dying won't help that goal be reached.

TWENTY-FIVE

"Evvie, eat your breakfast," I tell my sister for the second time this morning.

"I told you, I'm not hungry."

I recognize my own stubbornness in my little sister. "What's this protest really about, Ev? I know it's not about the toast or your stomach."

"It is about my stomach. Don't I have a right to be nauseated with you and Dad going into Miles again today?"

I wasn't looking for a smart-aleck response when I opened up the conversation, but I can't expect anything different from a worried, angry, and confused teenager. If I have a right to be nauseated, so does she.

"I still don't understand why you have to go," she says. "Last night you said you feel like you have to do all of this for our future, but I was thinking, isn't that our dad's job now?"

"It is Evvie, but it's mine too. I know it's hard to understand, but this is something that I have to do. I'm a part of this now."

"I think you're afraid." Though she looks down at her plate, she makes the statement with enough confidence for me to know she means it, not that she's just made it up as a last-ditch argument.

"Afraid of what?" I ask.

"You're afraid to be happy, Sydney. You could be enjoying this new life but instead, you're seeking out danger and destruction left and right."

I sit down next to my sister and talk to the neon-striped hair that she leaves hanging to hide her face. "I'm not afraid of being happy. It's what this fight is all about. We're working *toward* that. I can't just expect others to pick up the fight for me, Evvie."

Evvie turns her back to me as she takes her dishes away from the table and throws the untouched toast into the trash.

"Where are you off to today?" I ask her, trying to change the subject.

"Church first." My sister takes out her current hostility on the plate and glass that she scrubs.

"I'll come with you next time," I offer.

"Maybe," she says, brushing past me to shove a thick book into a bag. I stand when she turns to make for the door.

"Hey, Evvie..."

The calm in my voice finds its opposite in hers. "Don't! I don't want a hug and an *I love you*, Sydney. I'm tired of the *goodbye in case I don't come back*. I won't do it again because I wouldn't have to if you really loved me enough to stay."

My sister exits and slams the door behind her. I want to go after her, but what can I say that she'll understand? I scratch, "I love you *every* day," on a notepad and bring it into our room.

A dated trigonometry textbook lies on the floor next to her bed. They've placed her in trig? I suppose Evvie is smart and hardworking enough that she may have been enrolled in the same math course on EduWeb as me this year. I imagine I would have been asking her for help. More realistically, I would have found a way to copy her quiz entries. The way I saw it, the only math I needed to be able to do to survive was to accurately count the seconds for the camera to pass.

A piece of paper peeks out of the front cover when I pick up the heavy book. I slip it out and see that it's not math, but a writing assignment. If there were such a class back in Miles, I'd get better marks in handwriting than Evvie would. The paper is titled *Persuasive Essay Outline*. Evvie's topic: *Increasing the Enlisting Age*.

My eyes are drawn to her second main argument: *Why should someone die before they've had a chance to live?* My name is littered throughout her bulleted, supporting details. *Sydney started working at fifteen. Sydney struggled to live on her own at sixteen. Sydney became legally responsible for me at eighteen.* A starred point says: *She's never been able to play sports or be in clubs, spend time with friends or boys, or find out who she really is because she's been busy acting like someone twice her age. No matter how badly they want it, people shouldn't be allowed to volunteer to die before they know what it's like to live.*

Her summary sentence is flawed. I'm not volunteering to die; I'm volunteering to fight. There's a big difference—one my sister is not yet capable of seeing. I replace the paper and return the book to where I found it. Wishing she had let me speak its message, I place the note on her pillow before exiting.

"Hey, is the captain—" My gasp breaks Crewe's question. I know that people in Sheridan don't knock, but they ought to in wartime, especially considering that a BOT member let their self into this home once before. "I'm sorry." The hand he places on my shoulder soothes me, while the grin that cracks across his face reminds me of my feelings for him. "I scared you, huh?"

"You think?" I tease, matching his smile.

"Sorry." The momentary lightheartedness fades. "Has your dad already gone to town?"

"Yeah," I answer. The nerves have returned, but now they're in regards to something worth fearing.

"Do you know if he's set the squadrons?"

"He has," I answer.

"And are we...?"

"No, I'm in my own company."

"Your own? You mean you're not in the captain's group either?"

"He thought I would be safer if I wasn't with him."

"Why?" Crewe asks, too peeved to really consider any answer given.

"Well, because of what happened last time." When he doesn't understand my reference, I elaborate. "Cy and Decklin."

Crewe shakes his head in dissent. "That was different. We had a traitor among us then." He speaks to me as if I have the power to change the groupings. "If your dad is afraid you'll get hurt by being near him, fine, but why not put you with me then?" I have no answer to offer. After a few more paces he asks disapprovingly, "Who *are* you with then?"

"There are so many of us now that I only recognized Jaxon's name. He's from Neocropolis."

"I know Jaxon," Crewe says shortly. "He thinks on his feet. That's good. I assume you'll be in the tail group on your side. That must mean you'll be with a doctor."

"Yeah. The one from Braves."

"I assume you're traveling Bighorn River." I nod. Crewe apparently shares some tactical ideals with my father. "Am I

Powder then?" he asks.

"You're Bighorn too. You and Cheng are co-leading our side."

"I am?" He is both astonished by and satisfied with the decision. "I'm surprised your dad trusts mine and Cheng's tempers separately, let alone together. Who's co-leading the other side with the captain?"

"Braves," I answer briskly. Since the moment he startled me by being here, I've been longing for a comforting hug and for him to tell me that everything is going to be okay today. Instead, his business with me is an unwelcomed interrogation.

"Two town leaders on one side?" Crewe is not sold on the idea.

"Maybe Merick will be on the west side with us. My father didn't have time this morning to list everyone."

"No. Merick will stay behind as usual," Crewe states.

"Why is that?" I ask, interested in this one element of the conversation. "Merick is an experienced Veteran. He's not too old to fight."

"You're right, he's not too old—he's too sick. The cancer has gotten really bad the last few weeks."

"Cancer?"

Crewe nods. "Started in his lungs."

"Will he be okay?" I ask.

"No," Crewe answers with a peculiar, perhaps annoyed, expression. If the answer to my question were obvious to me, I wouldn't have asked it. "This is the wild, Sydney. We don't have treatments for many of the major illnesses. Merick won't live through the end of the year."

Once again, I've learned that Merick has deserved better appreciation from me. "I didn't know," I tell Crewe. "So do deaths out here outnumber the inside?" I ask. "A larger percent of the population, I mean."

"Our number of deaths each year is proportional to the region's average, which exclude the murders of those in their sixtieth year."

Math was never my strong suite, but something is not adding up. "How can they be proportional if the inside has better medicine? Shouldn't their death rate be much lower than Sheridan's when euthanasia isn't being counted?"

"I know you were taught county-created curriculum, but call it what it is, Sydney—murder."

I've always thought of euthanasia of the elderly that way, but maybe it's been too hard to say it that way out loud. "I'll learn more in this final year of my schooling than in all the other years combined," I tell Crewe.

"Wait," he says. "How is it that no one realized you're supposed to be in school for another year?" When I shrug my shoulders, Crewe smiles for a second before he returns to teaching me about the difference in survival rates between the counties and refugees towns.

"Many more county citizens get cancer and other illnesses that can become fatal. That's where the difference lies. Sometimes we wonder if it's natural—due to inside diet, chemicals, et cetera—or if it's by design." I nod, understanding that the counties may be infecting their citizens with deadly diseases. I'm no longer shocked by these facts. "You see, if everybody gets cancer—some several times—then the government has a stronger argument for the murders. The body can't recover from the treatment at older ages, they'll say."

"Before they're old enough to feel much hurt," I say, remembering my grandmother's words to me before her date came up.

"Exactly," Crewe says, thinking I've joined him in the *what the government would tell us* game. When I don't smile with him, he changes the subject. "Ready to head to town?"

"Yeah. I'm ready."

"Care to run there?" Crewe offers, knowing from the years of watching me in the wilderness that I run hard so I'm not able to focus on anything other than my breathing, the rocks in my path, and the branches that threaten to cross me. Crewe doesn't pry about what bothered me a moment ago. He offers me an escape from my problems instead.

"Absolutely," I answer.

Running is more of a necessity than an option, as the captain will be announcing the groups, leaders, and river routes shortly. This run into town is leg one of a lengthy journey whose halfway point—*not* the endpoint—is the main entrance of EPA 12-1.

After the captain's announcement, the teams will gather and pack their concealing and protective outerwear, weaponry, and gasoline, as well as hitch the boat trailers and boats. My father wants all the squadrons to have entered their respective rivers by noon. Since he wants the boats spaced significantly for the sake of satellite imaging, we'll have to either pack hastily or drive fast. Probably both.

The Bighorn River battalion has more miles to cover than those traveling the Powder River, but Bighorn flows more quickly and we'll be able to travel at a higher speed, with only four to a boat on our side as compared with five to most of the boats on the east side.

During the ten-hour boat ride, three members of my squadron will sleep while the other drives. I about laughed when my father told me that this morning. You want me to *sleep* on the brink of battle? Then he explained that Galvesten has pills to help us rest so we can be strong, alert, and precise throughout whatever nighttime combat will ensue. It's an extra bonus that the pills will lower our body temperatures a little during the longest leg of the journey, lessening our visibility to the BOTs.

The tarp we'll use to camouflage against the backdrop of the water will serve a purpose in relation to infrared imaging as well. They have each been lined with acetate sheets. My father and the seeksmen didn't have these when they traveled the Tongue to attempt to rescue me, but they did have neoprene suits. Even with additional suits from Braves and Idaho, we have less than half of what we'd need to cover everyone.

Sometime after each group's respective river merges with the Yellowstone, they'll have to ditch their motor and use only paddles or an oar. The boats on the Powder side have to paddle against the Yellowstone's current for a bit. They'll need more than one man at a time for that job, so they are getting two suits per boat.

On my side, only the man driving or rowing, in suit, will be able to be outside of the thermal energy blocking tarp. I'm worried about the chance one rower with only starlight to guide him stands against time. We need so many things just to keep us hidden, and all they ever seem to need is the time to find us, which this set up unavoidably allows them.

I wish we could take back the time the county has stolen from us and from our loved ones. If I were granted one second for every year that my grandmother would have lived after her sixtieth birthday, for every year my mother would have lived if she hadn't felt the need to commit suicide, for every year that I was separated from my father, who I believed to be dead, and for the years that Evvie and I spent apart under the jurisdiction of county parenting laws, I might have an extra minute to advance toward EPA 12-1 without an onslaught of BOTs. That single minute could make a world of a difference.

"Sydney," Crewe calls from a few paces behind me. He releases a frustrated grunt when I don't answer. "You're pushing too hard." Soon there is less time between the heavy thumps of his boots against the pavement. "Slow down. Save it, Sydney," he urges. I try to push myself to go faster yet and, judging by Crewe's irritated bellow, it works.

Just like with my initial capture, looking over my shoulder at Crewe allows him to capitalize. This time, he reaches out and grabs my bicep rather than lunging for my feet as he did before.

"Let me be!" I yell as I fight off his grip. I don't bother to run again when I'm free of it, however, because Crewe is not the enemy. He never was.

"No," he returns.

"Why not?" I growl.

"Because I never could. That's it." He shrugs. Crewe takes a deep breath, and then wipes the sweat from above his brow with his shirtsleeve. "I didn't know anything about your situation, but from the first time I saw you, Sydney, I knew that I couldn't let you go on living the way you were. Every time I was seeking, I was seeking for you. I wanted to know so badly what plagued you, and I wanted to do what I could to make it better. Things haven't changed any since then.

"Some might try to pick your brain, but I know that's the last thing you want. My brother tried a different route to get to you, the same I see your friend Red using. The jokes work, and

I like to see you smile." Crewe steps toward me and gently lifts my chin. "I do," he says as he gently strokes my cheek with his thumb. "But that happiness is desperate, not natural. It doesn't last. I want to make your pain go away forever, Sydney. Fighting is my avenue for reaching you, but you have to help me help you."

"What are you trying to say, Crewe?" I ask, somewhat softened by the spell of his touch.

"Slow down. Just take a breath," he pleads. "I know you couldn't before. I know what it's like to be responsible for someone you love—the only one you love. But you can ease the burden now. I won't let you be unless you let *it* be."

It's easy to pull away from him when I understand what he means to say. "Are you trying to tell me not to fight?"

"No, Sydney," he says, frustrated. "I'm telling you to be calm, patient. Don't rile yourself up so much that you can't recover physical or emotionally later, when it counts. I know you have a lot of spite—God knows we all do—but push it aside for now. Let it build at the right time, and *then* use it to propel you."

"Yeah. Fine," I agree.

"I wouldn't dare tell you that you can't fight for your sister. I tried that once, and I got tackled against the gravely ditch," he teases.

Sure, Cy goofiness made me smile and Red seemed to pick up where he left off, but the lightheartedness in Crewe is more rare, and extraordinarily precious to me, so I make it last. "You deserved it."

His smirk opens to a wide grin as he steps in close and whispers in my ear. "I didn't mind all that much."

Before he's pulled far enough away to see my flushed

face, I spin and take off toward town, unintentionally whipping my ponytail in his face.

"I meant to kiss you," he yells ahead.

"No time," I yell without turning back. My smile and ease are steadfast until I reach the laundromat from where the large gathering of soldiers at The Lot can be seen. Oddly, I'm not ashamed of my happiness on the threshold of war. It's given me something new to fight for. Me. Like Evvie mapped out for her school paper, my life is not a loss. I can still be happy. I just need the time. No one is going to give it to me. I have to do what I can to take it.

Twenty-Six

A splash of cold water on my face rattles me awake. Someone else under the tarp shushes me.

"Where are we?" I whisper.

"We're here," one of the men says.

Here? Judging by their whispers and the steady, alternating strokes of the oar in the water, we must be very near to EPA 8-9. Galvesten's sleeping pill really worked this time. He must have been flirting with safety when upping the dose of the sedation ingredient. My body sure feels like it's been completely comatose the last ten hours.

"How do you feel, Sydney?"

This voice I know, but it can't be. "Red?" I ask, shocked to be saying his name.

"You guessed it," he replies cheerfully. He is shushed harshly by one of the members of my squadron.

"What are you doing here?" My father was very clear that Red was too young, and would not be allowed to enlist without parental consent.

"I had to come, Sydney," he says seriously. "I was raised in Neocropolis. It's more than friends left behind down there; they're as much my family as my real family is." I understand the need he feels to help.

"Red here says he snuck under the tarp and rode in the boat," one of the soldiers says.

"It's true, Tate. It's too dark, but I probably already have the bruises to prove it. I sure feel them. Crewe drives like a maniac," Red says.

"You were in Crewe's trailer? How did you get in our boat?" I ask Red.

"When they stopped, I got out and hid. I ran north, but far enough away from the river that none of the boats could see me as they passed. After the third boat passed around the bend where I'd stopped to hide, I slipped into the water so that the last boat's driver would have no choice but to lift me out."

"I already reprimanded him for jeopardizing everything by running along the river without a suit," Tate says. "I also briefed him on the plan since we had no choice but take him along. I got to spend the rest of the day living the rumors I'd heard about crazy Red back in Neocropolis," Tate says bitterly. Tate began as our squadron driver, so he hasn't had much rest if he's been listening to Red talk for so long. I bet he wished Galvesten had sent an extra sleeping pill.

"Is Jaxon rowing now?" I ask. Just as I ask the question, I feel the nose of our boat brush onto land.

"Not anymore," Jaxon replies. "Stay down, and stay quiet," he orders. My groggy body falls clumsily against the others as Jaxon tugs the boat farther onto the riverbank. "Not yet." Metal clanks as he lines the grass with our weaponry. My senses recognize some fearful things after my familiarity with them over the past few weeks.

"For you and the kid," the older doctor from Braves says as he passes me a pair of padded vests.

"No," Red says. "I'm not supposed to be here. Give mine to whoever was supposed to have it."

"Oh shut up and put it on," the man says, taking one of the vests back from me and shoving it against Red's chest.

"There are only two?" I ask. "What about the three of you?" When nothing but silence follows my question, I decide I ought to shut up as well and do as I was instructed. I gave my bulletproof vest to Evvie after we rescued her from Miles the first time. I did without one then; I'll have to trust that my group mates will be safe without one now.

Moonlight accompanies Jaxon's face as he ducks under the tarp to give us his last-minute directives. "On my mark you come out, grab a gun, and sprint through the barrier. I guarantee they'll have infrared sensors lining the barrier, so expect company soon after. That means run with your weapon drawn, but if you approach a crowd, tuck it away and blend. Keep eyes out for each other. Questions?" When none of us raise any, Jaxon replaces the tarp and steps away.

Of course, I have questions. I have a million questions. What if the infrared sensors are connected to a bomb, which will target us the second we emerge from this tarp? What if, like other counties in Region Two, Miles has the technology to electrify even those without a chip as they cross the barrier, and has incited that power? What if someone from our company gets shot? When Jaxon said to keep eyes out for each other, did he mean that we should try to help them?

If one of us is pinpointed by them, hit, and falls, what use is a rescue attempt? In my eyes, there's no heroism in adding another body to the casualty count. I have to admit I'll be more likely to run away from a wounded soldier than toward them. That wouldn't be true for Crewe, though. When he thought I'd been shot by enemy fire, he sprinted to me and lunged across my body to protect me from further damage.

"Two minutes," Jaxon says.

I hope all the other teams have made it to their entering locations safely too. By Jaxon's watch, the entire company will be attempting to cross the barrier in under two minutes. It was Crewe who claimed that we'd all have better chances if we kept the county manpower dispersed.

Those of us who make it across safely will ambush EPA 12-1. Groups such as mine, who have entering locations far from EPA 12-1, will come as reinforcements to the battle which, by then, will be well underway. It's no wonder my father placed me in the boat that he did. I'll be in the back lines, and I'll be with Jaxon, the most promising new addition to Sheridan's army.

Part of me wishes we had broken the barrier a few minutes ago when we came ashore. The sooner we arrive to the scene of the battle, the more likely we are to be successful in freeing the prisoners from darkness. But, as my father reiterated this morning, if one group crosses the barrier before the others, it would either draw extra BOTs toward that team, making them dead bait, or, if the other units remained stationed, it will put them on higher alert, meaning more could be killed before ever reaching Neocropolis. We can't afford either situation. Crossing the barrier early would be a grave mistake.

"Now!" Jaxon orders in a hoarse whisper.

The boat is unstable as we burst from under the tarp and fight to find our bearings in the dark with, at least in my case, a half-asleep body. Red hands me a rifle, which I draw immediately. *God, show us you're on our side tonight*, I pray.

Jaxon's dark, neoprene suit blends almost too well with the night sky. I fight to follow his outline with my eyes. He's inside the barrier, and he's still running. One of my questions has been answered. Either Miles' barrier isn't yet capable of electrifying people without chips, or the county didn't foresee an attack tonight and turn it on.

Just as I cross EPA 8-9, I see a red, pulsing light on its wall facing the river. An alarm has been sounded. I know from climbing atop EPA 7-8 for many years that the rooftops don't house constantly vigilant snipers, as they perhaps should. The instant we crossed, they knew. If they were already stationed outside the building instead of watching media screens inside, they could take us out before we had a chance to get away and blend with the crowds. If they were smarter, I could be dead right now.

Jaxon clearly sees the same group of Miles' citizens that I see. He leads us toward them. The streets will become busier and busier as we cut across the county. This is buzz hour, when everyone starts gathering for nightlife affairs. There are no spotlights beaming from choppers overhead, so it should be easy for us to become lost in the crowd.

On the flip side, I know that if they lose us, they'll refocus their energy where they know we are most likely headed. The BOTs don't have to catch us now because they can beat us there.

I'm glad Crewe got me to stop running so hard this morning, and that Galvesten developed a pill that could knock me out. My legs have come back to life. They feel strong, powerful, and sure beneath me. I swerve swiftly through the people, careful not to let any see me long enough to recognize the weapon I hold tightly against my body. For once, I'm glad that they're too caught up in their gossip and bustle to notice me.

Somehow, I recall Jaxon advising us to keep an eye out for each other. I feel an eerie, overwhelming need to locate Red. Like he said, he grew up in Neocropolis, not in the streets of Miles. What if he loses sight of all of us, and doesn't know where to go?

When I spin around, the only member of my group that I see is Jaxon. I suppose with my speed and keen crowd navigation, I have passed all the others.

Noticing that I've slowed, Jaxon looks over at me. "I don't see Red," I yell to him.

"What?" he yells through the blurred faces.

"Red!" I shout. How I wish they didn't blare music from every last hub in the county's nucleus. Jaxon joins me in the search for our youngest team member, but it's short-lived when terror begins rippling through the crowd around us.

"Bomb! There's been a bombing!" a frantic woman screams. One of the front-line teams must have gotten into the EPA building and ignited their explosive. Jaxon starts to wave me on, but I've already turned to push my way through the frenzied crowd. If the panicked citizens don't clue Red in on the direction he needs to go, the smoke from the explosion soon should.

I notice a pair of young men from Miles running parallel to me. "Who do you think it is?" one asks the other. They'd never guess it's people of our own nation, former citizens of their very county, who have attacked. They also don't know the horrors that justify such an uprising.

Once I'm on the opposite side of the county's center, I start to feel vulnerable, even with the bulletproof vest. Jaxon, who has caught up to me now, doesn't seem to have any reservations. He is determined to see his friends freed and will stop at nothing to make that happen.

We're less than a half-mile from EPA 12-1 when scattered gunshots become audible. "Those aren't rifles," Jaxon yells to the others behind us. His words seem to squeeze my heart into a tight ball. My father, Crewe, Gauge, Edyn, and so many more whom I care about could be on the other end of the BOTs' sights.

Flashes of light enflame the sky above EPA 12-1 and linger in the smoke that saturates the air. Gauge's elevator bomb didn't produce smoke like this when we escaped from Neocropolis. This explosive was meant to destroy more than the barrier between the BOTs and the innocent people below. Unlike Gauge's bomb, it is no accident if this bomb succeeds in taking out the county agents in the process of freeing the prisoners.

I recognize Officer J. by his tattered suit as he blows by me. Although he was officer Q.'s right-hand, he too was a Level One or Two prisoner of Neocropolis. I'm glad our force didn't mistakenly kill him.

Not ten seconds go by before another Neocropolis resident comes sprinting toward us. "Go back!" a woman's voice shrieks. "Your orders are to turn back!" Astonishingly, it's Andriette, the woman I worked with in the laundry facility on Level Three. How did we get to people from the deepest levels? "Sydney," she says when she recognizes me, "it's done. Your whole company is fleeing. You need to get across the barrier *now,*" she urges the four of us, Tate and the doctor having now caught up.

"Are you coming with us?" I ask her.

"I'm staying," she replies solidly. I don't argue with her. She knows what she needs to do.

"We lost Red," I tell her.

"I'll find him," she says abruptly.

"We came across EPA 8-9," I say so that she has some direction in finding him, but Andriette has hit full speed again on the other side of us.

"Where can we find someone driving at this time of night?" Jaxon asks me.

"The streets belong to the people after ten," I answer.

"We need to carjack someone," Jaxon says hurriedly.

"It'll be reported, and they'll shut it down," I tell him.

"Someone you know then. Does anyone know someone with a car?"

"I know someone," I realize. "She's close too."

"Lead the way." Jaxon gives me a little shove, and we take off back toward the city center.

The streets have cleared considerably, but some, mostly men, remain gathered. Only now, instead of facetious numbness, they are alert and aware. Finally, something has awakened the drones.

Miles is the only county in Region Two, and maybe beyond, that still has a decent number of single-family houses. There simply isn't enough space for them, unless you're quite wealthy.

Through inheritance, the person we're going to see is wealthy enough to own both a house and a car. Most would argue that she had so much there was nothing she could've needed, but they'd be wrong. All the money and possessions in the world couldn't bring her happiness. Finally, that changed one day. It wasn't a possession, but a person to love, that the woman needed. She needed my sister.

Surprise is already written on Merideth Layton's face when she opens the door to unexpected visitors, but when she recognizes me, shock and disbelief overtake her.

"*Sydney?*" My name comes out in a whisper obstructed by the tightness of her throat.

"Ma'am, we need your car," Jaxon says straightaway.

"You're…you're dead," Merideth says, not hearing a word my leader has spoken.

"It's all lies, Merideth. I was locked below EPA 12-1 for knowing too much. Our father is alive too."

"Our? Where's Evvie? Is she okay? She's been missing for weeks." Merideth felt as if she were my sister's mother. The hysteria she's been feeling is very apparent in her untimely questions. "When you turned up dead, I thought…" Tears now drown out her words, giving me the chance to speak.

"Evvie's safe. Merideth, we need your car."

Merideth's face twists, and she moves back slightly. "You have a gun, Sydney," she states with unnatural calm. Merideth has never agreed with my sentiments and she disliked the impact they had on Evvie, but I've never seen her look at me the way she is now. She's afraid and distrusting of me.

"They had Evvie in the underground prison too, Merideth, and they messed with her memory. They're the ones not to be trusted!" I yell. "Now please, we need your help."

Merideth's tablet sounds. "It hasn't stopped," she says, referring to the call or message. "Sydney, what have you done?"

"She's aided in the freeing of at least a hundred innocent people," Jaxon says, his patience exasperated. "I was one of them. Listen, they're going to find and kill us if we don't get out now."

"Auntie Meri?" Brynn calls from the top of the stairs, horrified.

"It's okay, sweetie. Go back up to bed. I'll come up in a

minute." Merideth grabs her tablet and raises her car from the garage under her driveway. She starts it from her tablet too, but pushes through us to unlock it. She presses her thumb to the print reader above the door handle, and the doors unlock for us. "Where are you taking it?" she asks, ready to type the destination in her tablet.

"Nowhere it will take us," Jaxon says. "You need to unlock it to be driven manually." With a few additional strokes of her tablet, she enables manual use of her car for the maximum duration.

"Can we trust you not to say anything?" Tate asks.

Merideth nods. "What am I supposed to say if they find out?" she asks.

"Tell them I threatened you," I say. "They'll believe it."

Merideth follows me around to the other side of the car. "Be careful," she says, her eyes welling again. "Take care of Evvie and give her my love."

"She already has it," I say matter-of-factly before shutting the door.

"Drive slowly through town," I tell Jaxon. Though our hearts are racing with the need to be out of enemy territory, we have to travel nonchalantly through it in order to avoid raising suspicions.

I wonder if the other teams are exiting by vehicle too. With the possibility of choppers overhead, the boats aren't any good, and on foot is even worse. After tonight, they surely won't let anyone get away if they can help it.

This tiny car doesn't give us much cover and without the acetate sheets, we're defenseless against infrared technology. I hope we haven't made a mistake in choosing this mode of transportation. Only time will tell. Unfortunately, time never seems to be on our side.

Twenty-Seven

Jaxon's hardly able to increase our getaway speed after we cross the underground electric line around the county. The government decided on the wire rather than an electric fence because such would be imposing. Instead, they strategically transplanted a variety of trees around the county to help protect it from an outside land invasion, or so they said. It sure serves a double purpose in preventing anything sizeable from getting out.

The car takes a beating from several low-hanging branches, but Jaxon manages to maneuver the compact car through the trees and thicket.

"Who's the best marksman?" our leader asks the three of us. I'm not sure how long Tate had been locked up in Neocropolis before being freed, but he was from Miles, so the only shooting he could have done beforehand would be at the indoor gun range on the top floor of the sporting building. He's surely been shooting in Sheridan the last few days, but so have the rest of us. I assume the doctor from Braves has had shooting experience, but he isn't speaking up. "I hit my targets pretty well," I say finally.

"Moving?" Jaxon asks.

"I've never tried," I admit.

"Well, you will today." A popping sound makes my heart skip a beat. Stupid. It was only the trunk being opened. "Fold that seat down so she can get in the trunk," Jaxon tells the men in the back. "I want you to stay low and to the side so the car's frame gives you some protection. If something comes after us, you shoot at it."

"What if it's another one of our groups, or a group of escapees from Neocropolis?" I ask.

"You two help her decipher," Jaxon instructs the other two men. "Keep your eye trained," he tells me.

Pushing the button on the door, I release my seat belt. I pass my rifle to Tate, who is squatted on the floor. He slides it into the trunk, and I crawl in after it.

The shape of the trunk doesn't protect me well, but it's the only bunker I have. I eye-up to my weapon and practice shifting it to trees as we pass.

About ten percent of soldiers die by friendly fire, and that statistic comes from forces that have been trained well and trained together. Neither case is true for this Sheridan militia. We came together hastily by necessity. More time training and in larger groups would have tipped off the agents, who use imaging technology to spy on us. The former Neocropolis residents also feared the agents might impart Level-Five torture on our left-behind friends if they caught us training and wanted to threaten us through them.

"Get down!" Jaxon shouts as he slams on the brakes. The tires squeal, and I'm thrashed across the trunk as the car suddenly spins back the direction we came from. Even before I gain my bearings, I understand why. Headlights shine into the trunk and blind my focus as I fumble for my rifle.

This black utility vehicle came from the opposite direction we were traveling, so it's certainly not someone from our battalion driving it. I steady the nose of my gun on the edge of the trunk. There's also no way this bulky vehicle came through the tree line around Miles. I press the butt of the gun firmly into my shoulder. A county black-operations team was stationed out here, waiting for trespassers on this route between Miles and Sheridan. I cock the rifle.

"Sydney," Jaxon urges as the vehicle gains on us.

I know. I should be thinking of Evvie's capture, the murders of Cy and Decklin, and all the wrongful imprisonments, but instead I'm remembering that my father, a good man, used to be part of this force. I'm thinking of the agent who told me where to find the seeksmen when we escaped from Neocropolis. He bargained with us to get his family out of Miles. How many other agents are following orders out of necessity, but don't believe in the system they're supposedly protecting? Most present on my mind is the fact that they're not shooting at us, although they've likely spotted the open trunk and the muzzle of my gun, which protrudes from it.

"Shoot, damn it!" someone yells.

I adjust my gun. My team will think I missed, but I'll know I hit my target. I pull the trigger, and the cartridge explodes from the chamber. Hit. The vehicle sinks on the side of the tire I blew, swerves a little, and continues to follow us. I unload three more rounds on the other front tire before deflating it.

"Pull her in here," Jaxon orders. Tate grabs my jacket and rips me inside the car as it whips back into our original direction again. "Stay down," our leader warns us. He sinks lower into his seat and maximizes the car's speed.

As we pass the now-stopped utility vehicle, we are

bombarded with gunfire. My flesh seems to burn with the terror that spreads through me from the sounds of the successive rounds. I crouch into the space between the back bench seat and the center console, wrapping my arms tightly around my head. This is no game we're playing. This is war. I should have shot through their windshield. It's like Edyn said, when facing county agents, there's no waiting out the punches. Kill or be killed.

"Anybody hit?" Jaxon demands.

"No," Tate answers after checking.

"We've got a flat," Jaxon says. I can feel the ire in his voice. I made a dangerous mistake. Now the BOT's predicament has become ours, only they have superior artillery. The fire ceases.

"They're turning around," Jaxon informs us. In other words, we need to keep our heads low. They're coming after us. Our car careens severely as we drive the flat tire across the rumpled road. I imagine a straight path is difficult for them to maintain too, but I may have actually given them an advantage by lowering the second tire. Their vehicle is level, and ours is pulling hard to the left. I've done everything wrong, and so, the chase is far from over.

"You see that?" Tate calls to our driver.

Jaxon responds immediately to the dread in Tate's question by looking in the review mirror.

"Holy—"

"What is it?" Tate asks.

Like a kid who stretches their chip across the electric barrier just to know what the pain feels like, I tentatively lift my head just enough to turn and look at the sight behind us. A dark, boxy vehicle wider and twice the height of the utility vehicle plays backup for the BOT.

I watch as the monstrous vehicle slowly emerges as it sways to its left. This vehicle hasn't come as backup at all. It's come to get the job done itself. Is this how my life ends? They'll fire without knowing that Demetri Harter's daughter is one of the passengers of this lowly electric car. That's assuming they still have interest in keeping me alive to get to my father. That assumption could be unviable if the resistance was this bad or worse when the captain's team arrived at EPA 12-1. My father may already be dead.

Rapid gunfire erupts again. I close my eyes and tuck my head into the center of my being. *I'm sorry Evvie*, I think.

"They're shooting at it!" Tate screams over the blasts.

"What?" Jaxon replies.

"Goliath is shooting at the BOT. It must be one of ours!"

I lift my head just in time to see a standard Miles County garbage truck sideswipe the BOT utility vehicle, causing it to roll off the road into the ditch. The driver honks the garbage truck's horn and flashes its high beams in celebration of our rescue. Likewise, the three men in my car holler and cheer. With the miraculous aid of another Sheridan group, our fate just changed from certain death to life. Well, extended life, anyway.

The cabin of the garbage truck illuminates. When it gets closer to us, I see that it's Crewe, my Crewe, who came to our rescue. Jaxon clicks a dome light on in our car to identify our team to theirs. Crewe communicates a question to Jaxon, who answers it with a nod and a thumb pointed backward over his shoulder. The question could be *Are there others with you?* or *Is everyone all right?* but somehow I feel he's asked *Where's Sydney?* Crewe responds to Jaxon's gesture with a nod, and then waves us along.

We put over a mile of distance between the BOT utility

vehicle and our two teams before Jaxon wrenches the car to the side of the road. "Bring your weapons and ammo," he says.

Tate is the first to abandon the car. He sees that Crewe has opened the tailgate ram, so he leads all but Jaxon to the back of the garbage truck. Our squadron leader heads to the cab instead, where the other leaders are. A soldier from Crewe's team quietly helps us into the hopper. Then again, maybe he's from another squadron as there are about ten troops in the load, all equally silent.

Then the tailgate closes, I'm drawn to the only light in the trailer. The doctor from my team is drawn to the flashlight's beam too. He immediately pushes into the huddle around a soldier, who bleeds from the abdomen. My eyes don't adjust in time to make out the other faces in the trailer, but one of them recognizes me.

"Sydney." A male whose stature doesn't seem to be much more than my own embraces me quickly.

"Red?" I ask hopefully.

"*Red*? It's Gauge. Red's not out here," he reminds me.

"You didn't hear?" I ask. I'm afraid I have bad news for Red's best friend.

"Hear what?" Gauge asks nervously.

"Red hitched a ride to Bighorn Lake in Crewe's boat trailer. He hid while they launched, ran north along the river while other boatloads passed, and then waded in before my boat came along."

"Wait." Gauge takes a second to let the impossible settle. "Well, then where is he?"

There it is. The question I don't want to have to answer. "We lost him in the crowd at the county's center. I saw Andriette though. She said she would find him."

"That doesn't mean she will, or that she'll even try if it compromises her chance of making it to her family. Idiot kid," Gauge grumbles, but I know he's more worried than mad.

"Aren't others from Crewe's team with us?" I ask. It seems the whole load quiets down right before my question.

"His team was in a bad spot. Crewe is the only one who didn't get shot. Jarod's going to make it though," Gauge says. Jarod, one of the men that helped pull others out of Neocropolis when I escaped, must be the man the others were attending to.

"The others?" I whisper.

"One died on site and the other right before we picked your team up." This sad news explains the eerie silence when my team came aboard. A combination of reverence and dismay had come over them from the death of a comrade.

I don't want to know now who the deceased men are. My father and Red are the two men I care about most now. No one here has a better idea of Red's situation than I do, but they may know how the groups traveling up the other river faired.

"Have we heard anything about any of the other groups?" I ask Gauge.

"We probably only escaped a few minutes before you did, Sydney. I don't even know how we got out. We've been focused on keeping people alive. Now just Jarod."

Right. It's a good thing my group added a doctor with a small emergency kit. Hopefully, Jarod will make it to one of the hideaways where Della or Doctor McClain will have a fuller kit. I hope they aren't already busy trying to save the lives of other soldiers.

Sharing what we know is too important for it to wait until we get there. There's no way to get the big picture yet, but between the lot of us in here, we can create a snapshot. "Which squadron is everyone from?" I ask blindly. No responds initially so I decide to summarize my group's story first. "I was with Jaxon, who's with Crewe in the cab now. Someone I knew in Neocropolis relayed orders for us to retreat before we'd made it to 12-1. We got a car from someone I knew and weaved through the barrier. A BOT utility vehicle surprised us only a couple minutes outside the barrier. There was gunfire from both sides. None of us were injured, but that's because you all came along."

"I'm with Rodney," Gauge says. "He's up front too. Two guys from the boat in front of us stopped us from joining the fight just as we reached the back lines. Our foursome, intact, plus two others, sprinted northeast of our entering point, closer to the EPA and our fighting soldiers. I passed some people from Neocropolis, who said they were to scatter into the county and make the horrors of their imprisonment known to the Miles' citizens. Seconds later, we ran into Crewe and helped him with Jarod and the other man who'd been shot. Crewe hotwired this garbage truck, we loaded into it, and he drove us across the barrier. It felt like we went underground." Others in the group seem to agree with Gauge's theory.

"Me and two others here are from Neocropolis Level One," a man says. He clears his throat. "The direction to stay in Miles and spread the word about Neocropolis didn't reach all of us."

Sure, I think. Based on the level these three lived on, that statement can't be taken for credible.

"Say, Sydney?" the man calls. "Who was the Neocropolis resident you ran into out there?"

"Andriette, Level Three," I answer. "Why?"

"Never mind," he says passively. Everyone wants to know something about the people they care for.

"Were any residents shot during the first break?" I ask anxiously. I remember Edyn taking off, and then there was that sound.

"We just found out about the first escape. We were there, no doubt, but our memories of that night were erased. We just assumed that mischief occurred, and that's why people were missing from our level. We thought they'd been moved down."

"I was in Cheng's group," a militiaman provides. Good, Cheng's group was close to the frontline. The others from our side of the river who were involved in the fighting were Crewe, who is in the cab, Jarod, who is wounded and unconscious, a man who was shot and now lies dead in this very vehicle, and another who died on the battleground. This man's account of the events is the best I'll get until I can talk to Crewe.

"One of the Powder groups had just blown the hole when we got out of our boat," the man tells us. "Firing had already started by the time we got in range. Cheng had just turned to order us to draw our weapons when a few of them grabbed him and Rhoma."

I hadn't noticed it, but Cheng should have been sitting in the cab with Crewe. He wasn't, because they have him. But with shots having already been released, why would they have captured rather than killed Cheng and Rhoma? Maybe they seized him since he was rather high in the seeksmen's chain of command. That gives me hope for my father, who led the heavily fired-upon Powder side, if Ted and his agents are still set on gaining information rather than a higher casualty count.

"One came at me too," the man says, "but I hit him." I know he's not referring to a hit with his fist. He did what I couldn't—he shot one of them. *Someone.* "The two of us got closer, but then a stream of people came rushing out of the EPA, frantically scattering every which way." As with before, the first ones to escape had to have been the Innocents. I can picture their hysterical frenzy, especially the little ones, who have never been more terrified in their lives.

"The BOTs were very disorganized," Cheng's team member says. "Some captured prisoners, while others fired upon them or us. It was hard for us to take any of the re-capturers out with the citizens trapped in their grasps. Before the crowd hit us, we each shot a stationary agent who was firing on the Powder men, but then fire was returned our way. Thank God, they missed in the chaos. After that, the order to retreat was given. That's when we caught up with Rodney's group."

"Was it the captain that gave that order?" I ask anxiously.

"Yes, it was your father," the man says.

"But he'd been shot," a new voice says.

Shot? Instant panic constricts my chest, and I'm unable to breath. In my prior experience with Cy and Decklin, getting shot by a BOT equates to death.

TWENTY-EIGHT

A bit of grumbling tells me the unknown speaker wasn't supposed to disclose that my father had taken a bullet. Anger entwines itself with the terror running through me. "Where was he shot?" I demand. "Did he make it out?" No answer. "Did anyone see if he fell back with the others?" I yell, my throat dry and burning. Still, no one answers. I'll make him tell me what he saw, even if it's news I don't want to hear.

I take a powerful step to find and press the man who told me my father had been shot for more information, but Gauge reaches out and takes hold of my shoulder. "Calm down, Sydney."

"Don't touch me," I fume. "You knew," I accuse him, and judging by his silence, rightly so.

"I was ordered not to tell you," Gauge says, defending himself. There's alarm in his voice, but he's not hurt by my attack.

"By who?" I demand, but as soon as I've asked the question, I know the answer. I turn and stomp toward the wall closest to the cab of the garbage truck, not caring that I've plowed into a couple of troops. Thinking speed would be my greatest ally tonight, I selected a lighter, more flexible boot from the storehouse. Even so, I wind up and kick at the wall of the garbage truck load as if I wore combat boots as heavy as Crewe's.

"What are you doing?" someone grumbles. I make a few more thuds against the wall. "Talking to him now isn't going to do us any good," the man says.

"He's right, Sydney," Gauge agrees. "Crewe won't stop. He'll want to get to your father and get help for Jarod as soon as possible."

"This truck is a large enough target as it is," Tate says. "We sure don't need to make it an easier one to hit by stopping."

I lean against the wall and slump down to the floor. This can't be happening. Evvie and I just got our father back. We need him now. *I* need my father. I refuse to lose him for real.

Except for some hushed chatter at the other end, it is mostly silent, making the minute pass slowly. When I've finally cooled down, I decide to devote my energy to something that might actually help. *Please, God, let him be okay*, I say over and over in my head. *And Jarod too*, I add, beginning to realize how selfish I've been.

Footsteps approach me, and a man excuses himself in whispers as he shuffles around other soldiers in the dim light. He slides down the wall to sit beside me. Without looking over at him, I know it's Gauge. "You saw Andriette out there?" he asks.

"Yeah," I say. I've just had an embarrassing, selfish tantrum and yet Gauge has decided to come sit by my side. I should apologize or thank him for putting up with me, but I'm more comfortable in my scowl.

"Anyone else?"

"Officer J. and a couple of others, but I didn't know them," I tell him.

Gauge sighs. "I saw a few people too, from levels as deep as Three, but I didn't see my dad, and neither did anyone else so far," Gauge says. "The Innocents over there said they never knew of any additions, which can't be good."

Does my self-centeredness know no end? The man from Cheng's group had clearly told us that the BOTs fired upon many of the Neocropolis escapees, yet Gauge's father did not cross my mind. In fact, I haven't thought about his well-being since Gauge told Braves about him when we met to convince him to join us in tonight's undertaking.

"I'm sorry, Gauge," I offer. "Do you think your dad will go into the county like the other escapees tonight?"

Gauge lets out a heavy exhale. "I don't know." After a beat he adds, "And I'm sorry about your father too, Sydney. I would tell you if I knew anything more, but I didn't see him."

A low horn brings us all to attention, but we don't have a designated leader back here to tell us what to do.

"That's either a warning for the doctor or for us," someone says. "Maybe both. Everybody take hold of your weapons." The truck slows, and people begin to speculate that we've arrived, rather than that we are in danger.

The loading hopper begins opening before the garbage truck has come to a complete stop. We hear the doors of the cab slam shut and rushed footsteps coming toward the back of the trailer. Jaxon and the squadron leader from Idaho appear before the gate has finished opening. In these life and death situations, every second counts. Crewe knows this from Decklin's passing after he was shot in the back by a county agent.

Cy, however, had passed before reaching Galv and Della. For him, there was nothing anyone could do. The man whose lifeless body lies in the load now has a similar fate. There will probably be others tonight who won't make it to a doctoring station. I just hope my father is not one of them.

The doctor who was part of my squadron climbs out of the hopper first. Several shadowy men work together to get Jarod out of the truck as quickly and carefully as possible.

I get to the edge of the hopper just in time to watch the eyes of the Idaho squadron leader change from haste to confusion. He looks at the still body lying on the floor and up at us, who have given the deceased man space. His eyes change again, he cups his mouth, and then walks away. Just as my feet hit the ground, the man lets out an agonizing scream just on the other side of the truck. Gauge, one of his team members, crosses in front of me to go to him. I didn't know the man whose body lies there, nor do I know the team leader who's evidently from the same town, so I decide I have no place in comforting him.

I don't feel guilty about relieving myself of that responsibility. I have things I need answered, so I catch up to the others entering the generator-powered building in front of me. I've now been to three of the seeksmen's carefully planned safe houses. The first was a house, the second a nursing home converted into a hospital, and now this unidentified, boxy building.

Once inside, I see that we're in what used to be a dental or orthodontic clinic. Alix—Sheridan's only female seeksmen, exits a room neighboring the one that the others are entering. She cuts into the crowd just ahead of me, a shiny instrument in her hand. Over the heads of the others, I see her hand the tool to Della. Someone bumps Alix's bandaged arm as they place Jarod on what will become the operating table, and she suppresses a shriek.

"Keep pressure," Della tells one of the men. Her request is frantic, but much too sweet for the situation. "Start the anesthetic drip," she tells Alix. "Crewe, find his name in there," Della says, pointing to a binder on the counter. Crewe was leaning against the wall so close to where I stand in the doorway that I hadn't even seen him, though he was exactly the reason I stepped into this room. "Tell Alix his blood type." In the same breath, she directs Alix to another IV saying, "You get the transfusion going in this one."

"A positive," Crewe says. When he looks up from the binder, I see that his own blood has left his face. He passes me without a word as he hurries through the doorway. Maybe it's because he knows he won't need to say anything for me to follow him, or maybe it's because he doesn't want me to. That possibility doesn't hinder me, however.

"Thanks for ordering everyone *not* to tell me that my father had been shot," I snap to his back as he strides down the hallway.

"Sydney, I'm not in the mood," he returns curtly. Crewe pushes open a door and peels into a room on his right. The faded *Men's* sign on the wall doesn't deter me. I drive the door open with more force than needed and fumble for the light. I flick it on, revealing a sight that tears at my heart. Crewe is crumpled against the wall, his head hangs between his knees, and the same hand he injured by punching a hole in his bedroom wall after Cy died is bloodied.

Deep grief replaces my anger, but I still have to know about my father. "Where?" I ask. "Where was he hit?" When he doesn't respond, I fall to my knees and place my hands around the one that didn't smash the mirror. "Please tell me, Crewe. Please," I beg him.

"Chest, I think," he says, his voice so small it hurts. "But I was far away."

"No. No." I shake my head, but Crewe doesn't look up.

"He can't..."

"Could have been his shoulder," Crewe says. "His orders were strong." Crewe lifts his head some and nods. He turns to me and, for the first time, I see that Crewe has streaks of tears down his face. "I think he'll make it." He lifts his arm around me and wraps me into him, the moisture from his face rubbing off on my cheek. I realize he's holding me more for his comfort than mine when my brave, strong, rescuer completely breaks down.

"It's not even the same room, but I see him, Sydney. I *see* him," Crewe explains. "The captain and I bring Decklin in second but somehow Cy's gone. He's not where I'd laid him a minute earlier. I refused to believe it, so I...I think instead that he's come back to, that he's up and trying to help." Crewe snickers hauntingly. "But then I see him on the floor. Della's asking Decklin his blood type, he's shivering like mad, and the captain...he's pulling a sheet out of the cabinet." Crewe looks up at me and shakes his head. "I couldn't watch him cover my brother. And now, they might both be gone. My whole family." Crewe suddenly snickers again. "Twice over," he says, reminding me of the tragic deaths of each of his birth parents.

"Don't do that. Don't give up on my father. Galvesten was on the Powder side right?" I ask Crewe, begging him to give me hope.

"I miss him so much, Sydney. I wish it were me. Every day, over and over and over, I wish it were me. I traded boats with Cheng, you know," he confesses. "I had to be in those front lines." Something dark surges inside him. "I *needed* to kill as many of them as possible." Crewe thumps his head against the wall. "How did they miss me?"

When I realize Crewe regrets that they didn't shoot him

tonight, I break away from him and shove his shoulders against the wall. "What would Cy say, huh?" I yell. "You think you brother wants that? You think he wants you dead? You brother hasn't stopped trying to *protect* you, and this is how you repay him? By switching places with Cheng and *trying* to screw it all up!"

"My brother can't say anything, want anything, and he sure as hell can't protect me!" Crewe spits. Then anguish overtakes him again. "My brother is dead," he weeps. My heart breaks with him—both due to his sorrows and my own—but I can't let despair take him.

"Look at me," I say, lifting his chin. "When I was in Neocropolis, my roommate asked me about the young man in my life who had passed on. I don't normally believe in that stuff, Crewe, but I believe Cy had come *with me* when I went to Neocropolis. She said he was there to warn me that someone was in trouble. It was my father, *you*, and the other seeksmen who the county had spotted coming in. He was protecting you."

Crewe's eyes are too filled with pain for me to see any reaction. "You see, you can't give up. He wants you to finish his fight. To do that, you need to *live*." Like Crewe has done for me, I wipe his tears with my thumb, smearing them more than erasing them. "Don't forget that I..."

"You what?" he asks softly.

I've been feeling it, but I haven't said it outright, especially in the manner I mean it. "I need you, Crewe." Without him by my side, waiting for news on my father's state would be unbearable.

Crewe pulls me in close to him again. We sit that way quietly, comfortably, while we process our own sadness and worries. After a few minutes, Crewe says, "Thank you for being here, Sydney." He places such a soft kiss on top of my head that I wonder if I was even meant to notice it.

"Crewe," I say eagerly, a thought having occurred to me. "If you switched to the lead boat on your side, don't you have the other cell phone?"

"No," Crewe sighs. "I screwed a lot of things up, Sydney. Besides it all, I think I might have gotten Cheng captured."

"How?" I ask.

"I thought I saw something in the woods when I got out of the van, so I called to him just as he was launching his team, the first boat, into the water. I'd been thinking about switching the whole drive, but if I hadn't had a reason to call to him, our places wouldn't be switched right now. Maybe I wanted there to be a reason. Maybe I created it."

"There was a real reason," I tell him. "I guess you haven't heard yet that you had a stowaway."

"What? Who?" Crewe asks with growing concern.

"Red."

"Your friend from Neocropolis?"

I nod. "His heart was in the right place. He needed to go."

"What happened to him?"

"He disappeared in the crowd sometime during our run toward EPA 12-1. We lost him."

"It's not your fault; he shouldn't have been there. He'll turn up, though," Crewe adds, sensing my concern.

"I hope so. I hope everyone else is okay."

"Me too," Crewe agrees, both of us knowing it's too much to hope for.

Someone knocks on the door. "Yeah," Crewe calls, pushing any remnants of sorrow out of his voice.

Alix hesitantly pushes the door open. "Interesting," she comments. Whether she's referring to our togetherness or the fact that we're huddled away in the men's bathroom, I'm not sure. Either way, there is no malice detected in her voice, even though she and Crewe used to date. "We're done, and Jarod's stable. He can be transported whenever you're ready. The others are," she adds.

Without missing a beat, Crewe shifts into delegation mode. "Pack everyone in the van and go. We've got a doctor now; he and Della will be fine without you." Alix doesn't seem to be offended by her lack of need in this makeshift hospital. With her injury, I'm sure she was glad to be included in the force in any form.

"Staying behind?" It's more of a statement than a question, as Alix knows Crewe well too.

"We both are," he answers. "Just in case this is where the captain ends up coming." Alix nods and turns to exit. "Be safe, Alix," Crewe adds.

"You guys too," she returns before going on her way.

Crewe stands and offers a hand to me. "We should probably go back." After helping me to my feet, he washes his hands and wipes them on his pants. Just as I'm about to go out, he steps in front of the door. "I don't know when all of this will settle down," he says, somewhat awkwardly. "Maybe it's selfish, because I don't know how much I can be here for you, but I know I'll need you throughout this." Crewe gently lifts my hands in his cool, strong grasp. "Not just someone—you. I need you too, Sydney." When our eyes meet, I swear I feel his pulse in my hands. Maybe it's mine.

Despite everything bad around us, Crewe just gave me my reason to smile today. And now, I can return that reason to him. "I'm here for you."

Sure enough, a bashful smile spreads across his lips. The kiss we share is light, but heavy with our current burdens. Crewe pushes the door open for me. On the other side of it, he reaches for my hand.

Just as we reach the room where Della and the doctor from Idaho are exchanging the bloodied surgical tools with fresh ones, we hear the nearby sounds of an urgently honked car horn.

TWENTY-NINE

The instrument Della had in her hand clanks on the floor. Crewe and I rush outside, followed by the doctor from Idaho who was in my squadron.

Crewe pulls open the passenger door of a small truck, revealing two men. Adam, Cheng's seeking partner, is the driver, and the man sprawled across his lap is my father.

"Dad?" My nervous plea goes unanswered. No words are exchanged between the men as Crewe assumes the responsibility of lifting my father out of the truck. The way his arms and head fall limply tells me he is either unconscious or…

"Oh God, Demetri," Della whimpers when Crewe carries my father into the room. Thankfully, she quickly turns her uneasiness into action. "B negative."

When I realize Della's last statement was meant for me, I hurry over to the shelf where I saw Alix go to get a blood bag for Jarod's transfusion. I hand the cool pouch to her while Adam and Crewe cut away my father's shirt. The amount of blood is dizzying, so I only preview the wound on the left side of my father's bared chest. It's far too high to be fatal—at least, it wouldn't be in an inside hospital. Crewe snaps on a pair of gloves and puts direct pressure against the wound. My father has no reaction, and this concerns me.

"That syringe with red tape is saline," Della says, nodding at a tray behind her as she inserts the needle. "I need you to flush this," she says, pointing to some tubing that now rests near my father's neck. "Keep that pressure, Crewe."

I rush over to the doctors' side and grab the syringe. Shakily, I untwist the cap of the tubing and begin discharging the saline from the syringe.

"How long has he been out?" the doctor asks Adam.

"Less than ten minutes," he replies.

"That's good, sweetie," Della says, just as I begin to wonder whether I'm supposed to push all the saline into the line. I don't want to do something wrong that could cause complications that worsen his chances. "Increased heart and respiratory rates. Blood pressure is ninety over eighty-six," Della tells the doctor. Then to me, she says, "Now bring an IV stand over and hang the blood bag on the other side of the saline."

"The clavicle isn't shattered, but there are many fragments from the break that we'll need to remove," the doctor says. "I don't see the bullet, so it'll stay for now."

After securing the saline bag on the stand's hook, I ask, "Is he going to be okay?"

"You keep helping, and he'll be just fine." Della smiles. "Now undo that clamp, and when the saline covers the filter in that chamber, attach it to the line you flushed." I have new respect for Della after watching her compose herself and delineate the preparations for my father's surgery. "Another minute for the anesthetic," she tells the doctor. "Same thing for the blood line now." She nods to me.

"Prep for subclavian stymie and end-to-end suture of the suprascapular artery," the doctor tells Della. I want to know what that means, but I hold my tongue. My asking would do nothing to help save my father. "Alright Crewe, we'll take it from here."

"You sure?" Crewe asks worriedly. His hands remain pressed into a frame around the open wound.

"I'll stay," Adam says.

Della comes around to my side of the bed, adjusts the saline drip, and unclamps the blood line. "All set. Good work," she tells me. "Don't need to see this, especially you," Della tells me.

"He'll be alright," the doctor assures us. Crewe removes his gloves and exits the room slowly. I don't have to follow him far, as this time he sits just outside the room.

I take a breath and sit before I turn my questions on Crewe. "What do you know?" I ask him. "Anything. About the arteries, his chances, recovery time. I want to know anything you know."

"Even a nick to an artery isn't good if it goes untreated, and it sounds like one's been severed. That one has to be a small artery, though, or he wouldn't have made it here alive." Crewe lifts his eyes to the ceiling and rests his head against the wall. "Adam took too long getting him here."

Too long? What is he trying to say? "Is it worse than they're leading on?"

"I don't know," he says absently.

"They seem confident, so his chances must be at least fair," I say, seeking validation, and maybe even comfort, from him.

"He'll make it just fine," Crewe says, understanding that it's important that I hear this from *him*, and not just the doctor and Della. "But it'll be a long time before he can carry a weapon."

"So what then?" I ask the man who my father often places at his right hand.

"Well, we don't stop—I know that much. Too much has happened." Crewe turns and looks at me. "You were right, Sydney, about what I said earlier." Since he avoids repeating the thought, he must be referencing his earlier desire to be killed by a BOT. "It was stupid. Too many have died for this fight, and we're too close to give up now."

"I don't want you to lead it," I admit. I didn't like that my father was the county's principal target, but he was already the captain of the refugee towns when I met him. I knew that wasn't going to change. Crewe rising to that position, however, may be something I can prevent.

"And I don't want *you* anywhere near it," he says. "Neither does your father or Evvie."

"Don't go there, Crewe," I warn him.

"I'm not," he replies calmly. "I'm just reminding you that everyone's wants are beside the point—yours included. The only thing that matters is what we have to do."

"What do we have to do?" I ask him.

"Humankind has to be free. They'll rise up until they are or until they die trying. History has proven this over and over. The only thing you and I have to do is decide our role. I, for one, decide that I'll rise up so my sons won't have to."

"Or daughters," I say, reminding him of the many women, like Alix, Edyn, and Rhoma, who have helped us get this far.

"Yeah, I guess," he says, rolling his eyes. He's desperately trying to lighten our load, even temporarily. Worry seems to have seeped into my bones, making it hard to return anything but a forced smile. He reads it and nods. I love the way Crewe and I understand each other. We're sharing this small moment when the lights in the safe house all suddenly go out.

Crewe all but throws me back into the room where my father was being operated on. A magazine clicks as it's attached to a firearm. "Stay here," Crewe orders. "Close the blinds and get down." I hurry over and shut the blinds as directed. "Lower that chair too if you can. Sydney, find your dad's cell phone and hold it open over the wound for them. You two proceed as normal unless I give a different order or if you hear gunfire."

A pat to each of my father's pants pockets doesn't reveal the phone. I squat down and feel for his sticky, discarded shirt and jacket. In the inner breast pocket, I find the phone.

As if wartime surgery in a converted dental office with outdated supplies wasn't hard and stressful enough, now the doctors are being asked to work on their knees, in a faint glow of light, and with the potential for BOTs to quickly make the whole ordeal worthless.

I have to peer over the phone and focus on the wound in order to keep the light steady. Being this close to the operation, I should probably wear gloves and a cap like the others, but there's no time. I just have to hope that neither a hair, nor a bead of anxious sweat falls from my being.

"As steady as you can, sweetheart," Della requests in a wavering whisper. Her finger is pressed into my father's chest, just outside of where the flesh is torn. It appears she's functioning as the tourniquet as the doctor carefully stiches the second side of a graft to the artery.

"Relieve pressure slightly," the doctor mutters.

A burst of sound erupts in the terse quiet, and I nearly drop the phone—the source of the sound—into the open wound on my father's chest. I flip it toward me to stop the ring, but freeze when I read the name of the caller.

"It's Cheng," I tell the doctor, dumbfounded. Did he somehow get away?

"The rest can wait a minute; answer it," he urges.

I stop the ringtone and lift the phone to my ear. "Hello?"

"Sydney Harter, am I right? Where's your father?" There's a pang of familiarity in the man's voice, but there's no way it's Cheng. Something about the man's tranquility is very off-putting, like the eye of a storm that's catastrophic in its other half.

"He's in surgery," I answer.

"I thought so," he says facetiously. Whether he's referring to the fact of who I am or what state my father is in, I don't know. Either way, it's unsettling.

"Who is this?" I ask, hoping for an answer other than the one snaking in my heart.

"That was a nasty thing you all just did. I'm afraid you've really upset order this time."

No shadow of doubt remains. It's *him*. "Good, you should be afraid," I say, feigning courage.

He laughs. "Spirited one you are, Sydney, but you'll learn yet. I'm not afraid for me or for my county, I'm afraid for you and—more specifically—for your town," he says, biting into what little hope I still hold.

What am I supposed to say to him? Evvie is in Sheridan. I can't allow him to do anything to the town that could hurt her or anyone else, but I also won't cower and beg a belly-ridden snake. "What do you want me to do?" I ask, inviting him to help me find middle ground between our polar worlds.

"I want you to feel the same chaos you've sicked upon me," he says with a spike of heat in his relaxed demeanor. "Drive fast, but I cannot promise you that your town and loved ones therein won't already be ash." His venomous intentions shock my system. *No*. "Oh and Sydney," he adds, "do watch out for deer."

I hold the phone to Della after the call is ended. She shows me her bloodied gloves as if to refuse it, but I drop the cell phone in them anyway.

"Finish it. Fast," I command the two of them.

"What happened?" the doctor demands, no longer paying attention to the level of his voice.

"He's going to bomb them," I answer flatly.

"Who's going to bomb who?" Della cries. I find my rifle on the floor, grasp it, and walk out of the room. I'm going to find Crewe, help him kill any BOTs who are hidden in these parts, and then we're going to return to whatever is left of Sheridan. I'm not about to tell the others, but I heard it, somehow *felt it*, just before he hung up. My Uncle Ted doesn't *plan* to reduce Sheridan to ash as he noted. It's already been done.

THIRTY

After a couple of miserable hours with nothing but tormenting thoughts to pass the time, our speed finally slows. Adam rises to his feet and paces in the dark bed of the garbage truck. I shake my other backload companion, but it doesn't rouse her. "Della, wake up," I say.

"What? What's wrong?" Her words follow fast, but they are groggy, as if she's still dreaming.

"We're here." Della releases an afflicted sigh. Maybe she and Alix weren't able to rest during the hours that we soldiers crept toward Miles. Late in the night, she and the doctor from my team operated on Jarod. Not long after, they carried out a long and intensive operation on my father. I'm sure the stress from those surgeries alone was exhausting, but for almost an hour of my father's surgery, they also wondered whether BOTs were an outside threat.

A county agent was certainly responsible for destroying the safe house's generation of power, but they didn't stay to do any human damage. Their actions are strangely contradictory. Why would they *sneak* in and try to hinder his life-saving surgery? None of us had taken watch like we should have, so they could have sprung right in and killed him, or all of us. They shoot him outright first, and then try to finish the job in a roundabout way. It makes no sense.

I wish they had tried to harm us so they could've learned that I'm finished thinking of the black-operations agents as humans. They certainly don't think of anyone from Sheridan in that way. If Evvie so much as has an earache from a nearby explosion or if a single spark lands on her clothing, I'll do it. I'll channel all the anger I possess to terminate the next target in my sights.

For a change, I was the one asking Della a million questions at the beginning of our journey back here, and she graciously answered every one. She made my father's luck clear when I asked how close he was to not making it. They were solid in their capability to treat him given the bullet's entry point, but another centimeter lower and his major subclavian artery would have been severed. Luckily, the breaking of his clavicle deflected the bullet enough to help it steer clear of this artery. A bone fragment had only nicked it as it broke off.

The circumstances I've lived through are all but lucky but, considering the combat I've faced, I am lucky to be alive. I'm weary of wondering when my luck will run out, and they'll kill someone in my family or me.

The loading hopper opens. "We're out of gas," Crewe says. Adam turns in frustration so that only I can see his eye roll. "We're only a few miles out from the hospital."

"Yeah but we've expended all the gasoline from these parts," Adam complains. "We won't find a drop."

"I know," Crewe says, "The doctor is already on his way in."

"We don't know if any one of the doctors are back yet to help with whatever they've done, and now we have to waste twenty minutes—a half hour for Della—running there?" Adam criticizes.

"Well, we can stay here and whine about it," Crewe snaps, "or we can get our asses there as quickly as possible." Della makes her decision and slumps out of the hopper without a peep.

"And the captain?" Adam questions. I had the same thought on my mind.

"Stays," Crewe answers shortly. "It'll be faster and safer for us to come back for him than to carry him."

This I have to protest. "We can't leave him. They could—"

"I know," Crewe interrupts. "We need to decide who else will stay."

I love my father, but I have to leave him. "I need to get to Evvie," I tell Crewe.

"I know that too. Go," he says.

I take off down the abandoned highway. By the time I catch Della—which doesn't take long—I'm deeply regretting that I didn't show Crewe or my father any kind of affection before I left them. With the situation so volatile, I should have slipped in a quick and subtle goodbye, just in case.

Though it takes me until Main Street, I eventually catch the doctor as well. Everything is intact here, but I wouldn't expect any different. Sheridan industry is really only meant for sustenance, so bombing this part of town would bring no gain to my uncle. He was sure to specify that the ones I hold dear might be ash by the time I arrived. I have a nauseating feeling that he focused on devastating the other side of town. He knows that would hurt immeasurably more than anything else.

It's quite early, but this isn't Miles County; some of the Sheridans should be up and about as the day dawns. Instead, it is disquietingly still on this side of town.

The doctor and I detect a distressing scent at the same time. The smell petrifies him to a standstill, but it propels me to a feverish pace. Whether it's from terror or refusal to inhale the charred air, I don't breathe.

The wreckage is heart shattering. The houses haven't been bombed...they've been set on fire. Whether it's selective or random, I can't tell yet. House after house on the path to my own has been consumed by flame, only bits of blackened framing remaining. The little white house that my sister prepared for us, however, looks immaculate. He had to have known she wasn't staying there.

I weave through the devastation until I see it. Little but the concrete foundation remains of Gwen's two-story home. It looks worst of all, like the fire was started in multiple places to trap and quickly devour its occupants. Evvie. There's only one place to look for her—the hospital.

Before I've reached the building, I can hear the commotion inside. Arguments. Wails. This much pain and fear hours after it was all done can only mean that, as my uncle promised, people's loved ones have been reduced to ash.

Just before the hospital entrance, my toe catches on the cement and I plummet to the ground, my body scraping against it to slow my momentum. I begin to pull myself up, until the wind blows and wafts the reality of the scorched town into the center of my being. Then and there, it suddenly all becomes too much.

My father's death falsified. My grandmother murdered. My mother with no way to protect us other than to kill herself. My sister captured just after we gained hope for a better life. Cy and Decklin killed in effort to rescue her. My imprisonment in

Neocropolis. The round fired just after I escaped that tomb. My father shot and nearly killed. The very purposeful phone call from my uncle to let me know he has delivered me into the most tortuous existence because I refused to accept a tortured life.

I can't go on. Like Crewe, I can't bear to see my young sister covered in death. With each pained wail, I crumple back onto the earth and resign my life. I said it before anything got this bad—I won't live without my sister. I resolve to die by a shattered heart right there on the pavement until someone forces me up onto my feet.

"What happened?" Crewe demands, but I can't answer him. I fall against him, but he holds me up away from him. "Sydney," he says, trying to get to me.

"I knew it. I knew it on the phone," I sob, the agony unendurable. "She's dead, she's dead, my sister's dead!" I fall against his chest, but he holds me away from him.

"You don't know that." He grasps my shoulders firmly in his hands. "Don't you give up until you see it yourself, you hear me?" His words are so powerful as they escape him that he inadvertently shakes me. "You operate under the assumption that she *needs* you right now until you know differently. Come on," he says grabbing my hand and towing me inside.

The whole town has crowded into the hospital like they had when the seeksmen went after Evvie. Men flock to Crewe and me right away, firing one question after another. I push through them to scan the faces that line the hospital walls.

"I don't want us all here like this," Crewe shouts to the townspeople. "Makes it too easy."

"That's what I've been saying," an upset man near Crewe says.

With all eyes on Crewe now, and myself not far from

him, Evvie should have seen me if she were among the healthy.

"If you can help medically, stay. If you can't, go home. Or to someone else's if yours is gone."

"Have you heard anything about the captain, Crewe?" another man asks.

"Captain's going to be fine," Crewe tells everyone.

"Going to be?" someone questions.

"Just go," Crewe orders, raising his voice. "All of you go. Rest if you need to. Otherwise, find someone to help. The town is shut down until further notice." After most of the people have exited, Crewe asks one of the men who has stayed, "How many dead?"

"Three. You?" the man asks, wondering about the soldiers.

"At least that many," Crewe answers.

"You're going to want the rooms just before the end of the hall," the man tells us. His last words before departing are, "I'm sorry."

Crewe grabs my hand and together we walk down the ill-omened hallway. A shiver runs through me and numbs my soul. My feet tread the tiled floor, but only because I'm being pulled along. We arrive at the doors near the end of the hall faster than I want to. The one marked by melancholy moans is the one that Crewe decides we'll enter first.

The grief-stricken sobs come from Gwen. Part of her chin and most of her shoulder has been burned, the skin swollen, blistered, and wet looking. Some of her hair on the same side has been singed off. Two young girls were with Gwen in her home, but no one shares this room with her now. Crewe takes her hand and guardedly says, "Gwen?"

Gwen needs no more than this to answer what we

need to know. "They killed her," she cries. "They killed my baby." Lysia. Gwen's eight-year-old adopted daughter, such an animated, inquisitive child, is now dead.

As a result of dating her birth mother, Alix, for some time, Crewe was quite close to Lysia. A ghastly expression comes over him. Still, he asks the question I can't form. "Evvie?"

"I don't know," Gwen weeps. "I told her to stay outside, but she might have gone back in to look for Lysia after I did." Gwen's momentary composure breaks. "Why?" she wails, her body wrinkling into itself. "Why did she have to go?"

Crewe touches her back, which shudders with each aching cry. "I'm so sorry, Gwen," he forces through a tight throat. The two of us leave her in that inconsolable state. There's nothing we—or anyone—can do.

The room across the hall hosts Merick and two women, one of which is burned as badly as the agent above Neocropolis. Merick has also suffered a large burn on his chest.

"Where's my sister?" I ask Merick.

"Not here. No one's seen her in the hospital." Merick winces as he tries to prop himself up better. "I had a few guys check what's left of Gwen's house for remains, but there were none."

"Except for Lysia's," Crewe says, confused.

"Lysia was worried about Alix. Missed her. She snuck off to her house sometime in the night. That's where they found her."

"Where's Alix now?" Crewe asks.

"In any one of these rooms," Merick says. "She's been trying to attend to the wounds the way she remembers Della doing for her. She's in shock, Crewe."

"They've done it," Crewe says, devoid of emotion.

"They've broken us."

"What happened out there? You free those people?"

"Sounds like we freed as deep as the Threes."

"If those people went into the county, then you've broken them too. And they retaliated with this."

"We lost men out there too, though," Crewe explains. "At least two captured and two wounded."

"What about the captain?" Merick asks.

"He'll be alright." Merick frowns, so Crewe adds, "Shot through the clavicle. One artery severed and another nicked. We ran out of gas a couple miles out of town, but I've already sent someone to pick the captain and Adam up."

"Do you think they've taken my sister again?" I ask Merick.

"I think your uncle has a strange fascination with the two of you, so maybe," he answers. "The good thing is that I don't believe he'd hurt her."

Della enters the room with a bowl of clear liquid and a bag of supplies. "Alright, darling, you're next," she tells the woman with the most severe wounds. "Then it'll be your husband's turn," she tells the other woman, "so get your hands ready for some squeezing." The other woman gets off the bed from where she's been coughing, sits on the side of Merick's bed, and takes his hand.

"You keep looking for her," Merick tells me, "but be careful. And you make sure the captain is back and safe," he tells Crewe.

Alix comes out of the neighboring room at the same time that Crewe and I exit into the hallway. "Glad to see you two are okay. Did anyone else come after we left?" she asks Crewe as if it were an ordinary Monday morning, and her only child hadn't just been torn from the world by BOT-induced flame.

"Adam came with the captain," Crewe says uneasily. "He'd been shot, but he'll be okay." Crewe reaches for bowl of red-tinted liquid that Alix holds.

"No!" she snaps, drawing it away from him.

"Alix, let someone else do this," Crewe says.

"No," Alix begs him, her eyes flooding. "Please let me." She clears her throat and blinks away the tears that have not yet fallen. There was a fleeting break in her denial, but now it's consumed her once again. If Alix is anything like me, she sought for the deadness to return. She passes us and hurries into the room across from the technology station where Cy worked.

"Let's meet back here," I tell Crewe when we've reached the entrance to the hospital.

"Not a chance," he returns. "If your uncle has taken Evvie, then it's likely he's after you too. I'm coming with you."

"What about my dad?" I ask.

"I trust he's already being taken care of. Come on," Crewe says, taking my hand in his. "We'll check your house and then the place where the captain used to live before you and Evvie came along."

There are groups of people working at every turn as we jog through the homes. I even see a fresh Neocropolis escapee who still wears his jumpsuit.

Crewe stops when his home is in sight. All that remains is the collapsed roof. Maybe it smothered the flames when it fell. "Hey!" Crewe calls to a nearby group. "Make sure no one touches my house," he orders. We start jogging again, and then he explains to me, "I don't want anyone to touch Cy's things. If there's even a scrap to remember him by, I want it."

Finally, we reach the little house in which Evvie, my

father, and I only shared one night. Crewe shakes his hand from mine, ushers me behind him, and swings his rifle from his back to his hands. Focused on the house, he pushes me down below a window near the front steps. "Wait here," he says.

The minute that passes is painfully quiet. I wonder if Crewe's been tranquilized or shot with a silencer until I finally hear him call to me. "She's in here," he says when I come through the door, but his expression is troubled, not relieved. I cautiously round the doorframe to see my sister laying facedown on my bed, one arm hanging unnaturally over the edge.

THIRTY-ONE

"Evvie?" I rush to my sister, who isn't responding.

"She's alive," Crewe says, apparently having checked that before calling me in here. Crewe slings the rifle behind him to help me turn her over.

"Evvie?" I say again, patting her cheek. Crewe pulls his weapon back into ready position and watches the door.

"Hmm?" she returns without opening her eyes.

"What are you doing here? Look at me. Open your eyes, Evvie," I tell her. My sister finally opens her eyes. "How did you get here?"

"Where?" she asks dazedly.

"Our house. You were at Gwen's," I remind her.

"What?" she says, confused. She pushes herself up and envelops me in an abrupt hug, seeming to tire from the effort. Her eyes shift between Crewe and me in panic. They're the same wild blue eyes that belonged to my mother.

"Do you know where you are? Do you remember Crewe?" I ask her.

"Yes," she returns as an answer to both questions. Her quickened breaths cause her to cough. "Sydney, there was a fire."

"I know," I tell her. "Are you okay?"

"Did Gwen find Lysia?" she asks anxiously.

I didn't have to tell my little sister about Cy dying, because I was already in Neocropolis. Sharing this piece of tragic news, however, falls on me. I have no idea how to start. "She didn't make it," I say directly.

"What do you mean?" my sister asks, knowing well the answer.

"It's okay," I say, wrapping her in my arms. "We need to get you to the hospital. Dad's there too."

"What happened?" she asks me worriedly. A fit of coughing follows.

"He was shot but way up here," I say, touching my sister's clavicle. "Now come on."

Evvie stumbles a little and holds her head when she stands. With his gun still raised, Crewe takes hold of one of Evvie's arms to help me support her.

"Sydney, I feel really tired," Evvie tells me when we're two-thirds of the way to the hospital. I can tell. Her droopiness is making it difficult for us to get her there with any kind of haste. Red was like this after Doctor McClain sedated him so we could escape Neocropolis. He too was weak, heavy-eyed, and confused.

"Stay awake, Evvie. You want to see Dad, remember?" I say, although she never said the words.

The hospital is busier than when we left not long ago. That means there have been new arrivals from our force, some of them in poor condition.

"Find out where your dad is," Crewe tells me as he lifts my sister into his arms.

I don't recognize anyone in the first two rooms I enter, but I ask them about the captain anyway. One man says he knows he's here, but isn't sure which room. In the third room I enter, Doctor McClain attends to a soldier who I think is from Braves. "Do you know where the captain is?" I ask her.

"Second door from the end on the left," she says. Gwen's room.

I open the door for Crewe and follow him into the room. Gwen moves to sit at the end of my father's bed to make room for Evvie, who isn't responding anymore.

"You found her," my father says weakly. Evvie moans. "Get Galvesten," he orders Crewe, pointing across the hall. "Then Rico," he says before his soldier has made it out of the room. Gwen carefully gets up to follow Crewe. "Don't go," my father says to her. She squeezes his hand and then exits anyway.

My father releases a drawn-out sigh. "How am I supposed to fix this?"

"What happened?" Galvesten asks me

"We found her sleeping at our house," I tell the doctor. "She remembers the fire at Gwen's, but seems confused about the rest."

"Same thing I'm seeing with the rest," Galvesten says as he checks my sister's vitals. "Cough, drowsiness, dizziness, confusion, and nausea. Try to wake her up again so we can get a bronchodilator in her."

Hearing from the hall, Crewe comes over and lifts Evvie into a sitting position, which starts the coughing that wakes her. "The doctor is bringing you an inhaler and some oxygen," he tells her. "You need to stay awake."

"What's that?" my father asks Rico, who stands in the doorway with a few pieces of paper. He flips the first one around, revealing another picture of me. The photograph only hangs from Rico's fingers for a few seconds before Crewe snatches, crumples, and discards it.

Rico steps into the congested room to hand the other two papers directly to my father. While he reads the paper on top, I attend to Evvie, whose incessant coughs concern me. Having seen this with his other patients tonight, Galvesten passes me a trashcan. I place it just in time for my sister to get sick.

"Deep breaths, Evvie," Galvesten says after he secures the oxygen mask.

"Any chance he looked like that before?" my father asks Rico.

"I don't think so, Captain, but I can find out. Two from his squadron saw him and the girl get captured." Cheng and Rhoma. A picture of Cheng must have accompanied the one of me. My father studies the picture a moment longer and then passes it facedown to Rico, careful not to let anyone else see. I might be offended, if by sparing me the image, he weren't also protecting Evvie from it.

After Rico leaves, my father massages his forehead and brows. "Who's Edyn?" my father asks me.

"What does it say about her?" I abandon Evvie temporarily to lift the message from my father's lap. He sighs, but doesn't demand it back.

Demetri,

You have been away a long time, my brother. You can thank me when we next meet for watching over your beautiful and, dare I say, brave daughters after you deserted them. The pictures look awfully gruesome but, I admit, I never harmed Sydney. She had become too precious to me.
I am capable of many things, however. I felt you needed a

reminder of that. I began with one of your thicker-skinned men, but I have a plethora of weaker men, women, and children who I can move onto should you continue to refuse my offer for peace. I have options in Edyn, a champion boxer, Rhoma, a resolute young woman, and Red, an obliging boy. Two of these are already compromised, so I hope the persuasion that conveyed through Cheng has the potential to go farther.

Here, once again, is my offer—return all citizens to their natural county, or suffer the consequences twofold—to yours in Neocropolis and to yours in defenseless Sheridan.

Wishes of peace
Commander Theodore Harter

I feared Edyn could be dead, so receiving word that she's been compromised doesn't injure me as much as learning the same about Red. I assume since no one mentioned anything about Rhoma having been shot before she and Cheng were captured, that Red is the other of the two who are wounded.

He wasn't supposed to be there, but once he was, I should have seen to it to watch out for my untrained friend. Thinking of him suffering some injury in the depths of Neocropolis is bad enough; I don't want to imagine Red being a puppet for my uncle's *persuasion*.

Rico reenters and shakes his head, verifying that Cheng was perfectly healthy when he was captured. My father tenses in his rage, causing him to flinch with the pain from his broken clavicle and freshly repaired arteries.

"You should take something for the pain," Galvesten advises.

"Right now, I need to be alert," the captain responds. "Rico and Crewe, get Braves and Adam. That Jaxon fella from Neocropolis too, if you can find him." The two soldiers follow their orders as directed. "You two move Evvie out and Merick in," my father tells Galv and me. "Your ideas have been valuable in the past, Sydney, but if you want to stay with your sister, that's fine too."

With more strenuous effort than Crewe required, Galvesten lifts Evvie from the bed. I grab the oxygen concentrator and follow.

"You're wanted across the hall," Galvesten tells Merick.

"Hold on, not so fast," Della says. Merick bites his lip as she spreads a thick coat of ointment over the burned area of his chest. "Limit—"

"Motion. I got it," Merick says as he cautiously stands.

"Evvie, are you going to be okay?" I ask my sister. She's completely drained, but reaches for my hand anyway. She squeezes it once and nods before closing her eyes.

"I'll take good care of her," Della assures me.

Galvesten, Crewe, Adam, Braves, and Jaxon, all still dressed in their gear, stride down the hallway toward my father's room. "My, I'm not dressed for the occasion," Merick jokes, pulling a smirk from Jaxon, the newest member of the Sheridan militia.

"Grab that door," my father tells Adam after we've all assembled. "First of all, I want to tell you that I'm proud of each of you who bravely lead your teams. I'm proud of the way you saved men's lives, on the battlefield and off. As a whole, we may not be in good shape, but we've lasted because of your resilient courage." My father pauses to appreciate many of his soldiers, his eyes lingering on Braves.

"We're proud to be your seeksmen," Crewe replies for the bunch.

The captain nods in acknowledgement, but then his pride morphs into regret. "That's where I want to begin. You can all see I'm incapacitated. I'm also out of ideas," our leader admits. "I am taking a leave of absence as captain until further notice." In unison, the men grumble and plead for my father to reconsider. "Enough. Braves, I'm appointing you as my replacement if you'll accept." Braves forfeits his own doubts and agrees to the responsibility.

"Good," my father says. "I'm not going anywhere; I just can't do my job right like this. And leading this effort needs to be done cautiously and courageously. As I've already said, I know the second part comes easily for all of you." My father speaks this directly to Braves, which makes me think he's trying to inspire—not admire—the new leader's courage.

My father reaches for the message from his brother, wincing when he takes hold of it. "They mean to coerce us into the county by harming Cheng and the other prisoners in Neocropolis and our town like we suffered here tonight. I don't want to see either happen, but if it were still up to me, I wouldn't allow another townsperson to be killed."

"I say we get that plane running and do it right back to them," Adam fumes.

My father glowers at him. "We're no better than they are if we stoop to that level. Not to mention that a lot of the Sheridans still have family in the county. Think before you speak, *Jerus*," my father says, making his utmost dissatisfaction in Adam known in the worst way.

"Jerus is dead," I utter, not even meaning to.

"Serves him right," Crewe spews, needing to cut the

turncoat who got his brother and Decklin killed. The room becomes hushed as the other men probe me for an explanation. "He was working for them, but the agent that helped my group escape told me that Jerus wanted to flip to our side, but couldn't. After what happened to them..." I look at Crewe and shake my head.

"They didn't kill him," Merick notes. The room is silent for another moment, almost in reverence. Crewe, however, maintains his position. I can't blame him for that. If someone, even my father, lacked the courage to do what they knew was right and it ended up getting Evvie killed, I'd hate that person too.

"We're going to have to do something to stop or appease them," Braves says, relieving the tension. "In my town too, we've always thought their threats were empty. We now know that they're not. After all these years, we're finally at the breaking point. So the question is—how are we going to tip it in our favor?"

"I don't think the name release will be enough for people," Rico says. "I think people will want visitation rights." The men nod and murmur in agreement.

"What name release?" I ask.

"The escapees that were released did a good job of spreading the word in Miles," Crewe tells me. He must have gotten up to speed on this when he went to get Braves, Adam, and Jaxon. "Citizens are outraged. The county is pacifying them by releasing the names of Neocropolis' remaining residents tomorrow."

"They'll just make the names up," I tell the crowd.

Jaxon shakes his head. "No, everyone is watching this. People will dig to make sure that the names they release are people who actually existed."

A faint knock on the door interrupts our meeting. It's Della. "Galv, I need you," she says, not masking her worry well. "Bring that kit," she adds, before hurrying out of the room. The doctor gathers his tools and excuses himself from the meeting.

"I say we wait and see what happens inside," Braves suggests. "Maybe we buy ourselves time by having the people shut down their workplaces and pack up their homes. We can make it look like we're following their demands so that they don't punish Sheridan or our friends in Neocropolis. We need the time to properly plan our next move.

Della invades the room without knocking this time. "Captain, Sydney, Galv says you better come." Della stares at me, her eyes full of trepidation. "Something's wrong with Evvie."

THIRTY-TWO

I plow through the men at the door and rush into the room across the hall. The oxygen mask has been removed. The mask, Evvie's chin, and a streak of her neck are wet with vomit.

"What's wrong?" I ask the doctors frantically.

"Crewe, get Doctor McClain," Galvesten orders. Crewe hastily assists my father to the now-empty bed in the room, and then exits.

"This isn't normal," Galvesten tells my father more than me. "Her saliva isn't burnt enough for her to be puking like this, and she shouldn't be losing consciousness with the oxygen."

"Then what's wrong?" I ask urgently.

"We're trying to figure that out," Galvesten says harshly. "We're going to pump her stomach and do a blood transfusion to try and clean her system of anything hazardous."

"Like poison?" my father asks.

"She couldn't remember what happened after she got out of Gwen's house. Do you think they did something to her?" I ask helplessly.

"What is it?" Doctor McClain asks when she enters the room.

"Here." Della hands Doctor McClain a sample of my sister's blood, then continues to fill additional vials. "Test her type. That kit." She nods to the one Galvesten brought in. "We're going to start a transfusion, and then we'll use the centrifuge to run whatever tests we can."

Seeing my sister like this, and the doctor's unsure of how to make it better, sends my whole system into shock. I start to feel dizzy, sick, wheezy, and burdened. Crewe's cold, clammy hand massages my neck. If I'm not mistaken, his hand shakes some with the action.

Rico bursts in the room and frantically hands a piece of paper to my father, which I bend to read with him. It says:

A new pathogen has been developed nationally to help coerce citizens back to their respective counties. She can only be cured here. It is an augmenting disease, so act quickly. A helicopter will be at your service shortly. One relative may accompany her.

My father folds the message. His face is pale, vacant of emotion. "Can you write back?" he asks Rico. The messenger nods. "Tell him I'll come."

"No, Dad, I need to go with her," I tell him, my voice uneven.

My father ignores my statement and continues to deliver his message to Rico, while looking down at his hands. "Write that our families need a day to grieve. Tell him that after we bury our dead tomorrow, we will begin shutting down the town. Ten of our citizens who belong in Miles County will be ready for pick up two days from now. If it is proved to us that they are not harmed, the rest of our town will follow." My father looks up at Rico. "Make sure Braves gets a copy of the transcript." Rico exits to do what he's been commanded.

Then, suddenly, my sister starts convulsing. Drool slides from her white lips onto Della's hand as she tries to support Evvie's head.

"Dad, please," I cry. "I need to go with her."

"You and Evvie are my only responsibility now. My new job is to keep you each safe," he responds emptily.

"There has to be another way, Captain," Crewe says, craving for it to be true.

My father claps his soldier on the shoulder, swings his legs over the bed, and stands. Still gripping him, he looks Crewe in the eyes. With passion, he says, "Then you find it, Crewe. I have faith in you. Right now, this step has to be taken."

Crewe's jaw tenses, but he lowers his head and nods. When he looks back up at his reigning captain and fatherly figure, his eyes are wet with distress.

"Take care of her," my father says before parting with his beloved seeksmen. My father turns to me and brushes my cheek with his thumb. "Take care of my little princess," he says, still talking to Crewe.

"I love you, Dad," I tell him. I hug my father like I would have when I was child, if I knew he wasn't going to come back from work that day.

My father recoils a little from the pain. "I know it," he says. "Let's get her up," he directs Crewe.

Galvesten and Della have already shed Evvie of the tubing and needles they had inserted to prep for the cleansing. Crewe scoops my sister's lifeless body in his hands. Galvesten and I both offer my father an arm for support, but he refuses them. His expression has turned indomitable. He, the BOTs' most hunted and most despised man, will return to their clenches after fifteen years of freedom.

Shrieks outside let us know that the promised chopper has arrived to take my family away. "You're all to stay in here," my father demands. He holds out his arms for Crewe to pass him Evvie.

"Wait," I say, halting the exchange. I shuffle between my two dear men to say a few words to my beloved sister, who I don't know when I'll see again.

Crewe transfers Evvie weight and takes a knee. I join him in cradling my unconscious little sister. I run my fingers over the roots of her hair. "I love you, Evvie. I'm sorry I didn't stay to protect you, and I'm sorry I can't come with you now."

"It's time," my father says, motioning to the basket that's been lowered from the chopper. Crewe promptly stands and passes Evvie to my wounded, but unbroken father. Galvesten pushes the door open from inside. "Tell Gwen I'm sorry," my father tells Galvesten as he walks fearlessly out of the hospital.

Maybe he's trying to be brave for his men and me. Whether his courage is fronted or true, it helps me none. It's absolute torture for me to watch the only two people I love be lifted and taken away by the ruthless enemy. It feels like all the pieces of my shattered heart have evaporated, leaving a dark and cold void in the center of my being.

Braves tears into the hospital waiting room, stopping abruptly before the frozen three of us. "How could you let him go?" Braves accuses, focusing on Crewe.

"What choice did we have?" Crewe's voice is flat and dejected.

"What do we do now?" The new captain's words are more of a charge against us, the wrongdoers, than a survey for suggestions.

Crewe glares at Braves. "We tell our people," he says.

"Tell them what? That the captain is gone? That the BOTs are going to inject them with some new disease if they don't go into their county?" Merick, Adam, Rico, and Jaxon join us in the waiting room.

"We tell them that we have a new captain," Crewe returns. He addresses all of us as he continues. "Yes, we tell them the truth. They deserve to know it." No one contests this. "We gather volunteers to be taken to Miles. If we can't find ten, we draw names."

"We can't let them have that power over us, Crewe," Merick says. "It's bad enough that they got the captain."

"I think we should make the preparations in case we don't come up with a solution," he answers. "Apart from burying our dead tomorrow, I know every one of us will spend our time wracking our brains for a way out of this. We can share our ideas and put together a plan after the funerals tomorrow. Let's meet at the usual place."

I wonder if it's as clear to the others as it is to me who has really replaced my father.

"Let's bring a list of the people who agree to go into Miles," Merick says, confirming the meeting. When the others in the company agree, Merick turns and heads back into the hospital.

Crewe opens the door and the rest of us file out, Braves being the last. The seeksmen scatter this way and that to deliver achingly bad news to their already hurting townspeople. "What should I do?" I ask Crewe.

He takes my trembling hand in his and grasps it firmly. "Stay by my side," Crewe says. "That's the only thing you have to do. I'm going to figure this out."

Sheridan has become the deer in the middle of the road. Throwing in the towel and heading back is out of the question. So is standing still and trying to compromise. Like the deer, our enemy would overpower us, and lead us to certain death. The only way to survive is to push on, and quickly.

I will stay by Crewe's side—as one of the seeksmen. Through bullet or flame, I will fight until this war is won.

~The End~

ACKNOWLEDGEMENTS

Above all, I am grateful for life, family, friends, and all other gifts that the Lord has given to me.

I cannot express how deeply thankful I am for my mother. Being my principal beta-reader is only one of the countless ways she supports my dreams.

Just for believing in my story, I owe Rebecca Gober, Courtney Nuckels, Marya Heiman, and Dyan Brown of Clean Teen Publishing so much appreciation. Add their overarching creative, marketing, and organizational talents and their fun, upbeat personalities and you can see why I feel very blessed to be represented by this team.

Special thanks to CTP affiliates Cynthia Shepp, who enriched my writing with her editorial sharp-eye and enviable grammar, and Melanie Newton, who works her magic in the social media realms.

I have so much gratitude for the CTP street team whose members have read, reviewed, and shared news about the Concealed in the Shadows series. The same goes for my personal street team of close supporters who have done the above as well as given me guidance. Without each team's valuable feedback and promotion, I would not have the final party to thank.

To you, reader, I give my final acknowledgement. I sincerely thank you for your support. I hope you've enjoyed the journey thus far, and will embark on the last leg of it once I've laid the path!

ABOUT THE AUTHOR

Gabrielle Arrowsmith is a YA writer, a math teacher, an on-screen actress, and a soccer trainer who resides in Ham Lake, MN. Her favorite hobbies are reading, making and editing short films, running and other outdoor activities, watching movies, listening to music, playing piano, and scrapbooking. Gabrielle loves to spend time with her family, friends, and her adorable pets!

Connect with Gabrielle!

www.Facebook.com/ConcealedInTheShadows

www.GabrielleArrowsmith.com

CPSIA information can be obtained at www.ICGtesting.com
Printed in the USA
LVOW05s0724131014

408468LV00002B/3/P

9 781940 534558